NINETEENTH CENTURY GERMAN TALES

NINETEENTH CENTURY GERMAN TALES

Edited by
ANGEL FLORES

FREDERICK UNGAR PUBLISHING CO.
NEW YORK

Printed in the United States of America

Library of Congress Card Catalog No. 66-25110

Preface

These tales, newly translated for the present anthology, were extremely popular in all the German-speaking countries of their origin—Austria, Germany, Switzerland—when first published between 1793 and 1842, and their authors were well received in England and the United States when Carlyle, De Quincey, Coleridge, and Ruskin, among others, introduced them in translations and essays. In Hawthorne, Melville, Poe, and Poe's innumerable French progeny, their influence is unmistakable.

Today, however, these writers, with the possible exception of Hoffmann, have fallen into an unaccountable neglect, regrettable considering how strikingly modern are so many of their narratives which mingle fancy with realism, psychological analysis with suspenseful plots. Regarding them now, from the vantage point of a century's remove, it may be said that these remarkable writers not infrequently transcended what is often referred to as nineteenth-century "quaintness" to achieve precisely those qualities of mystery with myth-making, of atmospheric awesomeness shot through with matter-of-factness, of taut simplicity, which distinguish the art of some of our most contemporary writers, from Kafka to Buzzati, Holenia-Lernet, and Camus.

How can writers as powerful as Kleist, Mörike, Stifter, and these others have been forgotten, or relegated to the hands of specialists? Perhaps in the vagaries of literary history may the reasons be traced—changing fashions, the sociology of taste, and other intangibles, including the unfortunate vogue of their second- and third-rate imitators, after which realism and "documentaries" were almost inevitable. Thus we had the objectivity-at-all-costs of Flaubert, the Goncourts, Maupassant, and Zola, who set the stage for a long monopoly by a succession of Emma Bovarys and Zolaesque "human beasts." Like a tidal wave, the vogue of realism carried all before it, growing and proliferating in every country: in the England of Dickens, Bennett, and Galsworthy; in the United States of Howells, Norris, Sinclair Lewis, Upton Sinclair. . . . Only in comparatively recent years has a neoromantic trend begun to restore to imaginative writing its old prestige. Assuredly the time is at hand for a proper reappreciation of the authors whose works are represented in the pages which follow.

ANGEL FLORES

Queens College
Flushing, New York

CONTENTS

Life of the Cheerful
Schoolmaster Maria Wutz

JEAN PAUL RICHTER

TRANSLATED BY JOHN D. GRAYSON

O H happy Schoolmaster Wutz, how peaceful were your life and death, as calm and serene as a summer sea! The mild placid skies of Indian summer were cloudless for you and enveloped your life in a misty fragrance. You were altered by the years as a blossom changes, and your death was the decline of a lily whose petals flutter down upon surviving flowers. Yes, even on this side of the grave you were softly slumbering!

But now, my friends, first of all we must move our chairs closer to the fire and push the table with the water pitcher a little nearer so that I can reach it easily. Let us draw the curtains and put on our nightcaps, and just because I am going to tell you the story of the cheerful Schoolmaster, we must forget all about the Palais Royal and the *grand monde* across the way. And as for you, my dear Christian, because your heart is always open to the homely eternal joys of living, sit down here on the arm of my easy chair and lean on me whenever you like. You won't disturb me in the least.

Some member of the Wutz family had been schoolmaster of Auenthal ever since the Swedish Wars, and I do not believe that either the parson or his flock ever found fault with any of them. Eight or nine years after the marriage of a Wutz, he and his son would invariably be found in the village conscientiously performing their duties. Our Maria

Wutz taught the alphabet under his father's supervision
the very week in which he himself was learning that most
profitless accomplishment, the art of spelling. The person-
ality of our Schoolmaster Wutz, like the lessons of some
other schoolmasters, had something playful and childish
about it, but it reflected the joys of childhood rather than
its sorrows.

Even as a child he was somewhat childish. For there are
two kinds of children's games, you know, the childish and
the serious. The serious games are imitations of grownups
—playing salesman or soldier or craftsman—and the childish
ones are pretending to be animals. When Wutz played, he
was always a rabbit, a turtledove or its tiny fledgling, a
bear, a horse or even the wagon it pulled. Believe me! A
seraph sees no work in our colleges and lecture halls, only
play. And if he opens his eyes wide, these are the two kinds
of play he sees.

However, like all philosophers, Wutz had his serious moments and pastimes as well. Long before the Brandenburg
clergy wore multicolored vestments, had he not shown
himself to be above common prejudice by donning in the
morning a sky-blue smock?—a color not often seen on the
parson of the town, but in some cases the magic Faust-like
mantle on which he spirits himself into a livelihood. Attired in this blue surplice, Wutz would point out to the
housemaid the many sins that might jeopardize her salvation and send her to Hell. Sometimes he even attacked his
own father, but that would only happen in the afternoon.
Whenever he read to him from Cober's *Home Preacher*,
it particularly delighted him to add a couple of words, or
even lines, of his own composition and to read these inter-
polations along with the text, as if Herr Cober himself were
lecturing his father.

I think that these reminiscences of mine will shed much
light on Wutz's character and on a joke that he used to play
in the pulpit later on in life, when he would take the minister's place for an afternoon. It was his custom to read to
the congregation from the *Postilla*, but with so many addi-
tions and inventions of his own that he often succeeded

in rousing the drowsy churchgoers and routing the Devil. "Justel," he would say to his wife toward four o'clock, "you can't imagine from down in your pew how wonderfully fine it is up there in the pulpit, especially during the hymn just before the sermon."

We can easily see from his adult life what he was like in his youth. Later on he used to want the candles lit in December one hour later than usual, for in that hour he would relive his childhood, selecting each time a different day from the past. When the wind darkened his window with curtains of snow and the fire peered out at him through cracks in the stove, he would close his eyes and let the springtime of a former day descend again in dew-drops upon the frozen meadows. Once more he built a nest for himself and his sister, and as he rode homeward on top of the mountain of hay, he shut his eyes and tried to guess how far they had come along the road. In the cool of evening, as the swallows skirmished overhead, he flitted about like a twittering dove, trouserless and delighted at his bare-legged freedom, and by means of a wooden bill, he made a little circular depression in the mud. For his young one—a wooden cock with feathers pasted to it that he had received at Christmas—he brought feathers and straw to this nest for bedding.

On still another winter evening, he resurrected and enjoyed a splendid Trinity Sunday (I wish there were 365 Trinity Sundays in the year!), when, with spring ringing in him and around him, he marched out early through the village and into the garden, jingling his bunch of keys. There he cooled himself in the dew, thrust his shining face through the wet currant bushes, measured himself against the tall grasses, and with weak fingers picked some roses for the rector's pulpit. On the same Trinity Sunday (this was the second course he served up to himself on that particular December evening), with the sunshine at his back, he managed to squeeze off the organ keys the chorale "Glory to God on High," vainly trying to reach the pedals with his short legs, while his father pulled out the right stops for him.

What a jumble of incompatibilities these two hours would have held if he had gone on to recollect the whole December of his youth! But he was wise enough to postpone until a future third hour the memory of how he used to rejoice when the shutters were fastened and he could snuggle up securely inside the lighted room. He did not like to peer too long into that other room reflected in the shining windowpanes, the one that lay outside in the darkness. He remembered how he and his brothers and sisters would spy on, help with, and interrupt their mother's cooking, and how, from behind the breastworks of their father's legs, they would wait with tightly shut eyes to be dazzled by the candlelight. How safe and warm and cozy they felt in this small room, cut out of or built into the infinite vault of God's Universe! And every day, as often as he traveled backward to the December of his childhood, he would forget where he was. Then, when the lamp was lighted, he would discover to his astonishment that he was in the very room which he had transported, like a Loretto-cell, from the Canaan of his youth. At least, that is the way he himself describes these grand operas of memory in his *Promenades after Rousseau*. See, I have kept the book open on my lap to make certain that I tell his story accurately.

At this point, I fear I must skip over his advanced age and tell you at once about an extremely important circumstance; otherwise I may find myself entangled in a regular bramble patch! Afterward I shall begin in due order *a priori*, and follow Schoolmaster Wutz up the three ascending steps of life and then down the other side, until at last at the foot of the lowest step, he falls into the grave before our eyes.

Oh, if only I hadn't made that comparison! Whenever I have looked into Lavater's *Fragments* or Comenius' *Orbis Pictus* or seen the bloody and mournful scaffold of *The Seven Stages of Life* on someone's wall—whenever I watch that painted creature stretch itself and climb to the top of the pyramid and then, after looking about for a few minutes, creep down the other side and quake as it stumbles over the generations of corpses which lie strewn about this

Calvary—if I then turn to look at a rosy face, full of spring-time and thirsting to drink in the whole world, I am reminded that not a millennium, but a few decades alone, can make it into a shriveled, wrinkled symbol of outlived hopes. And as I grieve over others, I too am climbing up and down that same scaffold!—But come, we mustn't depress one another like this!

To resume, the important circumstance I was speaking about is this: that Wutz had actually written an entire library for himself. Indeed, if he had not, how could he ever have afforded to buy one? His desk was his little printing house, and whenever our Schoolmaster heard that a new title had appeared at the Book Fair in Leipzig, his own copy was as good as bought; for he would sit down immediately and compose it to be added to his fine collection—which, incidentally, like the libraries of the Greeks and Romans, was all in manuscript. For example, Lavater's *Fragments of Physiognomy* had scarcely seen the light when Wutz, in order to keep abreast of this prolific writer, folded his foolscap in quarto and sat down at his bench to produce his own physiognomical fetus. Its cradle was his bookshelf, and after three full weeks of industrious and almost unbroken labor, he discovered that his creation had actually made its debut before Lavater's. The Wutzian *Fragments*, however, bore Lavater's name, and in his Introduction our Schoolmaster stated that, while he did not actually object to the printed editions, he believed his own handwriting to be as legible, if not more so, than any pica type! He was no damned literary pirate who steals the original and usually copies the greater part of it! No, indeed; in fact, he never so much as laid a finger on the original.

When we realize that this was Wutz's method of procedure, it is easy to understand the two following facts: first, that he sometimes misunderstood the meaning of the title, and as a result was unable to make his subject matter correspond with what the author had in mind; and secondly, that he believed his copybooks to be the genuine and canonical documents. The printed ones were mere plagia-

risms! And there was one thing, he would complain, that
he could not comprehend, even if they were to offer him a
bailiwick; that is, why the plagiarist falsified and altered
the work so much that any reader who did not otherwise
know, would swear that the printed copy and the manuscript version had different authors. If, as sometimes occurred, a writer attempted to thwart him by writing profoundly (in square folio), or wittily (in duodecimo), his
fellow author Wutz could compete as capably as ever; he
folded his pages square or cramped his writing onto duodecimo, never daunted.

There was only one book he allowed in his house: the
Leipzig Fair catalogue. The rector would indicate the best
selections for him by drawing a black index hand in the
margin, and since there were two fairs yearly, a spring and
a fall, it was all he could do to dash off the Easter harvest
before the Michaelmas crop was ready to be gathered and
stored. I wouldn't have liked the job of writing his master-
pieces! Whenever the rector, his Friedrich Nikolai, marked
too many good books for him to compose (the black index
hand pushing along Wutz's hand, so to speak), the man so
weakened himself with his labors that he ran the greatest
risk of catching coughs and colds and his son often complained that for years on end his father had scarcely time
to sneeze between the pains of literary childbirth. At one
period, he had to bring into the world simultaneously
Sturm's *Reflections,* Schiller's *Robbers,* and Kant's *Critique
of Pure Reason.* This was his occupation by day. During
the evening after dinner, however, the good man had to
sail right around the South Pole, and on his journey à la
Cook, had barely any time to say three sensible words to
his son in Germany. For since our encyclopedist had never
ventured into the interior of Africa or into a Spanish stable
and had never even spoken to anyone who had, he had
that much more time and freedom to produce rich descrip-
tions of his travels to both of these places and many others.
There are, indeed, many traveler-authors who thus describe their voyages without making the trip, and so our
Wutz also found the source of his journals entirely in him-

self. He wrote about everything, and if the learned world was surprised when, five weeks after the publication of *The Sorrows of Werther*, he took an old feather duster, pulled out a quill, and immediately began to write the book himself, what of it? Did not all of Germany subsequently do likewise?—But now we shall return again to his youth.

In his tenth year he was transformed into a brown-gowned *alumnus* and upper fifth-grader in the city of Scheerau. His examiners must testify for me that I do not flatter my hero if I venture to state that he was only one page short of the fourth declension and that he could reel off like an alarm clock the whole list of nouns that were exceptions to the rule of gender—*thorax, caudex, pulexque* —before his peers; it was only the rule itself that he did not know. Of all the niches allotted to the students, there was only one that was as scoured and well kept as the kitchen of a Nuremberg housewife, and that was his. Happy people are the most orderly, you know. He bought two kreutzers worth of nails and studded his cell with them so that each article of his clothing might have its own nail. He moved his notebooks around until their backs made as symmetrical a formation as a platoon of Prussian soldiers, and he would rise from his bed by moonlight time and time again to look at his shoes and assure himself that they were exactly parallel to each other. As soon as everything was in order, he would rub his hands together, shrug his shoulders above his ears, jump about, nod his head and laugh in a most extraordinary fashion.

Before I give you further proof that he was happy as a student, I would like to mention that it was by no means easy to be so, but a veritable labor of Hercules. We consider a hundred Egyptian plagues as nothing merely because we suffer them in youth, when moral wounds and spiritual compound fractures heal as rapidly as physical ones; green wood does not break so easily as dry. In the old days, many of our boys' schools were monasteries, and their present regulations all indicate that they are in many ways still such. People ought to be content with that and not try to turn a reformatory into a pleasure palace. Aren't the inhabitants of such an institution required to take the three monastic vows? First, the vow of obedience, since the guardian of students and master of novices is constantly goading his black novice with unpleasant orders and mortifications of the flesh. Secondly, the vow of poverty, for they have neither scraps nor leftovers but only hunger to sustain them from day to day. Indeed, Carminati might have cured whole hospitals with the superfluous gastric juices from boarding schools like these! The vow of chastity we may take for granted, when a human being must run about and fast the whole day and is spared no other motion but the peristaltic.

Of all the students, only our Schoolmaster remained unaffected by the rigors of school life. Indeed, he was happy all day long. "Before getting up," he would say, "I am happy that I will soon have breakfast. All morning I look forward to lunch. Toward evening I anticipate the pleasure of tea, and then dinner." And so alumnus Wutz always has something to hope for. Whenever he took a long drink of water, he would say, "Didn't you enjoy that, Wutz!" and stroke his stomach. When he sneezed, he would say, "God bless you, Wutz!" In the frostiest November weather, as he stood in the street thrusting each cold hand in turn under his overcoat, he would comfort himself by picturing the warm stove indoors. If the day was stormy and windy—and there are such days for us poor wretches, when the whole world is in turmoil, and troubles, like playful water fountains, spray and soak us at every step—on such a day, our Schoolmaster was so clever that he would sit down in the torrent and not care in the least. This was not resignation, which accepts what is inevitable, nor indifference, which bears the unfelt, nor philosophy, which sweetens bitterness; it was not religion, either, which promises a reward. No, it was the thought of his warm bed. "Tonight," he would think, "I shall be under my cozy quilt for eight long hours; let them hound and drive me as they will."—And when he finally crept into his bed at the end of such a day of sorrows, he cuddled and drew his knees up under his chin, saying to himself, "You see, Wutz, at last it's all over."

When he reached the fifth grade, our Schoolmaster had a most important and profound experience: he fell in love. To elaborate on his emotions would be a pleasure for me indeed, but since this is the first time in my life that I have ever sketched a romantic picture, perhaps we had better stop here and continue again tomorrow evening at six. See how the fire has burned down!

If Venice, Rome, Vienna, and all the other cities of pleasure were to collaborate in giving me a carnival equal to the one we children enjoyed in the organist's dark parlor in Joditz, where we danced away from eight o'clock till eleven (a three-hour Saturnalia whereby we whetted our appetites for Lent), those great capitals would be giving themselves an absurd and impossible task. Yet they would probably have more success in this venture than if they were to try to match for schoolboy Wutz that festive Shrove Tuesday morning when he, a fifth-grade student home on vacation, actually fell in love in his father's schoolroom at about ten in the morning. Wasn't that a marvelous treat, my dear Schoolmaster! Indeed, he thought of nothing but his Justina, whom I shall seldom or never call by her Auenthal nickname of Justel. The schoolroom was being used for dancing that day, and although few boys of that age would have considered joining in, our Wutz, who was never proud though always vain, did so and perceived immediately in a quite impersonal way what Justina had to offer: that she was a pretty, graceful young thing who knew how to write a letter and had advanced to the rule of three in fractions; that she was fifteen and the grandchild of the rector's wife; and that she was in the ballroom only as a guest. He, being a guest himself, did in his turn what is proper under such circumstances: he fell in love, as I said before. It came upon him like a sickness during the very first dance, and as they stood waiting for the second, hand in hand and side by side, his condition grew progressively worse, and in no time at all he found that he had danced

his way right into the snares of love. Alas, when she undid
the red ribbons of her bonnet and let them flutter care-
lessly about her bare throat, he even stopped hearing the
bass viol, and when finally she began to fan herself with a
red handkerchief, waving it to and fro before his eyes, nothing could have saved him—not even a sermon by the four
greater and the twelve minor prophets! For just as a lion
gives way before a creaking carriage wheel and an elephant
flees from a mouse, Wutz always surrendered without re-
sistance to a handkerchief in a woman's hand. Country
coquettes make of their handkerchiefs the same cannon and
war engines that town coquettes make of their fans, you
know, but no rattling fan is as captivating as the soft waves
of a handkerchief.

Back to school went Wutz, his heart inflated like a balloon with the gas of love, but he said nothing to anyone
about it, least of all to the lovely lady with the handkerchief
herself. This was not because he was bashful, but because
he never desired more than the present moment. The fact
that he was in love was sufficient for him, and he did not
look ahead.

Why has Heaven ordained that the lustrum of love
should fall upon the young? Perhaps it is because that is
the time when we are gasping in schoolrooms, offices, and
other poison factories; then love climbs like a blooming vine
about the windows of those dungeons and reflects with its
shifting shadows the great springtime without. For I will
make a wager with you, Mr. Praefectus, and with you too,
most worthy educators: you may force a hair shirt onto
our cheerful Wutz (the truth of the matter is, he always
wears one), you may send him to move the wheel of Ixion,
to seek the philosopher's stone or push your baby's peram-
bulator; you may starve him half to death or have him
whipped; in short, so that you may win your damned wager, you can treat him like the very Devil (although I don't
believe you capable of it); Wutz will still be Wutz and he
will always hoard in his heart a little bit of happiness, even
through the dog days!

You will perhaps find that his summer vacation is nowhere better described than in his *Joys of Werther*, which his biographer need only copy. On Sundays after evensong as he walked home to Auenthal, he would pity all the people in the streets who had to remain behind. Out-of-doors his breast expanded with the sky above him, and doubly blessed, in the concert hall of the birds, he would give his attention now to the feathered choristers, now to his own fantasies. Sometimes, to give vent to his overflowing high spirits, he would gallop along for a quarter of an hour without stopping. He had always felt, before and after sunset, a certain voluptuous intoxicated yearning (for the night, like a lingering death, lifts man above the earth and removes it from under him), and so he would linger just outside of Auenthal until the setting sun over the cornfields embroidered his blue jacket with threads of gold and threw his shadow across the river to wander like a giant on the mountainside. He would reel into the village as the vesper bells rang in his ear like an echo from the distant past and his heart would warm to all mankind, even to his headmaster. Then he would walk around his father's house and watch the moon's reflection in the dormer window and, through another window, his Justina as she took her Sunday lesson in penmanship. Oh, if only he could have conjured away in this heavenly quarter of an hour room, lesson, and village and drawn round himself and the little scribe a dusky Vale of Tempe! If in this valley he and his intoxicated soul, which had thrown its arms about all mankind, could only embrace his loveliest of beings and with Heaven and Earth sink down and dissolve in a moment of fiery ecstasy!

And so, indeed, he did, dreaming in bed that night; and even earlier things did not go badly at all for him. He told his father, although actually he was telling Justina, about his studies and his political influence; he overrode all the corrections his father made to Justina's letters with the authority of an art critic; and since he had just come from town, he had a fine stock of clever stories to tell. Afterward, as he was falling asleep, his dancing mixed-up fantasies rang with the music of the spheres.

Oh Master Wutz, how well you may write of Werther's

joys, for your inner and outer worlds are joined snugly about you like the two halves of a mussel shell. Yet for us poor souls sitting here in front of the fire, the outer world is seldom the counterpart of our inner mood—or at best, only when our vocal organs have decayed and we groan and mumble. To use another metaphor, when our noses are congested, if all the flowers of the Garden of Eden were set before us, we could not catch their scent.

With every visit our Schoolmaster made his Johanna-Theresa-Charlotte-Mariana-Clarissa-Heloise-Justel the gift of a piece of gingerbread and a potentate; I shall satisfy your curiosity about both items. The potentates he manufactured in his own publishing house; but whereas the chancery of the nation creates its princes and counts out of a little ink, parchment, and wax, Wutz made his in a much more expensive fashion, with soot, grease, and twenty colors. In school they used to use the frames of a number of potentates for lighting the fires, all of whom Wutz, with the materials I mentioned, could copy and represent as well as if he had been their envoy. First he smeared the wax from a candle end all over a sheet of paper and then covered it with soot. Next he placed this sheet, black side down, over a blank one and on top of both he set some royal portrait. Then, with the tine of a broken fork, he drew over the face and body of the royal personage. This operation produced a copy of the potentate which was transferred from the black sheet to the white. And so he secured excellent copies of all the crowned heads of Europe. Nevertheless, I cannot deny that his grafting fork scratched and cut up the late Russian Empress and a score of crown princes so badly that they were only fit to go the way of their frames. His paint box gave the last finishing touches to the potentates, and when they had been suitably illuminated he presented them to the sovereign of his own heart, who had no idea what to do with her historical portrait gallery.

She knew, however, exactly what to do with the gingerbread, and she ate it. It's quite difficult, you know, to give one's sweetheart a present of gingerbread, because one often eats it oneself just before the presentation. Hadn't Wutz already paid three kreutzers for the first piece? Hadn't he put the small brown square into his pocket and carried it within an hour of Auenthal, the term of legal cession? And every fifteen minutes or so, didn't he take out his offering to assure himself that it was preserving its shape? But that was the trouble, you see, because when he handled it he always managed to break off a few insignificant almonds. Then, instead of squaring the circle, he set to work on the problem of how to restore the squared circle to its original form and bit off neatly the four right angles, thus making an octagon. Continuing the process, he produced a dodecagon, and so forth—for a circle is nothing more than a polygon with an infinite number of angles. After he had performed these mathematical operations, it was out of the question, of course, to offer the polygon to the young lady, whereupon Wutz would say with a sigh, "Ah, well! I'll eat it myself!" and in would go the geometrical figure. There are few Scotch professors and academicians alive who will not be eager to know by what miraculous means Wutz extricated himself from the difficulty. It was by means of a second piece of gingerbread that he always carried to keep the first company. While he ate the one, the other reached its destination in safety under the escort of its twin. He soon found, however, that in order for more than a crumb to reach Auenthal, it was necessary to increase the escort from week to week.

Wutz would have been promoted to sixth grade if his father had not been promoted at the time from our planet to another, or perhaps to some satellite. It occurred to him then to imitate his father's promotion and slip from his seat in the fifth grade to the teacher's chair. The church patron, however, Herr von Ebern, placed himself between the two seats and supported the claim of his cook, who had been serving him for some years, to a position for which his former job had eminently prepared him. For here, too, there were young suckling pigs to be whipped (they taste better, you know, when they are killed in that manner) and dressed, even if not to be eaten. I have already mentioned

in a note to my book on school reform that there lies latent
in every farm boy an undeveloped schoolmaster, who
would appear within the space of a few years; that just as
ancient Rome took her consuls, so also might our villages
take their schoolmasters from the plow and out of the fur-
rows. A man might as well be taught by his peers, just as
he is judged by them in England. After all, if a whole city
(Norcia in the Apennines) could be ruled by four unedu-
cated men (*i quatro illiterati*), it ought to be feasible for
the children of a village to be ruled and whipped by a
single unlettered man. It would be well for a legislative
body to study these facts and consider the matter. I wish
to add, however, that I said in my book that a village school
is adequately staffed. There are: (1) the gymnasiarch or
pastor, who puts on his vestments every winter or so and
visits the schoolhouse to terrify the students; (2) the rector,
conrector and subrector, all represented by the schoolmaster; (3) the schoolmaster's wife, who teaches the lower
grades and to whom, if to anyone, could be entrusted the
calisthenics in the girls' division; and her son, both third
instructor and pupil at the same time, whom his charges
must flatter and bribe so that they may be excused from
recitation, and who, when the schoolmaster is away, sometimes has the administration of an entire Protestant school
district on his shoulders; (4) finally, a whole caterpillar's
nest of collaborators, namely the schoolboys themselves,
because there, as in the celebrated orphanage at Halle, the
pupils of the upper grades are ready-made teachers of the
lower classes. So that they might satisfy the clamor of educational reformers for practical schools, communes and
schoolmasters espoused the cause and willingly did all they
could. The communes selected for their chairs of authority
only such pedagogical rumps as had formerly been installed
on weavers', tailors' or shoemakers' benches, and of whom
therefore something was to be expected; and doubtless
such men, by making before the attentive institute coats,
boots, creels, and other practical items, easily convert a
theoretical school into a practical one, where the art of
manufacture may be learned. The schoolmaster carries the

trend still further and meditates day and night on the management of a practical school. Indeed there are few tasks which normally fall to the head of a household or his servants for which he does not make use of his village stoa, and you may observe his practical seminary all morning long, hurrying in and out, chopping wood or carrying water, and so forth. It seems that apart from practical lessons, he gives none at all, and so he earns his bread by the sweat of his—schoolhouse. You don't have to tell me that in addition to these fine institutions there are also bad and unsatisfactory village schools; it is enough that the majority have all the advantages I have just described.

I will not attempt to excuse my digression, for if I did, it would take me even farther afield. To continue the story, Herr von Ebern would have appointed his cook schoolmaster if he could have found a successor to the cook's position. None appeared, however, and since the good gentleman thought that it might be too much of a novelty to have the kitchen and school supervised by the same individual, he retained the cook and appointed Wutz, who had been wise enough to remain in love.

I am guided here entirely by the praiseworthy testimonials which I have in my hands and which Wutz obtained from the rector, for his examination was perhaps one of the most rigorous and brilliant of our times. Did not Wutz have to repeat the Pater Noster in Greek, while the examining committee brushed its velvet trousers with a glass brush, and afterward the Athanasian Creed in Latin? Didn't the candidate enumerate the books of the Bible correctly and one by one without stumbling over the painted flowers and cups on his examiner's breakfast tray? Didn't he have to catechize a beggar boy who only stared at the penny he would receive as a reward and performed less like his brilliant instructor than like a block of wood? Didn't he have to dip his fingertips into five pots of warm water and to decide which was exactly right for an infant about to be baptized? And, last of all, didn't he have to pay three gulden and 36 kreutzers for the position?

On May 13, he walked out of his school as a pupil and

into his house as a public schoolmaster and out of the black
schoolboy cocoon there burst a bright organist into the
world.

On July 9, he stood before the altar in Auenthal and was
married to Justel.

But the Elysian interlude between the thirteenth of May
and the ninth of July! Never again will such a golden age
of eight weeks be granted by Heaven to mortal man! It was
only for our Schoolmaster that a dewy Paradise was made
to glisten on the star-decked fields of Earth. Floating
weightless on air, he found himself carried with Heaven and
sun around and around a transparent Earth. But to us
alumni of Nature no such eight weeks are granted, not one,
scarcely even a whole day, on which the Heaven above
and within us stains its clear blue only with the ruddiness
of dawn and sunset; on which we soar high above our daily
lives and are exalted as in a blissful dream—where the un-
ruly current of events cannot bruise or shake us in its
cataracts and whirlpools, but cradles us on sparkling ripples and carries us along under overhanging blossoms; a
day whose peer we seek in vain and of which we lament
at the close of every following one: we shall not see its like
again.

It will do us all good to hear these eight weeks or two
months of ecstasy described in detail. They consisted of a
series of days which were very much alike. Not a single
cloud was to be seen above the houses. All night long, the
red glow of evening remained in the sky, where the setting
sun had faded like a rose. The larks were already singing
by one o'clock in the morning, and a chorus of nightingales
filled the early hours with playful fantasies. The melodies
of the outer world penetrated into his dreams, and in them
he soared above the blossoming trees to which the real ones
outside his open window lent their flowery fragrance. At
dawn, his dream rocked him gently, as a crooning mother
would her child, out of sleep into waking, and he would step
out-of-doors with eager heart as the sun made the world
anew and as both poured forth in a surging sea of joy. From

this morning flood of life and happiness he turned back to his dark little room and sought strength in the small pleasures of life. He rejoiced at everything, at every bright and shadowy window, at the clean and tidy room, at his breakfast, which had been paid for out of his official stipend, at the fact that it was seven o'clock and he did not have to go to work, at his mother, who was happy every morning because he was a schoolmaster and she did not have to leave her old house.

As he drank his morning coffee, he cut his roll and, at the same time, the pens he would use to compose his *Messiad,* a work which he had quite finished by that time, with the exception of the three final cantos. He was very careful to cut his epic pens imperfectly, either like sticks or without a slit or with an extra slit which spattered the ink; for, since the *Messiad* was to consist of hexameters—and obscure ones, at that—it seemed to the poet that he might best achieve unintelligibility through illegibility; a very wise conclusion. By means of such poetic license, he succeeded in being obscure with a minimum of effort on his part.

At eleven o'clock he fed his birds and set the table (the four drawers of which held more than the table did) for himself and his mother. He cut the bread and gave the crust to his mother, although he didn't care to eat the crumb himself. Oh, my friends, why can't one dine as pleasurably at the Hotel de Bavière and at the Roemer as at Wutz's board? After dinner it was not the making of hexameters that occupied him, but of ladles for the kitchen—my sister still has a dozen of them. While his mother washed what he carved, their minds were not left idle; she told him little anecdotes about herself and his father and what had happened when he was away at school; and he laid before her his plans for future housekeeping, for he never tired of picturing himself as a *paterfamilias.* "I shall arrange my housekeeping most wisely," he would say; "we'll buy a piglet in preparation for the holidays, and we have so much potato and turnip peelings that it will become fat all by itself. And for the winter my father-in-law must get me a load of firewood, and the parlor door must be weather-stripped and reinforced—for, you know, Mother, we teachers are busy with our pedagogical tasks in winter, and cannot stand the cold."

On the twenty-ninth of May, there was a christening— it was his first—and it brought him his first fee. While at school he had prepared a large ledger in anticipation of this day. He examined and counted the couple of groschen twenty times, each time as if they were a new fee. At the baptismal font he stood in full vestments and the spectators stood in the gallery and the gentry's pews in their work-clothes. "It is the sweat of my brow," he said half an hour after the ceremony, as he drank a pint of beer (an un-common indulgence) bought from the christening fee. I ex-pect from his future biographers a couple of pragmatic hints, to explain why Wutz stitched himself a book to enter his fees, but none for his expenses, and why he provided columns in the former for louis d'ors, groschen, and pfen-nigs, although he never encountered the first denomination among his tuition fees.

After the ceremony was over and he had digested his beer, he carried out his table to a spot under the cherry tree and sat down to compose a few more illegible hexame-ters of his *Messiad*. Even as he was gnawing and polish-ing off his ham bone at dinner, he was mentally polishing still another line or foot of his epic, and I know very well that because of the fat, some of the cantos appear a little oily here and there. As soon as he saw that the sunshine had climbed from the street to the housetops, he gave his mother the money she needed for housekeeping and ran out-of-doors to picture in peace and quiet what the future held for him in autumn, in winter, and on the three great religious holidays of the year, as a schoolmaster and as a family man.

And still, these are only the weekdays; for him Sunday shone with a glory brighter than any altar painting! Indeed, no human soul of this century has so great a concept of Sunday as the souls that dwell in the persons of organists and schoolmasters; nor is it a wonder if they fail to appear modest on such an occasion. Even our Wutz could not help feeling what it meant to play the organ alone amidst a thousand people—to perform a real hereditary office and, as *valet de fantaisie* and body servant of the rector, to place the spiritual coronation robe on the clergyman's shoulders! To exercise territorial lordship over a sunlit choirloft and to rule over the poetry of a diocese from his organ as from a throne, even more absolutely that the parson commands its prose! To have the power to lean over the rail after the sermon to proclaim, or rather to promulgate, *sans façon*, his commands in loud and lordly voice! Indeed, one would think that here, if anywhere, I should admonish my Wutz: "Consider what you were just a few months ago. Consider that not all men can become organists, and make use of the happy inequalities of station without abusing them or belittling me and my listeners here at the fireside."

But no! Upon my honor, the good-natured little teacher never thought of such a thing. If only the country folk had been shrewd enough to look into your unspoilt overflowing heart, you funny smiling little man, what would they have found there? Nothing but happiness and joy in every compartment. Up in your choirloft you were counting your future schoolboys and girls in their pews and grouping them in your schoolroom before your little nose; and you were deciding that you would take a pinch of snuff morning and afternoon just so that you might sneeze and have the pleasure of seeing the whole company jump up like mad and call out, "God bless you, sir!" And in addition the country folk would have discovered the pleasure you feel every Sunday as you publish in large type on the blackboard the number and page of the next hymn (we authors appear in print with far worse testimony!) and the joy of showing off your singing voice before your father-in-law and your fiancée.

Indeed, it seems as if I shall never stop exclaiming over and praising our Schoolmaster! Why is it that this happy heart gives me—and perhaps you too—so much joy? Perhaps the reason is that we ourselves are never so completely happy, because the thought of life's vanities lies heavy on us and makes us breathless, because we have already

caught a glimpse of the black earth of the graveyard under the grass and flowers on which the little Schoolmaster
is dancing his way through life.

On Sunday evenings, the Communion wine still seemed
to sparkle in his veins, and I must tell you about this last
part of his Sabbath. It was only on Sunday that Wutz
might walk with Justina. Beforehand he would have dinner at his father-in-law's, although with little profit; for his
hunger seemed to abate while the grace was being said,
and by the time they reached the dessert, it had entirely
disappeared. If I were able to read it, I could find a complete description of these evenings in his *Messiad*, woven
into the Sixth Canto, where, just as all great writers incor-
porate in their *opera omnia* their careers, wives, children,
lands, and cattle, he has included them. He thought
that such evenings were likewise described in the printed
Messiad. In his own version, you may read his epical account of how the farmers from the edge of their fields
would scan the crop, measuring the growth of the corn-
stalks and shout greetings to him as their new organist from
across the river; of how the children made whistles out of
leaves and blew on little toy flutes; of how all the bushes
and blossoms and buds became a full-voiced orchestra, from
which something sang or hummed or buzzed; and finally,
of how everything became so festive that it seemed as if
the Earth herself were celebrating Sunday, while the hills
and forests enveloped this magic circle in haze. In the sky,
two triumphal arches appeared; a shining one, through
which the sun was setting, and a pale one, through which
the moon rose. O Thou Father of light! With how many
colors and balls of fire, with how much radiance dost Thou
invest Thy pale Earth!

Now the sunlight had dwindled to a single red beam
which mingled with the reflection of the sunset on the face
of his bride; and she, who seldom expressed her feelings,
told Wutz that as a child she had often longed to stand on
the ruddy mountains of the sunset and to descend with the
sun into the beautiful vivid country beyond. As his mother

rang the churchbell for evensong, he would lay his hat on his knee and gaze with unclasped hands at the red spot in the sky where the sun had last stood, and down at the deep shadowy stream; and it seemed to him that the vesper bell was ringing the world and his father once again to rest. For the first and last time in his life his heart surmounted the earthly scene; and he thought that something called to him from out of the chiming, that he would die of joy. With impetuous rapture he embraced his bride and murmured, "How I love you, love you forever." From the river came the sound of flutes and singing which drew nearer to them. Beside himself, he held her closer and closer, ready to die of love, and he imagined that the heavenly music would waft their two souls away from the Earth and scatter them like dewdrops on the fields of Paradise.

There appeared a gondola from the town, in which some young men were singing and playing on flutes. They sang:

> How beautiful is God's green earth!
> Therefore we must
> Enjoy its pleasures, know its worth,
> Ere we are dust.

He and Justina wandered along the river bank, hand in hand, following the moving gondola, and Justina tried to sing softly along with them. How lovely it all was! As the gondola was rounding a wooded bend in the river, Justina held him back so that they would fall behind, and when the little boat had disappeared, she put her arms about him and gave him the first blushing kiss. "Oh, that unforgettable first of June!" he writes. They followed the sounds of music on the water and both were lost in dreams, until she said, "It is late; the last sunlight is fading, and the village is quiet." They went home then. He opened the window of his moonlit room and with a soft "Good night," slipped past his mother, who was already asleep.

Each morning at sunrise, the thought came to him that the night's sleep had brought him one day closer to his wedding day—the eighth of June; and all day long he would rejoice, remembering that he would enjoy many more

heavenly hours before that date. And so, like the meta-
physical ass, he held his head between two bundles of hay
—the present and the future; but he was neither ass nor
scholar, and therefore could graze on and pick at both
bundles at once. Indeed, men should never be asses of any
sort—diaphorist, wooden, or Balaamitic—and I have my reasons for saying this.—But let me break off here; I must decide whether or not to picture his wedding day for you.
Of mosaic tiles I have more than enough, to be sure.

The truth is that I neither attended Wutz's marriage celebration nor my own, but I will describe it as best I can and
so make a little celebration for myself. Otherwise I am likely
to have none at all!

Let us take a peep into the schoolhouse and the bride's
house on the Saturday before the wedding, and clear the
ground for the wedding day itself by explaining the prem-
ises; tomorrow, Sunday, there will be no time for it. Likewise, according to the older theologians, the creation of the
world was effected in six days, rather than a minute, so
that the angels might better peruse the book of nature as
it was gradually unfolded. On Saturday the bridegroom
might be seen performing his dual role, dashing back and
forth between the rectory and the schoolhouse in order to
carry four chairs from the latter into the former. He borrowed these seats from the rectory for the accommodation
of the rector himself as his prince bishop, the rector's wife as
godmother of the bride, the subprefect of his school, and
the bride herself. Of the tin dinner service which the
bridegroom also obtained from his prince bishop the public
can be a better judge than I, when and if it should find its
way into the hands of the auctioneer. The wedding guests,
however, did know this much: that the salad bowl, the
sauce boat, the cheese dish, and the mustard pot were one
and the same piece, which, I should add, was washed each
time before it changed its function.

A regular Nile and Alpheus flowed over every board in
the room, some of which were soiled by earth tracked in
from the garden, over the bedposts and window sills, and
it left behind it the usual deposit—sand. The rules of ro-

mance now require that the little Schoolmaster should dress himself and lie down in a meadow beneath a rippling coverlet of grass and flowers to be overtaken by dreams of love; but this Schoolmaster was plucking chickens and ducks, grinding coffee and splitting firewood, roasting meats; and, attired in his mother-in-law's blue apron, his hair wrapped in horny curl papers, he ran about executing orders from the kitchen. "For of course," he said, "I'm not getting married every Sunday."

Nothing is more unpleasant than to hear and see a hundred footmen serving at some trifling celebration; on the other hand, nothing is sweeter than to perform this office oneself. The activity which we not only see but take part in, makes the pleasure of it like a fruit which we ourselves have planted and cultivated; and moreover we do not suffer the suspense of waiting.

Dear Lord, I would need a whole Saturday just to describe this one; all I can do is to take the briefest glance into Wutz's kitchen. Oh what writhings and clouds of smoke! Why are murder and marriage as close to each other as the two commandments that speak of them? Why must a middle-class wedding be such a massacre of fowls? But no one in the house passed these two joyous days more dolorously than two goldfinches and three bullfinches; these the cleanly and bird-loving bridegroom had personally incarcerated after chasing after them, waving his apron and throwing up his nightcap. Thus forced to leave their ballroom, they hopped about in two monastic cell-like wire cages which hung from the ceiling.

Wutz tells us, both in his *History of the Wutz Family* and his *Child's Intermediate Reader*, that by seven o'clock that evening, when the tailor brought his wedding trousers, waistcoat, and jacket to him for a final fitting, everything was in perfect order, clean and shining—Wutz himself excepted. An indescribable peace rests on each chair and table of a freshly cleaned room! In an untidy one we feel as if we were just on the point of moving out.

The sun and I will pass over that night and we will meet him again on Sunday morning when he trips downstairs,

flushed and tingling with the anticipation of the heavenly
day before him, into the happy wedding room we all decorated last night with so much care, with beauty baths,
mouchoir de Venus, and powder puffs (washcloths)—
powderboxes (sandbox) and other cosmetics. During the
night he had awakened seven times, in order to rejoice seven
times over the coming day; and he had risen two hours
before the usual time to feed on each passing minute. Even
now it seems to me that I am going through the door with
the Schoolmaster, before whom the minutes of the day
stand like honey-cells; he drains off one after the other, and
every moment brings him a fuller honeycup. The Schoolmaster could not have conceived of a house in the world in
which there was not Sunday, sunshine, and joy that day—
not even if you had offered him a life pension! After opening the door, he opened an upper window to let a fluttering
butterfly—a floating silver sequin, a flower petal, Cupid's
image—escape from the wedding chamber. Then, antici-
pating the busy day, he fed his choir of birds in their cages,
and before the open window he played on his father's violin
the waltzes to which he had danced from Easter week to
his wedding day. The clock is only striking five, my friend,
we have no need to hurry! We'll get into our two-yard
stock (into which you're already dancing yourself, while
your mother holds one end) quite easily and get our pigtail
ribbon on smoothly two full hours before the churchbell
rings. Oh, I would give my grandfather's armchair and
stove if I could transform myself and my listeners into invisible sylphs; then our whole company without disturbing
his quiet joy could follow the enraptured bridegroom into
the garden, where he is cutting real flowers, not diamond
ones, for a female heart which is also real; where he shakes
the shining beetles and dewdrops from the flower petals
and gladly waits for the bee to suck its last mouthful of
honey from the maternal leafy breast; where he thinks of
the Sunday mornings of his boyhood and of the too short
walk across the flower beds to the cold lectern on which
the rector used to place his bouquet. Go home, son of your
father, and on this eighth day of June, as evening falls, do

not look up to the spot where six silent feet of graveyard earth lie over many a friend; look rather toward this morning, where the sun is shining and Justina is just slipping in through the rectory door to have her godmother arrange her hair and help her to dress. I can see that my listeners would again like to be changed into sylphs, to flutter about the bride; but she would rather we did not.

Finally the sky-blue coat—the livery of millers and schoolmasters—with blackened buttonholes and all creases removed by his mother's ironing, is placed on our Wutz's person; he may now take up his hat and hymnal. And now —of course I know all about royal weddings, the cannonades, illuminations, drilling, and hair curling that goes on; but I would not even compare all of this pomp and glory with Wutz's wedding. Watch the man as he follows the sun's path through the clouds on the way to his bride; glancing at that other path that leads to his old school, he thinks, "Who would have imagined this four years ago?" Just look at him, I say! Doesn't the rector's maid stare at him, although she is carrying water, and doesn't she hang away in the clothes closet of her memory that magnificent full dress down to the last fringe? Isn't he powdered from head to foot? Aren't the red folding doors of his father-in-law's house standing open to him, and doesn't he stride through them, while his beloved slips out the back from the hands of her hairdresser? And aren't the pair of them so bedecked and bepowdered that they scarcely have the courage to bid each other "Good morning"? Have either one in their lives ever seen anything as gorgeous and aristocratic as themselves today?

I hope that the envious ladies will forgive me if I choose from my palette the brightest colors to paint the finery of the bride, the shining gold in her hair, the three gold medallions on her breast with miniature paintings of the German emperors and below the silver bars worked into buttons. But I could hurl my paintbrush at someone's head if I thought for a moment that my Wutz and his good bride would be laughed at by coquettes and other wicked people when this appears in print. Do you imagine, you city-bred

and tattooed female soul-sellers, who survey and love everything about a man except his heart, do you think that
I or my gentlemen readers could be indifferent to a girl like
Justina, or that we would not reject with amusement your
flushed cheek, your quivering lips, your brilliant lustful
eyes, and your ever waiting arms, even your sentimental
eloquence, for a single scene, where love is tempered by
modesty and the guiltless soul disrobes itself before every
eye except its own, where a hundred inner struggles ani-
mate the candid face—in short, for a scene like the very one
in which my bridal pair were the actors, when the bride's
father got hold of the two curled and powdered heads and
skillfully brought them together for a kiss? How you
blushed with pleasure, dear Wutz! And how embarrassed
you were, my dear Justina!

The noise of the children and the peddlers in the street
(and the thought of the critics in Leipzig) prevent me from
describing everything completely—the impressive flourishes
and lacy cadences with which the bridegroom festooned
every hymn he played on the organ; the wooden angel's
wings on which he hung his hat in the choirloft; the name
of Justina on the organ stops; his joy and happiness when
they each took the other by the right hand before the ceremony and he tickled her hand with his finger behind a bed-
screen; and their entrance into the bridal hall, where perhaps the greatest and most distinguished persons and
governors of the village met—a rector, a rector's wife, a subprefect, and a bride.

I am sure no one will mind if I change my pace and skip
over the wedding feast and the events of the afternoon to
tell what is happening that evening. The subprefect leads
off a couple of dances and everyone is leaping with excitement. The smoke from the tobacco and a regular steam-
bath from the soup roll around the three candles and
separate one feaster from another by banks of mist. The
'cellist and the violinist are less occupied with their instruments than with filling their own stomachs. All Auenthal
is peeping in at the window ledge, pushing and shoving
like the spectators in the second balcony of a theater; and

outside the young folk of the village are dancing rather prettily at a distance of some thirty paces from the orchestra. The old village *La Bonne* is screeching her remarks to the rector's wife, and the rector's wife is sneezing and coughing out her own, each wishing to ease herself first of the burden of historical fact and each unwilling to let the other have the floor. The rector looks like a bosom friend of the beloved disciple St. John—whom the painters portray with a wine cup in his hand—and is laughing louder than he preaches. The subprefect darts about like an elegant dandy, and no one can get hold of him. Our Maria splashes about in all four rivers of paradise, and is swung and tossed about on the all-powerful waves of a sea of joy. Only the lone bridesmaid, whose disposition is too tender and sensitive for her difficult role, hears the drums of gladness, smothered as if by an echo, or muffled with crepe as at a king's funeral, and expresses her quiet rapture by a sigh. Our Schoolmaster (who must certainly be allowed to reappear) steps with his helpmate through the house door, whose *dessus-de-porte* is a round swallow's nest, and looks up to the silent shimmering Heaven above him and thinks that every great sun there is peeping down at him like his village neighbors. Sail merrily over the evaporating drop of time that is yours, for well you may! Not all of us can do so. The lone bridesmaid cannot. Ah, if I had found like you a flower-like captive butterfly on a wedding morning, or a bee in a flower-cup; like you, the church clock stopped at seven; like you, the mute Heaven above and a noisy one below; the thought would have come to me that in this stormy world, where the winds uproot our little flowers, there is no resting place where a fragrance may encircle us, or an eye may be found free of the dust and raindrops which each storm hurls upon us. And had the shining Goddess of Joy stood as close to my side, I would still have had to turn my eyes to those handfuls of ashes to which her embrace reduces us poor mortals. And oh! if the description of such great delight has left me so sad, only think: if Thou, O God, hadst stretched forth Thy hand from the infinite Heaven to this low earth; if Thou hadst brought

me such joy, like a flower grown in the sun, tears of joy
would have fallen upon Thy fatherly hand and I would
have turned from my fellow men with weeping eyes.

But now, as I tell you this, Wutz's wedding is long past
and gone, his Justina is old and he himself is in the churchyard; the stream of time has carried him off and buried
him, together with all these shimmering days, under four or
five layers of earth. And so, around us too, there rises higher
and higher the earth of the grave; three minutes more, and
it has reached our hearts and stolen over us all.

While I am in this frame of mind, please don't ask me
to tell you about the Schoolmaster's many happy moments,
as he himself describes them in his *Book of Joy;* especially
those having to do with his Christmases or church and
school activities. Perhaps they may appear in a postscript
on some future occasion, but not today! Today it is better
for us to see the contented Wutz for the last time, living
and dead, and then go our way.

Although I must have passed his house thirty times, I
would really have known little about the whole man if old
Justina had not been standing by the door as I went by
last year on the twelfth of May. As she saw me writing in
my notebook while I walked, she asked me if I was not
also a maker of books. "Of course, dear lady," I replied,
"I produce one every year and present it to the public."
In that case, then, she asked, would I come into the house
and spend some time with her old man, who was also an
author, although he was now quite ill.

A stroke had paralyzed the left side of his body. He was
sitting in bed reclining on pillows and had about him on
the blanket a whole assortment of articles which I will tell
about shortly. A sick man is like a traveler—what else is
he?—in that he gets acquainted with everyone at once. We
no longer stand on ceremony in this wretched world when
we are on the threshold of the next. He complained that
he had sent his old woman out to look for a writer for the
past three days, but that she hadn't caught one until now.
He needed one, he said, to arrange, catalogue, and oversee

his library, and to add to his autobiographical notes, which
were scattered everywhere, a description of his last hours
—if these were his last. For his old wife was no scholar and
he had just sent his son to the University of Heidelberg
for three weeks.

The pockmarks and wrinkles in his little round face
seemed like merry little lights, each a smiling mouth; but
I was disturbed by the way his eyes burned, by the way
his eyebrows and the corners of his mouth twitched, and
by the trembling of his lips.

I must not forget that I promised to tell you about the
objects our Wutz had about him on the bed. First of all,
there was a child's cap of green taffeta with one ribbon
torn off; next, a child's toy whip on which there were still
some flecks of gold; a tin wedding band; a box with the
tiniest books imaginable; a wall clock; a dirty notebook and
a bird trap the size of one's index finger. They were the
souvenirs of his long-spent childhood. As precious to him
as an art gallery of Greek antiquities, they had been kept
for some years under the stairs. In a house which is, you
might say, the flowerpot or hothouse of a single family tree,
things sometimes remain in the same spot for fifty years.
And so, on the eve of his death—since it had been an in-
violable rule with him from his childhood to preserve all
his toys in chronological order and because no one except
himself ever ventured to look under the stairs—he was able
to arrange his mementoes about him, the funeral urns of a
life that had gone by; and to rejoice in looking backward,
for he could no longer rejoice in looking ahead. To be sure,
dear Maria, you could not enter Sans Souci or Dresden or
some other temple of antiquities to fall down before the
world spirit of artistic creation; but you were able to peep
into the tabernacle of the antiquities of your childhood under the dark staircase. And when you did so, the sunbeams
of your resurrected childhood played in the dark corners as
in a painting the light streams from the Christ child in the
manger! Oh, if only greater souls than yours could suck as
much honey from Nature's whole flower garden as you did
from the thorny green leaf on which Destiny hung you,

they would feast on gardens, not on leaves; and these better and yet happier souls would no longer ponder how a
schoolmaster can be so happy.

Turning his head toward the bookshelf, Wutz said,
"When I have tired myself with reading and correcting my
serious works, I spend hours looking at these old knickknacks. I hope that this is nothing for an author to be
ashamed of."

At this point perhaps I had best give my readers an explanation of the *objets d'art* and knickknacks as Wutz explained them to me. The four-year-old daughter of the late
rector had put the tin wedding band on his finger when
they were honorably and properly joined together by a
playmate. The worthless tin bound them more closely together than precious gold does the wealthy, and they kept
their vows for almost an hour. Later, as a black-gowned
student, when he would catch a glimpse of her as she
walked with bobbing plumes on the arm of some slim
young dandy, he would think of the ring and of former
days. Until now I have tried, though in vain, to conceal
this fact about my Schoolmaster: that he fell in love with
anything resembling a woman. All happy people of his
temperament do the same, you know; and perhaps it is because their love achieves a balance between the two extremes of love—the Platonic and the Epicurean—and bor-
rows something from both.

When he helped his father to wind up the clock in the
steeple (just as crown princes used to attend state councils
with their fathers), so trifling an operation was sufficient
to make a clockmaker of Wutz himself. He would make
holes in a little box of lacquered wood and thus transform
it into a wall clock. It had its long weights and its cog-
wheels, taken off the stand of a pair of Nuremberg horses
and thus elevated to a higher purpose, but unfortunately,
like many of our departments of state, it never functioned.
The green child's cap, with its lace trimming, was the only
surviving relic of his four-year-old son; the bust and plaster
cast of the little Wutz who had now grown into a man.
The everyday clothes of a dead man give us a much clearer

picture of him than his portrait. And so Wutz examined
the cap with nostalgic delight, and it seemed to him that
in the midst of the snow of old age there glittered a still-
surviving patch of greenery. "If I only had my old flannel
undershirt too," he said, "the one I used to wear tied under
my shoulders."

I know the King of Prussia's first notebook as well as I
do the Schoolmaster's, and since I have held them both in
my hand, I am able to affirm that the King's handwriting
grew worse with age, while Wutz's improved. "Mother," he
said to his wife, "just look how your husband wrote here
(pointing to the notebook) and there (indicating an account book—his calligraphic masterpiece—that hung from a
nail on the wall); I still can't help giving myself a pat on
the back, Mother!" He would boast before no one but his
own wife, you see, and I say it for what it is worth: that
one of the advantages of marriage is that the married man
acquires thereby a second self—an alter ego—before which
he may praise himself as much as he pleases. Oh, how I
wish that the German public were such an alter ego for
us writers!

The box was a bookcase for some Lilliputian tracts which
he had edited in his childhood by copying verses from the
Bible and compiling them in little volumes. Other authors
sometimes do likewise, but not until they are fully grown.
As he showed me his youthful compositions, he remarked,
"As a child, one is very foolish. However, the literary impulse was present even then, although in an immature and
ridiculous form"; and he beamed contentedly at his more
recent works. And so it was with the bird trap. Wasn't the
finger-length bird trap, which he smeared with beer and
whereby he caught the flies that crawled on his legs, the
forerunner of the arm's-length bird trap behind which he
spent his loveliest hours in late autumn?

It is quite understandable that his main pastime during
his illness was to look at a dreadfully printed old calendar.
He wandered through the pages representing eleven months
of the year, never taking notice of the current month, and
filled the woodcuts with the images that suited his needs

and theirs. On his sickbed, just as in his days of health, he enjoyed a climb up the bare black tree trunk on the page representing January, and loved to stand, in mind's eye, beneath that lowering sky that hung like a canopy over the winter sleep of meadows and fields. When he sat in reverie over the engraving of a June landscape, in which little crosses that were supposed to be birds flew about the gray paper and on which the engraver had reduced the summer foliage to a few skeleton leaves, the whole month of June, with its long days and long grasses, drew itself about him. The dreamer makes of every scrap a miraculous relic and a spring from the jawbone of an ass; the five senses afford him only the cartoons, only the outlines of pleasure or of sorrow.

The sick man skipped over May, for the house was surrounded by it. He could not smell the cherry blossoms which the lover's month wears in her green hair, nor the lilies she carries in her bosom; his sense of smell was gone. But he saw them and had some in a bowl next to his sickbed.

I have done what I set out to do—that is, to lead myself and my listeners five or six pages away from the sad moment in which Death steps up to the bedside of our sick friend before our eyes and with an ice-cold hand presses his warm breast and stops forever the heart that beat so joyfully. But still, that moment must come, and the phantom with it.

I spent the whole day there, and in the evening I said that I would sit up with him through the night. His excited brain and his twitching face had firmly convinced me that the stroke would return during the night; this did not happen, however, which was a great relief to myself and to the Schoolmaster. For he had said to me (just as he had written in his last tract) that nothing was easier and more beautiful than to die on a fine day, when the soul sees the sun up above through closed eyes and flies out of the withered body into the broad blue ocean of light. But to leave the warm body on a dark and stormy night, to plunge

into the lonely grave when all of Nature sits by dying—
that was, he thought, too hard a death.

About half-past eleven that night, there appeared again
at Wutz's bedside the two best friends of his childhood,
Sleep and Dream, who had come to bid him farewell. Or
hadn't they come rather to remain with him a while longer?
Are they not two friends of mankind who snatch the mur-
dered man out of Death's bloody hands and, cradling him
in their arms, carry him as would a mother through dark
subterranean caves and up into the bright land where a
new morning sun and new morning flowers breathe upon
him in a waking life?

I was alone in the room. I heard nothing but the sick
man's breathing and the ticking of my watch as it measured the last minutes of his life. The yellow full moon hung
large and low in the south and ringed with its dead light
the lilies by the bedside, the moldy wall clock, and the
child's green cap. The cherry tree with its delicate blossoms before the window cast upon the moonlit floor the
shadow of tremulous foliage. In the sky, a shooting star fell
from time to time, and passed away like a human soul. I
remembered that the next morning, the thirteenth of May,
would be the forty-third anniversary of the day on which
the sick man began his Elysian eight weeks in this very
room, now the black antechamber of the grave. I saw that
the man to whom the cherry tree had once brought fragrance and dreams, now lay scentless in the throes of a
dream. He was leaving us, perhaps this very day; and for
him, everything was over and would never return.

Just then, Wutz seemed to grasp at something with his
good arm. In the same trembling minute the month index
of my watch clicked and, since it was midnight, it moved
forward from the twelfth to the thirteenth of May. It
seemed that Death set my watch. I heard him grind man
and his joys to powder, and time and the world seemed
to plunge like an avalanche into the abyss and crumble to
nothingness. The dying man—we cannot call him that much
longer—opened his two burning eyes and looked at me for
a long time, trying to recognize me. He had dreamed that

he was a child again, rocking on a bed of lilies that sprang up under him. Then the lilies melted into a rosy cloud on which he skimmed along through the pink and gold sunrise over hazy fields of flowers. The sun smiled at him with the white face of a young girl and shone upon him; finally it seemed actually to become a young girl wearing a halo of light who disappeared behind a cloud bank, and he was angry because he could not embrace her with his useless left arm. This was what had awakened him from his last, or rather, his next to last dream; for on the long dream of life the bright little dreams of night are painted and embroidered like fanciful flowers.

The stream of life in his mind became faster and brighter every moment; once more it seemed to him that he was young. The moon he took for the overclouded sun and he thought he had become a carven angel with wings, hanging from a rainbow by a chain of buttercups which swung to and fro over an abyss and toward the sun, pushed by the hand of his four-year-old bride. Toward four in the morning, he could no longer see us, although the light of the dawn was already in the room. His eyes were glassy and his face scarcely stopped its convulsive twitching even for a moment; his mouth, however, seemed to smile more and more happily. Spring fantasies, unknown in this life and in the next, played with his sinking spirit and finally the Angel of Death covered his face with the pale shroud and bore away his blooming soul, its deepest roots now freed from the common clay.

Death is sublime! Behind black hangings he works his silent miracle for the other world, and the living stand by with wet but dull eyes, gazing at the divine scene.

"Dearest Father," said his widow, "if someone had told you forty-three years ago that you would be carried out on the thirteenth of May, the day when your eight weeks began!"—"His eight weeks are beginning again," I said, "but they will last longer."

At eleven o'clock, when I left the house, the very earth seemed holy to me and it seemed that I walked along accompanied by the dead. I looked up into the heaven, as if

I could find the dead man only there, in that one direction, in the infinite sky. And when I reached the top of the mountain from which one can see Auenthal, I looked back to the place of sorrow. When I saw among the houses with smoking chimneys the house of mourning—the only one whose chimney did not smoke—while up in the churchyard the gravedigger was preparing the grave; when I heard the tolling of the death bell and remembered the widow who, with brimming eyes, was herself pulling the rope in the silent belfry—I felt the nothingness of all of us and swore to despise, to deserve, and to enjoy this meaningless life of ours.

Hurrah for you, dear Schoolmaster Wutz! Whenever I go to Auenthal and seek out your grass-covered grave; when I mourn the fact that in this spot are also buried the cocoons from which the winged moths spring, that your grave is a playground for earthworms, creeping snails, busy ants, and nibbling caterpillars, while you lie deep below them all, your head motionless on your shavings of wood, and no caressing sunlight to break through your coffin boards and linen-bandaged eyes. Hurrah for you! because I can say of you, "While he still had life, he enjoyed it with greater pleasure than all of us!"

It is enough, my friends. It is twelve o'clock and the month index has sprung forward to a new day, reminding us of the twofold sleep—the sleep of the short and of the long night.

Michael Kohlhaas

HEINRICH VON KLEIST

TRANSLATED BY CHARLES E. PASSAGE

*In keeping with the subtitle "From an old chronicle,"
Kleist, who consistently wrote a difficult style in any case,
strove to compose the present story in such a way as to
give the reader the impression of reading in a book of an-
nals of long ago, perhaps in Petrus Hafftitius' Microchroni-
con, the very work from which the author drew his material.
Specific archaisms are few. The vocabulary is that of the
years 1805–1810 when the story was written. But a flavor
of antiquity is achieved by the immensely long paragraphs
that might correspond to a Latin author's caput (chapter),
by the immensely long periodic sentences, by the postponed
predicates, and by the subjects elaborately qualified by sub-
ordinate clauses. The result was the most difficult text in
standard German literature.*

*Many of the stylistic features are not tolerable to the
English language, but the translator has carefully retained
the original paragraphing and, as far as possible, the original sentence structure and punctuation. He has done so in
the belief that any simplification or modernization would
mar a significant beauty of the work and betray the author's
consummate plan.*

*Readers interested in this or other aspects of the story
are referred to the translator's interpretive article, "Michael
Kohlhaas: Form Analysis,"* in The Germanic Review, XXX,
3 (October 1955), *pp. 181–97, which also contains information as to the facts of the actual "Kohlhaas case" of the
sixteenth century.*

From an old chronicle

On the banks of the Havel there lived, around the middle of the sixteenth century, a horse trader named Michael Kohlhaas, the son of a schoolmaster, one of the most upright and at the same time one of the most abominable persons of his time. Up to his thirtieth year this extraordinary man could have passed for the model of a good citizen. In a village that still bears his name he owned a farmstead on which he quietly made his living by his trade. The children that his wife bore him he brought up in the fear of God to be industrious and honest. There was not one among his neighbors who had not enjoyed his generosity or his uprightness. In short, the world could not have done otherwise than bless his memory if he had not carried one virtue to an excess. His sense of justice, however, made him a robber and murderer.

One day as he was traveling toward foreign country with a string of young horses, all of them well fed and sleek, and pondering to what use he would put the profits that he hoped to make on them at the fairs—part, as good managers will, into new gains but part also into the satisfactions of the present—he reached the Elbe, and close by an imposing castle on Saxon territory encountered a tollgate which he had never found on that road before. At a moment when violent rain happened to be pouring down he halted with his horses and called for the gatekeeper, who

with a sullen face presently looked out from a window. The
horse trader told him to open the gate for him. "What's
this change here?" he asked as the customs official, after
some time, emerged from the house. "Seigneurial privilege,"
replied the latter as he opened the gate, "granted to
the Junker Wenzel von Tronka."—"So," said Kohlhaas,
"Wenzel is the Junker's name?" and took a look at the castle
which, with its gleaming battlements, looked out over the
field. "Is the old master dead?"—"Dead of a stroke," answered the customs official as he raised the toll bar.—"Hm!
Too bad!" returned Kohlhaas. "A worthy old gentleman
who took pleasure in association with people, assisted trade
and travel wherever he was able, and once had a pavement
put in because a mare of mine broke her leg down there
where the road goes into the town. Well, what do I owe
you?" he asked, and with some effort produced from beneath his wind-whipped cloak the coins which the customs
inspector required. "Yes, old man," he added further, while
the latter kept muttering "Hurry up! Hurry up!" and kept
cursing the foul weather, "if this bar had been left growing
in the forest, it would have been better for me and for you."
And therewith he gave him the money and started to ride
on. Scarcely was he beneath the toll bar, however, when
a new voice rang out behind him from the tower: "Hold
on, there, horse trader!" and he saw the castellan slam a
window shut and hurry down toward him. "Now what?"
wondered Kohlhaas and halted with his horses. The castellan, buttoning still another waistcoat around his ample person, came up and, standing sidewise to the storm, asked
for his exit permit. "Exit permit?" asked Kohlhaas. A little
taken aback, he said that, as far as he knew, he had no
such thing, but that if they would just describe what in
Heaven's name such a thing might be, he might just happen to be furnished with one. The castellan, looking at him
sidewise, replied that without a permit from the sovereign
lord of the district no horse trader would be allowed across
the border with horses. The horse dealer assured him that
he had crossed this border seventeen times in his life without any such permit; that he was thoroughly familiar with

all the legal regulations concerning his trade; that this must be a mistake; and that he requested time to consider it, but that, since he had a long day's ride ahead of him, he could not be held up any longer to no purpose. But the castellan replied that he was not going to slip through for the eighteenth time; that the ordinance had, for that very reason, appeared just recently; and that he must either procure the permit here and now or else return from whence he had come. The horse trader, who was beginning to get provoked at these illegal extortions, dismounted, after brief reflection, from his horse, turned it over to a groom, and said he would see the Junker von Tronka himself about the matter. And he walked toward the castle, the castellan following him, muttering all the way about hard-fisted money grabbers and the profitableness of letting blood from the same. Measuring looks with each other, they both stepped into the great hall. It chanced that the Junker was sitting over a glass with some jolly friends, and at some joke enormous laughter was resounding among them just as Kohlhaas approached him to present his grievance. The Junker asked what he wanted. The knights, at sight of the stranger, fell silent. But no sooner had the latter launched into his petition concerning the horses than the whole bunch of them cried, "Horses? Where are they?" and rushed to the window to get a view of them. At sight of the sleek string they hurried, at the Junker's suggestion, down to the courtyard. The rain had stopped. Castellan and overseer and grooms gathered around them and all were sizing up the animals. One praised the bay with the white star, a second liked the chestnut, a third stroked the dappled horse with the tawny spots, and they all were of the opinion that the horses were like stags and that none better were raised anywhere in the country. Kohlhaas jokingly replied that a horse was no better than the man that rode him and invited them to make their purchases. The Junker, who was much taken with the powerful bay stallion, asked him the price. The overseer urged him to buy a couple of blacks, which he thought could be used, given the shortage of horses, in the field work. But when the horse trader stated his terms, the

knights found him too dear, and the Junker said he would
have to ride to the Round Table and look up King Arthur
if he put prices like that on his horses. Kohlhaas, seeing
the castellan and the overseer casting meaningful glances at
the blacks and whispering with one another, and prompted
by a dark premonition, spared no pains to get them to buy
the horses. To the Junker he said, "Sir, I bought those
blacks six months ago for twenty-five gulden in gold; give
me thirty and they're yours." Two knights standing next to
the Junker declared with no uncertainty that the horses
were well worth that amount, but the Junker felt he might
well lay out money for the bay but not for the blacks, and
indicated that he was about to break off the bargaining.
Whereupon Kohlhaas said that perhaps he might do business with him the next time he was passing through with
his nags, respectfully took leave of the Junker, and seized
the reins of his horse preparatory to riding away. At that
moment the castellan stepped out from the crowd and said
he understood he could not travel without a permit. Kohlhaas turned and asked the Junker whether such was actually the case with this requirement, which would ruin his
whole business. With embarrassment on his face the Junker
answered as he turned away, "Yes, Kohlhaas, you have to
obtain the permit. Talk to the castellan and then go your
way." Kohlhaas assured him it was by no means his intention to circumvent ordinances that might govern the ex-
port of horses, promised to obtain the permit from the
Privy Secretariat on his way through Dresden, but requested that, since he had known nothing of such a requirement, he be allowed to go through just this one time.
"Well," said the Junker, just as the rain began pelting down
again and whistling through his withered limbs, "let the
beggar go through. Come on!" said he to the knights,
turned, and started for the castle. The castellan, turning to
the Junker, said that he had to leave behind a pledge at
least by way of guarantee that he would procure the permit.
The Junker halted again in the arch of the castle gate. Kohlhaas asked what amount of money or articles he should
deposit as pledge for the blacks. The overseer, muttering

in his beard, remarked that he could leave the blacks themselves. "Quite so," said the castellan, "that would be the most sensible thing. Once the permit is obtained he can come and get them any time." Startled at such an impudent demand, Kohlhaas turned to the Junker, who, half freezing, was holding the skirts of his jerkin up in front of him, and said that he was planning to sell the blacks. But the nobleman, driven inside the gate at just that moment by a whole mass of rain and hail, shouted, in order to put an end to the matter, "If he doesn't want to leave the horses, kick him back across the tollgate!" and walked away. The horse trader, seeing that he would have to yield to force, decided to meet the demand, since there was nothing else to do; he unhitched the blacks and led them to a stable pointed out to him by the castellan. He left a groom behind with them, provided him with money, cautioned him to take good care of the horses until his return, and with the remainder of his string resumed his journey toward Leipzig, where he intended to visit the fair, half sure, half unsure whether, with horse breeding in its infancy, such an ordinance could have been proclaimed in Saxony.

In Dresden, where he owned a house with several stables in one of the suburbs of the city because from there he could ply his trade in the smaller market towns of the province, he betook himself directly after arrival to the Privy Secretariat, where he learned from the Councilors, several of whom he knew, just what his first thoughts had told him, namely that the whole story about the permit was a fairy tale. Kohlhaas, upon whose application the displeased Councilors had given a written statement as to the unwarranted nature of the claim, smiled at the withered Junker's joke, although he did not exactly see what he was driving at with it; and, with the satisfactory sale of the string of horses that he had with him, he returned some weeks later, with no further feeling of bitterness beyond the general hardships of the world, to Castle Tronka. The castellan, to whom he showed the written statement, made no comment, and to the horse trader's question as to whether he might now have his horses back, he said that all he had to do was to go down and get them. Kohlhaas, however, had already had the unpleasant experience of finding out, as he was walking across the courtyard, that his groom had been beaten and driven away, on account of improper behavior, it was claimed, a few days after he had been left at Castle Tronka. He asked the boy who gave him this information what the fellow had done, and who had looked after the horses in the meantime; to which the boy answered that he did not know, and with that opened the stable where they were standing for the horse trader, whose heart was already heavy with foreboding. But what was his astonishment when, instead of his two sleek well-fed blacks, his eyes fell upon a pair of dry emaciated mares: ribs like racks to hang things on, manes and hair without attention or care, all matted together, the very picture of misery in the animal kingdom! Kohlhaas, toward whom the horses assayed a neigh with feeble motion, was outraged in the extreme and asked what had happened to his nags. The boy standing there beside him answered that no other misfortune had befallen them, that they had received the proper fodder, but that, since it happened to be right at harvest time, they had been used a little in the field for lack of draft animals. Kohlhaas cursed at this disgraceful and deliberate abuse, but, feeling his powerlessness, swallowed his anger, and, since there was nothing else to do, was making ready to take his horses and leave this robbers' nest when the castellan, attracted by the exchange of words, appeared and asked what was the matter. "What is the matter?" answered Kohlhaas. "Who gave the Junker von Tronka and his people permission to use my blacks that I left here, for work in the fields? Was this human?" he added, and trying to rouse the nags with a touch of the whip, showed him that they did not move. The castellan, after gazing at him for a time in defiance, replied, "Look at the brute! Why shouldn't the lout thank God that the mares are still alive at all?" He asked who was supposed to have been taking care of them since the groom had run away. Hadn't it been proper to make the horses earn in the fields the fodder that had been furnished them? He ended by saying that he needn't

pull any of his tricks here or he would call the dogs and
with them he would put an end to any trouble in the stable
yard.—The horse trader's heart was thumping against his
doublet. He felt an urge to throw the good-for-nothing fat-
gut into the mud and plant his foot on his coppery face.
But his sense of justice, which was like a gold scales, still
wavered. Before the bar of his own heart he was not yet
sure but that some guilt might still be pressing on his op-
ponent, and, swallowing the insults as he stepped over to
the horses and silently weighing the circumstances as he
smoothed out their manes, he inquired with subdued voice,
On the grounds of what oversight had his groom been
turned out of the castle? The castellan answered, "Because
the rascal was impudent in the stable yard! Because he
protested against a necessary change of stabling and for the
sake of his mares wanted to have the horses of two young
gentlemen, who had come to Castle Tronka, put out on the
open highway for the night!" Kohlhaas would have given
as much as the horses were worth to have the groom at
hand so that he could compare his statement with the statement of this big-mouth of a castellan. He was still standing
there smoothing out the mats of hair on the blacks and
pondering what should be done about the situation, when
suddenly the scene altered and the Junker Wenzel von
Tronka, returning from a rabbit hunt with a bevy of
knights, grooms, and dogs, galloped into the castle courtyard. When he asked what had happened the castellan
spoke right up, and, while the dogs, at sight of the stranger,
set up a frantic howl against him on one side, with the
knights ordering them to be still on the other, he informed
him, with the vilest misrepresentation of the case, what a
frightful row the horse trader was putting up because his
blacks had been used a little. With a scornful laugh he said
he was refusing to acknowledge the horses as his own.
Kohlhaas cried, "Those *are* not my horses, Your Worship.
Those are not the *horses* that were worth thirty gulden in
gold. I want my well-fed healthy horses back!" The Junker,
as a fleeting pallor crossed his face, dismounted and said,
"If the bastard won't take the horses back, he can leave it

at that. Come on, Günther!" he cried, "Hans! Come on!"
as with one hand he clapped the dust out of his breeches,
and, "Bring some wine!" he cried further as he was under
the arch of the door with the knights—and went inside.
Kohlhaas said he would call the knacker and have the
horses tossed into the carrion pit before he was going to
lead them back to his stable in Kohlhaasenbrück the way
they were. Without bothering with them, he left the nags
standing there, and, asserting that he would know how to
find justice, he swung himself up onto his brown horse and
rode away.

He was already posthaste on his way to Dresden when,
at thought of the groom and the complaint made against
him at the castle, he began to slow down to a walk, and
before he had gone a thousand paces turned his horse
around and headed in the direction of Kohlhaasenbrück for
a preliminary hearing of the groom, as seemed wise and
proper to him. For a correct awareness of the imperfect
ways of the world made him inclined, despite the insults
sustained, to make the best of the loss of his horses as a
just consequence, in case some kind of guilt were to be
attributed to his groom as the castellan had asserted. On
the other hand he was prompted by an equally admirable
feeling—and this feeling kept striking deeper and deeper
root the further he rode and the more he heard everywhere
he went about the injustices daily perpetrated at Castle
Tronka on travelers—to this effect: that, if the whole incident were merely premeditated, as it had all the appearances of being, then he with his strength was obligated
before the world to obtain satisfaction for himself for the
offense sustained, as well as guarantee for his fellow citizens
against future ones.

Arriving at Kohlhaasenbrück, and as soon as he had embraced Lisbeth, his faithful wife, and kissed his children,
who were crowding in glee about his knees, he asked directly for Herse, the head groom, and inquired whether
nothing had been heard from him. Lisbeth said, "Yes, dearest Michael, that Herse! Just imagine, that unlucky fellow
arrived here a couple of weeks ago, most pitiably beaten

up; no, so badly beaten, in fact, that he could not even draw a deep breath. We put him to bed, where he kept spitting blood violently, and at our repeated questionings we heard a story that no one understands: how he had been left behind by you at Castle Tronka with horses that were not permitted exit, how he had been forced by dint of the most disgraceful mistreatment to leave the castle, and how it had been impossible for him to bring the horses with him."—"So?" said Kohlhaas, laying off his cloak. "Is he well again now?"—"Pretty well, except for the blood spitting," she replied. "I was going to send a groom over to Castle Tronka right away to have him see to the care of the horses until you got there. For since Herse has always shown himself honest with us and, in fact, loyal as none other has been loyal, it never occurred to me to doubt his statement, supported as it was by so many marks of evidence, and to think that he might have lost the horses in any other way. But he implored me not to expect anyone to appear in the midst of that den of thieves and give up the animals unless I was willing to sacrifice a human life for their sakes."—"Is he still in bed?" asked Kohlhaas, freeing himself from his neckcloth.—"These last few days now," she replied, "he has been walking about in the yard again. In short, you will see," she went on, "that this is all quite true and that this incident is one of those outrages that they have been indulging in lately against strangers over at Castle Tronka."—"All the same I must investigate it first," answered Kohlhaas. "Call him in to see me, Lisbeth, if he is up." With these words he seated himself in the high-backed chair, and the lady of the house, who was very pleased at his calm, went and fetched the groom.

"What have you been doing at Castle Tronka?" asked Kohlhaas as Lisbeth stepped into the room with him. "It happens that I am not entirely satisfied with you."—The groom, on whose pale face a blotchy redness appeared at these words, was silent for a bit; then, "You are right, sir, there!" he answered. "For by God's dispensation I had a sulphur match ready to set fire to that den of thieves out of which I had been hounded, but upon hearing the wail of a child inside I threw it into the waters of the Elbe and thought to myself, 'May God's lightning reduce it to ashes, *I* won't!' "—Kohlhaas, startled, said, "But how did you incur your expulsion from Castle Tronka?"—To which Herse countered, "By a nasty trick, sir," and he mopped the sweat from his brow. "But there's no changing a thing once it's done. I didn't want the horses to be driven to death in the field work, and I said they were still young and hadn't done any heavy pulling."—Kohlhaas, still trying to conceal his perplexity, replied that on this score he had not told the whole truth, inasmuch as the horses had already been a bit in harness at the start of the previous spring. "You ought to have been obliging," he continued, "at the Castle, where, after all, you were a sort of guest, once or twice anyway, when it just happened to be necessary for getting the harvest in quickly."—"But," said Herse, "I did do just that, sir. I thought, as long as they were making sour faces at me, that it wouldn't cost me the blacks. The third forenoon I hitched them up and drew in three loads of grain." —With surging heart Kohlhaas lowered his eyes to the floor and remarked, "No one told me anything about that, Herse!"—Herse assured him it was so. "My failure to be obliging," he said, "consisted of my not being willing to put the horses back in yoke when they had hardly got through their noon feeding, and in my answering the castellan and the overseer when they proposed I should accept free fodder in return and pocket the money you had left with me for the price of fodder: I told them I would do something else to them, and I turned around and left."— "But you weren't driven out of Castle Tronka," said Kohlhaas, "for this discourteousness."—"God forbid!" exclaimed the groom. "For a godless deed of wickedness! That evening the horses of two knights, who arrived at Castle Tronka, were put in the stable and mine were tied to the stable door. And when I took the blacks from the hand of the castellan, who was quartering them there himself, and asked where the animals were supposed to stay now, he showed me a pigsty knocked together out of laths and boards against the castle wall."—"You mean," Kohlhaas in-

terrupted him, "that it was such a sorry cage for horses
that it was more like a pigsty than a stable."—"It was a
pigsty, sir," answered Herse, "an honest-to-goodness pigsty,
where the pigs ran in and out and where I couldn't stand
up straight."—"Perhaps there wasn't any other shelter to be
found for the blacks," said Kohlhaas. "The knights' horses,
in a way, had first call."—"Space was short," replied the
groom, letting his voice drop. "There were now seven
knights all told living at the castle. If it had been you, you
would have squeezed the horses in together a little. I said
I was willing to rent a stable in the village, but the castellan
said he had to keep his eye on the horses and I was not
to dare to take them out of the barnyard."—"Hm!" said
Kohlhaas. "What did you say to that?"—"Since the overseer
said the two guests would only be staying overnight and
would be riding on the next morning, I put the horses in
the pigsty. But the next day went by and nothing happened. And when the third day began, the word was that
the gentlemen would be staying on for a few weeks yet
at the castle."—"In the long run, Herse, it was not so bad
in the pigsty," said Kohlhaas, "as it seemed to you when
you first poked your nose in."—"True enough," answered
the other. "After I had swept the place out a little, it wasn't
so bad. I gave the girl a groschen to put the pigs some-
place else. And during the day I fixed it so the horses could
stand up straight by taking the upper boards off the laths
when dawn was breaking and putting them back on in the
evening. That way they stuck their heads through the roof
like geese and looked around for Kohlhaasenbrück, or
somewhere else where things were better."—"Well, then,"
Kohlhaas asked, "why in the world did they drive you out?"
—"I'll tell you, sir," replied the groom. "Because they
wanted to get rid of me. Because they couldn't work the
horses to death as long as I was there. In the stable yard,
in the servants' quarters, everywhere, they kept giving me
nasty looks. And because I kept thinking, 'Twist your faces
till you twist them out of joint!' they picked a quarrel and
kicked me out of the stable yard."—"But the excuse!" cried
Kohlhaas. "They must have had some excuse!"—"Oh, that

they did," answered Herse, "and a very justifiable one. On
the evening of the second day that I spent in the pigsty I
took the horses, which had gotten filthy in there after all,
and started to ride them to the horse pond. And just as I
am passing under the castle gate and ready to make the'
turn, I hear the castellan and the overseer rushing after me
with grooms, dogs, and clubs, and shouting, 'Halt there,
rascal! Halt, you gallows bird!' as if they are possessed. The
gate watch plants himself in my path, and just as I am
asking him and the crazy mob bearing down on me, 'What's
the matter?' the castellan says, 'What's the matter?' and
grabs both of my blacks by the bridles. 'Where do you
think you're going with those horses?' asks he and grabs
me by the front of my jacket. 'Where am I going?' say I.
'I'm on my way to the horse pond, damn it. Do you think
I . . . ?'—'To the horse pond?' cries the castellan. 'I'll teach
you, you swindling rogue, to pond your way along the
highroad to Kohlhaasenbrück!' and with a murderous blow
of spite he and the overseer, who has grabbed me by the
leg, knock me off the horse so I measure my length in the
mud. 'Death and damnation!' I cry. 'There are harness and
blankets and a bundle of my laundry up in the stable!' But
while the overseer is leading the horses away, he and the
grooms go at me with kicks and whips and clubs till I collapse half dead outside the castle gate. And as I am saying,
'The thieving dogs! Where are they taking my horses?' and
am getting to my feet, 'Get out!' screams the castellan. 'Get
out of this castle yard!' and 'Sick 'em, Caesar! Sick 'em,
Hunter!' goes the cry, and 'Sick 'em, Spitz!' and a pack of
more than twelve dogs goes after me. Then I break off a
fence lath or something, I don't know, and lay three dogs
dead beside me. And just as I, in pain with all those sorry
bites, have to give up, 'Tweet!' shrills a whistle; into the
courtyard go the dogs, the gate slams shut, and down goes
the crossbar—and I collapse in a faint on the road."—
Kohlhaas, his face pale and with forced raillery, said,
"Didn't you want to run away too, Herse?" And as the
latter looked down with a dark flush, "Admit it," he said.
"You didn't like it in the pigsty; you thought it was nicer in

the Kohlhaasenbrück stables."—"Damnation!" cried Herse. "I did leave harness and blankets behind, after all, and a bundle of laundry besides, in that pigsty. Wouldn't I have pocketed the three imperial gulden in the red silk handkerchief that I had hidden behind the manger? Hell and devils! When you talk this way, I would like to light that sulphur match again that I threw away!"—"All right, all right!" said the horse dealer. "I didn't mean anything bad by that. What you have told me, you see, word for word, I believe, and if it comes to a deposition, I'm ready to take the Eucharist on it myself by now. I am sorry you haven't fared any better in my service. Go, Herse, go to bed, have them bring you a bottle of wine, and console yourself: justice shall be done you!" With that he got up, made out a list of the articles which the head groom had left in the pigsty, specified their value, and even asked him how high he estimated his medical expenses. Then, after extending his hand to him once again, he allowed him to withdraw.

Thereupon he gave Lisbeth his wife a full account of the story together with its inner significance and declared that he had decided to enlist public justice for his cause and that he had the joy of seeing her support him in his project with all her heart. For she agreed that many another traveler, less patient perhaps than he was, would be passing by that castle, that it would be God's work to put a stop to wrongs like these, and that she would defray the expenses which the prosecution of his case might entail. Kohlhaas called her his stout-hearted wife and during this and the following day took his delight in the company of her and his children. Then, as soon as his affairs would permit, he set out for Dresden to present his complaint to a court.

There, with the help of an attorney whom he knew, he drew up a complaint in which, after circumstantial description of the outrage perpetrated upon him as well as upon his groom Herse by the Junker Wenzel von Tronka, he demanded punishment of the latter according to the law, restoration of the horses to their previous condition, and restitution for the injuries which he and his groom had sustained. The case seemed an open-and-shut one. The circumstance of the horses' having been illegally detained cast a decisive light upon everything else, and even if the claim were to be made that the horses had become sick by sheer accident, the horse dealer's demand to have them restored to sound condition would still have appeared just. Nor did Kohlhaas in any way lack for friends during the time when he was looking about in the capital, friends who promised active support for his cause. The extensive business which he carried on in horses and the honesty with which he conducted his affairs had gained him the good will of the most important men in the country. Several times he dined cheerfully with his lawyer, who was himself a man of repute, and deposited with him a sum of money to cover the costs of the trial. After the lapse of several weeks he returned to Kohlhaasenbrück and to Lisbeth his wife, completely reassured by him as to the outcome of his case. All the same, months passed and the year was about to end before he received from Saxony so much as an official notice about the suit he had initiated there, to say nothing of a decision. After appearing several times more before the tribunal he inquired of his lawyer in a confidential letter what was causing such inordinate delay, and learned that his suit had been absolutely disallowed by the Dresden court as the result of some superior instigation.—To the astonished return letter of the horse dealer asking what grounds there were for this, the lawyer stated that the Junker Wenzel von Tronka was related to two young gentlemen, Hinz and Kunz von Tronka, one of whom was Cupbearer, the other Chamberlain to the Sovereign's person. He went on to advise him to repossess himself of the horses, which were at Castle Tronka, without further efforts at the court of judicature, and signified to him that the Junker, who was now residing in the capital, seemed to have directed his people to surrender them to him. He closed with the request that, in case he was unwilling to be satisfied with this, he should spare *him* any further actions in the matter.

Kohlhaas happened to be just then in Brandenburg, where Heinrich von Gersau, Captain of the Civic Militia, within whose jurisdiction Kohlhaasenbrück was located, was engaged in establishing several charitable institutions for the sick and the poor, out of a sizable fund that had been bequeathed to the city. He was particularly concerned with establishing, for the use of the infirm, a mineral spring which flowed in a village of the area and in the curative powers of which more hope was placed than was justified by subsequent events. And since Kohlhaas was acquainted with him by virtue of numerous transactions at the time of his stay at court, he allowed Herse, the head groom, who was still troubled by pain in the chest when breathing ever since those bad days at Castle Tronka, to try the effects of the little curative spring now fitted out with a roof and an enclosure. It chanced that the Captain was present at the edge of the tank in which Kohlhaas had placed Herse, for the purpose of issuing certain directions, at just the moment when Kohlhaas received the disheartening letter from his Dresden lawyer which his wife had forwarded to him by messenger. The Captain, who had noticed, while he was talking with the doctor, that Kohlhaas had let fall a tear on the letter he had received and opened, approached him in friendly and cordial manner and asked him what misfortune had befallen him. And when the horse dealer handed him the letter without making a reply, this worthy man, who was familiar with the outrageous injustice perpetrated upon him at Castle Tronka, with the consequences of which Herse now lay ill, perhaps for the rest of his life, clapped him on the shoulder and told him not to be dispirited, *he* would help him obtain satisfaction! That evening, when, in accordance with his command, the horse dealer waited upon him at his castle, he told him he had only to draw up a petition to the Elector of Brandenburg with a brief description of the incident, enclose the lawyer's letter, and solicit his sovereign protection in the matter of the violence gratuitously practiced against him in Saxon territory. He promised him he would place the petition in the Elector's hands as part of another packet which was already made up, and that the latter, if circumstances permitted, would unfailingly intervene on his behalf with the

Elector of Saxony; further than this step nothing was
needed to obtain justice in the Dresden court in spite of
all the tricks of the Junker and his followers. Most heartily
delighted, Kohlhaas thanked the Captain for this fresh proof
of his good will and said he was only sorry he had not
initiated proceedings in Berlin in the first place, without
bothering with Dresden at all. Now, after drawing up his
complaint in proper form in the city chancery and entrust-
ing it to the Captain, he returned, with greater assurance
than ever before as to the outcome of his case, to Kohlhaasenbrück. Within a few weeks, however, he was grieved
to learn through a magistrate who was going to Potsdam
on business for the Captain that the Elector had turned the
petition over to his chancellor, Count Kallheim, and that
the latter had not gone directly to the court in Dresden,
as would have seemed appropriate, for investigation and
punishment of the outrage, but had gone for preliminary
and more detailed information to the Junker von Tronka.
The magistrate who stopped in his carriage outside Kohlhaas' residence seemed to be under instructions to make
this disclosure to the horse dealer, and in reply to his
startled question as to why this course of action had been
followed, he could give no satisfactory explanation. He
merely added that the Captain had bidden him tell him
to bide patiently, and seemed in a hurry to continue his
journey. Just at the close of the brief conversation Kohlhaas
divined from a few words dropped that Count Kallheim
was related by marriage to the House of Tronka. Kohlhaas,
who now took no pleasure either in his horse breeding or
in his home and farm, and scarcely any in wife or child,
awaited the new month in gloomy forebodings of the future.
In precise accordance with his expectations, Herse, to
whom the baths had afforded some relief, came back from
Brandenburg at the end of that period and brought with
him a rather lengthy decree accompanied by a letter from
the Captain to this effect: he regretted being unable to do
anything about his case, he was enclosing a decision of the
city chancery handed down to him, and advised him to
go and fetch the horses which he had left at Castle Tronka

and, in any event, to let the matter rest. The decision read to this effect: that, according to the report of the Dresden court, he was a good-for-nothing troublemaker; that the Junker with whom he had left the horses was in no way holding them back from him; he should send to the castle for them or at least notify the Junker where to send them to him; in all events, however, he was to spare the chancery such nuisance and wrangling. Kohlhaas, who was not concerned about the horses—he would have been equally aggrieved if a couple of dogs had been in question—was wild with rage when he received this letter. Every time a noise was heard in the courtyard he would glance toward the gate with the most irritated expectation that had ever stirred his bosom to see whether the nobleman's people might be there and, perhaps with an apology, might be bringing back his starved and wasted horses—the one instance where his soul, for all the discipline in which it was trained by the world, was quite unprepared to face the thing his feelings led him to expect. Shortly after, however, he learned through an acquaintance who had traveled that road that his nags were being used at Castle Tronka, now as before, just like the Junker's other horses, for field work. And amid the grief of glimpsing the world in such monstrous disorder darted the pain of beholding his own heart no longer at peace with itself. He invited a bailiff, a neighbor of his who had for some time been entertaining the notion of enlarging his property by the purchase of adjacent lands, to come and see him, and after the latter was seated, he asked him what he would be willing to give for his properties both in Brandenburg and in Saxony, land and buildings, goods and chattels, lock, stock, and barrel. Lisbeth, his wife, grew pale at these words. She turned and swept up her youngest child that was playing on the floor behind her, and as she did so darted glances that bore the mark of death past the rosy cheeks of the boy playing with her neckerchief and on toward the horse dealer and a paper he was holding in his hand. The bailiff, looking at him in surprise, asked him what had all of a sudden put such strange thoughts into his head. To which the latter

replied with as much cheerfulness as he was able to muster
that the idea of selling his farm on the banks of the Havel
was not exactly new; that the two of them had often discussed this matter before; that, compared with it, his house
in the Dresden suburb was a mere appendage not worth
bothering about; and that, in short, if he were agreeable
to taking over both parcels of land, he was ready to close
the contract with him. With a somewhat forced humor he
added that Kohlhaasenbrück was after all not the world;
that there might be ends compared to which that of
presiding over a household like a regular father was sub-
ordinate and insignificant; and in short he must tell him
that his soul was set upon great things about which he
might perhaps soon be hearing. The bailiff, reassured by
these words, spoke in jolly tone to the wife, who kept kissing the child over and over again, to the effect that: Surely
he wouldn't ask payment right away? laid his hat and cane,
which he had been holding between his knees, on the table,
and picked up the paper which the horse dealer was holding in his hand, in order to read it over. Kohlhaas, moving
closer to him, explained that it was a contingent bill of sale,
drawn up by himself, with a four weeks' right of cancella-
tion, and pointed out that it lacked nothing but the signa-
tures and the insertion of the amounts both of the actual
sales price and of the forfeiture sum, i.e., the amount for
which he was willing to pledge liability in case he backed
out of the bargain within four weeks. Once again he cheer-
ily urged him to make an offer, assuring him he would be
reasonable and not make much ado about it. His wife kept
pacing back and forth in the room. Her bosom was heaving
so that the neckerchief at which the little boy had been
tugging threatened to fall completely off her shoulder. The
bailiff said that, of course, he could not judge the value of
the property in Dresden at all; whereupon Kohlhaas, pushing toward him some letters that had been exchanged at
the time of the purchase, replied that he estimated the
value at 100 gulden in gold, although, as would be evident from these, it had cost him almost half as much again.
The bailiff, having read through the bill of sale again and

finding the right of withdrawal stipulated, quite unusually, on his part also, said, with his mind half made up already, that of course he wouldn't have any use for the stud horses that were here in the stables. But when Kohlhaas answered that he was not by any means prepared to part with the horses and that he wanted to retain some weapons also that were hanging in the armory, the other hesitated and then hesitated some more, and finally repeated an offer he had recently made him once before, half in jest, half in earnest, during a stroll—an offer quite unworthy of the value of the property. Kohlhaas pushed pen and ink toward him for writing, and when the bailiff, not trusting his senses, asked him again if he was in earnest, and when the horse dealer answered a little irritated, Did he think he was just playing a joke on him? the other picked up the pen—with a serious face, be it said—and signed. He struck out the clause, however, where it spoke about the forfeit in case the seller should withdraw from the transaction, pledged himself to a loan of 100 gulden in gold to Kohlhaas against the mortgage on the Dresden property, which he absolutely did not wish to acquire by purchase, and allowed him complete freedom to withdraw from the bargain for a two months' period. Touched by this act, the horse dealer shook his hand with much cordiality, and after they had agreed on a principal point at issue, namely that one quarter of the purchase price was to be paid in cash immediately and the remainder in the Hamburg Bank within three months, he called for wine to celebrate the bargain so happily concluded. To a maidservant who came in with the bottles he said that his groom Sternbald was to saddle his chestnut horse, alleging he had to ride to the capital where there were matters to be attended to, and he let it be understood that he would express himself more frankly when he returned presently about what for the time being he was obliged to keep to himself. Then, as he was filling the glasses, he inquired about the Poles and the Turks who happened to be at war just then, involved the bailiff in all sorts of political conjectures on that topic, finally toasted him once more by way of conclusion on the thrift of their enterprise, and saw him out. Once the bailiff had left the room, Lisbeth fell on her knees before him. "If you hold me at all," she cried, "if you hold me and the children I have borne you dear to your heart, if we have not already been rejected, for whatever reason I do not know, tell me what is the meaning of these dreadful steps!"—"Nothing, dearest wife," said Kohlhaas, "that need distress you yet, as far as matters stand. I have received a court decision in which they tell me that my complaint against the Junker Wenzel von Tronka is good-for-nothing troublemaking. And since some misunderstanding must be involved, I have decided to present my complaint once more in person to the Sovereign himself."—"Why do you want to sell your house?" she cried, as with a gesture of consternation she rose to her feet. Clasping her tenderly to his bosom, the horse dealer replied, "Because, dearest Lisbeth, I do not want to remain in a country where they are not willing to protect me in my rights. Better be a dog, if I am to be kicked, than a human being! I am sure my wife thinks on this point the same as I."—"How do you know," asked the other frantically, "that they will not protect you in your rights? If you approach the Sovereign humbly, as befits you, with your petition, how do you know that it will be brushed aside or that it will be answered by a refusal to hear you?"—"Very well," answered Kohlhaas. "If my fear proves groundless, then my house is not sold yet either. The Sovereign himself is just, I know, and if I can just get through the people around him and get to his own person, I have no doubt but that I will get my rights and return before the week is out to you and to my old pursuits. May I then," he added as he kissed her, "remain with you to the end of my life! All the same it is advisable," he continued, "for me to be prepared for any eventuality, and for that reason I should like to have you withdraw, if that may be, for a time and take the children to your cousin's in Schwerin, whom you have been wanting to visit for a long time anyway."—"What!" cried his wife. "I go to Schwerin? With the children over the border to my cousin's in Schwerin?" And terror choked her speech.—"Of course," answered

Kohlhaas, "and that, if possible, right away, so that I shall not be deterred by any considerations from the steps I mean to take for my cause."—"Oh, I understand you!" she cried. "You now need nothing but weapons and horses; the rest can go to anyone who wants to take it!" With that she turned, flung herself down upon a chair, and wept. Taken aback, Kohlhaas said, "Dearest Lisbeth, what are you doing? God has blessed me with wife and child and worldly goods: am I to wish for the first time today that it were otherwise?"—He sat down beside her as, with a blush at hearing these words, she had fallen upon his neck. "Tell me," said he as he stroked her hair back from her forehead, "what am I supposed to do? Shall I give up my cause? Shall I go to Castle Tronka, beg the knight to give me back my horses, jump on their backs, and ride them here to you?"—Lisbeth did not dare say, "Yes! Yes! Yes!" She wept and shook her head, clasped him in a vehement embrace, and covered his bosom with fervent kisses. "Well, then," cried Kohlhaas, "if you feel that justice must be done me, in case I am to continue my occupation, then allow me the liberty I need in order to obtain it!" And with that he stood up, and to the groom who announced that the chestnut was standing ready saddled he said that tomorrow the browns would have to be hitched up also to take his wife to Schwerin. Lisbeth said she had thought of something! She rose, wiped away the tears in her eyes, and asked him as he was now sitting at his desk whether he would give the petition to her and let her go in his place to Berlin to submit it to the Sovereign. Kohlhaas, touched for more than one reason by this turn, drew her down upon his lap and said, "Dearest wife, that is not wholly possible. The Sovereign is hedged many times about, and anyone approaching him is exposed to vexations of many sorts." Lisbeth countered that in a thousand instances it was easier for a woman than for a man to approach him. "Give me the petition!" she repeated. "And if knowing that it is in his hands is all you want, I guarantee you he will receive it!" Kohlhaas, who had many proofs of her courage as well as of her sagacity, asked how she intended to go about it;

to which she replied, as she shamefacedly lowered her eyes, that the castellan of the electoral palace had, in previous times when he was in service at Schwerin, paid her court, that he was of course married now and had several children, but that she was nevertheless not entirely forgotten yet, and—in short, that all he had to do was leave it to her to take advantage of this and many another circumstance too long to describe. Kohlhaas kissed her with much joy, said he would accept her proposal, instructed her that nothing was needed but to take lodgings with the man's wife in order to speak to the Sovereign in the palace itself, gave her the petition, had the browns hitched up, and sent her off, well bundled in, with Sternbald, his trusty groom.

But of all the unsuccessful steps he had taken in his case, this journey was the most ill-fortuned. For only a few days later Sternbald entered the courtyard again, with slow step escorting the wagon in which the horse dealer's wife lay prostrate with a dangerous contusion of the chest. Kohlhaas, approaching the vehicle and pale, could make nothing coherent out of what had been the cause of this mischance. The castellan, by the groom's report, had not been at home; they had, therefore, been obliged to stop at an inn situated in the vicinity of the castle; Lisbeth had left this inn the following morning and had instructed the groom to remain behind with the horses; not until evening had she returned—in this condition. It seemed that she had pressed too boldly forward toward the Sovereign's person and, through no fault of his but merely from the rough zeal of the bodyguard surrounding him, she had received a blow from a lance butt in her chest. At least that was the report of the people who brought her toward evening to the inn in unconscious state, for she herself was unable to say very much, impeded as she was by the blood flowing from her mouth. The petition had been taken from her afterward by a knight. Sternbald said it had been his wish to jump on a horse immediately and bring him news of this mishap, but she had insisted, in spite of the remonstrances of the surgeon who had been summoned, on being transported to Kohlhaasenbrück and to her husband without any prior notification. Kohlhaas put her to bed, more dead than alive from her journey, and there, amid painful efforts to draw her breath, she lived on for a few days. In vain they sought to bring her back to consciousness in order to get some clews as to what had happened; she only lay there, her staring eyes already set in death, and made no answer. Just before her death she did rouse once more to her senses. Then, when a pastor of the Lutheran religion—to which faith, then in its first growth, she had been converted, following her husband's example—was standing beside her bed reading to her a chapter from the Bible in a loud and perceptibly solemn voice, only then did she suddenly glance at him with a dark expression and, as though there were no need to have any of it read to her, took the Bible out of his hands, and leafed through it page after page seemingly in search of something; then, to Kohlhaas, who was sitting beside her bed, she pointed with her index finger to the verse, "Forgive thine enemies; do good unto them that hate you." So doing, she pressed his hand with a look of uncommon tenderness, and died.—Kohlhaas thought, "May God never forgive me as I forgive the Junker!" kissed her as the tears streamed down his face, closed her eyes, and left the room. He took the hundred gulden in gold which the bailiff had already sent him for the stables in Dresden and ordered a funeral that seemed less appropriate for her than for a princess: an oaken coffin heavily studded with metal, silken pillows with gold and silver tassels, and a grave eight ells deep lined with fieldstone and mortar. He himself, with his youngest child in his arms, stood beside the tomb and watched the work. When the burial day came, the corpse, white as snow, was displayed in a room which he had had draped with black cloth. The pastor had just concluded a moving address at her bier, when there was placed in his hands the Sovereign's decision in the matter of the petition which the deceased had transmitted, to this effect: he was to pick up the horses at Castle Tronka, and, on pain of imprisonment, to press this case no further. Kohlhaas pocketed the letter and had them put the coffin into the wagon. As soon as the grave mound had been heaped, a cross planted upon it, and the funeral guests bidden adieu, he threw himself down once again before her now desolate bed and then forthwith began the task of revenge. He sat down and composed a decree in which, by virtue of authority innate in him, he condemned the Junker Wenzel von Tronka, within three days of receipt, to bring to Kohlhaasenbrück the black horses which he had taken from him and ruined with field work, and to feed them personally in his stables until they were fat again. This decree he despatched to him by mounted messenger, instructing the latter to be back in Kohlhaasenbrück immediately after delivery of the paper. When the three days had gone by without delivery of the horses, he summoned Herse, disclosed to him what he had enjoined upon the nobleman concerning the fattening of the horses, and asked him two things: whether he was willing to ride with him to Castle Tronka and fetch the nobleman, and whether, if the nobleman once fetched proved reluctant about fulfilling the decree in the Kohlhaasenbrück stables, he were willing to use a whip on him. And when Herse, as soon as he understood him, shouted exultantly, "Sir, this very day!" and, tossing his cap aloft, assured him he would have a thong plaited with ten knots in order to teach him how to curry-comb—then Kohlhaas sold the house, sent his children, loaded into a wagon, across the border; with nightfall he summoned the other grooms together, seven in number and every one of them as true to him as gold, issued them weapons and horses, and set out for Castle Tronka.

And with this small band he did attack the castle at nightfall of the third day, riding down the tolls collector and the gatekeeper as they stood in conversation under the gate, and, while Herse, amid a sudden burst of flames from all the castle area outbuildings to which they had set fire, raced up the circular stairs to the tower quarters of the castellan and with blows and thrusts fell upon the castellan and the overseer as they sat there, half undressed, over a game, Kohlhaas rushed into the castle in search of the Junker Wenzel von Tronka. Thus does the Angel of Justice descend from Heaven; and the Junker, who, amid much laughter, was just in the midst of reading aloud to the pack of young friends, his guests, the decree which the horse trader had sent him, had no more than heard the latter's voice in the courtyard before, deathly pale, he shouted suddenly to the gentlemen, "Save yourselves, brothers!" and vanished. Kohlhaas, who upon entry into the room grabbed a Junker Hans von Tronka by the shirt front as he came toward him and pitched him into the corner of the room so that his brains splattered on the stones, kept asking, while the grooms overpowered the other knights, who had now reached for their weapons, and routed them, Where was the Junker Wenzel von Tronka? And when, confronted with the ignorance of the stunned men, he kicked open the doors of two rooms leading into the side wings of the castle, made his way in all directions through the rambling structure and found no one, he descended, cursing, to the courtyard to post guards at the exits. Meanwhile, taking fire from the outbuildings, the castle and all its adjacent structures were in flames and billowing dense smoke toward the sky, and, while Sternbald and three other grooms were busy dragging together everything that was not nailed down tight and pitching it out among the horses as good plunder, the corpses of the castellan and the overseer came hurtling out of the open windows of the castellan's quarters, together with their wives and children, to the jubilation of Herse. Kohlhaas, coming down the castle steps and meeting the old gout-plagued housekeeper that managed the Junker's household, asked her, as she threw herself at his feet, and as he stopped on that step, Where was the Junker Wenzel von Tronka? and when with weak and trembling voice she answered that she thought he had fled to the chapel, he called two grooms with torches, had them open the doors with crowbars and axes, for lack of keys, overturned altars and benches, and once again, to his fierce regret, did not find the Junker. It chanced that, at the moment when Kohlhaas was coming back out of the chapel, a young groom belonging to the Castle Tronka staff was rushing up to lead the Junker's stallions out of a large stone stable now threatened by the flames. Kohlhaas, glimpsing at that very

moment his own two blacks in a little thatched shed, asked
the groom why he didn't rescue the blacks; and when the
latter, inserting the key in the stable door, answered that
the shed was already on fire, Kohlhaas yanked the key out
of the stable door, threw it over the wall, drove the groom
with a hail of blows from the flat of his sword into the
burning shed, and forced him, amid the ghastly laughter
of the men standing around, to rescue the blacks. And yet,
when the groom came out pale with terror leading the
horses in his hand a few minutes before the shed came
tumbling down behind him, he could not find Kohlhaas;
and when he went down among the grooms in the castle
courtyard and spoke to the horse dealer, who repeatedly
turned his back on him, and asked him what he was supposed to do now with the animals, the latter lifted his foot
with such a ferocious gesture that the kick would have
been the death of him if it had been delivered, bestrode
his brown horse without answering him, and took up a position under the castle gateway to wait, while the grooms
continued their business, in silence for the coming of daylight. When dawn broke, the entire castle was burned down,
even to the walls, and no one was left within it except
Kohlhaas and his seven grooms. He dismounted and in the
bright sunlight that now illuminated the entire spot in all
its corners once again examined the place thoroughly, and
when, hard as it was for him, he was forced to admit that
his expedition against the castle had failed, he despatched
Herse and several other grooms, his heart heavy with grief
and sorrow, to ascertain the direction taken by the Junker
in his flight. Particularly disturbing to him was a wealthy
convent called Erlabrunn, which was located on the banks
of the Mulde and the Abbess of which, Antonia von Tronka,
was known in the area as a pious, charitable, and saintly
woman; for to the unhappy Kohlhaas it seemed only too
probable that the Junker, deprived as he was of all neces-
saries, had taken refuge in this convent, inasmuch as the
Abbess was his own aunt and his teacher in earliest childhood. After being informed of this circumstance, Kohlhaas
mounted the castellan's tower, within the confines of which

one room still remained habitable, and composed a so-
called "Kohlhaas Manifesto," in which he called upon the
country to provide neither aid nor comfort to the Junker
Wenzel von Tronka with whom he was engaged in just warfare, but rather obligated every inhabitant, not excluding
his friends and relatives, to hand him over to him on pain
of death and ineluctable reduction to ashes of anything that
might pass for property of theirs. This declaration he distributed in the district through the agency of strangers and
travelers; in fact, he gave a copy of it to the groom Waldmann with the explicit order to deliver it to Erlabrunn into
the hands of the Lady Antonia herself. Then he talked with
several Tronka grooms who were dissatisfied with the
Junker and who, allured by the prospect of booty, wished
to enter his service, armed them foot-soldier-fashion with
crossbows and daggers, and taught them to ride behind the
mounted grooms; then, after converting into money everything that the band had lugged together and dividing the
money among them, he rested for several hours beneath
the castle gate from his sorry labors.

Toward midday Herse came and confirmed what his
heart, ever disposed to the gloomiest forebodings, had already told him, namely, that the Junker was to be found in
the convent at Erlabrunn with the elderly Lady Antonia
von Tronka, his aunt. It seemed he had escaped through a
door that opened out of the back wall of the castle and
down a narrow stone stairway leading, underneath its small
roof, to some boats on the Elbe. At least Herse reported
that he had arrived around midnight by boat, with neither
oars nor rudder, in an Elbe River village to the wonder of
the people who had gathered on account of the fire at Castle Tronka, and that he had traveled on from there to
Erlabrunn in a village cart.—Kohlhaas fetched a deep sigh
at this news. He asked whether the horses had fed, and
when they told him yes, he had the band mount their
horses and within three hours was standing before Erlabrunn. He was just riding into the convent yard with his
troop amid the mutterings of a distant storm on the horizon
and by the light of torches which he had lighted outside

the place, and the groom Waldmann, approaching, was just
reporting to him that the manifesto had been duly delivered, when he saw the Abbess and the chapter warden
coming up in distraught conversation through the convent
portal; and while the chapter warden, a little old man with
snow-white hair, was having his armor put on, darting
fierce glances toward Kohlhaas the while, and bidding the
servants around him with sharp voice to sound the tocsin,
the directress of the convent walked down the ramp, a silver image of the Crucified One in her hand and pale as
linen-cloth, and threw herself, together with all her nuns,
down in front of Kohlhaas' horse. While Herse and Sternbald overpowered the chapter warden, who had no sword
in his hand, and were leading him captive among the
horses, Kohlhaas asked her, Where was the Junker Wenzel
von Tronka? and when she, unfastening a great ring of keys
from her girdle, replied, "In Wittenberg, Kohlhaas, worthy
man!" and with quivering voice added, "Fear God and do
no evil!" Kohlhaas, hurled back to the hell of unrequited
revenge, turned his horse around and was on the verge of
shouting, "Lay fire to the place!" when a tremendous thun-
derbolt struck the earth right near him. Turning his horse
back around to face her, Kohlhaas asked her whether she
had received the manifesto, and when the Lady answered
with faint and barely audible voice, "Just now!"—"When?"
—"Two hours, so help me God, after my cousin the Junker's
already accomplished departure!" and after the groom
Waldmann, toward whom Kohlhaas turned with grim
looks, stammeringly confirmed this fact, saying that the
rain-swelled waters of the Mulde had prevented him from
arriving any sooner than just now—then Kohlhaas mastered
his emotions. A suddenly fierce gust of rain that doused the
torches and came splashing down upon the pavement of
the courtyard dissolved the anguish in his unhappy bosom;
lifting his hat to the Lady, he faced his horse around, and
with the words, "Follow me, my brothers, the Junker is in
Wittenberg!" dug in his spurs, and departed from the
convent.

At nightfall he stopped at an inn on the highway, where,

on account of the great fatigue of the horses, he was forced to rest for a day and where, realizing that with a troop of ten men—for he was that strong by now—he could not challenge a place like Wittenberg, he drew up a second manifesto, in which, after a brief account of what had happened to him in the country, he called upon "every good Christian," as he termed it, to take up his cause against the Junker Wenzel von Tronka as the common enemy of all Christians, "upon his pledge of a bounty and other military emoluments." In still another manifesto that followed hard upon this one, he referred to himself as "a gentleman free before the Empire and before the world, responsible to God alone." Nevertheless, a kind of morbid and misdirected fanaticism brought him recruits aplenty, at the jingle of his money and the prospect of plunder, from among the rabble left without bread by the peace with Poland, so that he actually counted thirty-odd men when he returned to the right bank of the Elbe for the purpose of burning Wittenberg to the ground. He camped, horses and followers together, under the roof of an old dilapidated brick kiln in the solitude of a dismal forest which at that time surrounded that city, and no sooner had he learned through Sternbald, whom he had sent into the city in disguise with the manifesto, that the manifesto was already public knowledge there, than he started out with his troop on the holy eve of Pentecost and set the town on fire at several points while the inhabitants were lying in deepest slumber. While the grooms were plundering in the suburb he pasted up a paper on the doorpost of a church, which said that "he, Kohlhaas, had set fire to the city, and that if they didn't surrender the Junker to him, he would reduce it to ashes in such a way that," as he expressed it, "he would not have to look behind any walls to find him."— The horror of the inhabitants at this unparalleled outrage was indescribable; and the flames, which on that fortunately rather still summer night had destroyed no more than nineteen houses, including, however, one church, had hardly been brought more or less under control toward daybreak, when the old Governor, Otto von Gorgas, sent out a

detachment of fifty men to bring in this monstrous ruffian.
The captain in command, however, Gerstenberg by name,
managed things so badly that the whole expedition, instead
of precipitating Kohlhaas' fall, led rather to his gaining the
reputation of a highly dangerous warrior; for when this
commander divided his force into several squads, in order,
as he fancied, to encircle and crush him, Kohlhaas, keeping
his own band together, attacked him at separate points and
beat him so badly that by the evening of the following day
there was not left in the field one single man of the whole
detachment upon which the hopes of the province were set.
On the morning of the following day Kohlhaas, who had
lost several men in this fight, set fire to the city again, and
his murderous plans were so well conceived that once again
a number of houses and almost all the outbuildings of the
suburb were laid in ashes. Then he put up the well-known
manifesto again, this time at the corners of the City Hall
itself, and to it he appended a report of the fate of Captain
von Gerstenberg, whom the Governor had despatched and
whom he had utterly defeated. The Governor, irritated in
the extreme by this insolence, placed himself with several
knights at the head of a force of a hundred and fifty men.
To the Junker Wenzel von Tronka, upon the latter's written
application, he assigned a bodyguard to protect him from
the violence of the people, who flatly demanded to have
him removed from the city; and, after posting guards in
all the villages of the area and stationing sentinels along
the city wall to protect it from surprise attack, he set out
in person on St. Jarvis' day to capture the dragon that was
laying waste the land. This force the horse trader was
shrewd enough to avoid; and, after luring the Governor by
astute maneuvers five miles away from the city, and after
misleading him by dint of various tricks that he played into
thinking that, under pressure of superior strength, he was
going to flee into Brandenburg, he suddenly wheeled
around on the third nightfall, reached Wittenberg by a
forced march, and set the city on fire for a third time.
Herse, slipping into the city in disguise, carried out this horrible feat; and the fire, by virtue of a sharp north wind

blowing, was so destructive and spread so fast that, in less than three hours, two-and-forty houses, two churches, several convents and schools, and the building of the electoral government itself lay in rubble and ashes. The Governor, thinking his adversary in Brandenburg by daybreak, returned in swift march upon being informed of what had taken place, to find the city in general uproar; the populace by the thousands had taken up position before the Junker's house, now barricaded with beams and piling, and was demanding in frantic howls his removal from the city. Two burgomasters, Jenkens and Otto by name, present in their robes of office as spokesmen for the entire corps of magistrates, demonstrated in vain that they would simply have to wait for the return of a courier who had been sent to the President of the State Chancery for permission to take the Junker to Dresden, where he himself wanted to go for several reasons; to these words the unreasoning mob armed with pikes and staves would not listen, and just as they were laying violent hands on several aldermen who were urging measures of force, and simultaneously were on the point of storming the house where the Junker was, with the intention of leveling it to the ground, the Governor, Otto von Gorgas, appeared in the city at the head of his mounted troops. This worthy Lord, accustomed to inspiring respect and obedience in the people by his mere presence, had succeeded in capturing right outside the city gates three stray men from the incendiary's band, by way of recompense, as it were, for the failure of the expedition from which he was returning; and when, once the fellows were laden with chains in the sight of the people, he assured the magistrate in a shrewd speech that he was planning to bring Kohlhaas in before long in chains, since he was on his trail, he succeeded by virtue of these reassuring details in allaying the people's terror and in quieting them more or less on the score of the Junker's presence among them until the return of the courier from Dresden. Dismounting and accompanied by several knights, he betook himself, after removal of the posts and barricades, into the house, where he found the Junker, who kept falling into one fainting fit after another,

in the hands of two physicians who were striving to restore
him to life by means of aromatics and stimulants; and since
Knight Otto von Gorgas felt this was not the moment to
bandy words with him on the point of the riot he had occasioned, he merely told him, as he glanced at him with
quiet contempt, to get dressed and follow him for the sake
of his own safety to the Knights' Prison. When they had
put a doublet on the Junker, and placed a helmet on his
head, and left his chest half exposed because of his gasping
for breath, and when he appeared on the street supported
by the arms of the Governor and his brother-in-law, the
Count of Gerschau, monstrous and blasphemous curses
rolled up against him to the heavens. The mob, restrained
only with difficulty by the lansquenets, called him a blood-
sucking leech, a wretched plague on the land and a tor-
mentor of men, the curse of the city of Wittenberg and the
ruination of Saxony; and after a sorry parade through the
city's ruins, in the course of which he several times lost his
helmet without missing it and a knight repeatedly put it
back on his head from behind, they finally reached the
prison, where, under the protection of a strong guard, he
vanished into a dungeon. Meanwhile the return of the
courier with the electoral decree threw the city into new
alarm. For the government, to which the citizenry of
Dresden had appealed directly in an urgent petition, refused to hear of the Junker's presence in the capital before
the capture of the incendiary villain; rather, it enjoined
upon the Governor to keep him where he was, as long as
he had to be somewhere, and to protect him with all the
power at his disposal; simultaneously it announced to the
good city of Wittenberg, to calm its fears, that a column
of five hundred men under the command of Prince Friedrich von Meissen was on its way to safeguard it from the
further molestations of this man. The Governor realized that
a decree of this sort would by no means reassure the people,
for, not only had several small victories which the horse
dealer had gained at various points before the city spread
extremely unpleasant rumors about the strength he had at-
tained, but the warfare he was practicing in the dark of

night with disguised ruffians and with pitch, straw, and
sulphur, unheard of and unparalleled as it was, would have
frustrated a larger protective force than that with which
the Prince of Meissen was advancing. After brief reflection
the Governor decided to suppress completely the decision
he had received. He merely posted a letter, in which the
Prince of Meissen announced his arrival, at certain points
in the city. At daybreak a covered carriage emerged from
the courtyard of the Knights' Prison and drove down the
road toward Leipzig with a guard of four heavily armed
knights, the latter having let it be known, though not in
so many words, that it was bound for Castle Pleissen. And
with the people now reassured about the ill-fated Junker,
whose presence entailed fire and sword, the Governor set
out with a force of three hundred men to join Prince Friedrich von Meissen. Meanwhile Kohlhaas had, as a matter of
fact, seen his own strength swell to a hundred and nine
men by virtue of the curious position he had gained in the
world; and having rounded up a supply of weapons in
Jessen with which he armed his band to the teeth, and having received intelligence of the double storm now bearing
down on him, he determined to meet it with the swiftness
of the gale wind before it broke over him. Accordingly he
fell upon the Prince of Meissen the very next night in a
nocturnal attack near Mühlberg. In this encounter he lost
Herse, to his intense sorrow, when the latter fell at his side
amid the very first volley; but, embittered by his loss, he
so thrashed the Prince in a three-hour battle, unable as
the latter was to form up his men in the town, that he was
obliged by several serious wounds and the complete disorder of his forces to strike out on the road of retreat toward
Dresden. Heady with victory, he turned back to the Governor, before the latter could learn of it, attacked him near
the village of Damerow in broad noonday in the open field,
and fought with him, with murderous losses but also with
equal gains, until the descent of night. In fact, he would
certainly have attacked the Governor, who had taken up
position in the Damerow churchyard, the following morning with the remnant of his force, if the Governor had not

been informed through scouts of the defeat suffered by the
Prince at Mühlberg and consequently deemed it wiser to
return to Wittenberg until a more favorable time. Five days
after the routing of these two forces he was standing before
Leipzig and setting fire to the city on three sides.—In the
manifesto which he issued on this occasion he termed himself "a lieutenant of the Archangel Michael who was come
to punish by fire and sword all who had embraced the
Junker's cause in this conflict and the wickedness into
which the whole world had fallen." Simultaneously, from
Castle Lützen, which he had taken by surprise and where
he had established himself, he called upon the people to
join him in setting up a better order of things, and the
manifesto, with a kind of madness, bore the subscript,
"Given at the seat of our provisional world government,
the arch-castle of Lützen." Such was the good fortune of
the inhabitants of Leipzig that, because of a steady rain
falling from heaven, the fire did not spread, so that, with
the speed of the available fire-fighting organizations, only
a few stores around Castle Pleissen went up in flames. In-
expressible, however, was the dismay in the city at the
presence of the raging incendiary madman and the illusion
he cherished about the Junker's being in Leipzig; and when
a troop of a hundred and eighty men that had been sent
against him came back to the city in rout, there was nothing for the magistracy to do, since they were unwilling to
jeopardize the city's wealth, but to bar the gates completely and keep the citizenry on guard night and day outside the walls. In vain the magistracy had declarations
posted in the villages of the outlying area with definite as-
surances that the Junker was not inside Castle Pleissen;
the horse dealer insisted in similar notices that he *was* in
Castle Pleissen, and he declared that, if he were not to be
found there, he was going to proceed as if he were to be
found there until such time as they indicated to him by
name the place where he was to be found. The Elector, informed by courier of the distress in which the city of Leipzig stood, announced that he was already gathering an army
of two thousand men, and that he would take command

of it himself in order to apprehend this man Kohlhaas. To the Lord Otto von Gorgas he issued a severe rebuke for the ambiguous and ill-considered device he had used to get the incendiary out of the vicinity of Wittenberg; and no one could describe the consternation of all Saxony and of the capital in particular when it was learned that in the villages around Leipzig a notice addressed to Kohlhaas had been posted, no one knew by whom, to the effect that "Wenzel, the Junker, was with his cousins Hinz and Kunz in Dresden."

It was amid these circumstances that Doctor Martin Luther, relying on the prestige conferred upon him by his position in the world, undertook the task of forcing Kohlhaas, by the compulsion of reassuring words, back within the dykes of human order, and counting on a sound element in the heart of the incendiary, he issued a notice to him which was posted in all the cities and hamlets of the Electorate, saying:

"Kohlhaas, who do claim to be sent to wield the Sword of Justice, what, O Presumptuous Man, are you about in the Frenzy of purblind Passion, you who are yourself filled with Injustice from the Crown of your Head to the Sole of your Foot? Forasmuch as the Sovereign, to whom you are subject, has denied you your Right, your Right in your Contention for a valueless Possession, you do rise up, Wretch, with Fire and Sword and, like the Wolf of the Wilderness, do break into the peaceful Community which he protects. You who do lead Men astray with this Allegation full of Untruth and Deceitfulness, do you imagine, Sinner, that you will therewith prevail before God on that Day which will cast its Light into the Folds of all Hearts? How can you say that your Right has been denied you, you, whose savage Breast, provoked by the Tickle of vile Personal Vengeance, after the first facile Attempts which came to naught, wholly renounced the Effort to procure it? Is a Bench of Constables and Beadles who suppress a Letter brought to them, is the Holding back of a Judgment which they were to have delivered,

your final Authority? And must I inform you, Abomi-
nated of God, that your Authority knows nothing of your
Cause—nay, what am I saying, that the Sovereign against
whom you are in Rebellion does not know so much as
your Name, so that, when you shall step forth before the
Throne of God with the Mind to accuse him, he, with
cheerful Countenance, will be able to say, To this man,
O LORD, I did no Wrong, for his Existence is a Stranger
to my Soul? Know, then, that the Sword that you wield
is the Sword of Brigandage and of Bloodthirstiness, you
are a Rebel and no Warrior of the just GOD, and your
Goal on Earth is the Wheel and the Gallows which is
suspended above the Misdeed and above Godlessness.

Martin Luther.

Wittenberg, etc."

At the Castle of Lützen Kohlhaas was just revolving a
plan within his bosom to reduce Leipzig to ashes—for by
the notice posted in the villages saying that the Junker
Wenzel was in Dresden he set no store, because it had not
been signed by anyone, let alone by the magistracy, as
he had required—when Sternbald and Waldmann caught
sight of this notice, to their great dismay, which had been
affixed during the night to the castle's entrance gate. For
several days they kept hoping in vain that Kohlhaas, whom
they did not wish to approach on the subject, would catch
sight of it himself, but he turned up at the evening hour,
somber and withdrawn, merely to issue his brief commands,
and noticed nothing; thus, one morning when he was about
to have a couple of henchmen strung up for having pillaged
in the neighborhood contrary to his orders, they determined
to bring it to his attention. He was just returning from the
place of execution and the people were timidly yielding
way on either side for the processional which had become
customary with him since his last manifesto—a great angelic
sword was carried before him on a red leather cushion
adorned with tassels of gold and twelve men followed him
with burning torches—when the two fellows, with their

swords tucked under their arms, marched, in a manner that could not help but startle him, around the pillar on which the notice was posted. Kohlhaas, lost in thought and walking with his hands clasped behind his back, glanced up as he came under that gateway and gave a start; and when the two fellows, perceiving his glance, stepped respectfully aside, he walked up to the pillar with a few quick steps, gazing absent-mindedly at them as he did so. But who could describe the agitation of his soul when he saw there the paper whose purport was an accusation of *him* for injustice, and signed by the most precious and revered name he knew, the name of Martin Luther! A dark flush mounted to his cheeks; he read it over twice from beginning to end, having meanwhile removed his helmet; turned with looks of uncertainty and went back among his men as if he were about to say something, but said nothing; took the placard down from the wall, read it through again, and then cried, "Waldmann! Have my horse saddled!" and then, "Sternbald! Come with me into the castle!" and vanished. No more than these few words were needed to disarm him instantly in the total corruption amid which he stood. He put on the disguise of a Thuringian tenant farmer, told Sternbald that business of signal importance obliged him to make a trip to Wittenberg, and, in the presence of several of the leading henchmen, entrusted him with the leadership of the troop now remaining behind in Lützen; then, with the assurance that he would be back within three days and that no attack need be feared during that period, he rode off in the direction of Wittenberg.

Under an assumed name he took quarters at an inn, where, as soon as night had come, he went, wrapped in his mantle and armed with a pair of pistols which he had looted from Castle Tronka, to Luther's room. Luther, who was sitting amid papers and books at his writing desk, saw the strange man open the door and bolt it behind him, and asked him who he was and what he wanted. The man, holding his hat respectfully in his hand, had no sooner replied, with a timid presentiment of the fright he was about to cause, that he was Michael Kohlhaas, the horse dealer, than

Luther shouted, "Be gone from here!" and, rising from his desk and hurrying to get a bell, added, "Your breath is pestilence and your presence ruination!" Kohlhaas, without budging from the spot, drew his pistol and said, "Most Reverend Sir, if you touch that bell, this pistol will lay me lifeless at your feet! Sit down and listen to me; among the angels whose psalms you are writing, you are not safer than with me." Sitting down, Luther asked, "What do you want?" Kohlhaas replied, "To refute your opinion of me, that I am an unjust man! In your notice you said that my Authority knows nothing of my case: very well, obtain safe conduct for me and I will go to Dresden and present it to them."—"Godless and abominable man!" cried Luther, simultaneously confused and reassured by these words. "Who gave you the right to attack the Junker von Tronka in pursuance of decrees issued on your own authority, and, when you did not find him in his castle, to visit fire and sword upon the entire community that affords him shelter?" Kohlhaas answered, "No one, Most Reverend Sir, from this time hence! A communication which I received from Dresden deceived me, misled me! The war which I am waging against the community of mankind becomes a crime as soon as I have not been cast out from it, as you assure me I have not been!"—"Cast out!" cried Luther, looking at him. "What madness of ideas seized you? Who could have cast you out from the community of the state in which you live? Yea, where is there an instance, as long as states have existed, that anyone whosoever has been cast out from them?" —"Cast out," answered Kohlhaas, clenching his hand, "is what I term the man who has been denied the protection of the laws! For I require that protection if my peaceful trade is to prosper; indeed, it is the thing for whose sake I take refuge in that community myself together with the totality of my possessions; and anyone who denies it to me, casts me forth unto the savages of the wildernesses; he puts into my hand—how can you deny it?—the club of my own protection."—"Who has denied you the protection of the laws?" cried Luther. "Did I not write you that the complaint which you submitted is unknown to the Sovereign

to whom you submitted it? If state servants suppress law-
suits behind his back or otherwise make a mockery of his
sacred name without his awareness, who, save God, is permitted to bring him to account for the choice of such servants? Are you, abominable and accursed man, empowered
to judge him on that account?"—"Very well," returned
Kohlhaas. "If the Sovereign has not cast me out, I shall
return to the community of mankind which he protects.
Obtain for me, I repeat, safe conduct to Dresden, and I
will disband the force I have assembled in Castle Lützen,
and I will once again present before the tribunal of the
land that complaint with which I was turned away."—
With a look of annoyance, Luther swept the papers lying
on his table into a pile and was silent. He was vexed by
the posture of defiance which this man assumed in the state,
and, pondering the declaration of war issued from Kohlhaasenbrück against the Junker, he inquired, What, then,
was he asking of the Dresden court? Kohlhaas replied,
"Punishment of the Junker according to the laws; restitution of the horses to their previous condition; and compensation for the injury which I, as well as my man Herse who
died at Mühlberg, have sustained from the deed of violence
perpetrated upon us."—Luther exclaimed, "Compensation
for the injury! You have borrowed sums into the thousands,
from Jews and Christians, on notes and securities, for the
prosecution of your wild personal revenge. Will you add
that amount to the total bill when it comes to making your
demand?"—"God forbid!" replied Kohlhaas. "I do not ask
to have back my house and land and the wealth I once
possessed, any more than the expenses of my wife's funeral!
Herse's old mother will submit a bill of medical expenses
and a specification of what her son lost at Castle Tronka;
and the losses which I suffered from the nonsale of the
blacks the government can have estimated by an expert."
—"Mad, incomprehensible, and dreadful man!" said Luther,
and gazed at him. "After your sword has taken vengeance
on the Junker, the fiercest vengeance imaginable, what im-
pels you to insist on a judgment against him, the severity
of which, if it does fall on him finally, will strike him with

so slight a force?"—Kohlhaas, as a tear rolled down his
cheek, answered, "Most Reverend Sir, this has cost me my
wife: Kohlhaas means to show the world that she did not
perish in any unjust affair. Yield to my will on these points
and have the court render sentence; in all other points that
may possibly be at issue, I will yield to you."—"Look," said
Luther, "what you are asking is just, assuming circumstances otherwise are as public rumor reports; and if you
had been able to take your quarrel to the Sovereign for
decision before proceeding on your own authority to personal vengeance, I have no doubt but that your demands
would have been met, point by point. But, all things considered, would you not have done better to have forgiven
the Junker for your Redeemer's sake, taken the blacks, thin
and emaciated as they were, and ridden them back to your
stable in Kohlhaasenbrück for fattening up?"—"Maybe,"
answered Kohlhaas as he walked over to the window, "and
maybe not. Had I known I would get them on their feet
again only at the cost of my wife's heart's blood, maybe
I would have done as you say, Most Reverend Sir, and not
begrudged a bushel of oats. But, as long as they came to
cost me so dear, I thought, Let matters take their course;
let the judgment be pronounced, as I deserve, and let the
Junker fatten the blacks for me."—Luther, pondering many
thoughts, reached once more for his papers and said he
would initiate procedures on his behalf with the Elector.
Meanwhile he would be so good as to remain quiet at Castle
Lützen; if the Sovereign granted him safe conduct, he
would be notified of it by the device of public advertise-
ment.—"Of course," he continued as Kohlhaas bent down to
kiss his hand, I do not know whether the Elector will grant
mercy instead of justice, for I hear that he has assembled
an army and is about to seize you at Castle Lützen; meanwhile, as I have already told you, I shall not be idle in
my efforts." And therewith he rose and prepared to dismiss
him. Kohlhaas said that his intercession completely reassured him on that score. Whereupon Luther raised his
hand in farewell, but the other suddenly fell on one knee
before him and said he had still another request on his

heart, namely, that at Pentecost, when he was accustomed
to approach the Table of the Lord, he had omitted going
to church on account of his warlike enterprise; would he,
then, have the kindness to receive his confession without
further preparation and in return grant him the beneficence
of the Holy Sacrament? After a brief reflection during
which time he peered sharply at him, Luther said, "Yes,
Kohlhaas, that I will do! The Lord, however, whose body
you crave, forgave His enemy.—Are you willing," he asked,
as the other looked at him startled, "likewise to forgive the
Junker who has harmed you, and to go to Castle Tronka,
mount your blacks, and ride them home to Kohlhaasenbrück for fattening?"—"Most Reverend Sir," said Kohlhaas,
blushing, as he groped for his hand.—"Well?"—"Even the
Lord did not forgive all His enemies. Let me forgive my
two Lords the Electors, the castellan and the overseer, the
Lords Hinz and Kunz, and anyone else I may have injured
in my cause, but let me compel the Junker, if that may
be, to feed my black horses fat again."—At these words
Luther, with a glance of displeasure, turned his back on
him and rang the bell. While a body-servant answered its
ring by a light in the antechamber, Kohlhaas, taken aback,
rose from his knees, drying his eyes as he did so; and when
the body-servant worked in vain at the door because the
bolt was shot, and since Luther had seated himself again
before his manuscripts, it was Kohlhaas who opened the
door for the man. Luther, casting a quick side-glance at
the stranger, said to the body-servant, "Bring light!" whereupon the latter, a little puzzled at the visitor whom he now
perceived, took the house key from the wall and returned
to the half-opened doorway, waiting for the stranger to
withdraw.—Kohlhaas, taking his hat nervously in both
hands, said, "Then I cannot share, Most Reverend Sir, in
the blessing of atonement which I requested of you?"
Luther curtly replied, "With your Savior, no; with your
Sovereign—that will depend on an effort, as I promised
you!" And with that he beckoned to the body-servant to
carry out without further ado the task he had called him
for. In the expression of painful emotion Kohlhaas placed

both hands on his bosom, followed the man who was lighting him down the stairs, and disappeared.

On the following morning Luther addressed an epistle to
the Elector of Saxony, in which, after a bitter allusion to
the Lords Hinz and Kunz, Cupbearer and Chamberlain, von
Tronka, who attended his person and who, as was commonly known, had suppressed the complaint, he represented to the Sovereign, with that frankness peculiar to him,
that in such vexatious circumstances there was nothing else
to do but accept the horse dealer's proposition and grant
him amnesty for what had taken place, with permission to
renew his litigation. Public opinion, he remarked, was in a
most dangerous way on this man's side, to the point where,
even in Wittenberg to which he had thrice set fire, there
were still voices raised in his behalf; and since he would
inevitably bring his proposal to the knowledge of the people
in case it was refused, and enhance it with the most acid
commentary, the people might well be perverted to the
point where the state would be powerless to move at all
against him. He concluded by saying that, in this extraordinary instance, they would have to disregard the impro-
priety of negotiating with a citizen who had taken up arms;
that the man in question, by virtue of the wrong perpetrated upon him, had actually been placed, in a way, outside the social union; and, in brief, to get out of the difficulty, he would have to be considered not so much as a
rebel as a foreign power who had invaded the country, for
which status he was more or less qualified, given the fact
that he was an alien subject.—The Elector received this letter at just the time when there were present in the castle
the Prince Christiern von Meissen, Generalissimo of the
Realm and uncle of that Prince Friedrich von Meissen who
had been defeated at Mühlberg and was still convalescing
from his wounds; the Lord High Chancellor of the tribunal,
Count Wrede; Count Kallheim, President of the State
Chancery; and the two Lords Hinz and Kunz von Tronka,
the latter Chamberlain, the former Cupbearer, and childhood friends of the Sovereign. The Chamberlain, Lord
Kunz, who, in the capacity of a Privy Secretary, looked

after the Sovereign's private correspondence and had authority to use his name and seal, spoke first, and after once
again detailing at length how he had submitted to the
court the complaint presented by the horse dealer against
the Junker, his cousin, and would never have suppressed
it on his own authority if, misled by false representations,
he had not considered it a wholly unfounded and worthless
nuisance, finally touched on the present state of affairs. He
remarked that neither by divine nor by human law would
the horse dealer have been justified on the basis of this
error in so monstrous a personal revenge as he had allowed
himself; he described the glory that would redound to the
accursed man by treating with him as an actual military
power; and the disgrace thereby reflected upon the sacred
person of the Elector seemed to him so intolerable that in
the ardor of his rhetoric he claimed he would rather see
the worst, the fulfillment of the mad rebel's war decree and
the conducting of the Junker, his cousin, down to Kohlhaasenbrück to fatten up the black horses, sooner than see
acceptance of the proposal made by Doctor Luther. The
High Chancellor of the tribunal, Count Wrede, half turning toward him, expressed his regret that such tender concern as he was now displaying over the reputation of the
Sovereign upon the outcome of this decidedly sorry affair,
had not exercised him at an earlier opportunity. He explained to the Elector his reluctance to enlist the power of
the state to enforce a patently unjust ordinance; observed,
with a meaningful glance at the following which the horse
dealer continued to find in the country, that the chain of
crimes was threatening to project itself into infinity; and declared that it was to be broken, and that the government
could extricate itself successfully from this ugly business,
only by a forthright act of honesty which would directly
and without regard for persons make good the error which
they had incurred to their guilt. Prince Christiern von Meissen, at the Sovereign's question, What did he think of the
matter? turned respectfully to the High Chancellor and
said, The opinion voiced by him filled him with the utmost
respect; but, by wishing to help Kohlhaas get his rights, he

was not taking into consideration the fact that he had im-
pinged upon Wittenberg and Leipzig, and upon the entire
country which he had mistreated, in his just claim to restitution, or at least to punishment. The order of the state had,
by dint of this man, been so dislocated that it could hardly
be set right by an axiom borrowed from the science of juris-
prudence. Therefore he was in favor of invoking, concur-
rent with the Chamberlain's opinion, the measure established for such cases: convoking a military force of adequate
size and capture or annihilation of the horse dealer, whose
position was at Lützen. The Chamberlain, bringing over
chairs from against the wall for him and for the Elector
and obligingly placing them in the room, said he was delighted that a man of his integrity and acumen agreed with
him on the method of dealing with this ambiguous matter.
The Prince, holding on to the chair but without sitting
down, assured him he had no reason at all for being delighted, inasmuch as the concurrently involved steps were
necessarily those of first issuing a warrant for *his* arrest and
then of bringing him to trial for misuse of the Sovereign's
name. For if necessity required the lowering of a veil before
the throne of justice to conceal a series of outrages which,
stretching out further than the eye could reach, could no
longer find room to appear before it, the same did not hold
for the first one which had given rise to the others: only
a life-and-death accusation against *him* could empower the
state to destroy the horse dealer, whose cause, as was well
known, was entirely just, and into whose hands they had
themselves placed the sword that he was wielding. The
Elector glanced with a start toward the Junker upon hearing these words, then, as his whole face became red, turned
away and walked over to the window. After an embarrass-
ing pause on all sides, Count Kallheim said that in this
fashion they would never get out of the magic circle in
which they found themselves charmed. By the same token,
his nephew, Prince Friedrich, might be brought to trial, for
he too, in that strange expedition which he had undertaken
against Kohlhaas, had in various ways overstepped his instructions, so that, if anyone were to inquire into the ex-

tensive list of those responsible for the embarrassment in which they now found themselves, he would be likewise named among that number and would have to be called to account by the Sovereign for what had happened at Mühlberg. While the Elector with looks of uncertainty stepped over to the table, the Cupbearer, Lord Hinz von Tronka, spoke up and said he could not comprehend how the decision to be reached could escape men of such wisdom as were assembled here. As he understood it, the horse dealer had promised to disband the force with which he had invaded the country in return for nothing more than safe conduct to Dresden and a renewal of the investigation into his case. But it did not follow from that by any means that an amnesty had to be granted him for this outrageous personal revenge of his—two legal concepts which seemed to have been confused by Doctor Luther as well as by the State Council. "When once," he went on, laying his finger alongside his nose, "sentence has been passed on the score of the black horses, whatever that sentence may be, by the Dresden court, there is nothing to prevent the arrest of Kohlhaas on the charge of his murderous acts of arson and brigandage, a politic step which combines the advantages of both statesmen and is certain to get the approval of the world and of posterity."—When both the Prince and the High Chancellor answered this speech of the Cupbearer, Lord Hinz, with a mere glance, and the bargain seemed to have been closed therewith, the Elector said he would ponder privately the various opinions proposed to him until the next session of the State Council.—Those preliminary measures mentioned by the Prince had apparently had the effect upon his heart, which was highly sensitive where friendship was involved, of quenching all pleasure in carrying out the campaign against Kohlhaas for which all preparations had already been made. At any rate he had the High Chancellor, Count Wrede, whose opinion he felt to be the most practical, stay behind after the others had left; and when the latter showed him letters indicating that the horse dealer's strength had, in fact, swelled to four hundred men, and that, given the dissatisfaction prevalent in the country

on account of the improprieties of the Chamberlain, Kohlhaas might shortly be able to count on doubling and tripling
that strength, then the Elector determined without further
ado to accept the advice that Doctor Luther had given him.
Accordingly he turned the entire handling of the Kohlhaas
affair over to Count Wrede; and a few days later there appeared a proclamation which we reproduce here in its essentials:

"We etc., etc., Elector of Saxony, in particularly gracious consideration of the intercession made to Us by
Doctor Martin Luther, do grant to Michael Kohlhaas,
horse dealer in territory of Brandenburg, safe conduct to
Dresden for the purpose of renewed investigation of his
case, on condition that within three days of sight of this
document he lay down the arms he has taken up; with
the understanding that if the aforesaid party should, as
is improbable, be denied by the Dresden court in his suit
anent the black horses, proceedings shall be initiated
against him to the full extent of the law because of his
willful undertaking to attain his rights by himself; in the
contrary event, however, justice shall be tempered with
mercy for him and for his entire force and plenary amnesty shall be granted for the acts of violence committed
by him in Saxony."

No sooner had Kohlhaas received, through Doctor Luther, a copy of this proclamation which had been posted
in all the towns of the country, than, despite all the conditions attached to the statement, he disbanded his entire
force, dismissing them with gifts, expressions of gratitude,
and appropriate admonitions. All money, weapons, and
equipment he had taken as loot he deposited with the courts
in Lützen as electoral property; then, after sending Waldmann with letters to the bailiff in Kohlhaasenbrück concerning the repurchase of his farm, if that should prove feasible,
and after sending Sternbald to Schwerin to fetch his children, whom he wished to have with him once again, he
left the castle at Lützen, and with the remainder of his

small fortune, which he carried on his person in the form
of banknotes, made his way unrecognized to Dresden.

Dawn was just breaking and the entire city was still
asleep when he knocked at the door of the little house located in the Pirna suburb which, thanks to the bailiff's honesty, still belonged to him, and told Thomas, the aged
manager of the place, who opened the door with amazement and confusion, that he should go to the Gubernium
and announce to the Prince of Meissen that he, Kohlhaas
the horse dealer, was there. The Prince of Meissen, who
felt that it behooved him, on receipt of this news, to ascertain immediately in what relation they stood with this man,
found an immense throng of people gathered already in the
streets leading to Kohlhaas' dwelling when he arrived there
soon afterward with a retinue of knights and grooms. The
news of the arrival of the Avenging Angel who pursued the
people's oppressors with fire and sword had brought out
all Dresden, city and suburbs; the house door had to be
bolted against the crush of the curious mob, and the young-
sters were clambering along the windows to get a view of
the arsonist-murderer at breakfast inside. As soon as the
Prince had penetrated the house with the help of the bodyguard, who opened a path for him, and had entered Kohlhaas' room, he asked him as he stood there half undressed
by a table, whether he was Kohlhaas, the horse dealer;
whereupon Kohlhaas, producing a wallet from his belt con-
taining several documents dealing with his circumstances,
handed it respectfully to him and answered yes, and went
on to say that he had come to Dresden in accordance with
the safe conduct granted him by the Sovereign, having
meanwhile disbanded his forces, in order to present his
claim concerning the black horses against the Junker Wenzel von Tronka in the court. The Prince, after a fleeting
glance that scanned him from head to toe, looked through
the papers in the wallet, had him explain the significance
of a receipt, which he found among them, issued by the
Lützen court acknowledging deposits to the credit of the
electoral treasury; and, after sizing up what manner of man
this was by means of various questions about his children,

about his fortune, and about the kind of life he intended
to live in the future, and after having found him on all
counts such a person as one might be reassured about, returned him his wallet and said that no hindrance stood in
the way of his trial, and that, in order to initiate it directly,
he had only to apply to the High Chancellor of the tribunal,
Count Wrede. "Meanwhile," said the Prince, after a pause
during which he stepped to the window and with wonder-
ment surveyed the mob that had collected in front of the
house, "you will have to accept a bodyguard for the first
few days to protect you, both in your house and when you
go out!"—Disconcerted, Kohlhaas cast down his eyes and
was silent. "No matter," said the Prince, coming away from
the window again; "whatever happens, you will have only
yourself to blame for it!" and therewith turned toward the
door with the intention of quitting the house. Kohlhaas,
having reflected, said, "My Lord, do as you will! Give me
your word that you will withdraw the guard as soon as I
desire it, and I will have no objection to make against this
step!" The Prince replied that this required no discussion;
and after he had signified to the three lansquenets detailed
for this purpose that the man in whose house they were
being left was free, and that they were to follow him when
he went out only for his own protection, he saluted the
horse dealer with a condescending wave of his hand, and
departed.

Toward midday Kohlhaas betook himself to the High
Chancellor of the tribunal, Count Wrede, accompanied by
his three lansquenets and followed by a crowd that extended as far as the eye could reach, but which, because
they had been warned by the police, attempted to harm
him in no way. The High Chancellor, who received him
with gentleness and amicability in his antechamber, con-
versed for two whole hours with him, and after having him
narrate the whole course of the affair from beginning to
end, he referred him to a famous lawyer of the city, dele-
gated to the court, for the immediate drafting and submission of his complaint. Without further delay, Kohlhaas
made his way to the latter's residence; then, after the com-

plaint had been drawn up precisely in accordance with the earlier suppressed one, invoking punishment of the Junker according to law, restoration of the horses to their previous condition, and compensation for *his* damages as well as those sustained by his groom Herse who had died at Mühlberg, these latter made out in favor of Herse's aged mother, he returned to his house, followed by the still gaping mob, determined now not to leave it again unless unavoidable business so required.

Meanwhile the Junker too had been released from his Wittenberg jail, and after recovery from a dangerous case of erysipelas which had inflamed his foot, had been peremptorily summoned by the provincial court to present himself in Dresden to answer charges brought against him by the horse dealer Michael Kohlhaas for illegal detention of his black horses and their ruin by overwork. The Chamberlain and Cupbearer brothers von Tronka, cousins of the Junker, at whose house he came to stay, received him with the utmost embitterment and contempt; they called him a wretched good-for-nothing who was bringing shame and disgrace upon the whole family, announced to him that he was unquestionably going to lose his case now, and demanded that he make arrangements immediately for the producing of the black horses, to the fattening up of which he would be sentenced by the scornful laughter of the world. With weak and quavering voice the Junker said that he was the most pitiable man in the world. He vowed he had known but little of the whole accursed business that was now plunging him into grief, and that the castellan and the overseer were to blame for everything by virtue of their having used the horses in the harvest without his remotest knowledge or desire and by their having ruined them by immoderate exertion, partly in their own fields. As he was saying this, he sat down, and he begged them not to thrust him deliberately back by their abuse and insults into the illness from which he had only just recovered. On the following day the Lords Hinz and Kunz, who owned estates in the vicinity of burned-out Castle Tronka, wrote, upon the supplication of the Junker their cousin, and because, frankly,

there was no help for it, to their overseer and tenants located there to make inquiries concerning the black horses,
which had been lost sight of since that unhappy day and
had simply not been heard of since. But, with the total
devastation of the place and with the massacre of almost
all the inhabitants, all they could find out was that a groom,
forced on by blows from the flat of the arsonist-murderer's
sword, had rescued them from a burning shed where they
were standing, but that afterward he had received from the
raging madman a kick by way of answer to his question of
where he was supposed to take them and what he was supposed to do with them. The aged, gout-plagued housekeeper of the Junker, who had fled to Meissen, assured him,
in her answer to his written inquiry, that on the morning
after that ghastly night the groom had gone with the horses
in the direction of the Brandenburg border; but all inquiries
instituted there proved futile, and an error seemed to have
underlain that report, inasmuch as the Junker had no groom
whose place of residence was in Brandenburg territory or
even on the road thither. Some men from Dresden who had
been in Wilsdruf a few days after the burning of Castle
Tronka stated that around the specified time a groom had
arrived there leading two horses by the bridle, and that he
had left them, since they looked very bedraggled and could
not walk any further, in the cow barn of a shepherd who
had indicated willingness to get them back in condition.
For various reasons it appeared highly likely that these were
the black horses in question; but the Wilsdruf shepherd, as
people who came from there declared, had sold them on
to someone else, no one knew whom; and a third rumor,
whose originator proved unidentifiable, flatly claimed that
the horses had already departed this life and were buried
in the Wilsdruf bone yard. The Lords Hinz and Kunz, to
whom this last turn of affairs was, as may easily be understood, the most appealing, inasmuch as it obviated the necessity of their fattening up the blacks in their own stables
—for the Junker their cousin had no stables any longer—
wished nevertheless, for the sake of greater certainty, to
verify this report. Accordingly Lord Wenzel von Tronka,

as hereditary, enfeoffed, and jurisdictional lord of the area, despatched an epistle to the Wilsdruf courts, in which, after an extensive description of the black horses—which he said had been entrusted to his keeping and by mischance had been lost—he most humbly implored them to search out the current whereabouts of same and to urge and prevail upon their owner, whoever he might be, to deliver them, in return for handsome compensation for all expenses, to the stables of the Chamberlain, Lord Kunz, in Dresden. As a result there did actually appear, some days afterward, the man to whom the Wilsdruf shepherd had sold them and who now led them, shrunken, stumbling, and tethered to the tail bar of his cart, into the market place of the city; but, as Lord Wenzel's ill-luck would have it, and even more as the ill-luck of the honorable Kohlhaas would have it, this was the knacker from Döbbeln.

As soon as Lord Wenzel, in the presence of his cousin the Chamberlain, had heard by uncertain rumor that a man had arrived in the city with two black horses that had escaped from the Castle Tronka fire, they both made their way, accompanied by several servants hastily assembled from the household, to the palace square where he was, in order to get them from him, in case they were the ones belonging to Kohlhaas, reimburse him for his expenses, and bring them home. But how startled the knights were when they caught sight of a crowd of people that had been attracted by the spectacle and that was growing larger by the minute around the two-wheeled cart to which the animals were tied; amid infinite laughter the people were shouting to one another that the horses for whose sake the state was tottering had already gone to the flayer's! The Junker, having walked around the cart and taken a look at the woebegone beasts that seemed ready to die at any minute, said with embarrassment that those were not the horses that he had taken from Kohlhaas; but Lord Kunz, the Chamberlain, casting a glance of speechless fury at him that would have crushed him if he had been made of iron, and flinging back his mantle so that his orders and chain were revealed, stepped up to the knacker and asked him

whether these were the black horses which the Wilsdruf
shepherd had brought to him and which the Junker Wenzel
von Tronka, to whom they belonged, had requisitioned
from that place. The knacker, who was busy with a pail
of water in his hand watering the fat stocky horse that
pulled his cart, said, "The black ones?"—He put the pail
down, slipped the bit out of his nag's mouth, and said that
the black horses tied to his cart tail had been sold to him
by the swineherd from Hainichen. Where *he* got them, and
whether they came from the Wilsdruf shepherd, he didn't
know. The Wilsdruf court messenger had told *him*, he said
as he picked up the pail again and braced it between his
knee and the wagon tongue, the Wilsdruf court messenger
had told *him* that he was supposed to bring them to
Dresden to the house of the Lords von Tronka; but the
Junker he had been referred to had the name of Kunz. With
these words he turned with what was left of the water that
the nag hadn't touched in the pail and emptied it out on
the street pavement. The Chamberlain, surrounded by the
glances of the jeering crowd and unable to get this fellow,
who kept on about his business with phlegmatic diligence,
to look at him, said that he was Chamberlain Kunz von
Tronka; that the horses he was supposed to be bringing
him must belong to the Junker, his cousin; that they had
gotten to the Wilsdruf shepherd through a groom who had
escaped at the time of the Castle Tronka fire; and that
originally they were two horses belonging to the horse
dealer Kohlhaas. He asked the fellow, who stood there with
legs braced apart and hitching up his pants, if he didn't
know anything about all this. Hadn't maybe the Hainichen
swineherd bought them—and on this point everything depended—from the Wilsdruf shepherd, or from some third
party? The knacker, after standing up to the cart and passing his water, said that *he* had been sent to Dresden with
the horses to get money for them in the house of the Lords
von Tronka. What he was talking about, he didn't understand; and whether before this the swineherd from
Hainichen had owned them, or Peter, or Paul, or the
Wilsdruf shepherd, made no difference to him, so long as

they weren't stolen. And with that he struck out, with his whip slung over his broad back, toward a tavern situated on the square, with the intention, hungry as he was, of getting some breakfast. The Chamberlain, who didn't know what in God's world to do with horses sold by the Hainichen swineherd to the Döbbeln knacker in case they were not the ones on which the Devil rode through Saxony, demanded that the Junker say something; but when the latter with pale and quivering lips replied that the most sensible thing to do was to buy the blacks whether they belonged to Kohlhaas or not, the Chamberlain, cursing the father and mother who had borne him and flinging his mantle back, stepped rearwards out of the crowd, completely at sea as to what to do or not to do. He called over Baron von Wenk, an acquaintance of his who happened to be riding down the street, and, determined not to leave the square, precisely because the rabble was staring at him in mockery and, with their handkerchiefs crammed into their mouths, seemed only to be waiting for his withdrawal to burst out, he asked him to stop off at the High Chancellor's, Count Wrede's, and by his agency to get Kohlhaas down here to inspect the black horses. It just happened that Kohlhaas was present in the High Chancellor's room—he had been summoned by a court messenger in the matter of certain clarifications needed from him relative to the deposition in Lützen—when the Baron entered the room on the aforementioned errand; and as the High Chancellor rose from his seat with a look of annoyance and left the horse dealer, whose identity was unknown to the other man, standing off to one side with the papers he was holding in his hand, the Baron outlined for him the perplexity in which the Lords von Tronka found themselves. The knacker from Döbbeln, in response to unclear orders from the Wilsdruf court, had turned up with horses whose condition was so hopeless that the Junker Wenzel could not help but hesitate in recognizing them as the ones belonging to Kohlhaas; so that, in case they were to be accepted from the knacker anyway and an attempt made to recondition them in the noblemen's stables, ocular inspection by Kohlhaas would first be necessary in order to place the aforementioned circumstance beyond any doubt. "Be so kind, therefore," he concluded, "as to have Kohlhaas fetched from his house by a detail of guards and brought to the market place where the horses are standing." The High Chancellor, removing his spectacles from his nose, said the Baron was laboring under a twofold misapprehension: first, in thinking that the matter under discussion could not be resolved in any other way than by ocular inspection by Kohlhaas; and second, in fancying that he, the Chancellor, was authorized to have Kohlhaas fetched by a detail of guards to whatever place the Junker pleased. Therewith he introduced him to the horse dealer standing behind him, and, as he sat down and put his spectacles back on, he requested him to address himself in this matter to the man himself.— Kohlhaas, allowing no expression to betray what was going on in his mind, said he was prepared to follow him to the market place for an inspection of the black horses that the knacker had brought to town. As the Baron turned back to him in confusion, he stepped up once again to the High Chancellor's table, and, after extracting several papers from his wallet with information relative to the deposition in Lützen and giving them to him, he bade him good day; the Baron, who, completely red in the face, had stepped to the window, likewise bade him good day; then both of them, accompanied by the three lansquenets detailed by the Prince of Meissen, made their way, trailed by a crowd of people, down to the palace square. The Chamberlain, Lord Kunz, who meanwhile, despite the representations of several friends who had joined him, had stood his ground among the people in opposition to the knacker from Döbbeln, stepped up to the horse dealer as soon as the latter came into view with the Baron, and, holding his sword with pride and dignity under his arm, asked him whether the horses standing behind the cart were his. The horse dealer, after a courteous turn toward the gentleman addressing the question, with whom he was not acquainted, and raising his hat to him, stepped over, without replying and followed by all the knights, to the knacker's cart. From

twelve paces off, where he had stopped, he swiftly measured the animals that stood there on shaky legs, with their
heads drooping, and refusing the hay that the knacker had
put down for them. "Merciful God!" he cried as he turned
back to the Chamberlain. "The knacker is quite right; the
horses that are tied to his cart belong to me!" And therewith, as he gazed around the entire circle of lords, he
lifted his hat once again and departed from the square,
with the detail of guards following him. At these words
the Chamberlain, with a swift step that set his helmet
plume waving, advanced toward the knacker and threw
him a purse of money; and while the latter, with the purse
in hand, was sweeping his hair back from his forehead with
a lead comb and kept looking at the money, he ordered a
groom to untie the horses and lead them home. At his
master's summons, the groom had left a circle of friends
and relatives that he had among the people, and now,
slightly red in the face, did actually step toward the horses,
crossing, as he did so, a considerable pile of horse manure
that had formed at his feet; but he had scarcely taken hold
of the bridles in order to untie the animals when his cousin,
Master Himboldt, grabbed him by the arm and with the
words, "You're not going to touch those glue-factory nags!"
he hurled him away from the cart. Then, turning back with
unsteady steps across the manure heap toward the Chamberlain, who stood there speechless at this incident, he went
on to say that he would have to send for a knacker's man
to perform any such service for him! Foaming with rage,
the Chamberlain, after staring a moment at the Master,
wheeled around and over the heads of the knights surrounding him shouted for the guard; and as soon as an
officer followed by several electoral men-at-arms had appeared, at Baron von Wenk's order, from the castle, he
briefly related the shameful incitement to rebellion that the
citizens of the city were permitting themselves and called
upon the officer to arrest the ringleader, Master Himboldt.
Grabbing the Master by the shirt front, he accused him
of mishandling his groom who was untying the black horses
at his command and of knocking him away from the cart.

The Master, with an adroit turn that set him free, shoved the Chamberlain back and said, "Sir, telling a chap twenty years old what he is supposed to do does not mean inciting him to rebellion! Ask him if, contrary to tradition and propriety, he wants to have anything to do with those horses tied to the cart; if, after what I have said, he still does want to—so be it! For all I care, he can skin them and gut them right now!" At these words the Chamberlain turned around to the groom and asked him whether he had any objection to carrying out his order and untying the horses belonging to Kohlhaas and taking them home; and when the latter, retreating among the citizens, timidly answered that the horses would first have to be made respectable again before such could be expected of him, the Chamberlain went after him, knocked off his hat, that was adorned with the emblem of his house, and after stamping on the hat, whipped out his sword and with furious blows of the blade drove him instantly out of the square and out of his service. Master Himboldt shouted, "Get the murdering madman!" and, as the crowd, outraged by this scene, closed in and forced the guard away, he knocked the Chamberlain down from behind, tore off his mantle, collar, and helmet, twisted the sword out of his grasp, and hurled it with a fierce heave way across the square. In vain did the Junker Wenzel shout to the knights to run to his cousin's aid, while he himself dodged out of the mêlée; before they had taken a single step for that purpose they were scattered by the rush of the crowd, so that the Chamberlain, who had hurt his head as he fell, was exposed to the full frenzy of the mob. The only thing that saved him was the appearance of a troop of mounted lansquenets that happened to cross the square and whom the officer of the electoral guardsmen called over to support him. After dispersing the crowd, the officer seized the raging Master, and while he was being haled off to jail by several of the horsemen, two friends picked up the unlucky, blood-bedaubed Chamberlain from the ground and took him home. Such was the sorry outcome of the honest and well-meant attempt to provide satisfaction for the horse dealer in compensation for the in-

justice that had been visited upon him. As the crowd began
to drift away, the Döbbeln knacker, whose business was
finished and who did not want to wait around any longer,
tied the horses to a lamp post, where they remained standing all the rest of the day without anyone's paying any
attention to them, a butt for the mockery of street urchins
and loafers, so that, for lack of any care or tending, the
police had to take charge of them; with the coming of
evening they sent for the Dresden knacker to take them to
the city slaughter yards and look after them until further
disposition had been made.

This incident, however little the horse dealer was actually to blame for it, nevertheless aroused a feeling, even
among more moderate and better spirits, in the country
that was extremely dangerous for the outcome of his litigation. His position relative to the state was found to be intolerable, and in private houses and public places alike the
opinion developed that it was better to do him an open
wrong and to suppress the whole case once more than to
permit him justice, extorted by violence, in such an insignificant matter, merely for the gratification of his mad obstinacy. To the total ruin of poor Kohlhaas, the High Chancellor himself, by his too great honesty and the hatred for
the von Tronka family that derived therefrom, unavoidably
contributed to the confirmation and spread of the feeling.
It was highly unlikely that the horses, which were now being looked after by the Dresden knacker, could ever be
restored to the condition in which they had come from the
stables in Kohlhaasenbrück; but, assuming it were possible
by virtue of skill and unremitting care, the disgrace that
fell upon the Junker's family as a result of the existing
circumstances was so great that, considering the civic dis-
tinction that they had as one of the first and noblest families
in the country, nothing seemed more fair and reasonable
than a payment in money by way of restitution for the
horses. Nevertheless, when, a few days later, the President,
Count Kallheim, acting for the Chamberlain whose illness
prevented him from writing, made this proposal in a letter
to the High Chancellor, the latter also sent a letter to Kohl-

haas urging him not to reject such an offer out of hand if it
should be made to him; but, in a curt, barely civil reply,
he begged the President to spare him any private commis-
sions in this case and urged the Chamberlain to have recourse directly to the horse dealer himself, whom he described as a very sensible and modest man. The horse
dealer, whose will had indeed been broken by the incident
of the market place, was only waiting, in accordance with
the High Chancellor's advice, for some overture on the part
of the Junker or of his people in order to meet it with
complete readiness and forgiveness of all that had happened; but precisely this overture the proud knights were
sensitive about making, and, profoundly embittered by the
answer they had received from the High Chancellor, they
showed it to the Elector, who on the morning of the following day had visited the Chamberlain as he lay in his room
ill from the wounds he had received. In a faint voice all
the more touching on account of his condition, the Chamberlain asked him whether, after risking his life to settle
this affair in accordance with his wishes, he was now going
to have to expose his honor to the world's censure by appearing with a request for terms and for indulgence before
a man who had brought all imaginable shame and disgrace
upon him and his family. After reading the letter, the Elector asked Count Kallheim in embarrassment whether the
court was authorized to take its stand, without further consultation with Kohlhaas, on the point that the horses could
not be restored to their former condition, and accordingly
to render a verdict immediately, as though they were already dead, for mere compensation in money. The Count
replied, "Sir, they *are* dead, dead from a legal point of view
because they have no value, and they will be physically
dead before they can be gotten out of the knacker's yard
and into the knights' stables." To which the Elector, pocket-
ing the letter, said that he would talk to the High Chancellor himself about it, reassured the Chamberlain who had
half raised himself up and seized his hand in gratitude,
and, after again recommending that he take good care of

his health, rose with great dignity from his seat and left the room.

Thus did things stand in Dresden when over poor Kohlhaas broke another and more serious storm from Lützen, the lightning bolt of which the cunning knights were clever enough to divert upon his ill-fated head. Johann Nagelschmidt, namely, one of the henchmen gathered by the horse dealer and subsequently released with thanks after publication of the electoral amnesty, had found it worth while a few weeks afterward to regather a portion of this rabble, with its proclivity toward any shameless doings, along the Bohemian border and to continue on his own hook the business on whose traces Kohlhaas had set him. This worthless fellow termed himself a lieutenant of Kohlhaas, partly in order to inspire fear in the bailiffs who were after him, partly to seduce the peasantry in the usual manner to participate in his rascalities; with cleverness learned from his master, he spread it abroad that the amnesty was not being observed in the case of several henchmen who had quietly returned to their homes, in fact, that Kohlhaas himself, with a perfidiousness that cried aloud to Heaven, had been imprisoned upon his arrival in Dresden and committed to the charge of a guard; so that, in manifestoes that were very similar to those of Kohlhaas, his arson-and-murder crew appeared as a military force that had risen up for nothing but the honor of God with the mission of guaranteeing the observation of the amnesty that had been promised them by the Elector; all this, as has already been noted, was by no means for the honor of God, nor from attachment to Kohlhaas, whose fate was utterly indifferent to him, but merely in order to burn and pillage the more easily and with greater impunity under the protection of such allegations. As soon as the first reports of this reached Dresden, the knights could not repress their delight at such a turn of events which conferred a different form upon their whole enterprise. With wise side-glances of disapproval they recalled the mistake that had been made in granting Kohlhaas an amnesty in spite of their urgent and repeated warnings, just as though it had been the intention to give all

scoundrels the signal thereby to follow in his ways; and
not content with lending credence to Nagelschmidt's claim
of having taken up arms solely for the support and security
of his oppressed master, they vented the definite opinion
that his entire appearance on the scene was nothing but a
plot concocted by Kohlhaas to intimidate the government
and to force and rush through a verdict suitable point by
point with his insane obstinacy. Indeed the Cupbearer,
Lord Hinz, went so far, for the benefit of several hunting
companions and courtiers gathered around him after table
in the Elector's antechamber, as to represent the disbanding
of the robber band in Lützen as a damned humbug; and
while poking great fun at the High Chancellor's love of
justice, he demonstrated from various cleverly assembled
pieces of evidence that the band was ready now as before
in the forests of the Electorate and waiting only for a sign
from Kohlhaas to break forth anew with fire and sword.
Prince Christiern von Meissen, highly displeased at this
turn of affairs which threatened to smirch his master's reputation in the most grievous way, betook himself immediately to the palace to see him; seeing clearly through the
knights' interest in ruining Kohlhaas, if possible, on the
grounds of fresh offenses, he requested and received permission to organize a hearing at once for the horse dealer.
The horse dealer, not without surprise, and escorted to the
Gubernium by a constable, appeared with his two little
boys, Heinrich and Leopold, in his arms; for Sternbald,
the groom, had arrived the previous day with his five children from Mecklenburg where they had been staying, and
a variety of thoughts too far reaching to explain caused him
to pick up the lads, who amid an outburst of childish tears
at his departure had begged him to do so, and to take them
along to the hearing. The Prince, after looking benevolently
at the children, whom Kohlhaas had seated next to him,
and after inquiring in a friendly way about their names
and ages, detailed for him what kind of liberties his former
henchman Nagelschmidt was taking over in the Erzgebirge
valleys; then, passing over to him the latter's so-called manifesto, he called upon him to make whatever statements he

was able to make in his own defense. However dismayed
he was at these shameful and treacherous documents, the
horse dealer had little difficulty in establishing the base-
lessness of the accusations made against him before so upright a man as the Prince. As matters now stood, not only
did he not need any help from a third party in obtaining a
decision in his litigation, which was now progressing ex-
cellently, but, from some papers which he had with him
and which he showed the Prince, there was made apparent
quite a different kind of unlikelihood that Nagelschmidt's
heart was set on furnishing him with that sort of aid, by
virtue of the fact that he had been on the verge of having
the fellow hanged shortly before the dispersal of the troop
in Lützen on account of rape committed in open country
and other outrages; only the publication of the electoral
amnesty, by dissolving their whole relationship, had saved
him, and the two of them had parted mortal enemies on
the following day. Upon the Prince's suggestion, Kohlhaas
sat down and directed an epistle to Nagelschmidt in which
he branded as a shameless and infamous fabrication the
latter's allegation of having risen in revolt for the purpose
of maintaining the amnesty which had been violated with
respect to him and his followers; stated that upon his arrival in Dresden he had neither been imprisoned nor put
under guard and that his lawsuit was proceeding precisely
as he desired; and delivered him to the full vengeance of
the law, as a warning to the rabble that had rallied about
him, for the acts of arson committed in the Erzgebirge since
the publication of the amnesty. In addition there were
appended to the letter several extracts from the criminal
proceedings conducted against him at Castle Lützen by
the horse dealer on the count of the aforementioned outrages, for the information of people concerning this worthless fellow who had already been sentenced to the gallows
at that time and rescued, as previously mentioned, only by
the edict which the Elector had promulgated. Accordingly
the Prince reassured Kohlhaas as to the suspicion which
had unavoidably been voiced in his regard under the compulsion of circumstances; assured him further that as long

as *he* was in Dresden the amnesty accorded him was not
going to be violated in any way; shook the hands of the
boys once more, as he made them a present of the fruit
standing on his table; bade Kohlhaas adieu, and dismissed
him. The High Chancellor, however, aware of the danger
impending above the horse dealer, did his utmost to bring
the case to a conclusion before it became complicated and
confused by any new events, but such complication was
precisely what the politically cunning knights desired and
intended; instead of silent acknowledgment of their guilt
as heretofore, and instead of limiting their opposition
merely to obtaining a reduced sentence, they now began,
by means of evasions of the sliest pettifogging sort, to deny
their guilt altogether. Presently they gave out that Kohlhaas' blacks had been detained at Castle Tronka only as a
result of the arbitrary action of the castellan and the overseer about which the Junker was uninformed or only imperfectly informed; then again they asserted that the animals had already been sick with a violent and dangerous
cough at the time of their arrival there, and on this score
they invoked witnesses whom they pledged themselves to
produce; and when, after extensive investigations and ex-
planations, they were forced to retreat from these argu-
ments, they fell back on an electoral edict whereby, for a
period of twelve years previous, importation of horses from
Brandenburg into Saxony had actually been prohibited on
account of a cattle disease, crystal-clear evidence not only
of the Junker's authorization but of his duty to impound
the horses which Kohlhaas had brought across the border.
—Kohlhaas, who meanwhile had reacquired his farm by
purchase from the honest bailiff at Kohlhaasenbrück upon
payment of a small sum compensatory for losses sustained,
wished to leave Dresden for a few days and to go to this
native region of his, apparently for the purpose of legal
settlement of this business, a decision which, urgent as it
might actually be for the ordering of the winter seed grain,
was dictated less, as we can hardly doubt, by the aforementioned errand than by the intention of testing his position which was now so hedged about with odd and dubious

circumstances. Perhaps further reasons of another kind contributed to it, which we leave to be divined by each person with wisdom in his heart. Thus, abandoning the guard
assigned to him, he betook himself to the High Chancellor
and, with the bailiff's letter in his hand, explained to him
that, in the event he was not needed at the court, as now
seemed likely, he was of a mind to leave the city and to
travel to Brandenburg for a period of eight or twelve days,
within which time he promised to be back. The High Chancellor, staring at the floor with a look of displeasure and
doubt, replied that he was forced to confess that his presence was more sorely needed now than ever, inasmuch as
the court needed his statements and elucidations in a thousand unforeseen instances as a result of the cunning and
quibbling objections of the opposing party; but when
Kohlhaas referred him to his attorney who was well posted
on the case and with humble firmness insisted on his request, promising to limit himself to eight days, the High
Chancellor, after a pause, curtly said as he dismissed him
that he hoped he would apply to Prince Christiern von
Meissen for a passport.—Kohlhaas, who could read the
High Chancellor's face very well, sat down immediately
only the more confirmed in his resolve, and, without offering any reason, made application to the Prince of Meissen
as head of the Gubernium for an eight-day pass to Kohlhaasenbrück and back. To this request he received a gubernial resolution, signed by Governor of the Palace Baron
Siegfried von Wenk, to the effect that his application for a
pass to Kohlhaasenbrück would be submitted to the Elector's Serene Highness, and upon the latter's supreme authorization, as soon as it was forthcoming, the pass would
be sent to him. Upon Kohlhaas' inquiry to his attorney how
it happened that the gubernial resolution was signed by a
Baron Siegfried von Wenk and not by Prince Christiern
von Meissen to whom he had applied, he received the
answer that the Prince had ridden out to his estates three
days ago and that during his absence the affairs of the
Gubernium had been entrusted to Governor of the Palace
Baron Siegfried von Wenk, a cousin of the previously men-

tioned nobleman of the same name.—Kohlhaas, whose
heart was beginning to beat uneasily amid all these circumstances, went on waiting for several days for the decision
relative to his application, which had now been submitted
with surprising formality to the person of the Sovereign;
but a week went by, and more than a week went by, without either an answer's arriving or a decision's being reached
at the court, for all that the latter had been definitely
promised him, so that, firmly determined to force the government to declare its attitude toward him, be it whatever
it might, he sat down on the twelfth day and once again
applied to the Gubernium in an urgent petition for the
requested passport. But how startled he was on the evening
of the following day, which had likewise passed without
the expected answer, when, pondering the situation and
especially the amnesty procured for him by Doctor Luther,
he stepped to the window of his little back room and could
see no trace in the small building in the courtyard of the
guard detail that had been assigned to him on his arrival
by the Prince of Meissen. Thomas, the old porter whom he
summoned and asked what this signified, answered him
with a sigh, "Sir, everything is not as it should be; at nightfall the lansquenets, of whom there are more today than
usual, took up stations around the whole house; two are
standing with shield and pike at the front door that opens
onto the street, two are at the rear door in the garden, and
there are two others besides who are lying on a straw pallet
in the vestibule and who say they are going to sleep there."
Kohlhaas changed color, turned, and replied that it did
not matter, just so long as they were there, and that when
he went down to the vestibule he should put a lamp there
so they could see. After once again opening the shutters
of the front window, on the pretext of emptying a vessel,
and verifying for himself the truth of the details reported
by the old man—for there was being effected at just that
moment a noiseless relief of the guard, a measure no one
had thought of all the time the arrangement had been in
operation—he went to bed, although he had little wish for
sleep, and his decision for the coming day was immediately

made. For to the government with which he had to deal
he begrudged nothing so much as the appearance of justice while it was breaking the amnesty it had promised
him; and in case he was actually a prisoner, as there now
seemed to be no longer any doubt, he intended to force
out of them the definite and unequivocal declaration that
such was the case. As soon as the morning of the following
day dawned, therefore, he had Sternbald, his groom, hitch
up the wagon and bring it to the door in order to go to
Lockewitz to see the bailiff, who, as an old acquaintance,
had talked to him a few days since in Dresden and invited
him to come with his children some time to call on him.
The lansquenets, having observed with heads put together
the stir caused in the household by these preparations, sent
one of their number secretly into town, and within a few
minutes there arrived an official of the Gubernium at the
head of several constables, acting as if he had an errand
in the house across the street. Busy with getting his children's clothes on, Kohlhaas had likewise observed these
movements and purposely had the wagon wait longer than
necessary in front of the house; then, as soon as he saw
that the police had finished their dispositions, walked out
the door with his children without paying any attention
to them; in going past the crew of lansquenets standing
in the doorway he remarked in passing that they didn't
need to follow him, then he lifted the boys into the wagon
and kissed and consoled the little girls, who were in tears
because, in compliance with his instructions, they were to
stay behind with the daughter of the old porter. Hardly
had he climbed into the wagon himself, however, when
the official from the Gubernium, followed by his attendant
constables, came heading this way from out of the house
across the street and asked him where he was going. To
Kohlhaas' reply, that he was going to Lockewitz to see his
friend the bailiff who had invited him a few days before
to come and visit him in the country and bring his two boys
along, the Gubernium official returned the answer that, in
that case, he would have to wait a few minutes and that,
in accordance with orders from the Prince of Meissen, sev-

eral mounted lansquenets would escort him. With a smile
down from the wagon Kohlhaas asked if he thought his
person would not be safe in the home of a friend who had
made the offer of entertaining him for one day at his table.
With a cheerful and good-humored air the official answered that the danger was admittedly not great, and then
he added that the lansquenets were not to discommode
him in any way. Earnestly Kohlhaas replied that, upon
his arrival in Dresden, the Prince of Meissen had left him
free choice as to whether he wished to avail himself of
the guard or not; and when the official expressed amazement at this fact and with cautiously chosen words referred
to the custom in effect during the entire term of *his* association with the case, the horse dealer recounted the circumstances that had occasioned the stationing of a guard
in his house. The official assured him that the orders of
Governor of the Palace Baron von Wenk, who at this time
was chief of police, required from him as a duty the uninterrupted protection of his person, and requested him,
in case the escort was not to his liking, to go to the Gubernium himself to rectify the error that must be involved.
Casting an eloquent glance at the official, and determined
to make or break the matter, Kohlhaas said he would do
just that, climbed down with pounding heart from the
wagon, had the porter carry the children into the vestibule,
and, while the groom kept the vehicle waiting at the door,
made his way, together with the official and his guards, to
the Gubernium. It just so happened that Governor of the
Palace Baron Wenk, was in the midst of an inspection of
a band of Nagelschmidt henchmen that had been brought
in the night before after capture in the area of Leipzig and
the fellows were being interrogated by the knights present
there concerning a number of things that they wanted to
find out from them, when the horse dealer entered the room
with his escort. As the knights suddenly fell silent and de-
sisted from their interrogation of the henchmen, the Baron
stepped up to Kohlhaas as soon as his eye caught sight of
him and asked him what he wanted. And when the horse
dealer had respectfully presented his plan of dining with

the bailiff in Lockewitz and his desire to leave the lansquenets behind, inasmuch as he had no need of them on this occasion, the Baron changed color and, while seeming to be swallowing back a quite different speech, said he would do well to remain quietly in his house and to postpone for the time being this little feast at the Lockewitz bailiff's.—Then, cutting short the whole colloquy, he turned to the official and told him that there was a particular point in the orders he had issued him in respect to this man, and that the latter was not permitted to leave the city other than with an escort of six mounted lansquenets.— Kohlhaas inquired whether he was a prisoner and whether he was to consider that the solemn amnesty granted him in the whole world's sight was now broken; whereat the Baron, with his face red as fire, turned toward him, and then stepping right up to him and looking him straight in the eye, answered, "Yes! Yes! Yes!"—Then he turned his back on him, left him standing there, and went back to the Nagelschmidt henchmen. Herewith Kohlhaas left the room, and although he realized that by the step just taken he had seriously increased the difficulty of the sole salvation now remaining to him, namely escape, he nevertheless found his action good, because he saw himself absolved henceforth from the obligation of observing the terms of the amnesty. Arriving at his house, he had the horses unhitched, and, accompanied by the Gubernium official, repaired very gloomy and upset to his room; and while this man, in a manner that aroused the horse dealer's disgust, was assuring him that everything was undoubtedly the result of a misunderstanding which would shortly be cleared up, the constables, at his sign, were locking and bolting all exits of the house leading to the courtyard; whereat the official assured him that the front, main entrance was open, now as formerly, for his use whenever he chose.

Meanwhile in the forests of the Erzgebirge Nagelschmidt had been so harried on all sides by constabulary and lansquenets that, in view of the total lack of means to carry through a role such as he had undertaken, he hit upon the idea of actually enlisting Kohlhaas' assistance; and since

he was informed with tolerable preciseness about the state
of his litigation in Dresden through a traveler who was
journeying along the highroad, he felt it would be possible
to persuade the horse dealer to enter into a new alliance
with him in spite of the open hostility that existed between
them. Accordingly he despatched a henchman to him with
a letter drafted in barely readable German, to the following
effect: "If he would be willing to come to Altenburg and
resume command of the band which had gathered there,
made up of remnants of the dispersed one, he, Nagelschmidt, would be agreeable to coming to his assistance
with horses, money, and men in escaping from his arrest
in Dresden; in which case he promised him to be more
obedient to him in the future and better and more orderly
generally than previously, and by way of proof of his loy-
alty and submission he guaranteed to come in person into
the Dresden area to effect his liberation from prison." Now
the fellow entrusted with the letter had the misfortune of
collapsing in a village right near Dresden of a seizure of
an ugly kind to which he had been susceptible since childhood, and on this occasion the letter, which he was carrying
tucked in his doublet, was discovered by people who came
to his aid, while he himself, as soon as he had come to,
was arrested and transported by a guard and followed by
a great crowd to the Gubernium. As soon as Governor of
the Palace von Wenk had read this letter, he betook himself immediately to the palace to see the Elector, and there
he found Count Kallheim, President of the Chancery, and
also the Lords Kunz and Hinz, the former having by this
time recovered from his injuries. The gentlemen were of
the opinion that Kohlhaas must be arrested without further
delay and that proceedings must be initiated against him
on the grounds of secret collusion with Nagelschmidt, inasmuch as no such letter could have been written without
foregoing ones having proceeded from the horse dealer and
without there having been a criminal and outrageous understanding between them toward the end of concocting
fresh atrocities. The Elector stoutly refused to violate merely
on the grounds of this letter the safe conduct he had prom-

ised Kohlhaas; he was inclined rather to the opinion
that a kind of likelihood was evident from Nagelschmidt's
letter that no previous connection had existed between
them; and the most he would countenance, in order to get
to the bottom of the affair, at the President's suggestion
and only after great hesitation, was to allow the letter to
be delivered by Nagelschmidt's man as if the latter were
free now as formerly, and to see whether he would answer
it. The henchman, whom they had committed to prison,
was accordingly brought next morning to the Gubernium,
where the Governor of the Palace returned the letter to
him, and amid promises that he was to be free and that
the punishment he had incurred was to be remitted, ordered him to deliver the letter to the horse dealer as though
nothing had happened; for which evil deception this fellow
allowed himself to be used without any ado, and with apparent secrecy, on the pretext of selling crabs—with which
the gubernial official had supplied him at the market—he
presented himself in Kohlhaas' room. Kohlhaas, who read
the letter while the children were playing with the crabs,
would surely under other circumstances have taken the
rascal by the collar and turned him over to the lansquenets
standing outside the door; but since, given the present temper of people's minds, even such a step was liable to an
equivocal interpretation, and since he had become convinced that nothing in the world could save him from the
business in which he was entangled, he gazed with a look
of sadness into the fellow's well-known face, asked him
where he lived, and made an appointment with him for a
few hours hence, when he would make known to him his
decision in respect to his master. He had Sternbald, who
happened to be standing in the doorway, buy a few crabs
from the man who was in the room, and after this transaction was completed and both had withdrawn without
either recognizing the other for what he was, he sat down
and wrote to Nagelschmidt a letter which went as follows:
"First, that he was accepting his proposal relative to the
chief command of the band in Altenburg; that he should
therefore send him a wagon with two horses to Neustadt

near Dresden for his liberation from the present detention
in which he, together with his five children, was being
held; that, for the sake of swifter escape, he needed another team of horses on the road to Wittenberg, by which
detour alone, for reasons too long to explain, he could get
to him; that he thought he could bribe the lansquenets
that were guarding him, but that, in case force was necessary, he would like to be able to count on a couple of
stout-hearted, able, and well-armed fellows in Dresden-
Neustadt; that, to cover the expenses involved in all these
arrangements, he was sending him a roll of twenty gold
crowns by the henchman, the disbursement of which he
would like to discuss with him after the business was completed; that furthermore he absolutely declined the offer
of his presence as unnecessary for his liberation in Dresden,
in fact, that he was rather issuing him the specific order to
stay behind in Altenburg as provisional leader of the band,
which could not be without a commander."—This letter he
entrusted to the henchman when the latter arrived toward
evening, gave him a generous gratuity, and impressed upon
him the need to be careful.—His intention was to take his
five children and go to Hamburg and thence to take ship
to the Levant or to the East Indies, or as far as the sky
arched blue over human beings other than those he knew,
for, quite apart from the repugnance he felt at making
common cause with Nagelschmidt, his sorely tried soul had
given up the restoration of the black horses to health.—
Scarcely had the fellow delivered this answer to the Governor of the Palace when the High Chancellor was removed
from office, the President, Count Kallheim, named in his
stead as chief of the tribunal, and Kohlhaas, arrested by a
cabinet order of the Elector, brought heavily laden with
chains to the city dungeon.—On the grounds of this letter,
which was posted in all corners of the city, a trial was
instigated against him; and when before the bar of the
court he faced the magistrate who was holding the letter
up before him and in answer to his question as to whether
he recognized the handwriting, said, "Yes!" and when in
answer to the question of whether he had anything to say

in his own defense he cast his eyes to the floor and said, "No!" he was sentenced to have his flesh torn by the knacker's men with red-hot pincers, then to be drawn and quartered, and finally to have his body burned between the wheel and the gallows.

Thus matters stood with poor Kohlhaas in Dresden when the Elector of Brandenburg intervened to rescue him from the hands of superior and arbitrary force by advancing the claim, in a note submitted to the electoral chancery of that city, that he was a Brandenburg subject. For, during a stroll on the banks of the Spree, that noble-hearted captain of the civic militia, Lord Heinrich von Gersau, had related to him the story of this curious and not reprehensible man, and, pressed on that occasion by the questions of his astonished master, he was unable to avoid mentioning the guilt that attached to his own person as a result of the improprieties of his Arch Chancellor, Count Siegfried von Kallheim; whereupon the Elector, highly incensed, after summoning the Arch Chancellor to an interview and discovering that his relationship with the House of Tronka was the cause of all the trouble, relieved him of his post forthwith and with various signs of his displeasure, and then named Lord Heinrich von Gersau to the arch chancellorship.

Now it chanced that at precisely this time the crown of Poland, being involved in a dispute with the House of Saxony, over what issue we do not know, had sued to the Elector of Brandenburg in repeated and urgent expostulations to ally himself with them in common cause against the House of Saxony; thus the Arch Chancellor, Lord Gersau, who was not unskilled in such matters, might well hope to fulfill his master's desire to achieve justice for Kohlhaas at any cost without jeopardizing the peace of the whole commonwealth in a way more harmful than is warranted by consideration of the individual. Therefore the Arch Chancellor not only demanded unconditional and immediate release of Kohlhaas on grounds of wholly arbitrary procedures displeasing to God and man, in order to try him, in the event he was guilty, by Brandenburg law on charges

which the Dresden court could proffer through an attorney
in Berlin, but he even demanded passports for an attorney
whom the Elector was of a mind to send to Dresden to
plead the cause of Kohlhaas against the Junker Wenzel von
Tronka on the grounds of the black horses which had been
taken from him on Saxon territory and on the grounds of
other mistreatment and outrages that shrieked to Heaven.
The Chamberlain, Lord Kunz, who in the redistribution of
state posts in Saxony had been appointed President of the
State Chancery, and who, in the strait where he now found
himself, had various reasons for not wishing to offend the
Berlin court, answered in the name of his master—who was
greatly distressed by the note received—that they were
much astonished at the unfriendliness and unfairness with
which the Dresden court was being denied the right to
try Kohlhaas by law for crimes committed by him in
that country, inasmuch as this person, as everyone knew,
owned a considerable parcel of land in the capital and in
no wise denied his qualification for being a Saxon subject.
But, in consideration of the fact that the Polish crown was
already gathering an army of five thousand men on the
borders of Saxony preparatory to fighting out their claims,
and in consideration of the fact that the Arch Chancellor,
Lord Heinrich von Gersau, had declared that Kohlhaasenbrück, the place from which the horse dealer derived his
name, was situated in Brandenburg territory and that the
execution of the death sentence pronounced upon him
would be looked upon as a violation of international law,
the Elector, upon the advice of the Chamberlain, Lord
Kunz, himself, who wished to extricate himself from this
affair, summoned Prince Christiern von Meissen back from
his estates, and after a few words from that shrewd gentleman, determined to comply with the demand and turn
Kohlhaas over to the Berlin court. The Prince, who had to
take over the direction of the Kohlhaas case at the wish of
his hard-pressed master, although he was ill pleased with
the improprieties that had transpired, asked him on what
grounds he now wished to have the horse dealer charged
before the Berlin tribunal; and inasmuch as they could not

base their charges on that wretched letter to Nagelschmidt because of the ambiguous and unclear circumstances in which it had been written, nor on the previous pillagings and acts of arson because of the amnesty by which they had been forgiven, the Elector decided to lay before His Majesty the Emperor in Vienna a report of Kohlhaas' armed invasion of Saxony, plead the breaking of the public peace which he had established, and appeal to His Majesty, who was of course not bound by any amnesty, to prosecute Kohlhaas in the Berlin courts through the person of an imperial prosecutor. A week later, still in chains as he was, the horse dealer was loaded into a wagon together with his five children, who at his plea had been reassembled from foundling homes and orphanages, and transported to Berlin by the Chevalier Friedrich von Malzahn, whom the Elector of Brandenburg had despatched to Dresden with six horsemen. It chanced that the Elector of Saxony had journeyed to Dahme for a great stag hunt that had been organized to divert him, on the invitation of District Magistrate Count Aloysius von Kallheim, who at that time had extensive estates along the border of Saxony, and in the company of the Chamberlain, Lord Kunz, and his spouse, the Lady Heloise, daughter of the District Magistrate and sister of the President, not to mention other lords and ladies, gentlemen of the hunt, and courtiers who were present; thus beneath the shelter of pennant-adorned tents pitched on a hillside diagonally across the road, the entire company, still dusty from the chase, was seated at table and was being served by pages and youthful squires amid sprightly music that came from beneath an oak tree, when along the highway from Dresden came the horse dealer slowly traveling with his escort of horsemen. For the illness of one of Kohlhaas' frail little children had obliged the Chevalier von Malzahn, who was accompanying him, to tarry three days in Herzberg, a step of which he had not deemed it necessary to notify the Dresden government since he was solely responsible for it to the Prince whom he served. The Elector, who, with shirt open at the throat and with his plumed hat adorned hunter-fashion with sprigs of fir, was sitting

next to the Lady Heloise, who had been his first love in
the times of his youth, was in a cheerful mood as a result
of the charm of the fête resplendent about him, and to the
Lady he said, "Let us go down and give this goblet of wine
to the luckless fellow, whoever he may be!" The Lady
Heloise rose immediately, casting a sumptuous glance at
him as she did so, and plundering the entire table, heaped
a silver salver, which a page handed to her, with fruit and
cakes and bread; the entire company had already come
thronging forth from the tent with refreshments of every
sort when the District Magistrate came up to them with
a look of embarrassment and asked them to stay back. To
the Elector's startled question, What had happened to
cover him thus with confusion? the District Magistrate
stammered, as he turned toward the Chamberlain, that
Kohlhaas was in the wagon: at this news which flabber-
gasted everyone, for it was universally known that he had
departed six days ago, the Chamberlain, Lord Kunz, took
his goblet of wine and, turning back toward the tent,
spilled the wine into the sand. The Elector, flushing scarlet,
set his down on a plate which was held out to him for that
purpose by a page at a sign from the Chamberlain; and
while the Chevalier Friedrich von Malzahn passed slowly
through the rows of tents that stretched across the road
and respectfully saluted the company, whom he did not
know, and rode on toward Dahme, the company returned
inside the tent at the invitation of the District Magistrate
without taking any further notice. As soon as the Elector
was seated, the District Magistrate sent in secret to Dahme
to arrange with the magistracy there for the immediate
speeding of the horse dealer on his way; but since the
Chevalier absolutely insisted on spending the night in the
village because the day was already so far advanced, they
had to be satisfied with noiselessly installing him in a farmhouse that belonged to the magistracy and which was hidden in bushes off to one side. Now it chanced that toward
evening, when the noble company had again forgotten the
entire incident in their diversion with wine and the enjoy-
ment of a luxurious dessert, the District Magistrate pro-

posed the notion of taking up positions once more for the sake of a herd of stags that had been sighted. The entire party seized upon the proposal with delight, and after providing themselves with guns they hurried, in pairs, across ditches and hedges, into the nearby forest, and in this fashion it came about that the Elector and the Lady Heloise, who had accepted his arm to come and watch the sport, were conducted by a guide assigned to them, and to their astonishment, right across the courtyard of the house where Kohlhaas was lodged with his Brandenburg troopers. When the Lady heard this, she said, "Come, my Lord, come!" and coyly tucking inside his silken doublet the chain that hung about his neck, she added, "Let us slip into the farmhouse before the crowd comes back and have a look at this odd man spending the night there." Blushing and grasping her hand, the Elector said, "Heloise! What are you thinking of!" But when she looked at him in surprise and said no one would ever recognize him in the hunting costume he was wearing, and pulled him along with her, and when at precisely that same moment a couple of gentlemen of the hunt, who had already satisfied their curiosity, stepped out of the house and assured them that, thanks to an arrangement of the District Magistrate, neither the knights nor the horse dealer knew *what* company was assembled in the region of Dahme, then the Elector with a smile pulled down his hat over his eyes and said, "Folly doth rule the world and hath its dwelling place on lovely ladies' lips!"—When the Lord and the Lady entered the farmhouse to pay him their visit, Kohlhaas happened to be sitting on a bale of straw with his back to the wall feeding bread and milk to his sick child, and when, in order to start a conversation, the Lady asked him Who he was? and What was the matter with the child? and What crime he had committed? and Where they were taking him with such an escort? he tipped his leather cap to her and to all her questions returned unfulsome, though adequate, answers, continuing meanwhile with what he was about. The Elector, from where he was standing behind the gentlemen of the hunt, noticed a small leaden capsule hanging around

his neck on a silk thread, and for lack of anything better
for conversation, asked him what it signified and what was
in it. "Oh yes, Your Worship, this capsule," replied Kohlhaas—and hereupon he slipped it from around his neck,
opened it up, and drew forth a little piece of paper sealed
with wax—"There is a very strange story connected with
this capsule! Seven months or so ago, the very next day
after the burial of my wife, I had started out from Kohlhaasenbrück, as you perhaps know, to seize the Junker von
Tronka who had done me grievous injustice, when, for
some business unknown to me, the Elector of Saxony and
the Elector of Brandenburg were holding a meeting in
Jüterbock, a market town through which my route took me;
and when toward evening they had reached agreement in
keeping with their wishes, they were strolling down the
streets of the town in friendly conversation to view the fair
which was then going on merrily. There they came upon
a gypsy woman who was sitting on a stool and telling the
fortunes of the people around her from a calendar, and
they asked her in jesting fashion whether she didn't have
something nice to disclose to them. I had just dismounted
with my men at an inn and was there in the square when
the incident took place, but from behind the crowd where
I was standing beside a church door, I was unable to hear
what the strange woman was saying to the gentlemen, so
that, when the people laughed and whispered to one another that she didn't impart her wisdom to everyone, and
crowded around to get a view of the scene that was about
to take place, I climbed up on a bench that was hewn out
of the church entryway, less for curiosity's sake actually
than to make room for the curious. From that point of vantage and without any obstruction of view I had scarcely
caught sight of the Lords and of the woman who was sitting on the stool and seemed to be scribbling something,
when suddenly she got up on her crutches, gazed around
over the people, and fastened her eye on me, who had
never exchanged a word with her nor ever in my life craved
any of her wisdom; right through the dense throng of people she came straight to me and said, 'There! If the gentle-

man wants to know his fortune, he may ask me about it!'
And with that, Your Worship, she handed me this slip of
paper in her withered and bony hands. And when I, with
all the people turning around to look at me, said in surprise, 'What's this you're honoring me with, old woman?'
she muttered a lot of stuff I couldn't make out but in the
midst of which I did hear, to my great astonishment, my
name, and then she said, 'An amulet, Kohlhaas the horse
dealer; take good care of it, it will some day save your
life!'; then she vanished.—Well!" continued Kohlhaas good-
humoredly. "To tell the truth, as close a call as I had in
Dresden, it still didn't cost my life; and as for how I shall
fare in Berlin, and whether I'll pull through there too, the
future will tell."—As he heard these words the Elector sat
down on a bench, and though in reply to the Lady's startled question, What was the matter with him? he answered, "Nothing! Nothing at all!" he nevertheless had collapsed on the floor in a faint before she had time to rush
to his aid and support him in her arms. The Chevalier von
Malzahn, who stepped into the room on an errand at just
that moment, said, "Merciful God! What is the matter with
the gentleman?" The Lady cried, "Fetch some water!" The
gentlemen of the hunt picked him up and carried him into
the adjoining room and laid him on a bed; and consternation reached its peak when the Chamberlain, whom a page
had summoned, declared after all efforts to revive him had
proved futile, that he bore all the signs of having suffered
a shock. While the Cupbearer sent a mounted messenger
to Luckau to fetch a physician, the District Magistrate had
him placed in a wagon as soon as he opened his eyes and
transported at walking speed to his hunting lodge located
in the vicinity; but after arrival there the journey resulted
in two more fainting spells, so that not until late the following morning, upon arrival of the Luckau physician, did
he somewhat recover, although he now displayed definite
symptoms of the onset of a nervous fever. As soon as he
regained control of his senses, he half rose in the bed and
his first question was, Where was Kohlhaas? The Chamberlain, misconstruing his question, clasped his hand and said

he had no cause to distress himself over that horrible man, inasmuch as that person had remained behind in accordance with his orders in the farmhouse in Dahme and under Brandenburg guard, following that strange and incomprehensible incident. Then, with the assurance of his keenest sympathy and with the protestation that he had most bitterly reproached his wife for her irresponsible frivolity in confronting him with that man, he asked him what had so uncannily and so overwhelmingly come over him in the conversation with him. The Elector said he would have to confess that the sight of an insignificant piece of paper which the man had in a lead capsule on his person was to blame for the whole unpleasant occurrence that had befallen him. By way of explanation of this matter he added a great deal more besides, which the Chamberlain did not understand; suddenly insisted, as he pressed his hand between both his own, that possession of this piece of paper was of the utmost importance to him; and begged him to mount instantly and ride to Dahme and barter the piece of paper away from him, no matter at what cost. The Chamberlain, who had difficulty hiding his embarrassment, assured him that, if this piece of paper had some value for him, nothing on earth was more necessary than keeping that fact from Kohlhaas, for, as soon as the latter got wind of it by an indiscreet disclosure, all the wealth he possessed would not suffice to purchase it from the hands of this ferocious fellow of insatiable greed for vengeance. To pacify him, he added that a third means must be thought up and that perhaps by cunning, with the help of a third party who was completely disinterested, they might get possession of this paper by which he set such store, as long as the scoundrel apparently attached very little importance to it for its own sake. Mopping the sweat from his brow, the Elector asked whether they couldn't send immediately to Dahme for this purpose and for the time being hold up the further transportation of the horse dealer until, in some way or other, the paper was obtained. The Chamberlain, mistrusting his own senses, replied that unfortunately, by all likely reckoning, the horse dealer had already left

Dahme and must by now be over the border and on
Brandenburg soil, where attempts to stop the man's further
transportation or to make him turn back would occasion
the most unpleasant and far-reaching, indeed, perhaps, insurmountable difficulties. And now, as the Elector silently
leaned back onto his pillow with the gesture of one who
utterly despairs, he asked him, What, then, did the paper
contain? and, By what odd and inexplicable coincidence
had he happened to be aware of the contents? But to these
questions the Elector returned no answer, though he cast
ambiguous glances at the Chamberlain, whose obliging-
ness he mistrusted in this instance. He lay there rigid and
with pounding heart and kept looking down at the corner
of the handkerchief that he was holding pensively between
his hands. Suddenly he requested him to call into the room
Gentleman of the Hunt von Stein, a sturdy clever young
Lord whom he had rather frequently employed on secret
missions, on the pretext that he had another matter of business with him. The Gentleman of the Hunt, after having
the matter explained to him and after having had made
clear to him the importance of the paper in Kohlhaas' possession, was then asked whether he wished to win eternal
claim to his friendship by procuring that paper before the
horse dealer reached Berlin; and when the Gentleman of
the Hunt, as soon as he had to some extent grasped the
situation, odd as it was, assured him that he was at his
service to the utmost of his abilities, the Elector bade him
ride in pursuit of Kohlhaas, and, since the latter was apparently not to be lured by money, to engage him in a conversation devised with subtlety and to offer him his freedom and his life, in fact, if he insisted upon it, to propose
directly, though with caution, to help him with horses,
men, and money in escaping from the hands of the Brandenburg horsemen who were transporting him. After procuring a letter from the Elector's hand by way of creden-
tials, the Gentleman of the Hunt set out immediately in the
company of a few grooms, and by dint of not sparing the
horses' wind, had the good luck to catch up with Kohlhaas
in a border village, where the latter, together with his

five children and the Chevalier von Malzahn, was eating a
midday meal that was being served out-of-doors in front
of a house. The Chevalier von Malzahn, to whom the Gentleman of the Hunt introduced himself as a stranger passing through and wishing to have a glimpse of the strange
man he was escorting, immediately and in the most courteous way had him sit down at table, and at the same time
presented him to Kohlhaas; and since the Chevalier kept
going back and forth on errands, and since the horsemen
were being served at a table situated on the other side of
the house, it was not long before an opportunity offered
itself where the Gentleman of the Hunt was able to reveal
who he was and on what special errand he had come to
see him. The horse dealer already knew the name and rank
of the person who had fainted at the farmhouse at sight
of the capsule and needed nothing further to crown the excitement into which he had been thrown by his discovery
than to inspect the secret of the paper, which, for various
reasons, he was determined not to open out of mere curiosity. Recalling the ignoble and unprincely treatment he
had been compelled to endure in Dresden despite his total
willingness to make all possible sacrifices, the horse dealer
said he was going to keep the paper. To the Gentleman of
the Hunt's question, What made him persist in this odd
refusal when he was being offered nothing less than life
and liberty? Kohlhaas replied, "Noble sir! If your Sovereign
were to come to me and say, 'I shall annihilate myself and
I shall annihilate the whole pack of them who help me
wield my scepter'—annihilate, you understand—which is, of
course, the supreme desire cherished by my soul—I would
still refuse him this piece of paper, which is worth more
to him than his life, and I would tell him, 'You can have
me sent to the scaffold, but I can do you injury, and I
shall!'" Then, with death on his face, he called over a
trooper with the invitation to accept a considerable portion
of food that was still left on his plate; and for all the rest
of the hour that he spent in the village treated the Junker
sitting there at the table with him as if he did not exist,
turning to him again only as he was mounting the wagon,

and then with a glance that expressed farewell.—The condition of the Elector, when he received this news, worsened to the point where for three fateful days the physician was in the utmost anxiety for his life, which had been simultaneously assailed from so many directions. Nevertheless, by dint of the strength of his natural constitution, he recovered after several weeks spent painfully on his sickbed, or at least recovered sufficiently so that he was able to be loaded into a wagon and to be transported, well provided with pillows and blankets, back to Dresden and his governmental duties. As soon as he arrived in that city, he had Prince Christiern von Meissen summoned and asked him how matters stood with the plans for departure of Attorney Eibenmayer, whom they had planned to send to Vienna as legal representative in the Kohlhaas case to lay the complaint of violation of the imperial peace before His Imperial Majesty. The Prince's reply was that this person had left for Vienna in accordance with the orders issued at the time of his trip to Dahme and directly after the arrival of the jurist Zäuner, whom the Elector of Brandenburg had sent to Dresden as attorney to present his complaint against the Junker Wenzel von Tronka in the matter of the black horses. The Elector, flushing and stepping up to his desk, expressed surprise at this haste, inasmuch as, to the best of his knowledge, he had made it clear that he wished Eibenmayer's definitive departure to be postponed, pending more exact and more precisely timed orders because of the need for prior consultation with Doctor Luther, who had obtained the amnesty for Kohlhaas. As he said this, he made a gesture of repressed irritation by sweeping into confusion several letters and documents that were lying on the desk. The Prince, after a pause during which he stared at him wide-eyed, answered that he was sorry if he had failed to give him satisfaction in this matter, but meanwhile he could show him the State Council's decision which had made obligatory the despatch of the attorney at the aforesaid date. He added that there had been no mention whatsoever in the State Council about a consultation with Doctor Luther; that earlier there might perhaps have been some point in

taking the churchman's views into account, considering the
efforts he had made toward intercession in Kohlhaas' behalf, but not now, after they had broken the amnesty before the eyes of the whole world by arresting him and turning him over to the Brandenburg courts for sentence and
execution. The Elector said the oversight in sending Eibenmayer off was not really a serious one; meanwhile, however, it was his wish that he should not act in Vienna in
his capacity as prosecutor until further orders were issued,
and he asked the Prince to send him the requisite instructions immediately by a courier. The Prince replied that this
command came unfortunately one day too late, since
Eibenmayer, according to a report just received today, had
already presented himself in his capacity of prosecutor and
had submitted the complaint before the Vienna chancery.
To the Elector's startled question of, How had all this been
possible in so short a time? he answered that three weeks
had already elapsed since the man's departure and that his
instructions had made it his obligation to attend to this business without delay and immediately upon arrival in Vienna.
Any delay, the Prince observed, would have been all the
more awkward in this case, since the Brandenburg attorney
Zäuner was proceeding with the most belligerent insistence
against the Junker Wenzel von Tronka and had already
petitioned the court for provisional withdrawal of the black
horses from the hands of the knacker and, despite all objections of the opposing parties, had put it through. The
Elector rang the bell and said, No matter! It didn't make
any difference anyway! and after addressing some unimpor-
tant questions to the Prince about how things were, otherwise, in Dresden and about what had transpired during
his absence, he gave him a sign with his hand to indicate
dismissal, and, incapable of concealing his inner state of
mind, dismissed him. On the pretext that he wished to attend to the case himself because of its political significance,
he asked him that very same day in writing for all documents having to do with Kohlhaas; and since the thought
was intolerable that the one person from whom he could
get information about the secrets of the capsule should be

destroyed, he composed a letter to the Emperor in his own handwriting, in which he begged him most urgently and with all his heart for permission to withdraw the complaint which Eibenmayer had submitted against Kohlhaas, for the time being and until further decision could be reached, because of important reasons which he would perhaps set forth to him presently in greater detail. In a note drafted through the state chancery the Emperor answered that the change which seemed to have taken place suddenly in his heart surprised him excessively; that the report submitted to him on the initiative of Saxony had made the Kohlhaas case a matter of concern to the entire Holy Roman Empire; that he, therefore, the Emperor, as supreme head of that realm, had felt himself bound to appear before the House of Brandenburg as plaintiff in this case; and that inasmuch as Court Assessor Franz Müller had already gone to Berlin in his capacity as prosecuting attorney to bring Kohlhaas to justice there for his violation of the public peace, the complaint absolutely could not be withdrawn and the matter would have to take its course in accordance with the law. The Elector was utterly prostrated by this letter, and when in due time private reports arrived to his extreme distress from Berlin, announcing the initiation of the trial in the supreme court of judicature and remarking that, in spite of all the efforts of the lawyer assigned to him, it looked as though Kohlhaas would end on the scaffold, the unhappy monarch decided to make one more effort, and in a letter written in his own hand he begged the Elector of Brandenburg for the horse dealer's life. He alleged that the amnesty granted this man would not rightfully admit of the carrying out of a death sentence on him; assured him that, despite the apparent severity with which they had proceeded against him, it had never been his intention to allow him to die; and described to him how desolated he would be if the protection which they had claimed to bestow upon him from Berlin should finally take an unexpected turn and work out to still greater disadvantage for him than if he had remained in Dresden and his case had been decided according to Saxon law. The Elector of Bran-

denburg, to whom a great deal in these allegations seemed
ambiguous and unclear, answered to the effect that the
vigor with which His Imperial Majesty's council was proceeding would simply not permit of any departure from the
strict prescription of the law in order to comply with the
wish he had expressed. He observed that the misgivings
expressed really went too far, inasmuch as the complaint
relative to the crimes for which Kohlhaas had been forgiven during the period of the amnesty had not been laid
before the supreme court of judicature in Berlin by the
person who had proclaimed the amnesty, but by the supreme head of the Empire, who was in no wise bound by
it. At the same time he pointed out how necessary it was
to make an example in this case, given the fact that the
continuing outrages of Nagelschmidt were now extending,
with unparalleled insolence, even to Brandenburg territory, and advised him, in the event he did not wish to
take all these things into account, to have recourse to the
Emperor's Majesty itself, since, if a sentence were to be
passed in Kohlhaas' favor, it could only come as a pro-
nouncement from that quarter. From chagrin and vexation
over all these unsuccessful attempts, the Elector fell ill
anew, and when the Chamberlain was visiting him one
morning he showed him the letters he had sent to the Viennese and to the Berlin courts in the effort to save Kohlhaas'
life, or at least to gain time to get hold of the paper he had
in his possession. The Chamberlain threw himself down
upon his knees before him and begged him by all he held
dear and sacred to tell him what that paper contained. The
Elector told him to bolt the door and sit down on the bed;
then, after grasping his hand and pressing it with a sigh
to his heart, he began as follows: "Your wife, I understand,
has already told you that the Elector of Brandenburg and
I encountered a gypsy woman on the third day of our meeting in Jüterbock; and since the Elector, lively as he is by
nature, decided to play a trick on the fantastic woman,
about whose skill there had just been an immense lot of
talk at table, and to destroy her reputation in the eyes of
the people, he stepped up with folded arms in front of her

table and asked her for a sign that would confirm the
prophecy which she was about to make for him, a sign
that could be put to the test that very day, protesting that,
unless she did so, he could not believe in her words even
if she were the Roman sibyl herself. The woman quickly
eyed us from head to toe and said that the sign would be
this: that the great horned roebuck which the gardener's
son was raising in the park would come to meet us in the
market place where we then were, before we had left it.
Now you have to understand that this roebuck, which was
destined for the Dresden kitchen, was kept under lock and
key in an enclosure of high palings shaded by the oak trees
of the park, and that, on account of the other, smaller game
and fowl, the park as a whole and the garden that led up
to it were always kept carefully locked, so that it was quite
impossible to see how the beast could come to meet us in
the square where we were standing, and thus fulfill her
specific prediction; all the same, fearing there was some sly
trick behind it all, the Elector, after a brief consultation
with me, and determined once and for all to make a mockery of whatever she said, sent down to the palace in keeping with his jest and gave orders that the roebuck should
be slaughtered instantly and prepared for table on one of
the next few days. Then he turned back to the woman, in
front of whom this matter had been discussed aloud, and
said, 'All right now! What have you to reveal to me about
the future?' The woman looked into his hand and said, 'Hail
to my Elector and Lord! Your Grace will have a long reign,
the house from which you come shall long endure, and your
posterity shall become great and splendid, attaining power
before all the Princes and Lords of the world!' After a pause
during which he gazed thoughtfully at the woman, the
Elector said softly as he took a step toward me that he was
almost sorry now for having sent a messenger to undo the
prophecy; and while from the hands of the knights in his
retinue gold rained down in heaps, amid much jubilation,
into the woman's lap, he reached into his own pocket and
added another gold piece to the rest, asking her as he did
so whether the greeting which she had to give me would

be of just such a silvery sound as his own. After she had opened a box that was standing beside her, and after she had sorted the money by denomination and quantity carefully and at length, and then shut the box up again, the woman raised her hand to shade her eyes from the sun, as though it were burdensome to her, and then looked at me; and as I repeated the question to her and jokingly said to the Elector, while she was gazing into my hand, 'It seems she has nothing to foretell for me that would be especially pleasant!' she seized her crutches, slowly raised herself up from her stool, and as she pressed up close to me with mysteriously folded hands, whispered audibly in my ear, 'No!' —'So?' said I, confused, and fell back a pace before that form which now sat down again on the stool behind her with a cold and deathly glance as though her eyes were made of marble. 'From what direction does danger threaten my house?' Taking a piece of charcoal and a paper and crossing her knees, the woman asked me whether she should write it out for me; and when I, really embarrassed now because there was simply nothing else to be done under the existing circumstances, answered, 'Yes! Do that!' she said, 'Very well! I shall write down three things for you: the name of the last ruler of your house, the year when he shall lose his kingdom, and the name of the person who shall wrest it from him by force of arms.' And having done this, in sight of all the crowd, she got up, sealed the paper with wax, which she moistened with her withered mouth, and impressed into it a leaden signet ring which she wore on her middle finger. Just as I was about to seize the paper, curious, as you can well imagine, more than words can tell, she said, 'Not at all, Highness!' and turned and picked up one of her crutches. 'From that man yonder, the one with the plumed hat, standing on a bench behind the crowd and next to the church door, from him you may redeem the paper, if it so please you!' And with that, before I had really grasped what she was saying, she left me standing there in the square, speechless with amazement; and slamming shut the box standing behind her and slinging it over her shoulder, she disappeared into the crowd of peo-

ple around us without my being able to see anything more
of what she did. Now, to my really heartfelt relief, there
stepped up at that moment the knight whom the Elector
had sent to the palace and reported with laughter that the
roebuck had been slaughtered and carried off before his
eyes by two huntsmen to the kitchen. The Elector cheerfully took my arm intending to lead me away from the
square, and said, 'Well, so much for that! Her prophecy
was a common everyday swindle and not worth the time
and money it cost us!' But how great was our astonishment
when a shriek went up all around the square just as he
was pronouncing those words and all eyes were turned toward a great butcher's dog trotting down from the palace
courtyard: in the kitchen it had grabbed the roebuck by
the neck as fair game, and three paces away from us, pursued by scullions and maids, dropped it on the ground;
thus the woman's prophecy, the pledge for everything she
had told us, was fulfilled, and the roebuck, even though
dead, to be sure, did come to meet us in the market place.
The lightning bolt that falls from the sky on a winter's day
could not have struck me more crushingly than that sight,
and my first effort, as soon as I was free of the company
I was with, was to search for the man with the plumed
hat whom the woman had indicated to me; but for all that
they sent out constantly for information for three days, not
one of my people was able to give me the slightest word
of him: and now, friend Kunz, three weeks ago, at the
farmhouse in Dahme, I beheld that man with my own
eyes."—And with that he released the Chamberlain's hand;
then, as he wiped the sweat from his brow, he sank back
again upon his bed. The Chamberlain, who deemed it a
waste of effort to confront his own view of this incident
with the Elector's view, or to try to rectify the latter, urged
him to seek any means whatsoever to possess himself of
the paper and thereafter leave the fellow to his fate; but
the Elector answered that he simply did not see any way
of doing it, though the thought of having to be deprived
of it, or even of seeing the man die without having obtained the information, was driving him to grief and de-

spair. To his friend's question, Had he made attempts to
seek out the person of the gypsy woman herself? the Elector replied that, in compliance with an order issued by him
on a false pretext, the Gubernium had been searching in
vain through all the towns of the Electorate right up to
the present day; he himself, for reasons he declined, however, to elaborate, doubted very much whether she was to
be found in Saxony. Now it chanced that the Chamberlain
was about to make a trip to Berlin to see about several
considerable estates that had been inherited in Neumark
by his wife from the property of the deposed and subsequently deceased Arch Chancellor, Count Kallheim; and
thus, since he was genuinely fond of the Elector, he asked
him after a brief reflection whether he would be willing
to give him a free hand to deal with this matter; and when
the latter pressed his hand with heartfelt emotion to his
bosom and said, "Assume you are my very self, and get
me that paper!" the Chamberlain, after turning over his
affairs of office, advanced his departure by several days,
then, leaving his wife behind and accompanied only by a
few servants, set out for Berlin.

Kohlhaas, who meanwhile, as aforementioned, had arrived in Berlin and, on special orders from the Elector, had
been placed in a Knights' Prison, which made him and
his five children as comfortable as possible, had been summoned before the bar of the supreme court of judicature
on charges of violating the public, imperial peace, directly
upon the appearance of the Imperial Prosecutor from Vienna; and though he pleaded in his own defense that he
could not be indicted for his armed invasion of Saxony and
the acts of violence there perpetrated, by virtue of the truce
concluded with the Elector of Saxony at Lützen, he was
appraised that His Imperial Majesty, whose representative
was conducting the prosecution here, could not take any
account of that; but when the matter was explained to him
and it was stated that full satisfaction would, on the other
hand, be done him on Dresden's part in his case against
the Junker Wenzel von Tronka, he readily signified that
he was agreeable. Thus it came about that, precisely on

the day of the Chamberlain's arrival, sentence was pronounced and he was condemned to be put to death by
being beheaded—a sentence which, given the complicated
state of affairs, no one believed would be put into effect,
in spite of its mercifulness, indeed which the whole city
hoped, considering the good will the Elector bore Kohlhaas,
would definitely be commuted by an electoral proclamation to a simple, if long and severe, term of imprisonment.
The Chamberlain, who realized at once that there was no
time to lose if the commission entrusted to him by his master was to be carried out, set about his business by letting
himself be seen in his usual court costume, clearly and
unmistakably, by Kohlhaas one morning when the latter
was standing at his prison window in innocent contemplation of the passers-by; and when he judged from a sudden
movement of his head that the horse dealer had noticed
him, and more especially observed with great satisfaction
the man's involuntary reaching of his hand to that point on
his chest where the capsule was, he felt that what had
gone through the man's mind at that moment was preparation sufficient for advancing one more step in his attempt
to get the paper. He made an appointment to see an old
huckster woman who went about on crutches and whom
he had noticed in the Berlin streets amid a pack of other
rabble that dealt in old clothes, since by her age and ap-
parel she seemed to tally fairly well with the one described
to him by the Elector; and on the assumption that Kohlhaas would not have retained very sharp recollection of the
features of the one who in her fleeting appearance had
handed him the paper, he decided to substitute the one
woman for the other and have her play the role of the
gypsy woman with Kohlhaas, if this could possibly be done.
To acquaint her with her part, he instructed her in detail
about everything that had transpired between the Elector
and the aforesaid gypsy woman in Jüterbock, not omitting
to impress upon her especially the three mysterious points
in the paper, since he did not know how far the woman
had gone in her statements to Kohlhaas; and after he had
explained to her what words she was to drop, in rambling

and incomprehensible fashion, concerning certain arrangements that had been made to procure by treachery or by
force this paper which was of the utmost importance to
the Saxon court, he instructed her to get the paper from
Kohlhaas, on the pretext that it was no longer safe with
him, in order to place it in safekeeping during a few fateful
days. At the promise of a sizable reward, part of which
the Chamberlain was obliged at her demand to pay her
in advance, the huckster woman immediately accepted the
task of carrying out the business in question; and since
Kohlhaas, with permission of the government, received
visits at times from the mother of the groom Herse, who
had died in battle at Mühlberg, and since she had been
acquainted with this woman for several months, she was
successful, by virtue of a little gift to the jailer, in gaining
access to the horse dealer a very few days later.—But when
this woman entered Kohlhaas' quarters, he thought he recognized the old gypsy woman who had given him the paper
in Jüterbock, the tokens being a signet ring that she was
wearing on her hand and a coral necklace hanging around
her neck. Now since appearances are not always on the
side of truth, it chanced that something had happened here
which we report forthwith, though we are compelled to
allow the liberty of doubting it to anyone so choosing to
do: the Chamberlain had committed a most colossal blun-
der, and in the old huckster woman whom he had picked
up in the Berlin streets to impersonate the gypsy woman,
he had hit upon that mysterious gypsy woman herself
whom he wished to have impersonated. At any rate, while
she leaned on her crutches and stroked the cheeks of the
children, who clung to their father in fear at her bizarre
appearance, the woman stated that she had returned some
time ago from Saxony to Brandenburg, and that, in reply
to an incautiously ventured question of the Chamberlain
in the streets of Berlin relative to the gypsy woman who
had been at Jüterbock in the spring of the past year, she
had immediately pressed forward and offered her services,
under a false name, for the business that he wanted done.
The horse dealer, who noticed an odd resemblance be-

tween her and his late wife Lisbeth, such that he could
have asked her if she were her grandmother, for he was
most vividly put in mind of her not only by the features of
her face, her hands still beautiful even in their bony state,
and especially by the way she used them as she spoke—he
even noticed on her neck a mole with which his wife's neck
was marked—the horse dealer, his thoughts strangely confused in his mind, asked her to be seated and inquired,
What on earth brought her to him on business of the Chamberlain's? While Kohlhaas' old dog sniffed at her knees and
wagged his tail as she scratched his head, the woman answered that the errand assigned to her by the Chamberlain
consisted of her revealing to him to what three questions
important to the Saxon court the paper contained mysterious answers, of her warning him of an envoy who was in
Berlin to get possession of the paper, and of her procuring
the paper on the pretext that it was no longer safe in his
bosom where he was carrying it. But her real purpose in
coming was to tell him that the threat of cheating him out
of the paper by trickery or by violence was absurd and a
futile lure; that he need not have the slightest concern
about it under the protection of the Elector of Brandenburg, in whose custody he was; in fact, that the paper was
far safer with him than with her, and that he should be
on his guard against being cheated out of it by turning it
over to anyone soever on any pretext soever.—Nevertheless
she concluded by saying that she would consider it wise
to put the paper to the use for which she had given it to
him at the Jüterbock fair, to lend an ear to the proposition
made to him at the border by Gentleman of the Hunt von
Stein, and to surrender the paper, which could now be of
no further use to him, to the Elector of Saxony in exchange
for life and liberty. Kohlhaas, exultant at the power given
him to deal a mortal wound to his enemy's heel at the very
moment when it trod him in the dust, answered, "Not for
the world, old woman, not for the world!" and pressed the
old woman's hand and sought to know what kinds of answers the paper might contain to those fearful questions.
As she picked up the youngest child, who had come to

crouch at her feet, and set him on her lap, the woman
said, "Not for the world, Kohlhaas the horse dealer, but
for the sake of this pretty little blond boy!" and then, as
she smiled at the youngster and caressed him and kissed
him, while he kept looking at her with large eyes, she
handed him with her withered hands an apple that she
was carrying in her pocket. Kohlhaas, in some confusion,
said that the children themselves would praise his action
when they had grown up and that he could do nothing
better for them and for their children's children than to
retain that paper. Besides, he asked, who, after all the experiences he had had, would guarantee him against a new
betrayal, and would he not wind up sacrificing the paper
for the Elector's sake to no purpose, just as he had sacrificed
his recently surrendered force of soldiery that he had assembled at Lützen? "Whoever has once broken his word
to me," he said, "with that man I never exchange another
one; and nothing but a definite and unambiguous demand
from you, good old woman, will ever part me from that
paper, through which in wondrous wise satisfaction has
been done for all that I have suffered." Then the woman, as
she set the child back down on the floor, said that in many
respects he was right and that he might do or not do whatever he saw fit. With that she took up her crutches and
started to leave. Kohlhaas repeated his question concerning
the contents of that strange paper. As she replied in passing that he could, of course, open it, although that would
be an act of mere curiosity, he said he wanted to ask her
about a thousand other things before she left him: Who
she was, after all; How she had come by the knowledge
that she possessed; Why she had denied the paper to the
Elector for whom it had been written; and Why she had
given this miraculous paper precisely to him among so
many thousands of persons.—Now it chanced that there
became audible at just that moment the sound of several
police officials coming up the stairs, so that the woman
was seized with a sudden concern of being discovered in
these rooms, and she said, "Until we meet again, Kohlhaas,
until we meet again! You shall not lack for knowledge of

all these things when we do meet again!" Then turning toward the door she cried out, "Farewell, children, farewell!" kissed the little brood one after the other, and departed.

Meanwhile the Elector of Saxony, wretched victim of his wretched thoughts, had summoned two astrologers named Oldenholm and Olearius, who stood at that time in great repute in Saxony, to consult them for advice in the matter of the contents of that paper which was so important to him and to the entire race of his posterity; and when, after a profound inquiry that went on for several days in the palace tower in Dresden, they were unable to agree as to whether the prophecy related to distant centuries or to the present time, and as to whether the crown of Poland was involved, with which relations were still in a warlike state, the disquiet, not to say despair, in which this Lord found himself was only intensified by their erudite argument, instead of being allayed by it, and finally heightened to the point where it was utterly unbearable to his spirits. On top of everything else, it so happened that the Chamberlain spoke at just this time with his wife, who was about to follow him to Berlin, and instructed her to convey in a discreet manner to the Elector before she left, how, after an unsuccessful effort he had made with a woman who had not been seen since, the hope of getting the paper in Kohlhaas' possession appeared most unlikely, inasmuch as the death sentence had now been passed on him, after a thorough examination of the dossiers, and, with the signature of the Elector of Brandenburg already on it, the day of execution had been set for the Monday after Palm Sunday; at which news the Elector, his heart consumed with grief and despair, shut himself up in his room like a lost soul, and, weary of life, refused all food for two days; on the third day, however, after curt notification of the Gubernium that he was going to ride to the hunt with the Prince of Dessau, he disappeared from Dresden. Where he actually went, and whether he traveled toward Dessau, we shall leave undecided, since the chronicles from which we have collated this report are in curious contradiction on this

point and refute one another. Certain it is that the Prince
of Dessau, quite incapable of hunting, was at this time
lying ill in Braunschweig in the home of his uncle, Duke
Heinrich, and that the Lady Heloise arrived on the evening
of the following day at the quarters of her husband, the
Chamberlain, Lord Kunz, in Berlin, in the company of one
Count von Königstein who, she claimed, was her cousin.—
Meanwhile the death sentence had been read to Kohlhaas
upon the command of the Elector, his chains were struck
off, and the documents pertinent to his property, which
had been withheld from him in Dresden, were restored to
him; and when the lawyers assigned to him asked what
disposition he wished to make of his effects after death, he
drew up a will, with the aid of a notary, in favor of his
children and named his good friend the bailiff of Kohlhaasenbrück as their guardian. Nothing thereafter could
equal the tranquillity and composure of his last days; for
by a special ordinance extraordinary of his Elector, the
prison in which he was being held was shortly thereafter
thrown open and free access to him granted day and night
to all his friends, of whom he had a great many in the city.
In fact, he had the further satisfaction of seeing the theologian Jacob Freising appear in his prison as a deputy of
Doctor Luther with a letter composed in the latter's own
hand, doubtlessly a very noteworthy letter which has, however, been lost, and of receiving from that churchman the
beneficence of the Holy Communion in the presence of
two Brandenburg deacons, his assistants. In these circumstances, and amid a general commotion of the city,
which still could not give up hope of a proclamation of
pardon, that fateful Monday after Palm Sunday came
around, when he was to be atoned with the world for his
all too rash attempt to achieve justice there by his own
hand. Escorted by a strong guard, his two little boys in his
arms—for he had expressly obtained this favor from the
bar of the court—and led by the theologian Jacob Freising,
he was just emerging from the gate of his prison when,
from amid a mournful throng of acquaintances who kept
shaking his hand and bidding him farewell, the castellan

of the electoral palace stepped up to him with haggard face
and handed him a paper which he said had been given to
him by an old woman. Looking in astonishment at the man,
whom he knew only very slightly, Kohlhaas opened the
paper, whose signet-ring impression in the sealing wax immediately put him in mind of the familiar gypsy woman.
But who could describe his astonishment as he read the
following communication: "Kohlhaas: the Elector of Saxony is in Berlin; he has already preceded you to the place
of execution and can be recognized, if that is of importance
to you, by a hat with blue and white plumes. I do not need
to tell you his purpose in coming; he means to dig up the
capsule as soon as you have been buried and open the
paper inside.—Your Elizabeth."—Turning in uttermost consternation to the castellan, Kohlhaas asked him if he knew
the mysterious woman who had given him the note. But
as the castellan answered, "Kohlhaas, the woman—" and
oddly broke off in the midst of his speech, he was carried
along by the procession which at just that instant had
started up again, and he could not hear what was being
said by the man, who seemed to be trembling in every
limb.—When he arrived at the place of execution, he found
the Elector of Brandenburg present with his retinue,
among whom was the Arch Chancellor, Lord Heinrich von
Gersau, all on horseback amid an incalculable throng of
people: at his right hand the Imperial Prosecutor, Franz
Müller, with a copy of the death sentence in his hand; at
his left hand, holding the decree of the Dresden court, his
own attorney, the jurist Anton Zäuner; in the middle of the
semicircle framed by the crowd, a herald with a bundle of
articles and with the two black horses, resplendent with
health now and pawing the ground with their hooves. For
the Arch Chancellor, Lord Heinrich, had observed the
complaint which he had submitted in Dresden in his master's name, and had followed it through point by point,
without the slightest concession to the Junker Wenzel von
Tronka. Thus the horses, after a banner had been swung
above their heads to make them honorable again, had been
withdrawn from the hands of the knacker who was feeding

them, fed fat once more by the Junker's men, and, in the presence of an expressly constituted committee, turned over to the attorney in the Dresden market place. Then when Kohlhaas, under guard, had come up the hill and approached him, the Elector said, "Well, Kohlhaas, this is the day on which justice is rendered unto you. See, I here restore to you everything that you lost under the compulsion of force at Castle Tronka and which I, as your Sovereign, was bound to restore to you: the black horses, the neckerchief, the imperial gulden, the bundle of laundry, even the medical expenses incurred by your groom Herse who fell in battle at Mühlberg. Are you satisfied with me?" —Kohlhaas, as with gleaming eyes he read over the decree handed to him at a sign from the Arch Chancellor, set his two children, whom he was holding in his arms, down on the ground beside him; and when he came to a clause in which the Junker Wenzel was sentenced to two years' imprisonment, he laid his hands crosswise on his bosom, and, completely overwhelmed by his emotions, knelt down from afar before the Elector. Joyously he assured the Arch Chancellor, as he rose to his feet again and as he laid his hand upon his heart, that his supreme wish on earth had been fulfilled. He stepped across to the horses, looked them over, and patted their sleek necks. Then, as he came back to the Chancellor, he cheerfully declared that he was presenting him with his two sons Heinrich and Leopold. The Chancellor, Lord Heinrich von Gersau, gazed down benevolently upon him from his horse and promised him in the Elector's name that his last wish should be considered sacred, then bade him make disposition according to his judgment of the articles contained in the bundle. With that, Kohlhaas called up out of the crowd the aged mother of Herse whom he had glimpsed in the square, and giving her the articles, said, "Here, little mother, these belong to you!"—and added to the money in the bundle the amount allotted to himself as compensation for damages, as a gift toward her care and comfort in her old days.—The Elector cried out, "Now, Kohlhaas the horse dealer, to whom justice has thus been vouchsafed, prepare to render satisfaction in turn to His

Imperial Majesty, whose prosecutor stands here present, for the breach of his imperial peace!" Kohlhaas, taking off his hat and throwing it upon the ground, said that he was ready; picked up his children once more and, after pressing them to his bosom, gave them over to the Kohlhaasenbrück bailiff; then, while they were being led away in silent tears from the place, he stepped up to the block. He was just in the act of unknotting his neckerchief and opening his doublet when, with a fleeting glance over the circle formed by the people, he perceived a short distance away from him the familiar man with the blue and white plumes standing between two knights who were half shielding him with their bodies. With a sudden step that startled the guards around him, Kohlhaas stepped right up in front of him and removed the capsule from his bosom; he extracted the paper, broke the seal, and read it; and with his eye fixed upon the man with the blue and white plumes, who seemed already to be indulging fond hopes, he put the paper into his mouth and swallowed it. Whereat the man with the blue and white plumes collapsed in a faint to the ground and passed into convulsions. While the man's bewildered attendants bent down and raised him up from the ground, Kohlhaas turned back toward the scaffold, where his head fell beneath the hangman's ax. Here ends the story of Kohlhaas. Amid general lamentation of the people his corpse was placed in a coffin; and as the bearers lifted it up to carry it to seemly burial in the cemetery of the outer city, the Elector called forth the sons of the deceased, and with the declaration to the Arch Chancellor that they were to be educated in his School for Pages, he dubbed them knights. Not long afterward, the Elector of Saxony, shattered in soul and body, returned to Dresden, where the sequel of his tale must be sought in history books. In Mecklenburg province, however, several happy and sturdy progeny of Kohlhaas were still living in the course of the century just ended.

The Mines at Falun

E. T. A. HOFFMANN

TRANSLATED BY PEGGY SARD

ONE clear bright July day, all the people of Göteborg were gathered at the water front. A rich East Indiaman, safely returned from far lands, lay at anchor in the roadstead, her ensign, the Swedish flag, flying joyfully out in the azure air, while hundreds of small boats filled with jubilant seafaring men went back and forth on the sparkling ripples of the Göta River, and the cannons of Masthugget Fort thundered out their widely echoing greetings over the open sea. The owners of the East India Company strolled on the shore. With smiling faces they calculated the rich profits coming to them, and reckoned with great happiness that their undertaking gave a larger profit each year, and that Göteborg thereby grew constantly more important in commerce. The townspeople looked at these enterprising men with pleasure, and rejoiced along with them, for their ventures brought energy and strength to the life of the whole city.

The crew of the East Indiaman, about a hundred and fifty men, came ashore in the many small boats which had rowed out to them, and got ready to hold their Hönsning. That is what the celebration is called which ships' crews hold on these occasions. It often lasts several days. Musicians in wonderfully gay-colored costumes went before them carrying fiddles, fifes, oboes, and drums, which they played loudly, while others of their band sang jolly songs.

The sailors followed two by two. Some, whose jackets and hats were decorated with brightly colored ribbons, were waving streamers; others danced; all romped and rejoiced, and the joyful sounds carried far and wide.

So the happy procession went along the docks and through the city to the suburb of Haga, to a tavern where there would be great merrymaking. Once they were there, the finest ale flowed in streams, and bumper after bumper was emptied. As always happens when seamen return home from long voyages, all sorts of brightly bedecked girls soon joined them. Dancing began, and wilder and wilder grew the excitement, and louder and more frantic the shouts of joy.

Only one sailor, a slender handsome boy of barely twenty, had withdrawn from the tumult, and sat outside on the bench at the door of the tavern. Two seamen came out to him, and one said, laughing, "Elis Fröbom, are you going to sulk again, and waste this happy time in foolish brooding? Listen, Elis, if you stay away from our Höns-ning, you may just as well stay away from the ship too! You'll never make a real hearty seaman at this rate. You have courage enough, and you are bold enough in the face of danger, but you can't drink, and you would rather keep your money in your pockets than celebrate with us and throw some to the landlubbers here. Drink, boy, or the sea devil or even the Troll himself will be on you."

Elis Fröbom sprang hastily from the bench, glared at the sailors with burning eyes, took a beaker filled to the brim with brandy, and emptied it with one pull. Then he said, "You see, Jöns, I can drink with any of you. And the captain can decide whether I am a good seaman or not. Now shut up and go away. Your wild frolic is hateful to me. It is none of your business what I do out here." "Now, now," answered Jöns. "I know that you were born in Nerike, and that the men of Nerike are all gloomy and mournful, and have no real love for life at sea. Just wait, Elis, I'll send somebody out who'll get you away from that bench the Fiend has nailed you to."

It was not long before a pretty girl came through the

door of the tavern and sat down beside Elis, who, silent and withdrawn, had sunk back on the bench again. It was plain from her finery and bearing what sort of life she led, but this wild life had not yet left its mark on the lovely gentle lines of her face. No trace of repulsive shamelessness, no, but instead a quiet yearning grief lay in the glance of her dark eyes. "Elis, aren't you going to take any part in your comrades' rejoicing? Don't you feel any joy that you have come back home—that you stand on the soil of your native land again, after having escaped the dangers of the treacherous sea waves?" Thus the girl spoke, in a soft gentle voice, as she put her arm around the young man.

Elis Fröbom, as if waking from a deep dream, gazed into the girl's eyes, then took her hand and drew her to his breast. It was plain to see that her soft whispers had reached his heart. "Ah," he began at last, as if recollecting himself, "there is nothing left now of my joy and my rejoicing. I cannot join in my comrades' happiness. Go inside, dear girl, rejoice and exult with the others, but leave sad Elis here outside alone; he will only spoil all your pleasure. Wait a minute—I like you very much, and I want you to think of me when I am back on the sea again." With that he took two shining ducats from his pocket, pulled a handsome East Indian shawl from his breast, and gave both to the girl. But bright tears came to her eyes—she stood up, laid the ducats on the bench, and said, "Oh, take your gold; it will only make me unhappy. But I will wear this beautiful shawl in memory of you. Next year you will probably not find me here, when you hold your Hönsning in Haga."

Then the girl, without going back to the tavern, went off down the street, holding her hands before her face.

Again Elis Fröbom sank back into his dark dreams. As the merrymaking in the tavern grew louder and wilder, he cried out, "Oh, I wish I were lying at the bottom of the sea —for there is no one left with whom I can rejoice!" A deep rough voice close behind him said, "You must have suffered a great misfortune, young man, if you are already wishing for death, when life should just be opening up for you."

Elis looked around, and saw an old miner, who was
standing with his arms folded, leaning against the walls of
the tavern and looking down at him with a grave, penetrating expression. As Elis studied the old man, it seemed to
him that a familiar form came comfortingly toward him
in the deep unrestrained loneliness in which he had believed himself lost. He pulled himself together, and told
how his father had been a good helmsman, but how he
had perished in a storm from which he himself had only
escaped by a miracle. Elis' two brothers, soldiers, had
fallen in battle, and Elis alone was left to support his poor
helpless mother, with the good wages which he received
from each trip to the Indies. For he had had to remain a
seaman; he had always followed the sea since he had first
begun as cabin boy, and he had considered it a great piece
of luck to be able to get into the service of the East India
Company. The profits had been greater than ever this voy-
age, and each sailor had received a sum of money in addition to his wages. Elis had hurried off in great joy, with
his pockets full of ducats, to the little house where his
mother lived.

But strange faces peered out at him from the window.
A young woman at last opened the door, and, when he
explained who he was, informed him in a rough heartless
way that his mother had been dead three months by now,
and that he could pick up at the town hall the few shabby
possessions left after the burial expenses had been paid.

His mother's death broke his heart. He felt himself for-
saken by all the world; alone as if cast up on a desert reef,
helpless and miserable. His whole life at sea seemed to him
a confused, useless effort—yes, and when he thought that
his mother had had to die alone, or perhaps badly nursed
by strangers, then it appeared to him wrong and wicked
that he had left to go to sea, and had not stayed at home
to cherish and care for her.

His comrades had carried him away to the Hönsning by
force, and he himself had supposed that the loud merrymaking around him there, and also the strong drink, would
dim his grief. But instead he soon began to feel as if all the

veins of his breast had burst from emotion, and he would bleed to death.

"Why," said the old miner, "you will soon put to sea again, Elis, and then in a little while your sorrow will pass. Old people do die, that is the way of the world, and as you yourself know, your mother has only left a miserable weary life." "Oh!" answered Elis. "No one realizes my unhappiness; people even think me weak-minded and foolish. That is just what has made me feel so cut off from the world. I can't go to sea again, that life disgusts me. In other days, my heart leapt when the ship, her sails spread out like magnificent wings, drove along over the sea, and the waves splashed and blustered in cheerful music, and the wind whistled through the creaking rigging. Then I could make merry with my comrades, on deck; and when I had the still dark midnight watch, I could think of the return home and my dear old mother, of how happy she would be when Elis came back again. Then I could certainly rejoice at the Hönsning, after I had poured out the ducats into my dear little mother's lap, after I had handed over the handsome shawls, and many other gifts from faraway places, and when I saw her eyes shine bright, when she clapped her hands with joy, when she trotted busily here and there, and brought out the finest ale, which she had been keeping for Elis. And in the evenings, I used to sit with my mother, and tell her about the strange peoples among whom I voyaged, about their customs and habits, and about all the marvels that I saw on the long journey. It was her greatest pleasure, and she used to retell to me the wonderful voyages of my father in the farthest north, and regale me with many exciting seamen's stories, which I had already heard a hundred times, and which I couldn't hear enough. Oh, who will bring me back this happiness! No, I won't go to sea again. What would I do among comrades who only treat me with scorn, and how could I enjoy work that to me would only seem a miserable struggle for no purpose?"

"I have been listening to you with satisfaction, young man," said the old miner, as Elis fell silent, "just as for some time I have been watching your behavior with satisfaction. Everything that you have done and said has shown that you have a thoughtful, retiring, childlike nature. A finer gift Heaven could hardly have given you. But it is certainly not your destiny to be a seaman. How can a serious, in fact melancholy, man from Nerike (for I see your origin in the cast of your face and in your bearing) be content with the unsettled, savage life at sea? You do well to give up that life. But you can't just be idle. Take my advice, Elis Fröbom. Go to Falun and become a miner. You are young and strong; you'll soon be a first-class miner, then a hewer, then a foreman, and then more than that. You have money in your pockets; invest it, draw profits from it. You may very well come into possession of a mining property; you will then have an owner's share in the mine. Take my advice, Elis Fröbom, become a miner."

Elis became almost frightened at these words from the old man. "What?" he cried. "What do you counsel me? Shall I leave the beautiful open world, under the bright sunny heaven which encircles me, refreshing and reviving me, and go down into the cold depths to burrow and grub like a mole for ores and metals, all for mere profits?" "That's typical," said the old man angrily, "people scorn things they don't know about. Mere profits! As if all the torments on the surface of the earth, which earning a living brings, were nobler than the work of the miner, whose patient industry and whose skill open for him the best hidden treasure chamber of Nature. You speak of profit, Elis Fröbom. There may be something down there worth much more than that. Although the blind mole burrows through the ground by blind instinct, it may well be that in the lowest depths, by the weak light of the miner's lamp, men's eyes see more clearly, yes, that finally, having become stronger and stronger, they are able to see in the beautiful minerals reflections of the things which on earth are hidden above the clouds. You know nothing of mining, Elis Fröbom; let me tell you about it."

With these words, the old man sat down on the bench beside Elis and began to tell him in detail how mining is

carried out, and, painting with vivid words, made it seem
very clear to Elis' ignorant eyes. He spoke of the mines at
Falun, in which he said he had worked from his early
youth. He described the great entrance shaft with its dark
brown walls; he spoke of the mine's immense wealth of valuable minerals. More and more vivid grew his words, more
glowing his face. He went through the shafts of the mine
as through the paths of an enchanted garden. The rocks
came to life; the fossils seemed to move; the wonderful
pyrosmalith and the almandine flashed in the light of the
miner's lamp; rock crystals gleamed and sparkled everywhere.

Elis listened attentively. The miner's strange way of describing these underground wonders, as if he were standing
right in the midst of them, seized the boy's whole being.
He felt his breathing oppressed, as if he had actually gone
down into the depths with him, as if a powerful magic held
him fast there, and he would never again see the friendly
light of day. And yet it also seemed to him that the old
man had revealed a new and unknown world, to which
Elis belonged. The enchantment of this world seemed already to have been disclosed to him in his earliest boyhood,
through strange secret presentiments.

"Elis Fröbom," said the old man at last, "I have laid before you all the wonders of a calling for which Nature has
certainly intended you. Take counsel with yourself, and
then do what your instinct inspires you to do." With that
he sprang quickly up from the bench and strode away,
without saying good-bye to Elis or looking back at him.
Soon he had disappeared from sight.

In the tavern meanwhile it had become quite still. The
power of the strong ale and spirits had triumphed. Many
of the crew had slipped away with their girls; others lay
in the corners and snored. Elis, who could not go back to
his old home, was, at his request, given a small room in
which to sleep.

Scarcely had he stretched himself out, weary and heavy,
on his bed when a dream stirred its wings over him. It
seemed to him that he was gliding in a beautiful ship in

full sail, on a mirror-bright sea, and that over them arched
a dark cloudy sky. Then when he looked down into the
waves, he realized that what he had taken for the sea was
a solid, transparent, glistening mass, in whose shimmer the
whole ship melted away in some mysterious fashion, so that
he stood on the crystal floor. Over him he perceived an
arch of dark glittering stone; that which he had first taken
for the clouded sky was rock. Impelled by some mysterious
force, he stepped forward, but in that instant everything
about him began to move, and like curling waves, beautiful
flowers and plants of shining metal rose about his feet. They
shot forth their leaves and blossoms from the depths, and
in a graceful way became intertwined. The floor was so
clear that Elis could even see the roots of the plants. Soon,
as his gaze reached deeper, he saw at the very bottom many
lovely girlish figures, standing with their gleaming white
arms entwined. It was from their hearts that these roots,
these flowers and these plants grew, and when the maidens
laughed, a sweet music went through the whole vault, and
the wonderful metal flowers sprang up higher and more
joyfully.

An indescribable feeling of grief and delight seized the
young man; a world of love, of longing, of burning desire
grew in his soul. "I'm coming down, down to you," he cried,
and threw himself with outstretched arms on the crystal
floor. But it sank away from him, and he was suspended
in a shimmering ether. "Now, Elis Fröbom, how do you
like all this splendor?" called a strong voice. Elis saw the
old miner near him; as he looked at him more closely, the
old man turned into a colossus, cast of glowing metal. Elis
began to shudder, but at that instant there was a flash like
sudden lightning from the depths, and the stern face of a
majestic woman became visible. Elis felt the delight in his
breast mount steadily to crushing anxiety. The old man
put his arm around him and cried out, "Beware, Elis
Fröbom, this is the Queen. You had better look away now."
Unwillingly Elis turned his head—and became aware that
the stars of the evening sky shone through a fissure in the
vault. A gentle voice called his name disconsolately. It was

his mother's voice. He thought he saw her form aloft above
the cleft. But it was a beautiful young woman, who
stretched her hand deep into the vault and called his name.
"Let me go!" he cried to the old man. "I still belong to the
upper world and its kind heaven!" "Beware," said the old
man heavily. "Beware, Elis Fröbom. Be true to the Queen,
to whom you have surrendered." When the young man
looked down again at the rigid face of the commanding
woman, he felt that his own being would turn into gleaming stone. He shrieked in dreadful fear, and woke from the
marvelous dream, whose rapture and terror echoed deep
in his soul.

"No wonder I dreamed such strange things," said Elis to
himself, as with difficulty he collected his thoughts. "The
old miner told me so much about the splendor of the underground world that my head was full of it; yet never in
my whole life have I felt as I do now. Perhaps I am still
dreaming. No, no—I am probably ailing. I'll go out into the
open air, the freshness of the sea wind will heal me."

He got up quickly and ran toward the water front, where
the jubilation of the Hönsning had started afresh. But he
soon realized that those pleasures meant nothing to him,
that he could not keep his mind on anything, while longings
and wishes which he couldn't name went through his soul.
He thought with deep melancholy of his dead mother, but
then it seemed to him that he yearned to meet the girl
who had spoken so kindly to him yesterday. And then he
became afraid that if the girl should come toward him from
this or that street, she would in the end turn into the old
miner, of whom he was afraid, without being able to tell
himself why. And yet he would have been glad to have the
old man tell him more about the wonders of the mines.

Carried here and there by this succession of thoughts, he
looked down into the water. Then it seemed to him that
the silver waves stiffened into a sparkling glimmer, in
which the beautiful large ships melted away, and that the
dark clouds, which were passing evenly by on the bright
sky, sank down and thickened into a stone vault. He found
himself in his dream again; he looked again on the severe

face of the majestic woman; and the troubled anxiety of most passionate craving gripped him anew.

His comrades roused him from this reverie; he was to follow their procession. But then a voice whispered repeatedly in his ear, "Why are you still here? Away, away—your place is in the mines of Falun. There all the splendor of which you dream will open before you. Go, go to Falun."

For three days Elis Fröbom walked about the streets of Göteborg, accompanied incessantly by the wonderful images of his dreams, urged incessantly by the mysterious voice. On the fourth day he found himself at the gate through which the road to Gefle leads. A large man walked out just ahead of him. Elis thought that he recognized the old miner, and, irresistibly attracted, hurried after him, but without catching him.

The pursuit went on and on, without a pause. Elis knew of course that he was on the way to Falun, and this even calmed him in a strange way, for he was certain that the voice of fate had spoken to him through the old miner, who would now lead him to his destiny. And indeed, especially when the route was uncertain, he often saw the old man appear suddenly from a ravine, from dense underbrush, or from the shadow of a rock and lead him on, without looking back; but then he quickly disappeared again.

At last, after many weary days, Elis caught sight of two large lakes in the distance; between them a thick smoke rose. As he climbed higher and higher up a hill to the west, he saw through the smoke a pair of towers and some dark roofs. The old man stood before him large as a giant, pointed with outstretched arm toward the fumes, and vanished again among the rocks.

"That is Falun!" cried Elis. "That is Falun, the goal of my journey!" He was right, for people on the road behind him confirmed it. There between the lakes Runn and Warpann lay the city of Falun, and the hill Elis was that minute climbing was the Guffrisberg, where the great main shaft of the mine was located. Elis stepped forward with good cheer, but when he stood before the enormous hellish chasm, his blood froze in his veins, and he grew stiff with fear in the face of the frightful destruction.

The great main shaft of the mine at Falun, as is well known, is twelve hundred feet long, six hundred feet wide, and one hundred and eighty feet deep. The dark brown side walls at first go down perpendicularly for the most part. Then they flatten out between huge piles of dirt and stone fragments at the middle level. In these piles and at the side walls pieces of timbering from older shafts are visible, laid strongly and closely together, with the ends fitted into each other as they are in log cabins. No tree, no blade of grass sprouts in the bare moldering chasm. Jagged masses of rock, resembling gigantic stone animals and colossal human figures, tower above on all sides. In the abyss lie mixed together in wild confusion stone, dross, and slag. A perpetual stupefying brimstone vapor rises from the depths, as if a hell's brew were cooking down below, whose reek poisoned all the green growth of Nature. It would be easy to believe that it was here that Dante had descended and had seen the Inferno with all its desperate torments, with all its horrors.

As Elis looked down into the huge abyss, there came to his mind something that had been told him a long while before by the old helmsman of his ship. That was, that as he lay in a fever, suddenly it seemed as if the waves of the sea rolled away, and beneath him an immeasurable chasm opened, so that he saw the frightful monsters of the deep, which floundered with hideous gulpings here and there among the thousands of curious shells, the coral growths, and the strange rocks until they lay quiet in death, their mouths gaping wide. Such a sight, in the opinion of the old seaman, portended that death in the waves would follow soon, and as it happened this old man pitched suddenly from the deck into the sea quite soon thereafter, and was lost. Elis thought about this, for the abyss seemed to him like the bottom of the sea when the waves were gone, and the dark stones, the bluish and red slag seemed like horrible monsters, which stretched their vicious octopus tentacles toward him. It happened that just then some min-

ers came up from the pits. Their dark clothing, their black
scorched faces made them appear to be hideous creatures
laboriously crawling out of the earth, trying to make a way
for themselves to the upper world.

Elis felt himself shaking with fear, and was seized with
dizziness, which had never happened to him at sea on the
rigging. It seemed to him that invisible hands were trying
to pull him down into the abyss. Closing his eyes, he ran
back a little distance. Only when he had gone down the
Guffrisberg again, far from the entrance shaft, and had
looked up at the bright sunny heavens, was he freed from
all the anxiety of that dreadful sight. Then he breathed
easily again, and he called from the depths of his soul, "Oh
Lord of my life, what are all the terrors of the sea, compared to the frightfulness there in that desolate cavern? At
sea, the storm may rage, dark clouds may reach down to
the furious waves, but the noble glorious sun soon triumphs,
and before her friendly face the wild uproar falls silent.
But she never appears in that dark cavern, and no fresh
breath of spring ever quickens the breast down there. No,
may I never join you, you black earthworms, never would
I be able to get used to your dark life."

Elis planned to stay overnight in Falun, and in the earliest morning begin the return trip to Göteborg. But when
he came to the market place, which is called Helsing Place,
he saw a number of people assembled. A long procession
of miners in holiday clothes, with miners' lamps in their
hands, led by musicians, had just stopped in front of a fine
house. A tall thin man in his middle years came out, and
looked around him with a pleasant smile. From his inde-
pendent bearing, his sincere expression, and his shining
dark blue eyes, you could tell him to be a real Dahlcarl, for
these, Elis saw, were the characteristics of the people of
this province. The miners formed a circle about him. He
shook hands heartily with each one, and spoke with each
a few friendly words.

Elis Fröbom learned by asking questions that this man
was Pehrson Dahlsjö, chief overseer of the mines, and
holder of a fine frälse at Great Copper Mountain. In Swe-

den, land which is leased out for copper and silver mining is called frälse. The holders of these frälse have shares in the mines, whose working they manage.

Elis was told also that this day the Court of the Mines had had its last sitting of the session, and that it was the custom for the miners then to go around in procession to the surveyor, the head of the smelting house, and the overseers, each of whom entertained them.

As Elis looked at the fine handsome men, with open friendly faces, he thought no more about the earthworms at the great entrance shaft. The evident pleasure that flashed up through the whole circle as Pehrson Dahlsjö came out was a different thing entirely from the wild raging merrymaking of the sailors at the Hönsning. The way these miners enjoyed themselves went right to Elis' quiet serious heart. He felt indescribably happy, but he could hardly hold back tears of emotion when some of the apprentices began to sing an old song, with a simple, deeply moving melody, in praise of the working of mines.

Pehrson Dahlsjö then threw open the doors of his house, and all the miners went inside. Elis followed involuntarily, and stood on the threshold, where he could look over the spacious room in which the miners had taken seats on benches. A hearty repast lay prepared on a table. Then the doors on the other side of the room opened, and a lovely young girl, festively dressed, came in. Tall and slender, her luxuriant dark hair braided around her head, her neat pretty bodice fastened with rich clasps, she was in the fullest flower of youth. All the miners rose, and a low murmur went through the group, "Ulla Dahlsjö. How God has blessed our Overseer, with this daughter as good and as beautiful as an angel!" The eyes of even the very oldest miners sparkled as Ulla clasped the hands of each in very friendly greeting. Then she brought handsome silver tankards and poured out choice ale, of a kind which at that time was made only in Falun, and served it to the happy guests, while her sweet innocent smile shone on them all.

When Elis saw the maiden, he felt as though a flash of lightning had struck right to his heart and set on fire all

the heavenly delight, the ache, of love—the fervor that lay
within him. For it was she, Ulla Dahlsjö, who in that portentous dream had reached out a rescuing hand. Elis
thought that he had now guessed the deeper meaning of
that dream, and forgetting the old miner, he blessed the
fate which had brought him to Falun.

But he felt, as he stood on the threshold, like an un-
wanted stranger, and wished he had died before he had
seen Ulla Dahlsjö, for now he would perish of love and
longing. He could not take his eyes off the lovely girl, and
when she passed close by him, he spoke her name in a gentle trembling voice. Ulla looked about her and discovered
poor Elis, who, his face fiery red, now stood there with
downcast eyes, speechless and motionless. She went up to
him and said with a soft laugh, "You must be a stranger
here. I see that from your seaman's clothes. But don't just
stand there on the threshold. Come in and enjoy yourself
with us." With that she took him by the hand, drew him
into the room, and gave him a tankard of ale. "Drink," she
said. "Drink, friend. You are heartily welcome here."

For Elis, it was as if he were in a blissful dream, from
which he might at any moment awake and find himself
miserable. Mechanically he emptied the tankard. At that
moment Pehrson Dahlsjö came up, and, taking him by the
hand in friendly greeting, asked from where he came, and
what brought him to Falun.

Elis felt the warming strength of the good drink in all
his veins. Looking into Pehrson's honest eyes, he grew
cheerful and courageous. He explained that he was the son
of a seaman, and had been a sailor himself since childhood;
that he had just returned from the East Indies to find his
mother, whom his wages supported, dead; that he felt completely alone in the world; that the rough life at sea was
now repugnant to him; that his deepest inclinations drew
him to mining, and that here at Falun he intended to try
to get employment as a miner. This last, so opposed to
everything which he had decided a little earlier, escaped
him quite unexpectedly. It seemed to him as if he could
not have said anything else to the Overseer, even as if he

had really spoken his inmost wish, of which he had not been aware until now.

Pehrson Dahlsjö considered the young man very seriously, as if he wanted to look right into his soul. Then he said, "I do not suppose, Elis Fröbom, that mere flightiness drives you from your former calling, or that you have not carefully weighed all the hardships, all the toil of a miner's life before forming the resolve to devote yourself to it. It is an old belief with us that the mighty elements over which the bold miner rules destroy him, if he does not strain his whole being to hold his mastery over them—if he gives room to other thoughts which weaken the forces he should turn undividedly to his work with earth and fire. But if you have really tested your inner calling and found it genuine, you have come at a good time. There is work at my claim. You can, if you like, stay here at my house from now on, and in the morning go down the shaft with the foreman, who will explain your work to you."

Elis' heart expanded at Pehrson Dahlsjö's words. He thought no more about the terrors of the frightful abyss into which he had looked. He would now see lovely Ulla every day; he would live under the same roof with her, and he was filled with joy and delight; he permitted himself the sweetest hopes.

Pehrson Dahlsjö informed the miners there that he had just taken on a young man as apprentice, and introduced Elis to them. They all looked with approval at the youth, and were of the opinion that with his slender strong frame, he had been born to be a miner, and that he certainly seemed industrious and honest.

One of the miners, an older man, drew near and shook Elis' hand heartily, saying that he was the foreman spoken of, and that he would be very glad to teach him everything that he needed to know. Elis was made to sit down by him, and the foreman began immediately over his tankard of ale to speak about a miner's work.

Then the old man from Göteborg came to Elis' mind, and he found that in a strange way he could repeat almost everything that the man had said. "Why," cried the foreman, full of astonishment, "Elis Fröbom, where have you gotten this knowledge? Why, in a short time you will surely be the most skillful miner of all!"

Pretty Ulla, going back and forth among the guests and speaking with them, often nodded to Elis in a friendly way, and encouraged him to feel at home. "Now you are no longer a stranger," she said, "but you belong to this house. Not the treacherous sea, but Falun, with its rich hills, is your home." A heaven of bliss and happiness opened to the young man at Ulla's words. The others noticed that Ulla often lingered near him, and Pehrson Dahlsjö too regarded him and his quiet serious ways with obvious approval.

But Elis' heart pounded when he stood, dressed in miner's clothes, with heavy iron-studded Dahlcarl's shoes on his feet, at the smoking abyss, and went down with the foreman into the deep pit. Soon he was nearly suffocated by hot vapors; then their miner's lamps flickered in the blasts of piercing cold wind which rushed through the shafts. Deeper and deeper they went, until finally they came to an iron ladder barely a foot wide, and Elis found that all the skill in climbing which he had developed as a sailor did not help him here a bit.

At last they stood in the lowest diggings, and the foreman showed Elis the work that he was to do there. Elis thought of lovely Ulla. He saw her floating over him like a shining angel, and he forgot all fear of the pit, all the difficulties of the hard work. He held fast to the belief that only if he devoted himself to mining with all the force of his will, with all the exertion that his body could stand, would his sweetest dreams have a chance to come true. And so it came about that in an unbelievably short time he did as well at his work as the most skilled of the miners.

Each day good Pehrson Dahlsjö grew more fond of the diligent worthy boy, and often told him openly that he had acquired in him not so much a first-class miner as a well-loved son. Ulla's feeling revealed itself more and more plainly. Often when Elis went to the mine, and anything at all hazardous was under way, she begged him with bright tears in her eyes to guard himself against accident.

And when he came home, she came to him full of happiness, and always had the best ale, or else a good dish, ready to refresh him.

Elis' heart trembled with joy when Pehrson Dahlsjö said to him one day that since he had brought a good bit of money with him, he could not fail, with his industry and economy, to come into possession of a share in the mine, or even to get a frälse, and that then no mine owner at Falun would refuse him if he asked for the hand of his daughter. Elis almost told him at that moment how much he loved Ulla, and how all his hopes were centered on her. But insurmountable timidity, or even more, uneasy hesitation whether Ulla really loved him too, as he usually thought, stopped his mouth.

It happened that one time Elis was working in the lowest pit, enveloped in thick sulphur vapor, so that his miner's lamp shone only weakly through it, and he could scarcely see the vein of the mineral. He heard a noise, a pounding sound, as if in a still deeper shaft someone were working with a rock crusher. But that sort of work could not very well be done in the pits, and also Elis knew that no one except himself had come down into the pits, for the foreman had just stationed all the miners at the winding shaft —so the pounding and hammering seemed very strange to him. He put down his own tools and listened to the hollow sounds, which seemed to be coming closer and closer. All at once he saw a dark shadow beside him, and recognized, as a violent current of air blew away the sulphur vapor, the old miner of Göteborg, who stood at his side. "Good luck!" called the old man in the traditional miner's greeting. "Good luck, Elis Fröbom, here below among the rocks! Now, how is life treating you, comrade?"

Elis wanted to ask in what miraculous way the old man had come into the pit, but he struck the rock with his hammer with such force that sparks of fire flew all about, and a sound like distant thunder echoed through the shaft, and then he cried out in a frightful voice, "Here is a magnificent trap vein, but you, worthless rascally fellow, see only a trumm, hardly as big as a blade of straw. Underground you are a blind mole, to whom the Prince of Metals will always be unfriendly, and in the world above you will not be successful either; you will work in vain for the metal of your heart. You want to win Pehrson Dahlsjö's daughter for your wife; it is for that reason only that you work here, without care or concern for the work itself. Beware, you false journeyman, lest the Prince of Metals whom you mock seize you and throw you down to break your bones on the sharp rocks! And I tell you, Ulla will never be your wife."

Elis' anger boiled up at the old man's disdainful words. "What are you doing here in my master Pehrson Dahlsjö's shaft, where I am working with might and main, and doing a good job too. Get yourself gone the way you came, or we will see which one can beat out the other's brains." With that Elis placed himself defiantly in front of the old man, and raised his iron hammer high in the air. The old man laughed scornfully, and Elis saw with relief that he leapt nimble as a squirrel up the narrow rungs of the ladder, and disappeared in the dark galleries overhead.

Elis felt paralyzed in all his limbs. He could not work properly, and he came up from the pit. When the old foreman, who came from the winding shaft just then, saw him he cried, "In Christ's name, what has happened to you, Elis? You are as pale and haggard as a dead man. What's happened? Is it the sulphur vapor, which you haven't got used to yet? Here, drink this, my boy, it will do you good." Elis took a hearty pull of brandy from the flask handed him, and, strengthened by it, related everything that had happened down in the pit, as well as the way he had first met the strange old miner at Göteborg.

The foreman listened quietly. Then he nodded his head reflectively and said, "Elis Fröbom, that must have been Old Torbern whom you met. Now I know that the tales we tell of him are not just fancies. One hundred years ago or more, there was a miner here named Torbern. He must have been one of the first who brought mining at Falun to full perfection, and in his time the yield was much richer than it is today. No one understood mining as well as Torbern, who, because of his expert knowledge, became director of mining at Falun. The richest veins disclosed themselves to him, as if he were endowed with an unnatural power, and since in addition he was a morose melancholy man, without wife or child, without even a home of his own in Falun, and almost never came into the light of day, but burrowed incessantly in the pits, soon the story went about that he was in league with the mysterious power which rules in the center of the earth, and boils up the metals.

"Heedless of Torbern's stern warnings, which prophesied dreadful misfortunes if anything other than genuine love for the wonderful minerals and metals impelled the miners to work, men widened the pits more and more, in avaricious greed, until at last on Midsummer Day in 1678 the dreadful landslide occurred which created our huge entrance shaft, and at the same time destroyed the whole workings to such an extent that many shafts were reopened only by great labor and great skill. Nothing was seen or heard of Torbern, and it seemed certain that, working in the pits, he had been buried in the landslide. But not long afterward, when the work was going along better, the miners asserted that they had seen Old Torbern in the pits, and that he had given them good advice of all sorts, and had pointed out rich veins. Other miners had seen the old man above ground, strolling around the entrance shaft, sometimes lamenting sadly, sometimes raging in anger. Young men came here as you did, and said that an old miner had urged them to take up mining, and had led them here. It always happened at a time when there was a shortage of miners, and it might well be that Old Torbern was taking care of the mines in these ways. If it was really Old Torbern with whom you quarreled in the pit, and if he spoke of a rich trap vein, it is certain that there is one there, and we will trace it out tomorrow. You have not forgotten, of course, that here we call the concentrated rusty-brown veins in the rock 'trap runs,' and that a 'trumm' is a streak of the vein which divides into several branches, and finally breaks up entirely."

When Elis Fröbom, confused by many thoughts, went

into Pehrson Dahlsjö's house, Ulla did not come up to him as usual, in her affectionate way. She sat inside with down-cast look, and it seemed to Elis that her eyes were red with weeping. Next to her sat a fine-looking young man, who held her hand fast in his, and busied himself with saying all sorts of friendly joking things, to which Ulla paid no attention. Pehrson Dahlsjö came up to Elis, who, gripped by troubled misgivings, fixed his staring eyes on the couple, and, drawing him into another room, said, "Now, Elis Fröbom, you can show your affection for me, you can give proof of your true feelings. I have considered you my son for a long time. Now you can really be a son to me. The man whom you see here is a rich merchant from Göteborg named Eric Olafsen. At his request, I shall give him my daughter to wife; he will take her away to Göteborg, and then you alone will be left to me, the only pillar of my old age. Why, Elis, you say nothing? You turn pale—I hope you don't find fault with my decision—that now, when my daughter must leave me, you don't want to go off too! I hear Mr. Olafsen calling me, I must go back to him." With that Pehrson went back into the room.

Elis felt his vitals cut by a thousand burning knives. He had no words, no tears. In wild despair, he ran out of the house and away—on, until he came to the great entrance shaft. If that enormous chasm was a frightful sight in day-light, it was much worse, when night had fallen and the disk of the moon was just rising, to look on the stony waste, as a numberless host of monstrous brutes, the horrible brood of the infernal regions, seemed to move and roll confusedly below on the smoking floor, and to look around with fiery eyes, and stretch their gigantic clutches up to-ward the poor human beings.

"Torbern, Torbern!" shrieked Elis in a dreadful voice, which echoed through the hideous gorges. "Torbern, here I am! You were right. I was a false journeyman, for I gave myself up to foolish dreams of the upper world. My love, my life, my all lie down below. Go down with me, show me the richest trap runs, there I will dig and drill and work and never care about the light of day again. Torbern, Torbern, go down with me."

Elis took flint and steel from his pouch, lit his miner's lamp, and went down the shaft where he had worked before, without the old man's showing himself. It seemed to Elis that he saw the trap run plain and clear in the lowest shaft, that he could make out its edge, direction, and angle. Then, as he stared harder and harder at the wonderful vein, it seemed as if a dazzling light went through the whole pit, and its walls became transparent as the finest crystal. Each portentous dream that he had dreamed in Göteborg returned. He saw in that paradisiacal region the wonderful metal trees and plants, on which jewels flashing like fire hung as fruits, blossoms, and flowers. He saw the maidens, he shivered at the proud face of the mighty Queen. She seized him, pulled him down, and drew him to her breast. A red-hot ray went through his heart, and he was conscious only of the feeling that he swam in the waves of a diaphanous blue glistening mist.

"Elis Fröbom, Elis Fröbom," a strong voice from above called down, and the flickering of torches shone into the pit. It was Pehrson Dahlsjö, who had come with the foreman to look for the young man, for he had been seen running madly to the entrance shaft. They found him standing as if paralyzed, his face pressed to the cold stone. "What are you doing down here at night, you foolhardy boy?" called Pehrson to him. "Pull yourself together and climb up with us. Who knows what good news you may hear up there!"

In complete silence Elis climbed up; in complete silence he followed Pehrson Dahlsjö, who never stopped scolding him for venturing into such danger. It was bright daylight when they came into the house. Ulla threw herself with a loud cry on Elis' breast, and called him loving names. But Pehrson Dahlsjö said to Elis, "You idiot! Haven't I known for a long time that you love Ulla, and work with so much industry and zeal for her sake? Haven't I known for a long time that Ulla also loves you truly, from the bottom of her heart? Could I want a better son-in-law than a capable, industrious, good miner—than you, in fact, my dear Elis?

But you were silent. That vexed me, it hurt me." "Did we,"
Ulla broke in, "did we ourselves realize that we loved each
other so much?" "However that may be," continued Pehrson Dahlsjö, "I was upset that Elis did not speak to me
frankly and openly about his feelings, and therefore, and
also because I wanted to test your love too, I worked up
that story with Eric Olafsen yesterday, which nearly drove
Elis to his grave. You foolish man! Mr. Eric Olafsen has
already been married for quite a while, and it is to you,
Elis Fröbom, that I give my daughter as wife, for I say
again, I couldn't want a better son-in-law."

Elis wept for joy. His dearest wish had come to him so
unexpectedly, he almost thought he was dreaming again.

At Pehrson Dahlsjö's invitation, the miners gathered for
a joyful celebration at midday. Ulla had dressed in her best
clothes, and looked more beautiful than ever, so that the
guests kept saying, "What a lovely bride our Elis has won!
May Heaven bless them both for their goodness and
worth." But the horror of that night still lay behind Elis'
white face, and he often stared before him, as if carried
away from his surroundings. "What is wrong, dear Elis?"
asked Ulla. Elis pressed her to his breast and said, "Yes,
you are really mine, and now everything is all right."

Yet in the midst of his happiness, it often seemed to Elis
as if an icy hand touched his heart suddenly, and a gloomy
voice said, "Is this still your greatest joy, to have won Ulla?
You poor fool, have you not looked on the face of the
Queen?" He felt nearly unmanned by an indescribable fear.
The thought tortured him that at any time one of the miners would rise up like a giant before him, and to his anguish
he would recognize Torbern, come to remind him awe-
somely of the underground kingdom of stone and metal to
which he had surrendered. And yet he hardly knew why
the specter should be hostile to him, or what his mining
should have to do with his love.

Pehrson noticed Elis' troubled air, and ascribed it to his
having suffered the shock, and having spent the night in
the pit. But Ulla, seized by a secret foreboding, urged her
lover to tell her what dreadful thing had happened to him,

to take him away from her. Then Elis thought his breast
would burst, for he struggled in vain to tell his beloved of
the wonderful sight which had been disclosed to him in the
pit. An unknown force closed his mouth. The awful countenance of the Queen seemed to look out from his heart,
like the Medusa's head, and to pronounce her name would
be to turn everything about him into the stone of the dismal
dark shafts. All the splendor, which in the pits had filled
him with the highest joy, now seemed to him like a hell
of desperate torments, deceitfully decked out to entice him
to ruin.

Pehrson Dahlsjö ordered Elis Fröbom to stay at home
for a few days, to recover completely from the sickness into
which he seemed to have fallen. During this time Ulla's
love, which now poured forth bright and clear from her
childlike innocent heart, drove away his memories of the
fateful adventure in the pit. Elis was revived by his joy
and happiness, and believed that his good fortune would
keep evil forces away from then on.

When he went down the shaft again, everything in the
depths appeared quite different to him from before. The
most splendid veins were revealed to his eyes. He worked
with redoubled zeal, he forgot everything else, and when
he came up to the surface, he had to make an effort to
recollect Pehrson Dahlsjö, and even Ulla. He felt divided
in two. He felt as if his real, better self descended to
the center of the globe and rested in the Queen's arms,
while the other self went back to a dismal couch in Falun.
When Ulla spoke to him of her love, and of how happily
they would live together, he would begin to speak of the
wonders of the world underground, of the immeasurably
rich treasures which lay hidden there, and in telling of it
entangled himself in such completely unintelligible talk
that the poor child was filled with fear and anxiety, and
couldn't imagine how Elis could have changed so in all his
ways. And Elis announced continually, with great pleasure,
to the foreman, and to Pehrson Dahlsjö too, that he had
discovered rich veins and magnificent trap runs, and when
they found only barren rock there, he laughed scornfully,

and said that, to be sure, only he understood the secret marks, the meaningful letters which the hand of the Queen herself engraved in the clefts in the rock, and that it was really enough to be able to understand these signs, without making them known to others.

The old foreman looked sadly at the young man, who spoke with wild glittering eyes about the glorious paradise that shone resplendent in the center of the earth. "Oh, sir," he whispered softly in Pehrson Dahlsjö's ear. "Oh, sir, Evil Torbern has bewitched the poor boy!" Pehrson Dahlsjö answered, "Don't believe these miners' tales, old man. Love has unsettled this serious Neriker's head, that's all. Just let the wedding be over, then we will hear no more about trap runs and treasures and the whole underground paradise."

The wedding day set by Pehrson Dahlsjö came at last. For several days beforehand, Elis had been quieter, more serious, more drawn into himself than ever, but at the same time, he had never seemed so much in love with Ulla as then. He could not keep away from her for a minute, in fact he did not even go to the mine. He seemed not to think about his mining life at all, for not a word about the underground kingdom came past his lips. Ulla was full of joy. All fear that the menacing Powers of the Underworld, of whom she had often heard ancient miners speak, would entice her Elis to destruction, vanished. And Pehrson Dahlsjö too said, laughing, to the old foreman, "You see, Elis was only giddy from love of Ulla!"

Early in the morning on the wedding day (it was Midsummer's Day), Elis knocked at his bride's door. She opened it, and drew back in alarm when she saw Elis, dressed in his wedding clothes, dead white, and with dark flashing fire in his eyes. "I want to tell you, dearest Ulla," he said in a low, unsteady voice, "that we are right at the point of the greatest good fortune that is given men here on earth. Everything was disclosed to me during the night. Down in the pit there lies enclosed in the chlorite and mica the cherry-red sparkling almandine with the tablet of our life engraved on it, which you must receive from me as a wedding gift. It is more beautiful than the gorgeous blood-red carbuncle, and when, united in true love, we look into its radiant light, we will see clearly how our spirits are intertwined with the wonderful branch which comes from the heart of the Queen in the center of the globe. I must just bring this gem up here aboveground, and I will do that right now. Farewell for this little while, my dearest Ulla. I will soon be back."

Ulla with hot tears entreated her lover to give up this chimerical undertaking, for she had a presentiment of great misfortune, but Elis Fröbom insisted that without this stone he would never have a peaceful moment, and that the trip down for it could not be considered at all dangerous. He pressed his bride to his breast, and went away.

The guests were soon assembled, to escort the bridal pair to Copper Mountain Church, where the wedding was to take place. A group of gaily dressed girls who as brides-maids, according to the custom there, would lead the bride to the church, laughed and joked around Ulla. The musicians tuned their instruments, and rehearsed a joyful wedding march. Soon it was nearly noon, but Elis Fröbom was nowhere to be seen. Suddenly some miners rushed up, fear and horror in their white faces, and informed the gathering that a terrible landslide had just buried the whole section of the mine where Pehrson Dahlsjö's workings were.

"Elis, my Elis, you are lost!" Ulla cried, and fell as if dead. Now Pehrson Dahlsjö learned for the first time, from the foreman, that early in the morning Elis had gone to the entrance shaft and down to the pits. No one else was working there, for all the miners and apprentices had been invited to the wedding. Pehrson Dahlsjö and the mining folk hurried to the mine, but all their searching, at great risk to their own lives, was useless. Elis Fröbom could not be found. It was plain that the landslide had buried the unlucky boy in stone. And so weeping and mourning came to the house of good Pehrson Dahlsjö, just at the time when he thought he had arranged to spend his old age in peace and happiness.

Pehrson Dahlsjö had now long been dead, and Ulla had been lost sight of. No one in Falun thought about them any more, for well on to fifty years had passed since that unlucky wedding day.

It happened that the miners, while they were trying to cut through an opening between two shafts, at a depth of nine hundred feet, came upon the body of a young miner, lying in sulphur water. The body, when they brought it up to daylight, seemed to have been turned to stone. It seemed as if the young man lay in a deep sleep, so well preserved were his features, so without trace of decay were his miner's holiday clothes, even the flower at his breast. All the people from thereabouts gathered around, but no one recognized him, and none of the miners could remember a comrade's ever having been entombed there.

They were intending to take the body on down to Falun, when out of the distance a crone, as old as the hills, struggled up on crutches. "Here comes the old woman of Midsummer's Day," called one of the miners. They had given her this name because for many years she had appeared just on Midsummer's Day, looking into the pits, ringing her hands, groaning and wailing around the entrance shaft in a woebegone way, and then disappearing again.

As soon as the old woman had seen the motionless youth, she dropped her crutches, reached her arms up to heaven, and in heart-rending tones of deepest grief cried out, "Oh, Elis, Elis Fröbom, my sweet bridegroom." And with that she crouched down beside the corpse, took his stiff hands, and drew him to her old breast, grown cold with age, in which a heart full of warm love still beat, as a holy flame burns beneath a covering of ice. "Ah!" she cried again, scanning the circle of people around her. "Ah, not one of you recognizes poor Ulla Dahlsjö, this youth's happy bride of fifty years ago. When I went away to Ornäs, because of my grief and distress, Old Torbern comforted me by saying that I should see my Elis, whom the slide buried on our wedding day, again on earth, and therefore year in and year out I have come back, and, full of love and longing, I have looked into the pits. And today I have seen him again, a corpse! Oh my Elis, my beloved bridegroom!"

Again she threw her withered arms around him, as if she would never let him go, and everyone standing there was deeply moved. Softer and softer grew her sighs, her sobs, until they faded away entirely. The miners stepped forward. They wanted to lift her up, but she had breathed out her life on the body of her bridegroom. Then they saw that the unlucky youth's body, which they had thought turned to stone, had begun to crumble into dust.

At Copper Mountain Church, where fifty years earlier the pair were to have been married, lie buried the ashes of the young man, and the body of the bride who had been true to him till bitter death.

The Black Spider

JEREMIAS GOTTHELF

TRANSLATED BY MARY HOTTINGER

In translating Gotthelf, the translator is faced with one al-most insuperable difficulty. Gotthelf's native tongue, the language he lived his daily life in, was Bernese, one of the many dialects of German which are the living languages of Switzerland today. In writing, like all Swiss, he used the form of High German which is the official language of Switzerland, though it differs considerably from High Ger-man proper.

Like Burns, who was in a similar linguistic situation, he made the best of both worlds by writing in Swiss High German, but using the homely, concrete, and vigorous Swiss words whenever it suited him. Anyone who has at-tempted to read the High German "translations" of Gotthelf (for the reading of the original is laborious to anyone quite unacquainted with Swiss dialect) will feel how flat and colorless they sound.

This is the problem the translator has to face. No dialect may be translated into any dialect of another language; its local associations are too strong. Gotthelf's translator must therefore abide by the literary language of his own country and sacrifice a great deal that lends relief and vigor to the whole. This is most painful in the case of the window post where the Spider is imprisoned, for Gotthelf used for it the old word Bystel, still current in certain parts of Switzerland and South Germany, instead of Fensterposten, the common and official word. Equally painful is the necessity of dis-carding Gotte and Götti, the homely Swiss words for god-mother and godfather.

There is nothing for it but to let these things go with a sigh and hope that the rich serenity and titanic vigor of Gotthelf's style will make itself felt without them.

THE sun rose over the mountain tops, pouring its radiance into a smiling but narrow valley and wakening to joyous life the creatures whose sole end is to rejoice in their life's sunshine. From the golden fringe of the wood the morning song of the blackbird rang out, the quail's monotonous love call rose from among the sparkling flowers in the dew-pearled grass, mating rooks danced their marriage dance above dark pines or croaked tender lullabies over the thorny cradles of their unfledged young.

Full on the sunny hillside nature had marked out a fertile sheltered spot. In the middle of it there stood a farmhouse, broad and bright, set in a splendid orchard where a few apple trees still wore the bravery of a late blossom. Some of the lush grass watered by the farm fountain was still standing, the rest had gone the way of all grass. The house was bathed in the Sunday glory which no hurried sweeping between night and day of a Saturday can bestow, but stands witness to the precious heritage of that ancient cleanliness which, like the family honor, must be tended day by day lest, in one heedless hour, blots might come on it, and persist from generation to generation, like bloodstains that no paint can conceal.

There was good reason why the earth built by the hand of God and the house built by the hands of men should shine in purest beauty. Over both a star shone in the blue

sky, for it was a solemn day. It was the day on which the
Son had returned to the Father, a sign to all men that the
ladder was still standing on which the angels had gone up,
like the souls of men who have sought their salvation with
the Father and not on earth. It was the day on which the
whole vegetable creation strives upward toward Heaven in
luxuriant bloom, a symbol, yearly renewed, of man's own
destiny. The air was full of sweet ringing sounds which
poured in over the hills on all hands. They came from the
churches outside in the wide valleys, where the bells were
calling that God's temples stand open to all whose hearts
are open to the voice of God.

Round the stately house a great bustle was going on. By
the fountain splendid horses were being groomed with special care—noble mares, their foals gamboling about them.
Mild-eyed cows were drinking from the great trough by
the fountain, and twice the farm lad had to take pan and
brush to remove the lingering traces of their contentment.
At the fountain, maids were scrubbing their faces with
rough drill rags, their hair twisted in knots over their ears;
others were hurrying through the open door with pails of
water, while the dark column of smoke panted straight and
high from the squat chimney into the blue air.

Leaning on the crook of his stick, the grandfather came
slowly round the house, silently watching the farm hands
and maids at their work, stroking a horse or warding off
the lumbering advances of a playful cow, and pointing out
to the heedless lad a forgotten wisp of straw here and there.
Every now and then he took from his deep vest pocket the
tinderbox to light his pipe, which he relished so much in
the morning, though it drew so badly.

On a spotless bench in front of the house sat the grandmother, slicing fine bread into a huge dish, every piece very
thin and just the right size, while hasty cooks and maids
cut slices fit to choke a whale. Fat hens strutted at her
feet, squabbling with stately pigeons for the crumbs, and
if some timid pigeon was pushed out of its share, she would
throw it a bit for itself with a kindly word to comfort it
for the grossness of the others.

Inside the house, in the great shining kitchen, a vast fire of pine wood was crackling, coffee beans were dancing in a big flat pan, stirred with a wooden spoon by a fine upstanding woman. Beside her the coffee mill was creaking between the knees of a freshly washed maid, while in the open parlor door there stood a beautiful pale woman with an open bag of coffee in her hand.

"Listen, midwife," she said, "mind that the coffee isn't roasted so black today. They might think I wanted to skimp it. Half a pound more or less is no matter today. And mind you have the wine soup ready in time. Grandfather'd think it was no christening if we had no wine soup for the company before they go to church. Spare nothing—do you hear me? There's saffron and cinnamon in the dish on the dresser, and sugar on the table. Take as much wine as you think is half too much. There's little fear it won't be drunk up at a christening."

So that was it. There was a christening in the house and the midwife was doing her work as a cook as doughtily as she had done it as a midwife. But she would have her work cut out if she was going to be ready in time and cook on the old-fashioned stove all that custom required.

Out of the cellar came a broad-shouldered man carrying a huge piece of cheese; he took from the spotless dresser the first plate that came to his hand and was just on the point of taking it into the parlor to set on the brown walnut table.

"Benz, Benz," cried the beautiful pale woman, "how they'd laugh if we'd no better plate for the christening," and going to the polished cherry-wood dresser where the glories of the house were displayed behind glass doors, she took out one of the handsome plates with blue edges and nosegays in the middle, surrounded by such sayings as:

'Tis more than human heart can utter,
Three halfpence for a pound of butter!

In Hell 'tis hot,
The potter turns his pot.

As the cow eats grass,
Man's life must pass.

Beside the cheese, she laid the huge züpfe, the true
Bernese loaf, plaited like the women's hair, brown and gold,
made of fine white flour, eggs, and butter, big as a one-year-
old and almost as heavy. Above and below it she set two
more plates piled high with oatcakes and scones. Hot thick
cream stood in a covered flowered jug on the stove and the
coffee was simmering in the shining three-legged pot with
the yellow lid. A breakfast was awaiting the company such
as princes never have on earth and no farmers but the
Bernese.

"If only they'd come, it's all ready," sighed the midwife.
"It'll take time for them to eat it all up and for everyone
to have his share, and parson's terrible strict and as sharp-
tongued as he can be if anyone's late."

"And Grandfather'd never let us take the gocart," said
the young mother. "It's his belief that a child that rides to
its christening'll grow up lazy and never be able to use its
legs properly. If only Godmother would come! She takes
longest. The men eat quicker. Besides, they could run."

The worry spread through the house. "Aren't they here
yet?" was heard at every turn, from every corner eyes were
on the watch, and Turk barked with might and main as if
to hurry them on. But the grandmother said: "In my time
it wasn't like this. People knew they had to rise betimes
on such a day and that the Lord waits for nobody."

At last the farm lad rushed into the kitchen—the godmother was in sight.

She arrived, bathed in sweat and laden like a Christmas
tree. In one hand she held the black strings of a huge
flowered bag with a vast züpfe, wrapped in a fine white
towel, sticking out of it—a present for the young mother.
In the other she carried another bag with an outfit for the
baby and some finery for herself, in particular beautiful
white stockings, and under one arm she held a box with
her wreath and the lace cap with the magnificent black silk
ribbons.

A chorus of joyful "God welcomes" greeted her. She could hardly find time to set down one of her loads to shake the hands stretched out to her. Eager helpers stood round to relieve her of her burdens, while the young wife stood in the doorway and it all began over again until the midwife warned them into the parlor—they could say what custom required in there.

And, mannerly but firm, the midwife got the godmother settled down at table, and the housewife came in with the coffee, though the godmother declared she'd had some already. Her aunt would never let her leave the house without bite nor sup, it was bad for young girls. But her aunt was an old woman, and the maids wouldn't get up in the morning and that was why she was late. If it hadn't been for them she'd have been here long ago. The thick cream went into the coffee, and though the godmother protested and vowed she didn't like it a lump of sugar went in too. And for a long time the godmother wouldn't hear of the züpfe being cut on her account, but all the same she had to let a large piece be cut and set before her. As for cheese, she would have none of it. But the housewife said she must be thinking it was only half cream, and that was why she wouldn't eat it, so the godmother had to give way. But she wouldn't touch the cakes, she wouldn't know where to put them, she said. But then there must be something wrong with the cakes, she was told, of course she was used to better, so what was she to do but eat cakes? While all this urging was going on she had drunk her first bowl of coffee in steady sips, and now a real dispute arose, for the godmother turned her bowl upside down, declared she hadn't any room left for any more good things and that they should leave her in peace. And this time she wasn't going back on it. Then the housewife said she was sorry the coffee was so bad, she'd given the midwife strict orders to make it as good as she could, she really couldn't help it if it was so bad nobody could drink it, it couldn't be the cream, she'd skimmed the milk with her own hands, and that was a thing she didn't do every day. So what was the poor godmother to do but submit to another bowl?

For a long time past the midwife had been bustling about impatiently, and at last she burst out:

"If there's anything I can do to help, just say so. I've got time."

"Why, there's no hurry," said the housewife.

But the poor godmother, who was steaming like a boiler, took the hint, swallowed the hot coffee as fast as she could, and, in the pauses forced on her by the scalding drink, remarked:

"I'd have been finished this long while if I hadn't had to take more than I can do with. But now I've finished."

She stood up, unpacked her bags, handed over the züpfe, the clothes, and the christening gift—a bright new thaler wrapped up in a beautifully painted christening text —with many an excuse that it was all so poor. But the young wife broke in upon her time and again, crying that it was a sin and shame to spend so much, she could hardly take it all, and if they'd known, they wouldn't have dared to bid her to the christening.

But now the girl set to work, helped by the midwife and the housewife, and did her best to make herself a bonny godmother from her shoes and stockings to the wreath on her precious lace cap. Everything had to be just so, in spite of the midwife's impatience, and the godmother always found something out of place. Then the grandmother came in, saying: "I must have a look at our bonny godmother." But she dropped a hint that the second bell had already rung and that both godfathers were already waiting in the outer parlor.

There indeed sat the two godfathers, the elder and the younger, scorning the newfangled coffee they could have any day, with the wine soup steaming in front of them, that old, traditional Bernese drink made of wine, toast, eggs, sugar, cinnamon, and saffron, that ancient spice that no christening must lack in the soup, in the stew, in the sweet tea. They smacked their lips over it, and the elder godfather, whom they called Cousin, cracked many a joke with the young father, telling him they would eat him out of house and home that day, but to judge from the wine soup he wouldn't grudge it them.

Now the godmother appeared like a bright rising sun, and the two godfathers bade her God welcome, and she was dragged to table and a huge plate of wine soup set in front of her; she was to drink it up, there was time enough while they were getting the baby ready. The poor girl warded it off with hands and feet, declaring she had had enough for many a day to come, she could hardly breathe. But it was all no good. Old and young set upon her, gravely or gaily, till she took up her spoon and, strange to say, one spoonful after the other found a bit of room somewhere.

But there was the midwife again with the baby in its fine swaddling clothes. She tied the embroidered cap with its pink silk ribbon on its head, laid it on its cushion, put its sweetened comforter in its mouth, then said she hadn't wanted anyone to be kept waiting, so she thought she would get the baby ready, then they could go when they liked.

All stood round the child, praising it duly, and indeed it was a wonderfully fine boy. The mother rejoiced in the praise, and said: "I'd have been glad to go to church and help to commit him to God. You can remember what you've promised so much better if you've been at the christening yourself. Besides, it frets me not to be able to go beyond the eaves for a whole week, just when we're so busy with the planting."

But the grandmother said they hadn't come to that yet, that her own daughter-in-law should have to go to church in the first week, and the midwife put in that she didn't at all like to see young wives going to church for the christening. They were always worriting lest something should go wrong at home, and hadn't their minds on what was going on in church, and on the way home they hurried for fear something should be forgotten, and got overheated, and many a one had taken ill of it and nearly died.

Then the godmother took the baby on its cushion in her arms, the midwife laid the fine white christening veil with

the black tassels at the corners over its face, taking care
not to brush against the nosegay on the godmother's breast,
and said: "Now go, in God's holy name." Grandmother
folded her hands and offered up a silent prayer for a blessing on them, but the young mother followed the procession
to the door, saying: "My little one, my little one! Three
whole hours without you! How shall I bear it?" And the
tears rushed into her eyes. Hastily wiping them away with
her apron, she turned back into the house.

The godmother stepped briskly down the hill and along
the road to the church with the sturdy baby in her arms,
followed by the godfather, the young husband, and the
grandfather. None thought of relieving her of her burden,
though the younger godfather wore a huge nosegay on his
hat as a sign that he was single, and there was in his eyes
something like great good will toward the godmother, all
masked, of course, by a show of complete indifference.

Grandfather told them about the terrible storm there had
been when he had been carried to church: what with hail
and lightning the churchgoers hardly thought they would
escape with their lives. Afterward people had prophesied
all manner of things on account of the storm, some a dreadful death, others that he would make his fortune at war.
And after all he had had a quiet life of it like anyone else,
and at seventy-five he would hardly die young or make his
fortune at war.

They were more than halfway when the maid came running after them who was to carry the baby home as soon
as it was christened, while the family and the rest of the
company stayed for the sermon in the good old fashion.
The maid, determined to make the best of herself that day,
had forgotten the time. She offered to take the baby, but
though the others urged her, the godmother would not give
it up. It was too good a chance to show the young godfather how strong her arms were and how much she
could carry. A proper countryman takes more pride in the
strength of his wife's arms than in useless little sticks which
the north wind can blow to bits at the first gust. A mother's
strong arms have been the saving of many a child whose

father has died, and she has had to heave the wagon of home out of all the ruts that threatened it.

Suddenly the sturdy godmother leapt backward as if somebody had tugged her plaits or clouted her over the head. She gave the baby to the maid, waited for the others to come up, and pretended to be in difficulties with her garter. Then she joined the men, interrupted their talk, and tried to distract the grandfather, now with this, now with that, from what he was saying. But as old people will, he stuck to his point and steadfastly picked up the broken thread of his talk. Then she set on the young father and tried to inveigle him into talking to her, but he was quiet and unresponsive. Perhaps he was busy with his own thoughts, as every father must be when his child is carried to its christening, especially the first son. The nearer they came to the church, the more people joined them. Some were already waiting in the road, their hymn books in their hands; others were hurrying down the narrow footpaths, and in a great procession they advanced on the village.

Next the church stood the inn, side by side as they often are in life, sharing joy and sorrow, in the good old fashion. There the company sat down, the baby was changed, and the father ordered wine, though the others protested—he shouldn't do it, they had just had all their hearts desired and needed neither bite nor sup. But once the wine was there they all fell to, especially the maid, thinking, most likely, that she had better drink wine when it was offered, for that didn't happen often the long year through.

Only the godmother resisted, in spite of endless urging, till the landlady told them they should stop, the girl was turning quite pale and a few drops of hartshorn would do her more good than wine. But the godmother wanted none of that either, could hardly be persuaded to drink a glass of plain water, but had to submit to a few drops of hartshorn on her handkerchief; innocent as she was, many a suspicious look was cast upon her and she could not help herself. For she was half dead with fear. No one had told her what the baby's name was to be, and it was an old

custom for the godmother to whisper the child's name to
the pastor as she handed it over; when there were many
children to be christened, he might easily confuse the
registered names.

In their hurry over all that had to be thought of and
their anxiety not to be late, nobody had told her the name,
and her aunt had once for all strictly forbidden her to ask,
if she didn't want to make the child unhappy for life, for
if a godmother asks the child's name it will be inquisitive
its life long.

So she didn't know the name and mustn't ask, and if the
pastor had forgotten too and were to ask her in front of
all the people, or, in his hurry, to christen the boy Anni
or Babi, all the people would laugh, and she would be put
to shame for all her life. She sat in mounting terror, her
sturdy legs quivering like bean poles in the wind and the
sweat pouring in streams from her pale face.

The landlady now came to warn them that it was time
to move if she wasn't going to be scolded by the pastor,
but to the godmother she said: "You'll never go through
with this, my girl. You're as white as a fresh-washed sheet."

It was only the hurry, declared the godmother, she'd feel
better in the fresh air. But she didn't feel better. The people in the church turned black before her eyes, and now
the baby began to scream, louder and louder. The poor
godmother rocked it in her arms, and the louder it screamed
the higher she rocked it, till the petals rained down from
the nosegay at her breast. And there was a tightness in her
throat and all the people could hear her labored breathing.
As her breast surged higher the child rocked higher, and
the higher it rocked the more thunderous grew the pastor's
prayers, till the voices re-echoed from the church walls. The
godmother no longer knew where she was, there was a
roaring in her ears like the waves of the sea and the church
began to dance round in the air with her. At last the pastor
said Amen, and now the dire moment had come, now she
would know whether she was to be a laughingstock to
children and children's children, now she had to raise the
christening veil, give the child to the pastor and whisper

its name into his right ear. In fear and trembling she raised the veil and held out the child; the pastor took it but never so much as looked at her, asked her no stern question but, dipping his hand in the water, let fall a drop on the forehead of the suddenly silent baby and christened it neither Anni nor Babi but Hans Uli, a good honest Hans Uli.

Then the godmother felt as if not only all the hills of the Emmental had fallen from her heart, but the sun, moon, and stars too, as if she had been carried from a fiery furnace into a cooling bath, but all through the sermon she trembled in every limb and could not keep still. The pastor gave a beautiful and moving sermon, all about how the life of man should really be an ascension all the time, but the godmother could not really feel moved, and by the time they left the church she had forgotten the text. She could hardly wait to tell the others about her secret terrors and the reason for her pale face. There was great laughter and many a joke about inquisitiveness, and how women fear it but all the same pass it on to their daughters, while it does no harm to the boys. So she might have asked after all.

Rustling fields of oats, pretty patches of flax, glorious growth in field and pasture, however, soon drew all eyes and occupied all minds. They found many a reason for lingering on the way. But the brilliant rising sun of May was hot, and when they reached home a glass of cooling wine did them all good, protest as they might. Then they sat down outside the house, while busy hands worked in the kitchen and the fire set up a great crackling. The midwife was glowing like Shadrach, Meschach, and Abednego. Before eleven there was a call to dinner, but only for the servants. They were to have their dinner first, and a good one too, but the people were glad when they were out of the way, especially the farm hands.

Outside the house the talk trickled in a thin stream, but did not dry up. Before dinner the stomach thwarts the mind, though no one will admit it and all pass it off with casual remarks on whatever comes into their heads. The sun was already past noon when the midwife, her face flaming but her apron still spotless, appeared on the threshold with the welcome news that dinner was ready if everybody was there. But most of the bidden guests had not arrived, and the messengers sent to fetch them, like those in the Gospel, brought back many answers, though in this case everybody was coming, but not yet. One had workmen in, another had business on hand, the third some errand to go, but nobody was to wait; dinner was to go on. The company soon agreed, for if they were to wait for everybody, they would be sitting there at moonrise. The midwife grumbled a bit; there was nothing more vexatious than to keep everything waiting, she declared. In their hearts they all wanted to come, but didn't want to show it. And she'd have the trouble of putting everything back to keep warm and wouldn't know if there was enough and would never get done.

But although they had soon reached an agreement about the absentees, there was more trouble with those present. It took a vast amount of urging to get them into the parlor and make them sit down, for nobody wanted to be the first to do this or that. When they had at last all got settled down, the soup was brought in, a rich broth colored and spiced with saffron and so full of the fine white bread the grandmother had cut that not much liquid was to be seen. Then every head was bared, hands were folded, and a long and solemn grace was offered up to the giver of all good gifts. Only then did they take up their pewter spoons, wipe them carefully on the fine white tablecloth, and fall to on the soup, and many a compliment was paid—if there was broth like this every day nobody would want anything else. When the soup was finished the spoons were carefully wiped on the tablecloth again, the loaves were sent round, everyone cut his own slice and watched the stew in saffron gravy being brought in—a stew of brains, mutton, and pickled liver. When that had been dealt with in leisurely fashion, the beef appeared, piled high in dishes, fresh and smoked, and each took what he liked best; then there were dried beans and stewed pears and a gammon of bacon and magnificent loins of pork from three-hundredweight pigs, red and white and juicy.

All these things followed each other in slow succession,

and when a new guest arrived, everything was brought in
again from the soup on, and everyone had to begin again;
not a dish was spared them. Benz, the young father, poured
wine out of the beautiful white flagons which were richly
ornamented with crests and mottoes. Where his arms were
too short to reach, he bade others be his cupbearers, and
urged all to drink, saying over and over again: "Drink up,
that's what it's there for"; and every time the midwife
brought in a new dish he gave her another glass, so that
if she had drunk them all there might have been curious
scenes in the kitchen.

The younger godfather had to put up with a good deal
of banter for not being able to persuade the godmother to
do more justice to the wine. If he didn't do better than
that, they said, he'd never get a wife. Oh! Hans Uli didn't
want one, opined the godmother, unmarried lads these days
had other things in their heads than marrying and most of
them couldn't even afford to.

"You're right there," said Hans Uli. "Slovens as most
girls are these days make terrible spendthrift wives and
most of them think that to make a good wife all she needs
is a blue silk kerchief on her head, gloves in summer, and
embroidered slippers in winter. If you've got no cows in the
byre, things are bad, but you can change them, but if
you've got a wife who's costing you hearth and home, the
law says you've got to keep her. So a man does better for
himself if he's got other things in mind than marrying and
leaves the girls alone."

"And that's a fact," put in the elder godfather, a small
nondescript man whom they treated with great respect and
called Cousin, for he was childless and had a farm of his
own and a hundred thousand Swiss francs out at interest.
"A fact it is," he went on. "It's a poor showing the women
make today. I'm not saying there isn't one here and there
who's the pride of the home, but they're few and far between. Most of them have nought in their heads but pride
and folly. They dress like peacocks, strut about like storks,
and if they have to do an honest day's work they take to
their beds with a headache for three days after. When I

went courting my old woman things were different. You didn't have to worry about getting a fool or a fury instead of a good manager."

"Nay, nay, Godfather Uli," said the godmother, who had been struggling to get a word in edgeways for a long time past. "Anyone'd think there'd been no good farmer's daughters since your time. You don't know the girls, and that's right and proper for an old man, but there's as good girls now as when you went courting. Self-praise is no recommendation, but Father's often said that if I go on as I'm going I'll be as good a housewife as my mother that's dead, God rest her soul, and she was a rare housewife. Father never took such fat pigs to market as he did last year, and the butcher often said he'd like to see the lass that fattened those pigs. But there'd be plenty to say about the young men nowadays—what in Heaven's name is the matter with them? Smoking, sitting in the sun with their hats on the side of their heads and staring like the town gates of Berne, and skittles and shooting and running after the wenches— that's about all they can do. But if they've got to milk a cow or plow a field they're done for, and with a tool in their hands they're as clumsy as a gentleman or a clerk. Often enough I've sworn I'll never take a husband till I know for certain how I'd get on with him, and even if one here and there does turn out to be a good farmer, you never can tell if he'll turn out a good husband."

The others laughed, the girl blushed, they chaffed her without mercy. How long would a man have to be on trial before she knew for certain he'd be a good husband?

And so, with laughter and joking, they put away a good deal of the meat, until the elder godfather said it seemed to him they'd had enough for the present, they should stretch their legs a bit, and a pipe never tasted so well as on top of meat. This advice was received with general applause, though the young wife and husband begged them again and again not to go. Once they'd gone there'd be no getting them back.

"Don't you trouble, Cousin," said the elder godfather. "Put something good on the table and you'll soon see us back and if we stretch our legs a bit we'll be handier at the eating after."

Then the men made the round of the stables, had a look into the hayloft to see if there was any old hay lying about, praised the fine grass, and looked up into the trees to see what kind of fruit crop they could hope for.

Under one of the trees which was still in bloom the cousin called a halt, saying that this was the best place for a rest and a pipe, it was cool, and when the women had got something tasty ready they wouldn't have far to go.

Soon they were joined by the godmother and the other women, who had inspected the garden and the vegetables. One after another they sat down in the grass, carefully lifting the hems of their gay jackets, but exposing their bright red petticoats to stains from the lush grass.

The tree round which the company had settled stood above the house just where the gentle slope began. In the foreground was the new house; beyond, the view spread to the other side of the valley, over many a fine rich farmstead and yet farther to green hills and other dark valleys.

" 'Tis a fine house you've got here, and everything shipshape," said the cousin. "And now you can live with room for all of you. I never could tell how you could live in that poor old house when you'd money and wood enough to build a new one like this."

"Nay," returned the grandfather. "There's none too much of either and building's a bad thing. You know where you start but you never know where you'll stop, and now one thing stood in the way and now another."

"It's a wonderful house to my thinking," said one of the women. "We should have had a new one this long while, but we're afraid of the cost. As soon as my man's here he'll take a good look at this one. If I had one like it I'd think myself in Heaven. But there's one thing I'd like to know, and no offense meant in asking. What's that old black window post doing there next to the new one? It spoils the whole look of the house."

Grandfather looked very grave and puffed away still more vigorously at his pipe, then said there wasn't enough wood for the building, they'd had nothing else at hand, and in their haste they'd taken some wood from the old house.

"But look," said the woman, "that black window post was too short; you've had to piece it together above and below, and any neighbor'd have given you a new post."

"Well we just didn't think of it and we couldn't go on plaguing the neighbors, they'd helped us enough as it was with wood and the loan of their carts."

"Come, come, Granddad," said the cousin. "Don't beat about the bush. Tell the whole story just as it was. I've heard plenty of talk and never could get to the bottom of it. And now it'd be the very thing to while away the time till the womenfolk have the roast ready. So out with it!"

Grandfather took a deal of persuading, but the cousin and the women gave him no peace till he promised, though with a warning that what he told should be kept among themselves and go no further. Things like that set a lot of people against a house, and he wouldn't like to do ill by his own folk at his age.

Whenever I look at that post, began the venerable old man, I can't help wondering how it happened that men came from far away in the East, where the human race is said to have come into being, and found this nook here in this narrow valley, and I think how much those who found their way or sought refuge here must have suffered and who they can have been. I've asked and asked again, but never could find out anything but that there were men in these parts in very early times, indeed that Sumiswald was a township before our Saviour was born, though that's written down nowhere. But one thing we do know, and that's that the castle which used to stand where our hospital is was there six hundred years ago, that most likely there was a house here too at that time, which belonged to the castle along with most of the neighborhood, and had to pay tithes and rent to the castle, and do labor for it. Indeed, the men were serfs and not men in their own right, as every man is these days when he comes of age. Very different were the lives of men at that time, and side by side there lived serfs who made a fine living and others who were sorely, maybe unbearably oppressed and went in fear of their lives. It all depended on their overlords; they could do as they liked with the men, while the men had no one they could complain to without fear or with any hope of redress. It's said that the serfs who belonged to this castle were worse off at times than most of the others. The other castles mostly belonged to a single family and were handed down from father to son; the lord and his men knew each other in their boyhood and many a lord was a father to his serfs. But in early days this castle came into the hands of knights called the Teutons, and the lord who commanded here was called the Comthur. Now these overlords changed from time to time. Once there would be a Swabian, the next time a Saxon, and no love could grow up and each brought his own ways with him from his own country.

Their real business was to fight the heathen in Poland and Prussia, and although they were really spiritual knights, they lived more in heathen fashion and treated their serfs as if there were no God in Heaven, and when they came back to live here carried on as if they were still in heathen lands. Those who preferred a life of ease to fighting bloody battles, and those who had wounds to heal or needed to restore their strength were sent to the estates which the Teutonic Order, for that was the name given to the company of knights, possessed in Germany and Switzerland, and each one of them went his own way and did as he pleased. One of the worst of them, they say, was called Hans von Stoffeln, and it was under him that there happened what you want to know, and has been handed down in our family from father to son.

It came into this Hans von Stoffeln's head to build a great castle up there on Bärhegen Hill, where even today, when a storm is brewing, you can see the castle demons sunning their treasures. Generally the knights built their castles overlooking the roads, just as innkeepers do today, and both so as to make it easier to rob passers-by, though in a different way. But why the knight wanted a castle up there

on that wild ugly hill in the wilderness we don't know. Anyway, he wanted it and the peasants who belonged to the
castle had to build it. The knight never troubled his head
about any work the season required, whether haymaking,
or harvest, or sowing. So many loads must be carried, so
many hands must work, at such and such a time the last
tile must be on the roof and the last nail driven home. And
he would not let them off a single sheaf of tithes corn, not
a doit of rent, not a carnival hen, nor even a carnival egg.
There was no mercy in him; and he knew nought of the
needs of poor men. In his heathen fashion he drove them
on with blows and curses, and when one was tired, slackened in his work or sat down to rest, the bailiff was after
him with the whip, and neither age nor weakness was
spared. When the savage knights were up there they loved
to hear the whip crack, and they plagued the laborers in
many other ways too. If they could double their labor for
pure sport, they did so with a will, and then made merry
over the serfs' sweat and toil.

At last the castle was finished; five ells thick were the
walls, nobody knew why it was up there, but the peasants
were glad it was standing at last where it had to stand
and that the last nail had been driven in and the last tile
was on the roof.

They wiped the sweat from their brows and looked round
their own fields with heavy hearts, sighing to see how far
behind the accursed building had put them. But a long
summer lay before them, God was above them, and they
took heart and laid strong hands to the plow, speaking comfort to their wives and children who had so nearly starved
and now saw only fresh torment in work.

But hardly was the first furrow driven when a message
came that all the serfs were to appear at a certain time
in the castle at Sumiswald. They trembled and hoped.
True, they had never known kindness, but only hard and
bitter cruelty from the present inmates of the castle, but
it seemed to them only right that their lords should do something to reward their terrible labors, and because they
thought so, many a one thought that the knights must think

so too, and make them some present, or promise some respite that evening.

They arrived at the castle in good time and with beating hearts, but were kept waiting a long time in the courtyard, a laughingstock to the castle servants. These men had been in heathen lands too. Besides, it was most likely the same then as now, when any half-baked squire thinks he has the right to mock and despise the old farmers who have tilled the soil for centuries.

At last they were summoned to the banqueting hall. The heavy door opened before them. Inside, round the huge ash table, sat the swarthy knights, their savage dogs at their feet, and at the head of the table sat Stoffeln, a big fierce man with a head like a double quart pot, eyes like plow wheels, and a beard like an old lion's mane. None of the men wanted to be the first to go in, and everyone pushed his neighbor. Then the knights laughed till the wine splashed out of the tankards and the dogs dashed out in fury, for when dogs see trembling legs, they scent good quarry. The men's hearts sank, they wished themselves back home again, and each tried to hide behind his neighbor. When silence had at last been restored among the dogs and the knights, Stoffeln spoke, and his voice was like the roaring of a century-old oak.

"My castle is built, but one thing is lacking. Summer is coming and there is no shady walk up there. Within a month you must plant one for me. Take a hundred full-grown beeches from the Münneberg with boughs and roots and plant them on Bärhegen Hill, and if a single beech is lacking you shall pay for it with land and limb. There is food and drink for you below, but see to it that the first beech is standing on Bärhegen Hill tomorrow."

One of the peasants, hearing the words food and drink, thought the knight was in gracious mood and good humor, and began to speak of the work they had to do, and of their hungry wives and children, and of winter when the thing would be easier to do. Then the knight's head swelled up high with rage, and his voice bellowed out of it like thunder echoing from a mountain wall, telling them that he only had to show them a little kindness and they must needs turn stubborn. In Poland, if a man had his bare life he would kiss your feet for it, and here they had children and cattle, house and home, and were not content.

"But you shall learn to obey and quit your fat living, and if the beeches are not standing up beyond in a month, you shall be whipped till there is not a finger's breadth whole on you and your wives and children shall be thrown to the dogs."

Then none dared to say another word, neither did anyone touch the food and drink. Once the furious command had been given, they crowded out of the door, each trying to get out first, and the knight's thundering voice, the laughter of his fellows, the jeering of the servants, and the snarling of the dogs followed them far on their way.

When a turn in the road hid them from the castle, they sat down and wept bitterly. None could find a word of comfort for the other, none had even the heart to feel a righteous anger, for want and torment had quenched their courage till there was no room in their hearts for anger, but only for grief. Three hours' distance they would have to cart the beeches, with boughs and roots, over rough ways and up the steep hill, while close by the hill fine beeches grew in plenty, yet they must not touch them. Within a month the work was to be done, on two days three beeches, the third day four, to be dragged through the long valley and up the steep hill by their weary beasts. And above all it was May month, when the farmer must be at work in his fields from morning till night, must hardly leave them if he wants bread and food for the winter.

As they sat there helplessly weeping, none daring to look at the other and see his grief because each was drowning in his own, and none daring to go home with the tidings, none daring to carry his trouble home to wife and child, there suddenly appeared before them—they did not know from where—a green huntsman, tall and lean. A red feather waved on his jaunty cap, a little red beard flamed in his swarthy face, and between his arched nose and pointed chin, almost invisible, like a cave under overhanging rocks, a mouth opened to say:

"What's your trouble, goodmen all, that you sit there howling till the stones burst out of the earth and the boughs from off the trees?"

Twice he asked the question and twice no answer came.

Then the Green Man's swarthy face grew blacker still, his red beard redder till it seemed to crackle and sparkle like fire in pine logs, his mouth pursed up as sharp as an arrowhead, then it opened again to ask quite graciously and mildly:

"But, goodmen all, what good is it to sit there howling? You can howl a new flood down or burst the stars out of the sky, but little will it help you. When a man who means well by you and might help you in your trouble asks you what it is, it would be better to speak sense than to howl. It would help you far more."

Then an old man shook his white head and said:

"We mean no offense, but no green huntsman can relieve our trouble, and when the heart is swollen with grief, no words can rise from it."

Then the Green Man shook his head and said:

"There's truth in what you say, father, but that's not the way of it. You can beat what you will, stone or tree, it complains. And a man should complain too, tell all his trouble, tell it to the first man he meets, for maybe the first man he meets can help him. I am but a plain huntsman, but who knows if I haven't a stout team of horses at home to cart wood and stones or beeches and firs."

When the poor peasants heard the word team, it dropped into every heart, turning to a spark of hope, and all eyes were fixed on the Green Man, and the old man's tongue was loosened. It wasn't always best, he said, to tell the first man you met the trouble in your heart, but since they could see that he meant well by them and maybe could help, they would hide nothing from him. For two years they had had troublous times with the building of the new castle, and not a home in the domain but was sadly in want. And just when they had taken fresh heart, thinking their hands were free at last for their own work, the Comthur had commanded them to plant beside his castle an avenue of beeches from the Münneberg, and all in a month. How they were to do it with their worn-out beasts they did not know, and even if they did, what good would it be? They could sow nothing and must die of hunger if the work did not kill them first. And they dared not carry the tidings home and bring fresh trouble on top of the old.

Then the Green Man looked very compassionate, shook a long thin dark hand at the castle, and swore dire revenge for such tyranny. But he was ready to help them. His team, and there was not its like in the world, would cart all the beeches from the church hill on this side of Sumiswald— as many as they could bring—up to Bärhegen, for love of them and in defiance of the knights, and all for a small reward.

All the men pricked up their ears at this unexpected offer. If they could come to an agreement about the pay, they were saved, for they could cart the beeches to the church hill without delaying their work in the fields and so perishing. So the old man said: "Then name your reward and we'll make a bargain of it."

A sly look came into the Green Man's face, his beard crackled, and his eyes glittered at them like the eyes of snakes, and a grisly smile curled the corners of his lips as he parted them to say:

"I told you, it's little that I ask for, just an unbaptized child."

The word flashed through the men like lightning, the scales fell from their eyes and they scattered like chaff in the wind.

Then the Green Man laughed aloud till the fish hid in the waters, and the birds sought the thickets, while his little red beard wagged up and down.

"Take counsel among yourselves, or ask it from your womenfolk. The third night from now you'll find me here," he called to them as they fled, in a sharp ringing voice which made his words stick in their ears like barbed arrows in the flesh.

Pale, trembling in heart and limb, the men rushed home.
None looked round for the others. They would not have
turned their heads for all the riches in the world. When
the men came hurrying home in their plight like doves
frightened from the dovecote by a hawk, terror entered
every home, and all feared to hear the tidings which had
turned the men's knees to water.

Agog with curiosity, the women crept after the men until they had got them in some quiet spot where they could
speak undisturbed. Then every man had to tell his wife
what had been spoken in the castle, and the women listened
with rage and curses. Then the men had to tell who had
met them and the offer he had made. A nameless dread
seized the women, a cry of woe rose over hill and dale,
and every woman felt as if it were her child that must be
given to the being who knew no mercy.

Only one woman did not lament with the others. She was
a terrible valiant woman; they say she came from Lindau
and lived on this farm. She had fierce black eyes and feared
neither God nor man. She had already fired up because the
men hadn't simply refused to obey the knight's command.
If she'd been there she'd have spoken her mind to him, she
said. When she heard of the Green Man and his offer, and
how the men had fled before him, she raged and upbraided
the men for their cowardice and for not standing up to the
Green Man more boldly. Perhaps he would have been satisfied with some other reward, and since the work was for
the castle, it'd do no harm to their souls if the Devil did
it. She raged to the very depths of her soul that she hadn't
been there, if only to see the Devil and find out what he
looked like. And so this woman shed never a tear, but in
her anger spoke bitter words against her husband and all
the other men.

The next day, when the lamentation had died down into
quiet weeping, the men sat together, seeking counsel and
finding none. First they thought of a fresh petition to the
knight, but none was willing to carry it, for none held life
or limb cheap. One said they should send the women,
weeping and wailing, but he soon fell silent when the

women began to speak, for even in those days, when the
men sat in council, the women were not far off. In the end
they could see no way but to obey in the name of God,
to have masses said to obtain God's help; they would ask
neighbors to help in secret and at night, for their lords
would never suffer it by day. They would divide into two
companies, one working with the beeches, the other sowing
the oats and tending the cattle. In this way they hoped,
with God's help, to cart at least three beeches a day up to
Bärhegen Hill. Not a word was said about the Green Man.
Whether any man thought of him is not written.

So they divided into two companies, made their tools
ready, and at sunrise on May Day they assembled on the
Münneberg and set to work with a quiet courage. A wide
trench was dug round each beech, sparing the roots, and
the trees were carefully lowered to the ground so as to take
no harm. Morning was not yet high in the sky when three
lay ready to go, for they were to be carted three by three,
so that all the men could help on the hard road with their
work and their oxen. But the sun rose to noon, and they
still had not left the wood with the three beeches. It had
sunk behind the mountains, and the teams were not yet
beyond Sumiswald, and not till the new day had dawned
did they reach the foot of the castle hill on which the
beeches were to be planted. The stars in their courses
seemed to fight against them. Disaster followed disaster;
traces snapped, axles broke, horses and oxen stumbled or
turned stubborn. The next day was worse. Fresh troubles
brought fresh work, the poor creatures panted in unremitting toil, yet not a single beech stood on the hill, nor was
the fourth carted beyond Sumiswald.

Stoffeln raged and cursed; the more he raged and cursed,
the heavier grew their hearts and the more stubborn their
beasts. The other knights mocked and jeered and took their
pleasure in the peasants' struggles and Stoffeln's fury. They
had laughed at his new castle on the bare hilltop. He had
sworn that within a month a shady walk should stand
there. So the knights laughed and the peasants wept.

A terrible discouragement overcame them. Not a cart

was whole, not a team unharmed; in two days they had not brought three beeches to their place and all their strength was gone.

Night had fallen, black clouds were rising, the first lightning of the year was flashing. The men sat down by the wayside at the very turn in the road where they had sat three days before, though they did not know it. There sat the farmer of Hornbach, the Lindau woman's husband, with two farm hands, and others sat beside them. They were waiting for the beeches which were to come from Sumiswald, and they took time there to brood over their misery and give their aching limbs a rest.

Suddenly, with a noise like the whistling of the wind, a woman approached with a basket on her head. It was Christine, the Hornbach farmer's wife. He had come by her when he had followed his overlord to the wars. She was not the kind of woman to take pleasure in staying at home, going quietly about her work and caring only for her house and children. Christine had to know all that was going on, and where she had no say in a matter, it must go wrong, or so she thought.

Therefore she had not sent a maid with the food, but had loaded the heavy basket onto her own head, and had sought the men for a long time in vain. When she found them, she upbraided them bitterly. But she did not stand idle; she could talk and work at the same time. She set down her basket, took the lid off the porridge pail, set the bread and cheese out, stuck a spoon in the porridge opposite each man and each farm hand, and bade even those who had nothing to eat to join in. Then she asked about the day's work and what had been done these two days. But the men had lost both their hunger and their desire to speak, and none took up his spoon nor did any give her an answer. Only one lad, who did not care whether it rained or shone at harvest time if only the year went round and wage day came and there was food on the table at mealtimes, took up his spoon and told Christine that not a beech was planted—it seemed as if the Devil was in it.

Then Christine said it was all idle fancy, and the men

were no more good than women in childbed. Not a beech would be carted up to Bärhegen with working and weeping, with sitting and wailing. It would serve them all right if the knight vented his rage on them, but for their wives' and children's sakes they must set about it in another fashion. Then over the woman's shoulder there came a long, swarthy hand and a shrill voice cried: "She has spoken well." And there among them stood the Green Man, grinning, with the feather waving on his cap. Then fear drove the men away; they scattered down the hill like chaff in a whirlwind.

But Christine could not flee, for now she was to know what it means to face the Devil himself. She stood rooted to the spot, her eyes fixed on the red feather on his cap and on the red beard merrily wagging in his swarthy face. He sent a shrill laugh after the men, but on Christine he bent a loving look and took her hand graciously. Christine tried to pull it away, but she could no longer escape the Green Man; it was as if her flesh were hissing between red-hot tongs. Then he began to speak courteously to her, and as he spoke his little red beard wagged with desire. Not for a long time had he seen so fine a woman, he said; his heart was laughing within him. Besides, he liked a bold woman, and above all, he liked women who stood their ground when the men ran away.

And as he spoke, he seemed less terrible to Christine. This was a man you could talk to, she thought, and she didn't see why she should run away—she had seen far uglier men in her day. More and more she came to feel that this was a man you could drive a bargain with, and if she set about it the right way, he would do her a favor after all, or she might outwit him, as she had outwitted the other men. But the Green Man went on to say that he couldn't understand why they were all so terrified of him; he meant well by all men, and if they treated him so scurvily, they could hardly wonder if he refused to do what they wanted.

Then Christine plucked up courage and said that he frightened people out of their wits. Why had he asked for an unbaptized child? He might have asked for something else; it looked so suspicious. After all, a child was a human being and no Christian would hand one over unbaptized.

"That's the reward I'm used to nor will I stir a finger for any other. Who troubles about a child that knows nobody? It's just when they're young that people are most willing to give them away, before they've had any joy of them or trouble with them. But the younger they are, the better they suit me, and the earlier I can set about bringing up a child in my own way the more I can do with it. But I need no baptism and I'll have none either."

Then Christine knew that he would not be put off with any other reward, and it came home to her that this was a man who could not be tricked.

So she said that if a man wanted to earn a reward, he must be content with what could be given him, and at the moment there wasn't a single unbaptized child in any home, and none expected within a month, and by that time the beeches had to be planted. Then the Green Man said, with a most polite wag of his head:

"I'm not asking for a child in advance. As soon as I have the promise of the first one to be born, unbaptized, I shall be content."

Christine was highly delighted. She knew that no child was to be born in her lord's domain for a long time to come. Once the Green Man had kept his promise and the beeches were planted, they need give him nothing, neither a child nor anything else. They could have masses said and laugh at the Green Man boldly, or at any rate she thought so. So she thanked him heartily for his good offer, said it was worth thinking over and she would see what the men had to say.

"Gently there," said the Green Man. "The time for thinking and talking is over. I told you to be here today, and now I want my answer. I've got plenty to do elsewhere—I'm not here only for you. Yea or nay I must have, then I want to hear no more about the whole matter."

Christine tried to put him off, for she was unwilling to take everything on herself. She even made as if to caress him in order to gain time. But the Green Man was not in the mood and made no move. "Now or never," he said. As soon as the bargain for the child was struck, he would carry as many beeches up to Bärhegen as the men would bring to the bottom of the hill before midnight. He would wait for them there.

"And now, my beauty, no more shilly-shallying," he said, patting her cheek kindly. Her heart beat fast, and she would have been glad of the men to push in front of her and take the blame. But time was passing, there was no man there to be the scapegoat, and she still believed she was more cunning than the Green Man and would find a way to outwit him after all.

So she said that as far as she was concerned she would agree, but if, later on, the men would not, she couldn't help it and hoped she wouldn't have to pay for it. But the Green Man said that he was quite satisfied with her promise to do what she could. Then Christine shuddered, soul and body, for now, she thought, the dreadful moment had come when she would have to sign the pact with the Green Man in her own blood. But he made it easy for her and said he never asked a handsome woman to sign. A kiss was all he wanted. And therewith he pursed up his lips against Christine's face, and again she could not flee and again she stood rooted to the spot.

Then the sharp mouth touched her face, and it seemed to her as if the heat from a red-hot spit were pouring through her veins, and yellow lightning flashed between them, showing Christine the Green Man's face in a devilish grin, and thunder rolled over her as if Heaven had burst.

The Green Man had vanished, and Christine still stood there as if turned to stone, as if her feet had struck roots deep in the earth at that dreadful moment. At last the use of her limbs came back to her, but there was a roaring in her head as if a mighty river were plunging overtowering black rocks into a black gulf beneath. And just as we cannot hear our own voices in the thunder of the waters, Christine could not hear her own thoughts through the din in her soul.

She fled down the hill, and where the Green Man's lips

had touched her, there was a fire which grew. She rubbed, she washed, but the fire would not die down.

It was a wild night. The storm raged and howled in the heavens and in the valleys as if the demons of night were holding their wedding in the black clouds, the winds playing savage tunes to their dancing, with lightning for marriage torches and thunder for the marriage blessing. Never had such a night been seen at that season.

In the dark valley, the men were crowding round a large house, many taking shelter under its spreading roof. As a rule, fear for his own cattle drives the countryman under his own roof in a storm, and as long as the storm rages in Heaven, he watches over his own house. But now the need of all was greater than the fear of the storm, and that was what had brought them to this house, which was on the way both for those who had been driven from the Münneberg by the storm and for those who had fled from Bärhegen. Forgetting the terrors of the night in their own wretchedness, they loudly lamented their evil plight, and nature's rage merely swelled their own misery. Horses and oxen had shied in terror, had kicked the carts to pieces and fallen down precipices, and many a wounded man was groaning in his pain, and loud were the cries of those whose torn limbs were being set and bound.

Into this misery there rushed, in deadly fear, those who had seen the Green Man, and trembling they told how he had come again. Trembling the crowd listened, came huddling out of the dark corners of the room to the fire where the men were sitting, and when the wind roared through the rafters, or thunder rolled over the house, a cry went up and the people seemed to see the Green Man breaking through the roof into their presence. But when no Green Man came, when the dread of him waned, when the old misery remained and the groans of the sufferers rose again, there slowly entered into their minds the thoughts that can so easily cost a man his soul. They began to reckon how much more worth they were than one unbaptized child, forgetting that the guilt of one soul's destruction weighs far heavier than the saving of thousands and thousands of human lives.

Slowly these thoughts found a voice, and began to mingle, in words that all could understand, in the groans of the wounded. The people began to ask about the Green Man, complained that he had not been given a better answer. He had made away with nobody, and the less they feared him, the less harm he could do them. If their hearts had been in the right place they might have helped the whole valley. Then the men began to make excuses. They did not say that there is no tricking the Devil, and that whoever gives him an inch must soon give him an ell, but they spoke of the Green Man's fearful shape, of his flaming beard and the fiery feather on his cap, and of the frightful smell of sulphur that had robbed them of their senses. But Christine's husband, who always turned to his wife for support, said they should ask her, she could tell them whether anyone could have borne it, for she was a bold woman and everybody knew it.

Then they all turned to look for Christine, but she was nowhere to be seen. Every single one of the men had thought only of his own safety, and not of the others', and once he was safe, imagined the others must be safe too. Only now did they realize that Christine had not been seen since that ghastly moment and had not come into the house. Then her husband began to complain, and the others with him, for now it seemed to all as if Christine alone could help.

Suddenly the door opened and there was Christine in their midst; her hair was streaming, her cheeks blazing, and her eyes glowing darker than ever in unholy fire. She was bidden welcome with unwonted kindness, and every man tried to tell her what he had thought and how great had been his fear for her. But Christine soon saw through it all, and, in order to conceal the fire within her, taunted them bitterly for taking to their heels and having no thought for a poor woman, nor so much as casting a look behind them to see what the Green Man was doing to her. Then the storm of curiosity broke, and everyone wanted to be the first to hear what the Green Man had done to her, and those at the back stood up to hear and see better the woman who had been so close to the Green Man. By rights, Christine went on, she should hold her tongue, they didn't deserve anything from her, they had made her life a burden to her here in the valley because she came from foreign parts, and the women had given her a bad name, and the men had never stood up for her, and if she weren't better and braver than them all there'd be no comfort and no hope for them. For a long time she went on, calling the women hard names because they wouldn't believe her when she said that Lake Constance was bigger than the castle fish pond, and the more they begged the harder she seemed to grow, and again and again she told them that it was no use talking, they'd only take it ill, whatever she said, and if things turned out well, small thanks she'd get for it, and if they turned out badly, she'd get all the blame to bear.

When at last the whole assembly was almost on its knees before Christine, and the groans and prayers of the wounded came to swell the prayers of the others, she seemed to be mollified and began to tell how she had stood her ground and made a pact with the Green Man, but she said nothing about the kiss, nor of the burning in her face nor the roaring in her mind. But she told them what she had planned in her own crafty thoughts. The beeches had to be carted up to Bärhegen, that was the first thing. Once they were up there, the men would have plenty of time to see what was to be done next, for what really mattered was that, as far as she knew, no child was to be born among them till then.

Many a man's flesh crept as she spoke, but they were all glad to think that there was plenty of time for them to decide what was to be done later.

But one poor young woman wept so bitterly that they could have washed their hands at her eyes, though she said nothing. Then an old and venerable woman, tall of stature and with a face to bow to or flee from, stepped into the midst of them and spoke: to do this would be to forget

God, to stake the sure on the unsure, to play with eternal
life. The man who parleys with the Evil One will never be
rid of him, and to give him a finger means to give him the
whole body. Nobody could help them out of their plight
but God, but the man who abandoned God in his time of
troubles would drown in his troubles. But this time they
scorned the old woman's words, and bade the young one
cease her weeping; howling and crying would help nobody.
What they needed was help of another kind.

They soon agreed to try the plan. Even at the worst, no
great harm could come to them. It wasn't the first time that
men had tricked the most evil of spirits, and if there was
no other way out, the priest would give them counsel. But
in the dark depths of his heart many a man thought, as he
confessed later, that he would risk little money or trouble
to save an unbaptized child.

At the moment when they made up their minds to take
Christine's advice, it was as if all the whirlwinds had broken
loose over their heads, as if the ranks of the wild huntsmen
were galloping past. The pillars of the house quivered, the
rafters bent, and trees were splintered against the house like
spears against a knight's armor. Inside the house, the people turned pale and fear entered into them, but they did
not give up their plan. In the gray of dawn they put it into
action. The morning was clear and bright, the storm and
devilry were past, the axes struck deep, the soil was light
and free, every beech fell just as it should, not a trace broke,
the animals were strong and willing and the men protected
from all mishaps as if by an invisible hand.

There was only one strange thing about it all. Below
Sumiswald no road led into the valley at that time. It was
all swamp watered by the wild river. They had to ride up
through the village and past the church. In the same way
as on the other days, they drove three teams at a time so
that they could stand by each other with advice, strength,
and beasts. All they had to do was to ride through Sumiswald, and down the church hill outside the village where
a little chapel stood. But as soon as they were up the hill
and on the flat road leading to the church, the weight of

the carts did not ease off. It grew heavier and heavier, they had to bring fresh horses and oxen, as many as they had, and lash them without mercy, or even lay hold of the spokes themselves, and even the quietest horses shied as if an invisible presence from the churchyard stood in their way, and the muffled toll of a bell, almost like a wandering death knell, rang from the church, a nameless dread overcame even the strongest of them, and every time the men and beasts reached the church, they trembled. Once past the church, they could drive on in peace, unload in peace, and return in peace for a fresh load.

That day they unloaded six beeches side by side at the appointed place, and in the early morning six beeches stood on Bärhegen Hill, and throughout the valley no one had heard the creaking of an axle on its hub, nor the shouting of carters, nor the steady lowing of oxen. But six beeches were standing there for all to see, and they were the beeches the men had unloaded at the bottom of the hill, and no others.

Then there was great wondering in the valley, and many a one was agog to know how it had happened. Above all, the knights were curious to know what bargain the peasants had made and how the beeches had been brought to their place. They tried, with their heathen ways, to squeeze the truth out of the peasants, who they soon saw knew nothing themselves and were half terrified. Besides, Stoffeln forbade them to go on. He was not merely indifferent as to how the beeches had come to Bärhegen. On the contrary, if only they were there, he was glad if he could spare the peasants. He knew quite well that his knights' taunts had tempted him into folly, for if the peasants perished and there was no one to work in the fields, it was the master who had to pay for it. But what Stoffeln had once said he abode by. So he was quite pleased that the peasants had found help, and cared little whether they had sold their souls for it, for what were the peasants' souls to him once death had taken their bodies? So now he laughed at the knights and shielded the peasants from their mockery. All the same, the knights wanted to find out what was behind it all; they sent out squires to keep watch, but they were found next day half dead in the ditches where an invisible hand had flung them.

Then two knights came up to Bärhegen; bold men they were, and whenever a deed of daring was to be done in heathen lands they had done it. In the morning they were found senseless on the ground, and when they had recovered the use of speech, they said that a red knight had ridden them down with a flaming lance. Here and there some curious woman could not resist peeping through a slit or a crack when midnight had descended on the world. But at once a poisonous wind blew on her, her face swelled, for weeks neither nose nor eyes could be seen, and her mouth hardly at all. Then the people gave up spying and not an eye looked down the valley when midnight lay over it.

One night a man felt his last hour draw near, and lay in need of extreme unction, but no one dared go for the priest. Only his son, an innocent boy, dear to God and man, in his fear for his father ran unbidden to Sumiswald. As he approached the church hill, he saw how the beeches on it rose from the ground, each carried by two fiery squirrels, and beside them he saw a green man riding a black goat, with a fiery whip in his hand, a flaming beard in his face, and on his hat a fluttering feather, glowing red. Then they rose high up in the air over all the hills and as swift as a moment of time. So much the boy saw, but no harm was done him.

Not three weeks had passed when ninety beeches stood on Bärhegen Hill, making a beautiful walk, for all flourished gloriously and not a single one withered. But the knights, and even Stoffeln himself, seldom walked there, for every time a nameless dread overcame them. They would have been best pleased to put an end to the whole thing, but no one put an end to it, and each took comfort to himself, saying: "If evil comes of it, the other will be to blame."

But with every beech that stood on Bärhegen the peasants' hearts grew lighter, for with each one their hope grew that they might please their overlord and cheat the Green Man. The Green Man had no pledge from them, and when the hundredth beech stood on the hill, who was going to trouble his head about green men at all? Yet they were not quite sure in their hearts. Every day they dreaded that he would play some trick on them and leave them in the lurch. On St. Urban's day, they brought the last beeches to the church hill, and neither old nor young slept much that night. They could hardly believe that he would finish the work without child or pledge.

Next morning, long before sunrise, young and old were afoot, all moved by the same evil curiosity, but a long time passed before they ventured to the place where the beeches had lain. Would no trap be waiting there for men who had in mind to trick the Green Man?

In the end, a wild young goatherd who had brought the cheese from the pasture took heart, ran on ahead, and found the beeches gone from the church hill and no devilry to be seen anywhere. The people were still suspicious; they sent the young herd on to Bärhegen ahead of them. There everything was as it should be; a hundred beeches stood in ranks, none had withered, and no man had a swollen face or an aching limb. Then the men's hearts leaped within them, and they mocked the Green Man and the knights. For the third time they sent out the wild young goatherd, this time to tell Stoffeln that the work on Bärhegen Hill was finished, he could come and count the beeches. But his soul shrank within him and he sent to tell them to get away home. He would have preferred to order them to clear the whole walk away, but he dared not on account of his knights. They were not to say he was afraid, yet he knew nothing of the bargain and of who might have taken a hand in it.

When the goatherd brought the tidings, the people's hearts leapt within them, the young men and women danced madly in the beech walk, fierce yodels rang from gorge to gorge, from hill to hill, echoing from the walls of the castle at Sumiswald. Grave elders warned and prayed, but hard hearts have no ears for the warnings of grave elders, yet when trouble comes, it is the elders who have brought it upon them with their fears and warnings. The time is not yet come for men to realize that it is their own hard hearts that bring the trouble. The jubilation spread over hill and dale into every home, and wherever a handsbreadth of meat still hung on the rafters, it was boiled, and wherever a spoonful of butter was still in the jar, it went on fritters.

The meat was eaten, the fritters had gone, the day had passed, and once more the sun rose over Sumiswald. Nearer and nearer came the day when a woman was to bear a child, and the nearer the day came, the greater grew their terror. The Green Man would come again, demand his due or set some trap for them.

But who shall measure the grief of the young wife whose child it was? The house was filled with her lamentations and all who lived in it were moved, but none could tell what to do, though all knew that it was folly to trust their partner to the pact. The nearer her hour came, the closer the young wife clung to God's holy Mother, not only with her arms, but with her body, soul and spirit, beseeching protection for her blessed Son's sake. And day by day she grew stronger in the faith that in life and death, in every sorrow, the greatest comfort is in God, for where He is the Demon cannot be and has no power.

Day by day she came to see more clearly that if the priest of the Lord were present at the birth with the Holy of Holies, the blessed body of the Redeemer, and armed with powerful exorcisms, no evil could come near, and the priest could at once bestow on the child the sacrament of baptism, as custom then permitted; then the poor child would be wrested forever from the danger which the foolhardiness of the fathers had brought upon it. The others began to believe it too, and the grief of the young wife went to their hearts, but they shrank from confessing their pact with Satan to the priest, and no one had been to confession since that day and no one had told him the truth. A very devout man he was; even the knights at the castle played none of their pranks on him, while he, for his part, told them the truth. Once the thing was done, the peasants had thought, no one could prevent it, yet now nobody was willing to tell him about it, their consciences knew why.

At last one of the women could bear it no longer. She went and told the priest about the pact, and what the young wife wished. The good man's soul was seized with terror, but he wasted no time in vain words. Boldly he took up the struggle with his mighty adversary for the sake of one poor soul. He was a man who feared not the most grievous battle because he looked to be crowned with the crown of eternal life, and knew that none shall be crowned who has not fought lawfully.

Round the house where the woman lay awaiting her hour he traced with holy water the circle which evil spirits dare not enter. He blessed the threshold and the whole room, and the young wife bore her child in peace and the priest baptized it unmolested. Outside all was peace, the bright stars glittered in the sky, and the breeze played softly in the trees. Some declared they had heard a neighing laughter, but the others said it was only the owls at the edge of the wood.

Then all rejoiced; fear had vanished, they thought forever. If once they had cheated the Green Man, they could do it again.

A great feast was prepared and guests bidden from far and near. In vain the priest warned them against feasting and revelry, exhorted them to tremble and pray, for the adversary was not overcome, nor was their peace made with God. He felt in his soul that it was not for him to lay penance on them, as if a huge and grievous penance were coming from God's own hand. But they would not listen, and tried to silence him with food and drink, and he went sadly away, prayed for those who did not know what they did, and armed himself with prayer and fasting to fight like a good shepherd for his flock.

Christine too sat among the revelers, but she was unwontedly silent, with her burning cheeks and gloomy eyes. There was a strange twitching to be seen in her face. As an experienced midwife she had been present at the birth and had stood godmother at the hasty christening, with pride, but no fear, in her heart. But when the priest sprinkled the child with holy water and baptized it in the three Holy Names, she felt as if a red-hot iron were being driven into the spot where the Green Man had kissed her. She had started in sudden dread, nearly dropping the child, and since then the pain had not abated, but had burned more fiercely hour by hour. At first she had sat still, stifling the pain and mutely revolving her heavy thoughts in her awakening mind, but her hand kept moving to the burning spot; it was as if a venomous wasp were sitting there, plunging its glowing sting into the very marrow of her bones. But as there was no wasp to brush away, and the smarting grew fiercer with the horror in her mind, she began to show her cheek to the people and ask if there was anything to be seen on it. But nobody could see anything, and soon nobody was willing to waste the merry time with searching her cheek. In the end she induced an old woman to look; the cock was crowing, the day dawning, when the old woman spied an almost invisible spot on Christine's cheek. It was nothing bad, she declared, it would go away again, and she went on her way.

Christine tried to take comfort; it was nothing bad, it would go away again soon, but the pain did not abate and the little spot spread until all saw it and asked what the black thing in her face was. They meant no harm, but their questions stung her to the heart, bringing back her grievous thoughts, and she could not forget that the Green Man had kissed her on that very spot, and that the fire which had flashed through her limbs like lightning now sat fast there, burning and destroying. Sleep fled from her, her food tasted like glowing embers, ceaselessly she hurried hither and thither, seeking comfort and finding none, for the pain still grew and the black spot spread and spread, dark stripes crawled out of it, and near her mouth a little swelling seemed to be rising on the spot.

So Christine suffered and roamed about for many a long day and many a long night, but she had not confided to anyone the dread in her heart nor what she had received from the Green Man on that spot. Yet if she had known how to rid herself of the pain, she would have sacrificed anything in heaven and on earth. She was by nature a bold woman, but now, in her raging pain, she was like a wild beast.

Then it came about that a woman was again with child. This time there was no great fear among the people and they were in good spirits; provided they sent for the priest in good time, they thought, they could laugh at the Green Man.

Christine alone knew better. The nearer the day of the birth came, the fiercer grew the fire in her cheek and the huger grew the black spot. Distinct legs ran out of it, short hairs grew on it, gleaming spots and stripes came out on its back, and the little swelling turned into a head which glittered venomously as if from two eyes. When the people saw the evil Spider on Christine's face they screamed aloud and fled in fear and trembling, for they saw how firm it sat on the face it had grown out of. They talked, one advised this, another that, but all were content that whatever was to come should fall on Christine, and all shunned her and fled before her whenever they could. The more they fled, the more Christine was driven to follow them; she ran from house to house. She knew only too well that the Devil was reminding her of the promised child, and in her determination to make the people speak openly of the sacrifice, she pursued them in mortal dread.

But the others cared little, Christine's anguish caused them no pain; what she suffered, they thought, she had deserved, and when they could escape her no longer, they said to her: "Now listen. Nobody promised a child, so nobody will give one."

She set furiously on her own husband. He fled like the others, and when he could escape her no longer, said coolly that it would get better; it was a mole such as many people had, and once it was full grown they could tie it at the root and it would fall off.

But the pain did not cease, every bone was like the fires of Hell, and when the woman's hour came, it seemed to Christine as if there were a wall of flame round her, as if glowing knives were burrowing in the marrow of her bones, as if fiery whirlwinds were rushing through her head. But the Spider grew, and reared, and between the bristles, malignant eyes swelled up. When Christine, in her burning anguish, found no comfort anywhere, and saw the woman in childbirth well guarded, she rushed like a madwoman along the path the priest was to take.

Striding manfully, he mounted the slope, his burly sexton by his side. Neither the hot sun nor the steep hillside could check him, for there was a soul to be saved, an eternal wrong to be righted, and, coming from a distant sickbed, he trembled lest he should come too late. In despair, Christine threw herself in his path, embraced his knees, prayed for rescue from her hell, for the sacrifice of the child who had not yet known life, and the Spider swelled yet higher and more hideous in Christine's flushed face, and glared on the priest's holy vessels with baleful eyes. But he swiftly thrust Christine aside, making the sign of the cross; he could see the enemy, but abandoned the battle to save a soul. Then Christine started up and rushed after him, straining all her strength, but the sexton's strong hand held the raving woman from the priest, and the priest was in time to protect the house and to receive in his consecrated hands the child which he committed into the hands of Him whom death could not overcome.

Outside the house Christine had fought a desperate battle. She wanted the child unbaptized in her hands, and struggled to reach it, but the hands of strong men prevented her.

Gusts of wind smote the house, pale lightning licked round it, but the hand of the Lord was upon it, the child was christened, and Christine roamed about the house in vain. A prey to yet more mortal anguish, sounds came from her such as no human throat can utter; the cattle shuddered in the byres and tore at their tethers, and the oaks in the forest rose rustling in horror.

Inside the house the people began their rejoicing over this new victory, the powerlessness of the Green Man and the vain struggles of his accomplice, but outside Christine lay on the ground in agony, and in her face pains began such as no woman in childbirth has known on this earth, and the Spider in her face swelled yet higher and burned through her bones more fiercely than ever.

Then Christine felt as if her face had burst, as if red-hot coals were being born and coming to life in it; she felt a crawling over her face, over all her limbs, as if everything in her were coming to life and crawling in fire over her body. Then, in the livid light of the lightning, she saw, long-legged, poisonous, and countless, black spiders hurrying over her limbs and away into the night, to be followed by others, long-legged, poisonous, and countless. At last no more came, the fire in her face died down, the Spider settled and shrank into an almost invisible spot, gazing with dying eyes at the infernal brood it had borne and sent forth as a sign that there was no jesting with the Green Man.

Weak as a woman in childbed, Christine crept home. Though the fire no longer burned so fiercely in her face, the fire in her heart was burning still. Though her weary limbs craved for rest, the Green Man left her no peace. That is his way with those who have once become his.

Inside the house the people rejoiced and were glad, so that a long time passed before the lowing of the cattle in the byre came to their ears. Then they started up, and some men went to see. White with terror, they came back to say that the finest cow lay dead and the others were raging and plunging as had never been seen before. Something was wrong, some strange thing was afoot. Then the revelry ceased, all hurried to the cattle whose lowing rang over hill and dale, but none knew what to do. They tried to break the spell by exorcisms, spiritual and temporal, but in vain; before day had dawned, death had laid low all the cattle in the byre. But when silence came there, the lowing rose again, now here, now there, and those who were in the house heard, by the piteous cries of the cattle for their masters in their fear, how the calamity had descended on their own byres.

The men hurried away as if their homes were on fire, but they brought no help with them. On all hands, death struck down the cattle, the cries of man and beast re-

echoed far and wide, and the sun, which set on their rejoicings, rose upon terrible woe. In the light of the risen
sun, the people saw how, in the byres where the cattle had
fallen, countless black spiders were crawling. They crawled
over the cattle and the fodder, poisoning whatever they
touched, and any beast that was still alive began to plunge
and was soon laid low in death. Once the spiders had entered a byre, it could never be rid of them; they seemed to
grow out of the ground. Nor could any byre that had not
been attacked be protected; they crawled out of the walls
and fell in heaps from the ceiling. The men drove the cattle
to pasture, but only drove them into the jaws of death.
For as soon as a cow set foot on a pasture, the earth came
to life, long black spiders sprouted up like hideous Alpine
flowers, and crawled up the cattle, and a piteous cry of
pain echoed from the mountain to the valley. And all the
spiders were as like the Spider on Christine's face as children are like their mother, and the like of them had never
been seen before.

The cries of the poor beasts were heard in the castle too,
and soon cowherds came with the news that their cattle
had died of the poison, and with growing anger Stoffeln
learned how herd after herd had been lost, learned of the
pact with the Green Man, how he had been cheated a second time, how the spiders were as like the Spider on Christine's face as children are like their mother, and how the
Lindau woman had made the pact alone with the Green
Man and never told the truth about it. Then Stoffeln rode
up the hill, grim with anger, and thundered at the poor
men that he was not going to lose herd after herd for their
sakes, that they would have to make good all he lost, whatever happened, and whatever they had done they must bear
the consequences. He was not going to suffer loss by them,
or, should he suffer, they would pay for it a thousandfold.
Such was his manner of speech to them, careless of the
burden he was laying on their shoulders, nor did he think
that it was he himself who had driven them to it; what
they had done he laid at their own doors.

Most of them had slowly come to understand that the

spiders were a pest sent by the Evil One to remind them
that the bargain must be kept; they felt too that Christine
must know more about it and had not told them of all her
dealings with the Green Man. But now they shuddered at
the thought of the Green Man, ceased mocking at him and
trembled before their temporal lord, for if they made their
peace with him, what would their spiritual lord have to
say; would he allow it and would he lay no penance on
them? In their fear, the most respected of them assembled
in a lonely barn and sent for Christine to come and tell
them openly what bargain she had really driven.

Christine came, savage and revengeful, again a prey to
the growing Spider.

She looked at them and saw their fear, saw too that none
of the women were present. Then she told them exactly
what had happened, how the Green Man had promptly
taken her at her word and, as a pledge, given her a kiss
she had paid no more attention to than any other. How
on that very spot the Spider had grown in mortal agony
from the moment the first child was born. How the Spider,
when they had christened the second child and tricked the
Green Man, had given birth in agony to a countless brood,
for he would not be fooled for nothing, and how she had
felt that in her mortal pain. And now the Spider was growing again, and the pain with it, and if the next child was
not given to the Green Man, nobody could tell how deadly
the pestilence would be and how grim the knight's revenge.

Thus Christine spoke, and the men's hearts trembled
within them, and for a long time none would speak. Then,
little by little, broken sounds came from their oppressed
breasts, and when the sounds were put together, they
meant what Christine meant, yet no single one of the men
had agreed to her advice. Only one of them stood up and
spoke briefly and to the point. The best thing, he said,
would be to kill Christine; once she was dead the Green
Man would rest content with the dead, but he would have
no more hold on the living.

Then Christine broke out into savage laughter, strode up
to him, face to face, and told him to strike. She would not

complain, but what the Green Man wanted was not her, but an unbaptized child, and the mark he had put on her he could just as well put on the hand that did her harm.

Then the man who had spoken felt his hand twitch, he sat down and listened to the others. With no man saying all, and each something which mattered little, they agreed to sacrifice the next child, but none would put his hand to it, and none carry the child to the church hill where the beeches had been laid. None feared to make use of the Devil for the good of all, but none would have dealings with him in his own person. Then Christine said she would do it, for if anyone has had to do with the Devil once, the second time cannot do much harm. They knew who was to bear the next child, but none spoke the name and the father was not there.

Having agreed, with and without words, they parted.

The young wife who had trembled and wept without knowing why that dreadful night when Christine had come back with her tale of the Green Man was now awaiting her next child. She could draw neither comfort nor confidence from what had happened. A nameless dread lay upon her heart which neither prayer nor confession could dispel. A suspicious silence seemed to surround her. Nobody spoke of the Spider now; the eyes that rested on her looked wary, and seemed to be calculating the hour when they could get possession of her child and pacify the Devil.

And so she felt lonely and helpless. There was no one to stand by her but her mother-in-law, a devout woman, but what can one old woman do against a savage crowd? She had her husband, and he had comforted her with promises, but how he complained about his cattle and how little he thought about his poor wife's fears! The priest had promised to come as quickly as he could and as soon as they sent for him, but what might happen when he was on the way? And the poor woman had no trusted messenger but her own husband, who should have been her watch and ward. Besides, she lived in the same house as Christine, their husbands were brothers. She had no kin of her own, and had come to the house an orphan. There is no telling how great was the poor woman's terror. Her only comfort was prayer with the pious mother, and that died away when she looked into the wicked eyes.

And all the time the pestilence went on, keeping fear alive. True, it was only now and then that a cow died, and the spiders were seldom to be seen. But as soon as the horror quitted one farm, as soon as anyone said that the pestilence would disappear of itself and that they should think well before sinning against a child, Christine's agony returned, the Spider in her face swelled up high, and death came upon the herd of the man who had thought or spoken. The nearer the expected hour came, the greater grew the calamity, and they saw that they must at last settle how to get possession of the child. It was the husband they feared most, yet it went against the grain to do him violence. Then Christine undertook to win him over, and she did. He was willing to shut his eyes, to do his wife's will and fetch the priest, yet not hurry on the way and ask no questions about what had happened in his absence, and so he set his conscience at rest. He would settle his account with God by masses, and perhaps something could be done for the poor child's soul. Perhaps the pious priest could win it back from the Devil, then they would be shut of the whole matter, would have done all they could and yet fooled the Evil One. So the man thought, and in any case he felt he would be guiltless, whatever happened, if he did not put his hand to it.

And so the poor wife was sacrificed and knew nothing about it, hoped in fear and trembling that she might be saved while the council of the men had pronounced her death blow, but what He above had resolved was hidden in the clouds that veil the future.

It was a thundery year and harvest time had come. All hands were at work to bring the corn into safety as long as the sun shone. It was a hot afternoon, the clouds stretched black heads over the dark mountains, the swallows fluttered anxiously round the roof, and the poor young wife, alone in the house, felt cramped and afraid, for even the old grandmother was out helping in the field, though more with

will than with deed. Then pain struck through her like a
two-edged sword, the place turned black before her eyes,
she felt her hour approach and she was alone. Fear drove
her out of the house, heavily she moved toward the distant
field; she struggled to call, but her voice died in her throat.
Beside her was her little boy, who was just learning to walk
and had never yet been to the field on his own legs. And
this little boy was the only messenger the poor woman had
at hand, not knowing if he could find the field or his little
legs carry him to it. But the staunch little lad saw his
mother's fear and ran and fell and stood up again; his lamb
ran after him, gamboling and butting, the cat ran after his
rabbits, doves and hens ran under his feet. But the boy paid
no heed, would not be stayed, and loyally delivered his
message.

Panting, the grandmother came, but the husband delayed. He had just one more load to bring in, they said. An
eternity passed, at last he came, another eternity passed, at
last he set out slowly on his way, and in mortal fear the
poor woman felt her hour approach on hurrying feet.

Christine had watched all this from the field, rejoicing.
The sun shone hot on her labors, but the Spider hardly
burnt at all, and in the next few hours her steps were light.
She worked merrily and made no haste to go home, for she
knew how slow the messenger would be. Not until the last
sheaf was loaded and gusts of wind were heralding the
coming storm did she hasten to her prey, which, she
thought, was hers this time for sure. And as she went home
she nodded meaningly to many a one she met, they nodded
back and hurried home with the tidings. Then many a knee
turned to water and many a soul strove to pray in unwilling
dread, but could not.

Inside the house, the poor wife moaned, the minutes
dragged out to eternity and the grandmother could not
soothe her anguish with prayer and consolation. True, she
had bolted the door and piled heavy furniture behind it.
As long as they were alone in the house they could bear it,
but when they heard Christine come home, heard creeping
footsteps at the door, when more and more footsteps

crowded round, with muffled whisperings, when no priest
appeared, and the moment women wait for so eagerly came
ever nearer, there is no telling the dread which closed over
the women like boiling oil as they sat there without help
and without hope. They heard Christine keeping guard at
the door. The poor young wife felt the fierce eyes of her
sister-in-law burning through her, body and soul. At last a
child's first whimpering cry came through the door, stifled
at once, but too late. With one well-prepared thrust the
door flew open, and like a tiger on its prey Christine fell
on the mother. The old woman, who had thrown herself
in the way of the onslaught, was hurled aside. In the holy
dread of motherhood the young wife dragged herself up,
but her weakened body failed her, a scream of agony broke
from her heart, then the blackness of a swoon wrapped her
round.

When Christine appeared with the child, the men shrank
back in fear. The premonition of a terrible future came to
them, but none had the courage to say nay, and the fear
of the Devil's torments overcame the fear of God. Christine
alone did not waver. Her face glowed like a victor's after
battle. The Spider seemed to caress her cheek with a soft
and pleasant itching. The lightning which forked round her
on her way to the church hill were gleams of joy, the thunder a tender growl, the revenge-snorting storm a sweet
rustling.

Hans, the poor woman's husband, had kept his promise
only too well. He had gone slowly on his way, mustering
every field at his leisure, watching every bird, waiting for
the fish to rise before the coming storm. Then again he
would start forward, mend his pace, begin to run. There
was something in him that drove him on and made the
hair rise on his head: it was his conscience, warning him
of what a father deserved who betrays his wife and child;
it was the love he still bore his wife and the fruit of her
body. But then another and stronger power held him back;
it was the fear of men, the fear of the Devil, and the love
of what the Devil could take from him. Then he would
slacken his pace again and walk as slowly as a man on his

way to execution. No man knows, when he sets out,
whether it is for the last time or no. If he did, he would
go otherwise or not at all.

And so it had grown late by the time he reached Sumiswald. Black clouds were driving over the Münneberg,
heavy drops fell hissing in the dust, and the muffled toll
of the church bell was warning men to think of God and
beseech Him not to make His thunder a judgment on them.
The priest was standing in front of his house, ready for any
call if his Lord, striding over his head, should call him to
a deathbed, a burning house, or anywhere else. When he
saw Hans coming, he knew it was a summons to a grievous
errand. He girded up his loins and sent to tell his sexton
to find someone to take his place at the bell so that they
might set out together.

Meanwhile he set wine before Hans to refresh him after
his hurried walk through the sultry air. But Hans did not
need it; the good priest knew nothing of the malice of men.
Hans refreshed himself at his leisure. The sexton came unwillingly and was glad to take the share of the wine which
Hans offered him. The priest stood waiting beside them,
disdaining to drink; he had no need of it for such an errand and such a battle. He was loath to order them away
from the flagon he had set before them, for all guests have
privileges, but he knew a law which stood above hospitality,
and anger at their sloth boiled up in him in waves.

At last he told them he was ready, an afflicted woman
was waiting with a terrible wrong hanging over her head,
and it was his duty to avert that wrong with holy weapons;
therefore they should not delay, but come. There would be
drink enough when they arrived for any whose thirst had
not been already quenched. Then Hans, the woman's husband, spoke: there was no great hurry, his wife always had
a long labor. At that moment a flash of lightning blazed
through the room, dazzling them all, and a roll of thunder
pealed over the house till every post and wall in it quivered.

Then the sexton, having said his grace, spoke:

"Hark to the weather. Heaven itself is saying what Hans
has said. We should wait. What good would it be for us to

go? We should never reach the top of the hill alive, and he himself said there was no hurry about his wife."

It is true that a thunderstorm was moving toward them such as had not often been seen in mortal memory. From every gorge and hollow it rolled, racing in on all hands, swept together by all the winds over Sumiswald, and every cloud became a host of war, and every cloud stormed the next, was out for the blood of the next, and a battle of clouds began and the storm stood still and, flash after flash, the lightning struck the earth as if to blast its way through to the other side. Relentlessly the thunder rolled, the storm howled in rage, the womb of the clouds burst, the floodgates were opened, and the priest delayed for his companions' sake. But when the cloud battle had broken out, huge and sudden, he had given the sexton no answer. He had sat down, with rising dread in his heart. He felt he must fling himself into the raging elements. Then, through the dreadful voice of the thunder, he seemed to hear the piercing scream of a woman in childbirth, the thunder became God's terrible chiding for his delay, he set out in spite of the others. Out he strode into the flaming storm, into the rage of the cloudburst, armed against whatever might come. Slowly and unwillingly the others followed.

The storm screamed and howled and raged as if it were gathering itself together for the Last Trump which heralds the end of the world, and flame fell on the village in sheaves as if to set every house on fire, but the servant of Him who gives the thunder its voice and whose servant is the lightning has nothing to fear from that fellow servant of God, and he who walks in the ways of God can safely leave the thunder to rage. Therefore the priest strode undaunted through the storm to the church hill. But there was no faith in the hearts of them that followed him, for their hearts were not where his was. They did not want to go down the church hill, not in such weather and at that hour of night, and Hans had his own reasons for not wanting to go. They begged the priest to turn back, to take other paths; Hans knew shorter ones, the sexton better ones, and Hans warned him of the swollen Green Water in the valley. But the priest would not listen and paid no heed to what they said. Driven on by a wonderful power he hastened toward the church hill on the wings of prayer; his foot struck against no stone, no lightning dazzled him. Trembling, far behind, guarded, as they thought, by the Holy of Holies in the priest's own hands, Hans and the sexton followed.

But as they left the village, where the hill drops to the valley, the priest stopped short, his hand shading his eyes. Below the chapel a red feather gleamed in the lightning and the priest's sharp eyes discerned a black head with a red feather on it rising above the green hedge. As he looked, he saw on the opposite slope a wild figure flying at full speed toward the dark head on which the red feather waved like a pennant.

Then the lust of holy battle flamed up in the priest, that lust which enters into such as have, in the presence of the Evil One, dedicated their lives to God, as growth enters into the corn seed, pierces the bud when the flower is to unfold, and inflames the hero when the enemy draws his sword. And as the hart plunges into the cooling stream and the hero into battle, the priest rushed down the hill, hurled himself into the boldest battle of all, thrust himself between the Green Man and Christine, who was laying the child in his arms, thundered the three Holy Names into the Green Man's face, and the holy water he sprinkled on the child fell on Christine too. Then the Green Man fled with a howl of pain, flashing away like a crimson streak till the earth swallowed him up. At the touch of the holy water, Christine shrank together in a rain of sparks with a horrible hiss like wool in fire, like chalk in water, shrank down to the black, huge, swollen, hideous Spider in her face, shrank with it, hissed into it, leaving the Spider on the child's very body, bursting with defiance and venom and darting evil looks at the priest. He flung holy water at it; it hissed like well water on a hot stone. The Spider swelled and swelled, stretched its black legs over the child and glared yet more venomously at the priest, who, in the holy wrath of his faith, laid hold of it with a valiant hand. It was as if he had plunged his hand into red-hot thorns, but he grasped unshakably fast, flung the creature away, snatched up the child, and hurried on to the mother.

And when his battle was over, the battle in the clouds died down and they hurried back to their gloomy chambers. Where but a short time before the fiercest fight had raged, the valley now lay glimmering in the quiet starlight, and, almost at the end of his breath, the priest reached the house where the unholy deed had been wrought on mother and child.

There the mother still lay senseless; her senses had left her with her wild scream. Beside her the old woman sat praying. She trusted in God to be stronger than the Devil was evil. With the child, the priest restored the mother to life. When, awaking, she saw her child again, a warmth streamed through her such as only the angels in Heaven can feel, and in her arms the priest baptized the child in the name of the Father, Son, and Holy Ghost. And now it was wrested from the power of the Devil till it would yield itself up to him of its own free will. But God guarded it from that, while its body was poisoned by the Spider.

Soon its soul took flight again, and the little body was branded as if with fire. The poor mother wept indeed, but when each part returns to its appointed place, the soul to God, the body to earth, comfort will come, sooner to one, later to another.

As soon as the priest had performed his holy office, he felt a strange itching in the hand and arm which had hurled away the Spider. His hand came out in little black spots; they spread and swelled under his very eyes, and the fear of death trickled through his heart. He blessed the women and hurried home. Like a faithful soldier, he wished to restore his holy weapons to their proper place so that they should stand ready to the hand of his successor. His arm swelled high, black boils swelled yet higher on it, he struggled with the weariness of death but did not yield.

When he reached the church hill, he saw Hans, the God-forsaking father, whose fate no one had known, lying on his back across the path. His face was swollen and black with burning and on it there sat, bloated, black, and grisly, the Spider. When the priest approached it blew itself up, the hairs on its back bristled venomously, and its eyes glared and flashed poison; it might have been a cat gathering itself together to spring in its archenemy's face. Then the priest pronounced holy words and raised his holy weapons, and the Spider shrank away, crawled long-legged from the blackened face and was lost in the hissing grass.

Then at last the priest went home, and set the Holy of Holies in its place, and while fierce pains racked his body, his soul awaited in sweetest peace its God, for whom it had fought a good fight in God's holy warfare, and God did not keep it waiting long.

But the sweet peace which waits patiently upon the Lord was to be found neither below in the valley nor up in the mountains.

From the moment when Christine had rushed down the hill with the child to meet the Devil, a terrible dread had overcome all hearts. As the huge storm raged, the people shuddered in the fear of death, for in their hearts they knew only too well that, if God's destroying hand was upon them, they had more than deserved it. When the storm had passed, the tidings spread from house to house of how the priest had brought back the child, but neither Hans nor Christine had been seen.

When the gray of dawn came, it rested on livid faces, and the radiant sun restored no color to them, for all knew that the greatest horror was yet to come. Then they heard that the priest lay dead with black boils; Hans was found, his face distorted; and strange, confused tidings were spread of the Spider which was Christine.

It was a fine harvest day, but no man lifted his hand to work; the people gathered in knots, as they do on the morrow of some great disaster. Now in truth they felt in their shuddering souls what they had done in striving to buy themselves free of earthly pain and toil at the cost of an immortal soul, felt that there was a God in Heaven who took fearful vengeance for all wrong done to poor defenseless children. So they gathered together and stood lamenting, and no man who came to join them could tear himself away again, though there was strife and dissension among them and each blamed his neighbor, and declared that his had been the warning voice.

None minded punishment falling on the wrongdoers, but each was resolved that he and his house should go free. And if, in their dreadful loitering and strife, they had known of another innocent victim, not one but would have raised his hand against it to save himself.

Then one in their midst howled as if he had trodden on red-hot iron, as if his foot were nailed to the ground with a red-hot nail, as if fire were streaming through the marrow of his bones. They scattered, and all eyes turned to the man who had howled and on the hand which grasped his foot. But on the foot there sat, black and huge, the Spider, casting evil looks upon them. The blood froze in their veins, the breath in their throats, while, in unhurried malevolence, the Spider sat gloating, and the foot turned black and in the man's body, fire and water seemed to hiss and fight. Terror burst the bonds of fear, the group scattered. But in ghastly haste the Spider had left its first resting place and crept over one man's foot and another's heel, and fire coursed through their bodies and their dreadful cries lent wings to the feet of those who fled. On the wings of the wind, in the terrors of death, like the ghostly quarry before the ghostly hunt, they scattered to their homes, each feeling the Spider behind him. Then they bolted their doors and could not stop shuddering in mortal dread.

One day the Spider vanished. No cries of death were heard, and the men had perforce to leave their bolted houses to seek food for their cattle and themselves. But where was the Spider? Could it not be lying in wait, invisible, to appear unawares on a man's foot? And he who set down his foot most cautiously, and spied about him most keenly, suddenly saw the Spider sitting on his hand or foot; it crawled over his face, sat black and huge on his nose, glaring into his eyes, and red-hot stings burrowed into his bones, and the fires of Hell closed over him till death laid him low.

Thus the Spider was now nowhere, now here, now there,

now down in the valley, now up in the hills. It hissed through the grass, fell from the ceiling, rose from the ground. In broad daylight, as the people sat at their midday porridge, it sat gloating at the foot of the table, and before they could scatter in their fear, it had run over their hands, was sitting at the top of the table on the father's head, glaring gleefully over the table and the blackening hands. It fell on their faces at night, met them in the woods, sought them out in the byre. No man could avoid it; it was nowhere and everywhere. Awake or asleep, they could not ward it off. When they felt most safe, in the open air or up in a tree, fire crept up their backs, fiery feet were plunged into their necks, and the Spider glared at them over their shoulders. It spared neither the child in the cradle nor the old man on his deathbed. It was a dying such as had never been heard of before, and the death of it was more dreadful than had ever been known, and still more dreadful than death was the nameless horror of the Spider, which was everywhere and nowhere and which, when they thought themselves in safety, suddenly glared, death-dealing, into their eyes.

The tidings of the horror had, of course, soon reached the castle, and had stirred up fear and strife there too, insofar as might be within the rule of the Order. Stoffeln trembled lest the visitation should come upon them too, as it had come upon their cattle, and the dead priest had said many things which now disquieted his soul. For the priest had told him more than once that all the suffering he inflicted on the peasants would be paid home to him, but he had never believed it, thinking that God would know the difference between a knight and a serf, having created them so different.

But now he was afraid all the same lest things might be as the priest had said, and gave his knights hard words and told them that their wanton speech would be bitterly avenged. But the knights would not take the blame either; each blamed the other, and though none said so, thought it concerned Stoffeln alone, for, looked at properly, it was he who had brought the whole thing about. And beside

him their eyes rested on a young Polish knight who had
jested most wantonly about the castle and had been most
zealous in egging Stoffeln on to its building and to the planting of the flaunting avenue. He was very young, but the
fiercest of all, and when a deed of daring was to be done,
he was the first. He was no better than a heathen, for he
feared neither God nor Satan. He soon saw what was in the
others' minds, and marked their secret dread. Therefore he
taunted them, saying that if they feared a spider, what
would they do against a dragon? Then he armed himself
well and rode up the valley, boasting that he would not
return until his thrust had laid the Spider low and his fist
crushed it. Savage dogs leaped round him, his hawk sat
on his wrist, his horse reared spiritedly. Half in fear, half
in malice, the others watched him ride out of the castle,
and they thought of the night watch at Bärhegen, where
earthly weapons had availed so little against such an enemy.

He rode along the edge of a pine wood to the nearest farm, keeping a sharp lookout around and above him.
When the house came into sight, with people standing
round it, he called to his dogs and unhooded his hawk,
while his dagger rattled loose in its sheath. As the hawk
turned its dazzled eyes to the knight, awaiting his signal,
it suddenly flung itself from his wrist and soared up into
the air, the dogs howled aloud and fled, their tails between
their legs. In vain the knight galloped and called, he saw
his creatures no more. Then he rode toward the people to
ask for tidings. They stood still till he was near them, then
a hideous cry arose, they fled to wood and gorge, for on the
horseman's helmet there sat, unnaturally huge, the Spider,
glaring with baneful malice over the countryside. What
the knight sought he bore unwittingly with him. Afire with
rage he rode after the people, calling ever more fiercely,
till he and his horse fell over a precipice into the valley.
There they found his helmet and his body, and the Spider's
feet had burned into the knight's brain, where it had raged
in dreadful fire till he could die.

Then indeed fear entered the castle. They locked themselves in, but could not feel safe. They sought for spiritual

weapons, but a long time passed before they could find a
priest who would and dared to be their leader. He came,
and summoned them to sally forth with holy vessels and
holy water against the enemy. But he did not strengthen
himself in prayer and fasting; he sat at table early in the
morning with the knights, did not count the goblets he
drank, and lived well on venison and bear flesh. Between
times he would talk of his valorous spiritual deeds, while
the knights talked of their worldly ones, and no man
counted the goblets and the Spider was forgotten.

Then, in a moment, life was paralyzed, the hands stiffened round fork or goblet, mouths hung open and all eyes
were fixed on one spot. Stoffeln alone drank on, telling a
tale of a deed of daring in heathen lands, but on his head
there throned the Spider, glaring round the banqueting
table, and the knight did not feel it. Then the fire began
to course through his brain and blood. Raising his hand to
his head he uttered a dreadful cry, but the Spider was no
longer there, had, in its hideous speed, crawled over all
their faces, and one after the other they screamed aloud,
devoured by the fire, and from the priest's tonsure it gloated
over the horror. The priest strove to quench with the goblet
in his hand the fire which flamed through his bones. But
the Spider defied his weapon and sat upon its throne gloating on the horror till the last knight had uttered his last
cry and drawn his last breath.

Of all that lived in the castle only a few servants were
spared who had never scorned the peasants; they told the
dreadful tale. But the feeling that the knights had got what
they deserved was little comfort to the peasants; the horror
grew and spread and was more dreadful day by day. Some
set out to leave the valley, but it was just they whom the
Spider fell upon. Their bodies were found by the wayside.
Others fled to the high mountains, but the Spider was there
before them, and when they thought themselves in safety,
there was the Spider sitting on their necks or faces. Day
by day the creature grew more malevolent, more devilish.
It no longer took them by surprise, no longer burnt death
into them unawares; it sat in front of them in the grass,

hung over them in the trees, glaring at them with venomous eyes. But if any man who had taken flight slackened his pace, then only did it crawl toward him and strike him down.

Many, in their despair, tried to kill the Spider, dropped hundredweight-heavy stones on it as it sat in the grass in front of them, or struck at it with clubs or axes, but it was all in vain. The heaviest stone could not crush it nor the sharpest axe wound it, and there it was sitting on their faces or crawling unharmed toward them. To flee was as vain as to fight. All hope was at an end and despair filled the valley and sat on the heights.

Till then the creature had spared one single house and had never appeared in it. It was the house where Christine had lived and from which she had stolen the child. She had attacked her own husband on a lonely pasture; they found his body more horribly mutilated than any other, his features wrung with unspeakable pain. She had wreaked her most dreadful anger on him, preparing an awful re-union with her husband. But no man had seen it happen.

She had not yet come to the house. Whether she wished to save it to the last, or whether she shunned it, no one could guess. But dread housed there as in every other place.

The good young wife had recovered. She had no fear for herself, but only for her staunch little boy and his sister. Day and night she watched over them, and the grand-mother watched with her. Together they prayed that God would keep their watching eyes open, and give them light and strength to save the innocent children.

It often seemed to them, as they kept watch through the long nights, as if they could see the Spider glimmering and glittering in the dark corner, or glaring in through the window, and then their fear was great, for they knew of no way to shield the children from it, and they prayed all the more fervently to God for His counsel and help. They had laid all kinds of weapons ready, but when they heard that stones lost their weight and axes their edge, they put them away again. Then a thought began to take shape in the mother's mind, and grew clearer day by day. If anyone

dared to grasp the Spider in their hand, it could be overcome. She had heard too that some of the people, when
stone proved powerless, had striven to crush it in their
hand, but in vain. A stream of fire pulsing through hand
and arm swept all their strength away and carried death
to their hearts.

She did not think she could crush the Spider, but she
could lay hold of it, and God would give her the strength
to put it where it would be harmless. She had often heard
how wise men had imprisoned spirits in a hole in rock or
wood, which they had then shut fast with a nail, and as
long as no one drew out the nail, the demon remained in
the hole.

More and more the spirit moved her to attempt a like
deed. She bored a hole in the window post nearest her right
hand as she sat by the cradle, prepared a plug which exactly fitted it, sprinkled it with holy water, and laid a hammer ready, then prayed day and night to God for strength
to carry out the deed. But at times the flesh overcame the
spirit, heavy sleep pressed her eyes shut, and in dreams
she saw the Spider glaring at her boy's golden hair. Then
she would start up out of her dream and stretch out her
hand to her boy's curls. But no spider was sitting there, and
there was a smile on his face such as children smile when
they see their angel in a dream, but the mother saw the
Spider's venomous eyes glittering in every corner, and sleep
left her for many a long day.

Once more, as she kept strict watch, sleep had overcome
her, hanging her round with black veils. Then it seemed to
her that the priest who had died to save her child came
rushing toward her from far distances, crying: "Woman
awake! The enemy is at hand!" Three times he called, and
not until the third time did she cast off the clinging bonds
of sleep. But as she toilsomely opened her heavy eyelids,
she saw the Spider, bloated with venom, moving over the
cot to her boy's face. Then she thought of God and with a
swift hand seized the Spider. Streams of fire flowed from
it, through the faithful mother's hand and arm into her
heart, but her faith and love pressed her hand together and

God gave her the strength to endure. In a thousandfold agony of death she pressed the Spider into the hole with one hand, pressed in the plug with the other, and drove it home with the hammer.

Inside the room there was a roaring as when whirlwinds fight with the sea, the house rocked to its foundations, but the plug held, the Spider was a prisoner.

The faithful mother had time to rejoice that her child was saved and to thank God for His grace, then she died the same death as the others, but her mother-love quenched the pain and the angels led her soul to the throne of God, where all the heroes stand who have given their lives for others and dared all for God and their loved ones. Now the Black Death was over. Peace and life returned to the valley, and the Spider was seen no more at that time, for it sat a prisoner in that hole where it sits now.

"What, in that black post there!" screamed the godmother, leaping up from the ground as if she had sat on an anthill. Her back smarted, she turned round on herself, looked down her back, felt herself all over, but could not shake off the fear that the Spider was sitting on her neck.

The hearts of the others were oppressed too, but the grandfather sat silent. An awed silence had fallen on all. None dared to jest, yet none would yield easily to belief. Each thought it better to listen to what the others might say; it was the best way not to go wrong.

Then the midwife, who had called more than once without getting an answer, came running, her face flaming as if the Spider had crawled over it. She began to scold, telling them that no matter how loud she might call, nobody would come. She had cooked the dinner and now nobody wanted to come to table, and when everything was spoilt, she would get the blame, it was always the way. Nobody could eat meat as fat as was waiting for them if it had got cold; besides, it would be bad for them.

So they came, but very slowly, and nobody would go through the door first, and Grandfather had to lead the way. But this time it was not out of respect for the old custom of hanging back so as not to seem too eager. It was the shrinking which befalls all men at the entrance to a place of dread, and yet there was nothing dreadful to be seen. On the table the refilled wine bottles shone bright, two brave hams glistened, huge roasts of veal and mutton smoked, fresh züpfen lay between, plates of fruit tarts and three kinds of cakes were squeezed in between, and the pots of sweet tea had not been forgotten. It was a fine sight, but they paid little heed to it all and looked round anxiously to make sure that the Spider was not glittering in some corner or fixing venomous eyes on them from the top of a ham. It was nowhere to be seen, yet no one paid the customary compliments—whatever could the housewife have been thinking of to load the table that way?—anyone who ate all that would soon have too much, and so on. They huddled together at the foot of the table and none would go up higher.

In vain the guests were urged to move up, and empty chairs were pointed out. They stood as if nailed to the ground. In vain the young father poured out wine and called on them to come and drink healths; the glasses remained full.

Then he took the godmother by the arm, saying: "Come, Godmother, show your wits and set an example." But the godmother fended him off with might and main, crying: "I wouldn't sit there, no, not for a thousand pounds. My whole back is creeping and crawling as if someone were stroking it with nettles. And if I were to sit there in front of that window post I'd feel that dreadful spider in my neck."

"It's all your fault, Grandfather," said the grandmother. "Why do you rake up such things? Nobody believes them nowadays, and they might bring discredit on the house. The day the children come crying home from school, complaining that the other children have cast it up at them that their grandmother was a witch and is shut up in that window post, you'll see."

"Quiet there, Grandmother," said the grandfather. "People have short memories these days. They don't keep things in their minds as they used to long ago. The company wanted to hear about it all from me, and it's better for folk to know the truth just as it is rather than make things up for themselves. The truth can bring no dishonor on our house. But come and sit down, all of you. Look, I'll sit in front of the post myself. After all, I've sat there thousands of days without fear or trembling and then there's no danger. It was only when ill thoughts rose in me which might give the Devil a handle that I seemed to hear something purring behind me like a cat when you stroke its stomach. Then the goose flesh crawled up my back. But the rest of the time it sits in there as still as a mouse and as long as God is not forgotten here outside it'll have to wait inside."

Then the guests plucked up courage and sat down, but nobody moved up to sit by the grandfather. Now at last the young husband could carve. He laid a huge slice of roast on his neighbor's plate, stripping it off with his thumb. The slice went the rounds until one of the company said thanks, he'd keep it, there was more where that came from, then another slice was sent round. While the husband filled the glasses and the guests told him he'd have his work cut out that day, the midwife went round with the tea, strongly spiced with saffron and cinnamon, offering it to all and saying that anyone who liked it need only say so, there was plenty. And when anyone made an offer she poured the tea into the wine and said she was fond of it too, the wine lay better on the stomach and there was no fear of headaches.

They ate and drank, but hardly had the noise subsided which means that fresh dishes have made their appearance when silence fell again, faces grew grave, and it was easy to see that all thoughts were busy with the Spider. Furtive eyes sought the plug behind the grandfather's back, yet everybody was afraid of raising the subject again. Then suddenly the godmother screamed and nearly fell off her chair.

A fly had crawled over the plug; she seemed to see the Spider's black legs scrabbling out of the hole, and she was quivering in every limb from the shock. They hardly laughed at her. Her shock was a welcome pretext to begin again about the Spider, for once a thing has really gone home to people's minds, it is no easy matter to put it aside again.

"Now listen, Cousin," said the elder godfather. "Hasn't the Spider ever been out again? Has it stayed in there all these hundreds of years?"

"Ah!" said the grandmother. "It'd have been better not to bring the whole thing up at all. You've been talking about nothing else the whole afternoon."

"Now, Mother," said the cousin. "Let the old man have his say. He's kept us quiet and nobody's going to cast it up at you. After all, you're no kin of Christine's. But you won't stop us thinking about it, and if you won't let us talk about it we'll talk about nothing else and there'll be nothing to pass the time. Go on, Grandfather, your old woman won't grudge it us."

"Well, if you will have it then have it, as far as I'm concerned, but it'd have been better to start about something else, especially now night's coming on," said the grandmother.

Then the grandfather began again, and all faces turned toward him expectantly.

I don't know much more to tell, but I'll tell you what I do know. Somebody might take an example by it even today. In any case, there's plenty of people who'd come to no harm by it if they did.

When the people knew that the Spider was a prisoner and their lives safe again, it's said that they felt as if they were in Paradise, with the Lord God in His blessedness in the midst of them, and for a long time all was well. They walked in God's ways and shunned the Devil, and even the new knights who had come to the castle respected the hand of God and treated the people kindly, and helped them to prosper.

But all looked on this house with awe, almost as if it had been a church. It's true they shuddered at first when they looked at it and saw the Black Spider's dungeon and thought how easily it could break out and the calamity begin all over again by the Devil's power. But they soon saw that God's power was greater than the Devil's, and as a token of their gratitude to the mother who had died for them they looked after her children and worked the farm for nothing until the children were able to work for themselves. The knights would have let them build a new house so that they might get rid of the fear of the Spider, or in case it might get out again in a house that was lived in, and they'd have had help in plenty from the neighbors who couldn't shake off their dread of the creature they had so mortally feared. But the old grandmother wouldn't hear of it; she taught her grandchildren that here the Spider would be kept prisoner by God the Father, Son, and Holy Ghost. As long as the three Holy Names were venerated in that house, as long as food and drink were taken at that table in the three Holy Names, so long would they be safe from the Spider in its hole and no chance could change that. Here, at this table, with the Spider behind them, they would never forget their fear of God nor the greatness of His power, and so the Spider would turn their minds to God in spite of the Devil. But if they abandoned God, were it a hundred miles away, the Spider or the Devil himself would find them. The children understood and grew up in the fear of God, and God's blessing was upon the house.

The little boy who had stood so staunchly by his mother grew up to be a fine upstanding man, who was beloved of God and found favor with the knights. He was blessed with worldly goods, but never forgot God on their account nor closed his hand upon them. He helped others in need as he desired that others should help him in his last need, and when he grew too weak to help himself, he became all the more powerful an advocate with God and man. He was blessed with a wise wife, and between them was the peace that passeth understanding; therefore their children bloomed in piety and man and wife were granted a peaceful death. And after them the family continued to prosper in the fear of God and in righteous ways.

Yes, the blessing of God lay upon the whole valley, and there was plenty in field and byre and peace among men. They had taken the dreadful lesson to heart; they clung close to God, what they did they did in His name, and where one could help his neighbor he did so without delay. At the castle, no evil and much good was done them. The number of knights dwindled as the war with the heathen raged more fiercely and the need of every hand that could wield a weapon grew greater. But to those who remained in the castle, the great hall of death, where the Spider had vented its rage on knights and serfs alike, was a daily warning that God's power ruled equally over every man who abandoned Him, be he knight or serf.

Thus many years of happiness and blessing passed, and the valley was renowned above all others. The houses were stately, their storerooms rich, their money chests well-filled. Their cattle were the finest up hill and down dale, their daughters were famous far and wide and their sons welcome everywhere. And their fame did not wither overnight like Jonas's gourd, but endured from generation to generation, for the sons remained God-fearing and respected of men from generation to generation.

But just as it is the best-watered and most vigorous pear tree that the worm gnaws and blasts, it also happens that when the stream of God's blessing pours most abundantly over men, the worm enters the blessing, making them proud and blind, so that in the midst of God's blessing they forget Him who bestowed it, and become like the Israelites who, when God had succored them, forsook Him for golden calves.

And so, after many generations had passed away, pride and vanity entered the valley, and foreign wives came too, increasing both. More and more splendid grew their clothes, jewels glittered, and the vainglory spread even to the holy things, for instead of raising their eyes to God in prayer, they let them rest proudly on the gold beads of their rosaries. Then God's divine service became a show of pride, while their hearts hardened toward God and men. None troubled to keep God's commandments, all mocked His service and His servants, for where there is great pride or great wealth, men soon come to believe that their appetites are their wisdom, which is higher than God's. They, who had been so sorely oppressed by the knights in olden times, turned hard and cruel toward their own servants, and as the knights had built before them, they built now, and as the knights had once plagued them, they now spared neither man nor beast once the building devil had entered into them. The change had come over this house too, while the old plenty remained.

Nearly two hundred years had passed since the Spider had been shut in its hole. A clever and valiant woman was master here. She was not from Lindau, as Christine had been, but in many ways she was like Christine. She too came from foreign parts and was much given to show and pride. She had an only son; her husband had died under her rule. This son was a fine lad, kindly and gentle to man and beast, and she loved him, though she would not show it. Every step he took was ruled by her, and nothing he did was right unless she had allowed it. Though he was long since a grown man, he could not be with the other young men, or as much as go to the fair unless his mother went with him. When at last she thought he was old enough she gave him a wife from among her own kin and after her own mind. So now he had two masters instead of one, and because both were proud as peacocks they meant Christen to be like them. When he was kind and thoughtful for others, as was his true nature, he had to learn who was master.

The house had long been a thorn in their flesh. They were ashamed of it, for the neighbors, even though they were not so rich, had new houses. The memory of the Spider, and of what the grandmother had said, still lived in the minds of all, otherwise the old house would have been pulled down long before. But all the people forbade it. For their part, all the women could see in the ban on a new house was the envy that grudged it to them. Besides, they were growing uneasy in the old house. When they sat at this table, it was as if the cat were placidly purring behind their backs, or as if the hole had gently opened and the Spider were aiming at their necks. Theirs was not the spirit which had plugged the hole, and so their fear that the hole

might open grew. Thus they found good reasons for building a new house where they would need to fear the Spider
no longer; or so they thought. They decided to leave the
old house to the servants, who so often stood in the way
of their pride.

With a heavy heart, Christen consented. He remembered what the old grandmother had said; he believed that
the family blessing was bound up with the family house,
and his prayers were never so heartfelt as when he sat at
the head of this table. He said what he thought, but his
womenfolk bade him be silent, and because he was their
slave he did so, but when he was alone he often wept
bitterly.

Above the tree where we sat they planned to build a
house such as nobody in the whole parish possessed.

In the impatience of their pride, because they knew nothing about building and could hardly wait to show off their
new house, they drove men and beasts without mercy
while the building was going on. They would not let them
keep the holy feast days and even grudged them their sleep
at night. And there was no neighbor whose help pleased
them, and they wished them all ill when, having given their
help freely, as men did even in those days, they went home
to look after their own needs.

When the roof was on and the first peg was driven into
the threshold, smoke poured from the hole as it does when
damp straw is fired. Then the workmen shook their heads
gravely and said, in secret and aloud, that the new house
would never be old, but the women laughed and paid no
heed to the sign. When at last the house was finished they
settled in with unbelievable splendor, and for the house-
warming they gave a feast which children and children's
children still spoke of in the Emmental.

But the whole three days long there was heard all over
the house a strange noise like a cat purring with pleasure
when its stomach is stroked. But search as they might, no
cat could be found in the house. Then many a one grew uneasy and in spite of the splendor ran away in the midst of
the revelry. The women alone heard nothing or paid no

heed. They thought their battle won with the new house.

Yes, the blind man cannot see the sun, and the deaf man cannot hear the thunder. Therefore the women rejoiced in the new house, grew prouder every day, never thought of the Spider, but led, in their new house, an idle life of gluttony and finery. No one was a match for them, and of God they thought not at all.

In the old house the servants remained by themselves, living as they pleased, and when Christen tried to take them in hand, the women would not have it and scolded him, the mother chiefly from pride, the wife from jealousy. And so there was an end to all decent living among them, and with that all fear of God vanished, as is always the way where there is no master. When no master sits at the head of the table, no master holds the reins inside the house and out, he who behaves worst counts himself the greatest, and he who speaks most evilly the best.

So it went on in the old house and the servants soon came to look like a troop of wild cats. They had forgotten how to pray, and so they had no respect for God's will or His gifts. As the pride of their mistresses lost all bounds, the bestial wantonness of the servants knew no restraint. They outraged the bread without fear, threw the porridge at each other's faces across the table, and even fouled the food to spoil each other's appetites. They teased the neighbors, tormented the animals, mocked at Holy Mass, denied all higher power, and plagued to the top of their bent the priest who had warned them of retribution to come. In short, they forgot all fear of God and man and grew worse every day. Man and maid vied with each other in evil living, yet they plagued each other whenever they could, and when the men could find no new way of tormenting the maids, one of them hit on the idea of cowing them with the Spider in its hole. He threw a spoonful of porridge and milk at the plug, crying that the prisoner must be hungry in there after all those centuries of fasting.

Then the maids set up a terrible screaming and promised him everything. Even the other men were afraid. But since the game was repeated with impunity, it soon palled, the

maids stopped their screaming and the other men began in
their turn. Then the first farm hand began to brandish his
knife at the hole, declaring with the most hideous oaths
that he would take the plug out and see what was inside,
for they must have something new to see for once. That
was the signal for a fresh outburst, and the man who did
it was the master of all and could get what he wanted, especially from the maids.

He was, indeed, a strange creature, people say, and no
one knew where he came from. He could be as meek as a
lamb and as savage as a wolf. When he was alone with a
woman he was as meek as a lamb, but in front of the other
men he was as savage as a wolf, as if he hated them all
and only wanted to be their master in wickedness. And so,
in front of the other men, the maids were terrified of him,
but, people say, he was their favorite when they could get
him alone. His eyes did not match, but no one really knew
what color they were, and one eye hated the other and
never looked the same way, though he managed to conceal
it with his long hair and downcast looks. His hair curled
beautifully, but no one knew whether it was red or golden.
In the shade it was a perfect gold, but when the sun shone
on it no squirrel ever had a redder coat. He ill-treated the
beasts more than all the others, and they hated him accordingly. Each of the men believed he was his friend, but
he only stirred up strife among them. He was the only one
who could please the mistresses; he alone was often at the
upper house. Then the maids misbehaved down below, and
as soon as he noticed it, he would stick his knife into the
plug and threaten till the maids cringed before him.

Yet they soon tired even of this game. The maids got
used to it and said at last: "Do it if you dare, but you
daren't."

Christmastide and the Holy Night were approaching.
They had no thought for all that hallows it to us. They
planned to make a merry night of it. In the castle there was
only one old knight left, and he cared little for the things
of this world. A rascally bailiff managed everything to his
own profit. The servants had bargained with him for some

fine Hungarian wine in exchange for some roguery or
other, but they knew nothing of its strength and fire. A
terrible storm broke out, with lightning and wind such as
is seldom seen at that season. Not a dog would have been
driven from the fireside that night. It was not the wild
weather that kept them from church, but it was a good
excuse for them to stay alone in the old house with the
noble wine.

Christmas Eve began with cursing and dancing, with
wicked and worse things, then they sat down to a meal.
The maids had cooked meat, white pudding, and whatever
other dainties they had managed to steal. More and more
bestial grew their doings. All the food was outraged, every
holy thing blasphemed. The strange farm hand mocked at
the priest, distributed bread and wine as if presiding at
Holy Mass, baptized the dog by the fire, and carried on
till the others, wild as they were, were terrified. Then he
stuck his knife into the plug and vowed he would show
them far worse things.

When they would not be afraid because he had done the
same thing so often, and the plug in any case resisted his
knife, he snatched up an awl and, half raving, swore in
most unholy fashion that they should see what he could do
and pay for their laughter till the hair rose on their heads,
and with a savage thrust he screwed the awl into the plug.
Screaming shrilly the others rushed on him, but before they
could stop him, he laughed like the Devil himself and gave
a vigorous tug at the awl.

Then a huge clap of thunder struck the house to its
foundations, the evildoer fell on his back, a red stream of
flame burst out of the hole, and in the midst of it, huge,
black, and bloated with the venom of centuries, sat the
Spider, gloating balefully at the rabble who stood paralyzed
with fear, unable to move a limb to escape from the hideous
monster, which crawled with slow glee over their faces,
stinging them to fiery death. Then the house shook with
dreadful cries of pain such as a horde of a hundred starving
wolves could not utter.

Soon a like scream was heard from the new house.

Christen, who was just coming uphill from Mass, thought robbers had broken in and, trusting to his strong right arm, rushed to his family's help. He found no robbers, but death. His wife and mother were in their death throes, and no voice issued from their black and swollen faces. His children were sleeping peacefully, their bright faces flushed with health. A dreadful premonition came to Christen. He hurried down to the lower house; there he found all the servants lying dead, the parlor a death chamber, the grisly hole in the window post open, and in the hand of the hideously distorted man the awl with the dreadful plug on its point.

Then he knew what had happened. He raised his hands in horror and if the earth had opened and swallowed him up he would have been glad. Then something crawled out from behind the fireplace. He started away in fear, but it was not the Spider. It was a poor little boy he had taken in for God's sake and left among the savage servants. The child had taken no part in the servants' doings. He had fled in terror behind the stove, and he alone had been spared by the Spider and could tell the dreadful tale.

But even as he spoke, cries of fear from the other houses rang through wind and weather. In century-old glee the Spider sped through the valley, choosing first the finest houses, whose inmates thought least of God and most of worldly things, and were therefore least prepared to think of death.

Day had not yet dawned when the tidings were in every home. The Spider had broken out and was roaming through the parish, dealing death on its way. Many, it was told, lay dead already, and up the valley scream after scream was rising to Heaven from those already marked by death. No need to tell of the woe in the countryside, the dread in all hearts, or the kind of Christmas that was at Sumiswald. None could think of the joy it brings, and the affliction came from the evildoing of men. The calamity grew from day to day, for the Spider was bigger, swifter, and more deadly than before. Now it was at one end, now at the other, of the valley, and appeared in the valley and on the mountain tops at one and the same time. While before it had marked down one here, another there, for death, it seldom left a house now before poisoning all the inmates. Not until all were in their death agony would it settle on the threshold to gloat over its work, as if to say: Here I am, I have come back, however long I was a prisoner.

It seemed to know that its time was short, or perhaps it simply wished to save trouble. Wherever it could lay low many at a blow, it did so. For that reason it would lie in wait for the processions which carried the dead to church. Now here, now there, but most often at the foot of the church hill, it would suddenly appear in the midst of the company or sit on the coffin, glaring down on the men. Then a hideous cry rose from all, man by man they fell till the whole procession lay on the road in the throes of death, till no life was left in them and a heap of dead lay round the coffin as brave heroes lie round their banner when a greater power has struck them down.

Then the people ceased carrying the dead to church; none would carry and none go with them. The dead were left to lie where death had struck them down.

Despair filled the valley. Every heart was boiling with rage, and hideous curses were launched against poor Christen. He was to blame for it all.

Suddenly everyone knew that Christen should never have left the old house nor abandoned the servants. Suddenly it came home to them that the master is answerable for his servants, that he should keep watch over them at prayer and at table, should prevent them living a godless life, with godless speech and the outraging of God's gifts. All at once the people had enough of pride and vainglory. They banned them to the lowest parts of Hell and would hardly have believed God Himself if He had told them how shamelessly they had indulged in them but a few days before. Suddenly they were all devout again, wore their poorest clothes, took their old forgotten rosaries up again, and persuaded themselves they had always been devout, and if they could not make God believe it, it was not for want of trying.

Christen alone was the godless one among them, and on all hands curses as high as the hills were heaped on him. Yet he was perhaps the best of them all, but his will lay chained in the will of his womenfolk, and to be so bound is a grievous punishment for any man, nor can he escape his burden of responsibility for not being what God meant him to be. Christen's eyes were opened too; therefore he did not turn on the people and rend them, but took more guilt upon himself than was his by rights. But that did not pacify them, for now more than ever they screamed at each other how great his guilt must be, since he took so much upon himself and freely confessed his unworthiness.

Meanwhile Christen besought God day and night to avert the evil, but it grew more grievous every day. It came home to him that he must atone for his sin, must be the sacrifice himself, must do the deed his ancestress had done before him. He prayed to God till his heart was fired with the resolve to save the valley, and his resolution was strengthened by the steadfast courage that never fails, but is always ready for the one deed, morning and evening.

Then, with his children, he moved down into the old house, cut a new plug for the hole, had it consecrated with holy water and sacred words, placed the hammer beside the plug, and sat down by his children's bedside to wait for the Spider.

There he sat, watching and praying, and with a good courage fought against sleep and did not falter. But the Spider did not come, though it was everywhere else, for death spread day by day and the rage of the survivors grew fiercer. In the midst of the terror, a woman was to bear a child. Then the old dread came over the people that the Spider would fetch the child unbaptized as the pledge of their ancient pact. The woman was beside herself. With no faith in God, she had all the more hatred and revenge in her heart.

They knew how their forefathers had warded off the Green Man long ago when a child was to be born, and that the priest was the shield they had set up between themselves and the eternal adversary. They resolved to send for the priest, but who was to be the messenger? The road was barred by the unburied dead whom the Spider had struck down on the funeral processions, and would any messenger who took the path over the wild heights be able to escape the Spider? At last the woman's husband said that if the Spider meant to have him it would get him at home as easily as on the way. If he was marked for death, he could escape it nowhere.

He set out, but hour after hour passed and no messenger returned. As the hour of birth approached, the woman's rage and lamentation mounted. In the frenzy of despair she tore herself from her bed and rushed to the house of Christen, the thousandfold accursed, who sat beside his children, praying and waiting for the Spider. From far off her cries were heard, her curses thundered at Christen's door long before she flung it open. When she came rushing in with her terrible face, he started up, not knowing at first whether it was Christine herself. But in the doorway pain checked the woman's onrush, she writhed against the doorpost, pouring her curses over poor Christen. If he was not to be accursed by children and children's children, let him be the messenger. Then pain overcame her, and on Christen's threshold she bore a son. All who had followed her scattered far and wide, dreading the final horror.

Christen stood with the innocent child in his arms. In her riven face the woman's eyes glared piercing, wild and venomous, till he seemed to see the Spider itself crawling out of them.

Then God gave him strength, and a more than human will was born in him. Casting a look of love at his children, he wrapped the newborn child in his warm cloak, sprang over the glaring woman, and ran down the hill and along the valley to Sumiswald. It was he himself who would carry the child to the holy sacrament as an atonement for the guilt that was upon him, the head of his house. The rest he committed to God. The dead lay in his path. He had to place his feet with care. Then a light footstep caught up with him; it was the poor little boy who had feared the wild woman and had followed his master with

childish trust. Christen's heart was wrung by the thought
that his children were alone with the frantic woman, but
his foot stayed not and he hastened on to his holy goal.

He had already reached the foot of the church hill, and
the chapel was in sight, when suddenly fire barred his way,
a red feather waved in the bushes, and the Spider sat before him, rearing high to leap.

Then Christen called upon the Holy Trinity with a loud
voice, and a savage cry echoed from the bushes. The red
feather vanished, Christen laid the child in the boy's arms
and, commending his spirit to the Lord, laid hold of the
Spider with a strong hand, for it had sat motionless as if
spellbound by the holy words. Fire streamed through his
bones but he held fast, the way was open, and understanding was given to the little boy, who hurried on to the priest
with the child.

But Christen, fire in his strong hand, ran home as if on
wings. The fire in his hand was agony, the blood seemed to
freeze in his veins and his breath to stop, but he prayed
unceasingly with God steadfastly before him, and so the
pains of Hell could not overcome him.

His house came in sight, his hope grew with his pain,
the woman stood in the doorway. When she saw him coming without her child, she rushed on him like a tigress
robbed of her young, believing in a most shameful treachery. She paid no heed to his signals, was deaf to the words
which came from his panting breast, fell into his outstretched hands and clung to him. In the fear of death he
had to drag the raving woman into the house and struggle
himself free before he could push the Spider into the hole
and hammer it in with his dying hands.

With God's help it was done. His dying eyes rested on
his children; they were smiling sweetly in their sleep. Then
a lightness entered into him, a higher hand seemed to
quench his fire, and praying aloud he closed his eyes in
death. Those who came creeping anxiously to see what had
happened to the woman saw peace and joy in his face.
Amazed, they saw the hole plugged, but the woman lay

singed and distorted in death. She had taken the fiery death from Christen's hand.

The people were still standing, not knowing what had happened, when the little boy returned with the child and the priest, who had quickly baptized it according to the custom of those times. He was ready, well armed and of a good courage, to plunge into the very battle in which the priest of old had won victory with his life. But God required no such sacrifice of him. Another had already won the battle.

It was a long time before the people grasped the great deed that Christen had done. When at last belief and understanding came to them, they prayed joyfully with the priest, thanked God for the life He had restored to them and for the strength He had bestowed on Christen. But to the dead Christen they prayed for forgiveness for the wrong they had done him, and resolved to bury him with great honor, and his memory was enshrined in their hearts as gloriously as that of any saint.

When the hideous terror which had never ceased to quiver through their limbs suddenly vanished, and they could look up to the blue sky with joy, not fearing that the Spider was crawling over their feet, they could hardly believe their senses. They resolved to have many masses said and to make a general procession to church. First of all they wished to bury the two bodies, those of Christen and his savage besieger; then they would bury the other dead, as far as room could be found.

It was a solemn day when the whole valley moved to church; there was a solemn feeling in many a heart, many a sin was confessed and many a vow made, and from that day on there was little vainglory to be seen in faces or clothing.

When, in church and the graveyard, many tears had been shed, many prayers offered up, all those who had come to the burying—and all who could move their limbs had come—went to the inn for the funeral meal. According to custom, the women and children sat apart at one table, but all the grown men found room at the famous round table that can still be seen at the Bear Inn at Sumiswald. It was kept there to remind people that once there were only two score men where now nearly two thousand live, and as a warning that even the lives of two thousand are in the hands of Him who had saved two score. They did not linger long over that meal. Their hearts were too full for meat or drink. When they came out of the village onto the open height, they saw a glow in the sky, and when they reached home they found the new house burned to the ground. How it happened they never knew.

But the people never forgot what Christen had done for them and paid their debt to his children. They were brought up in piety and strength in the most devout homes. No hand touched what was theirs, and though no account of it was ever seen, it was well tended and multiplied, and when the children grew up, not only were they not cheated of their possessions, they were not cheated of their souls. They became godly and righteous men, who found favor with God and good will among men, who were blessed in this life and still more blessed in Heaven. And so it remained in the family, and no man feared the Spider because all feared God, and as it was then, so may it remain, if God will, as long as a house stands here, as long as children follow in the ways and thoughts of their forefathers.

There the grandfather stopped, and for a long time all were silent, some thinking over the story, others waiting for him to go on.

At last the elder godfather spoke:

"I've sat at that round table many a time myself, and I've heard of the dying and how after it there was room at the table for all the grown men in the village. But how exactly everything came about nobody could tell me. Some guessed this and some that. Now tell us how you came to know all about it."

"Ah!" said the grandfather. "It was handed down among us from father to son, and when the memory of it faded among the people in the valley, the family kept it secret and would not let it be known. Only the family spoke of it, so that no member of it should forget what builds a house and what destroys a house, what brings a blessing and what drives it away. You heard how unwilling our old grandmother was to hear it spoken of. But to my mind, the more time passes, the more it should be spoken of, so that men may know where pride and vanity can lead them. That's why I won't keep it all a secret, and it's not the first time I've told the story to friends. I always think that what has preserved the fortunes of my family for so many years will bring no harm to anybody, and it's not right to make a secret of what we can call ours by good luck and God's blessing."

"You're right there, Cousin," answered the godfather. "But there's one more question. Was the house you pulled down seven years ago the old one?"

"Nay," said the grandfather. "The house was nearly falling down three hundred years ago, and God's gifts from field and pasture could long since find no room in it. Yet the family did not want to leave it, and they dared not build a new one. They could not forget what had happened to that other new one so long ago. And so they were hard put to it, and at last turned for counsel to a wise man. He answered, so they say, that they might well build a new house in the same place as the old one, but nowhere else, and two things they must keep, the old window post where the Spider lived and the old spirit which had thrust the Spider into the old wood. Then the blessing would again rest on the house.

"They built the new house, and with care and prayer built the old window post into it, and the Spider did not stir, and the old spirit and the blessing did not forsake them.

"But even the new house grew old and cramped, and its wood was devoured of worms and rotten. Only the window post stayed firm and hard as iron. My father ought to have built. He put it off, then my turn came. I thought a long time, then I ventured. As my fathers had done before me, I built the old wood into the new house, and the Spider did not stir. But I will confess, never in my life have I

prayed as I prayed when I held that dreadful post in my
hands. My whole body was on fire, and I couldn't help
looking to see if there were any black spots coming out
on my hands or anywhere else on me, and a load fell from
my heart when at last everything was in its place. And I
was strengthened in my faith that neither I nor my children and children's children had anything to fear from the
Spider as long as we feared God."

Then the grandfather was silent, but they still felt the
shudder that had crept up their backs when they heard
that he had held the post in his hands, and they wondered
what they would feel if they had to take it in theirs.

Then the cousin spoke:

"It's only a pity that nobody knows how much truth there
is in such things. You can't believe the whole story, and all
the same there must be something in it or else the old post
wouldn't still be there."

"However that may be, there's still plenty to learn from
it," said the younger godfather, and went on that time had
passed so quickly, it seemed as if they had only just come
out of church.

But the grandmother said they shouldn't talk too much
or her old man would be beginning another story. They
should eat and drink now; nobody would eat and drink, it
was a disgrace. It must all be uneatable, though they had
done what they could, as far as in them lay.

So then they fell to, there was a great eating and drinking
and many a wise remark was passed, till the moon stood
high and golden in the sky, and the stars issued from their
majestic chambers to warn men it was time for them to
seek their humble ones.

The company saw the mysterious warners, but they sat
so contentedly together, and the hearts of all beat so
strangely in their breasts at the thought of going home, that
though nobody said so, nobody wanted to be the first to go.

At last the godmother stood up and made herself ready
to go with trembling hands, but there was no lack of
doughty protectors to go with her, and the whole company
left the hospitable house with many thanks and good

wishes, though the family pressed them hard to stay—it wasn't dark yet.

Soon the house lay still, and inside too was silence. Peacefully it stood there, shining pure and beautiful down the valley in the moonlight. With care and tenderness it guarded good people in quiet sleep, as those sleep who carry the fear of God and an untroubled conscience in their hearts, and will never be awakened from sleep by the Black Spider, but only by the kindly sun. But what power is the Spider's if their spirit should change is known only to Him who knows all, and bestows on all His power, on spiders as on men.

ADALBERT STIFTER

TRANSLATED BY HERMAN SALINGER

I. *Journey Through the Steppes*

CERTAIN things, certain relationships in human existence, are sometimes not immediately clear to us; it is impossible for us to explain to ourselves readily what their basis is. Their effect in such cases is mostly that of a beautiful, gentle, and especially mysterious charm upon our souls. In the countenance of the ugly person there is often an inner beauty which we cannot possibly ascertain from a hasty evaluation, whereas the features of another one may seem cold and empty to us even though everyone says that they possess the greatest possible beauty. In the same way we often feel ourselves drawn to someone whom we actually do not know at all; something in his movements pleases us, his manner is inviting; we are sorry when he has left us, we feel a certain longing, even love, toward him whenever in later years our thoughts turn to him—whereas we cannot get clear about another person whose value may lie open before us in the form of many deeds, even if we have been close to him for years. There is, in the last analysis, no doubt that there are moral reasons which the heart feels, but we cannot always find them and weigh them on the scales of consciousness and objectivity. The study of psychology has thrown light on many things, but many things have remained obscure to it, and quite remote. For this reason it is probably not too much to say that for us there exists a serene and measureless gap in which God and the spirits hold sway. In moments of ecstasy the soul often flies over it, or poetry at times blows across it in child-like unconsciousness—but science, with her hammer and straightedge, often merely stands at the brink and, in many cases, cannot even put a finger to the task.

I have been moved to make these remarks by something I experienced while still young in years, on the estate of an old major, and at a time when I still had a great wanderlust which drove me out into the world hither and yon because I still hoped to experience and investigate the Lord knows what.

I had come to know the Major during a trip. Even at that time he repeatedly invited me to visit him sometime in his home. However, I took this to be a mere form of speech, the kind of politeness travelers often exchange, and I should probably never have followed the matter up at all if, in the second year of our separation, a letter had not come from him. In it he inquired most eagerly about my welfare, finally ending with the old request to come and visit him, to pass a summer with him, or a whole year, or even five or ten years, if I wanted to do so. For, he said, he had finally decided to stick to one small spot on this earthly ball and not allow one other mote of dust except that of his homeland to settle upon his boots, now that he had found there the goal he had sought in vain everywhere else in the world.

Since it was spring, and I found myself curious to learn what this goal of his was, and not knowing where else to travel—I decided to give in to his wishes and accept his invitation.

His estate lay in eastern Hungary. I consumed two whole days with the weighing of plans, trying to figure how I could most easily make the journey. On the third day I was sitting in the stagecoach, rolling toward the east. Since I had never seen that landscape before, I was preparing my eyes for views of heath lands and forests. On the eighth day I was already wandering across an immense steppe, as splendid and as desolate as any Hungary has to offer.

At first my very soul was gripped by the immensity of

what I saw and felt: how the boundless air languished
about me, how the steppe exuded fragrance and a splendor
of loneliness was breathed out everywhere round about me.
But when everything was the same on the next day and
again the day after—forever and forever nothing at all but
the delicate ring where sky and earth kissed—my spirit grew
accustomed to it, my eyes began to be overwhelmed and
so cloyed with nothingness that they felt as if they had seen
too much. My sight turned inward, and while the sunbeams
played and the grass blades shimmered, various lonely
thoughts passed through my soul, old memories came
thronging across the heath, among them the picture of the
man whom I was on my way to see. I seized it gladly and
in the emptiness had time enough to piece together in my
memory all the features I had once known and to give them
a renewed freshness.

In southern Italy, in a wasteland as solemn as the one
I was crossing this very day, I had seen him for the first
time. He was, in those days, welcome in every gathering
and, although already nearly fifty years old, still the focus
of many beautiful eyes. A more handsome build and countenance could not be imagined, nor a person who knew
how to bear this exterior more nobly. I should like to call
it a gentle haughtiness which fairly flowed in all his movements and gestures, so simple and so victorious that more
than once it captivated even his male acquaintances. But
upon the hearts of women, so the talk went, he was supposed to have exerted in his day a truly bewildering effect.
People repeated stories of victories and conquests he was
supposed to have made and these were marvelous enough.
But there was one failing he was said to have which, for
the first time, rendered him really dangerous: namely, that
no one, not even the greatest beauty who trod this earth,
had succeeded in holding him longer than he himself chose
to be held. All the affection which every heart felt for him,
and the victorious bliss that went along with it, he accepted to the very end—whereupon he took leave, went on
a journey, and did not return. But this failing, instead of
frightening them away, endeared him all the more to

women, and many a quick-blooded southern heart burned
to cast its happiness and good fortune, the sooner the better, on this man's heart. Then, too, there was something
teasing about the fact that no one knew from whence he had
come or what his position was among men. Although all
agreed that the graces played about his mouth, still all admitted that upon his brow a kind of sadness hovered which
must be indicative of a significant past. But that, after all,
was the most alluring thing: that no one knew what this
past was. He was said to have been involved in affairs of
state; he was said to have been unhappily married; he was
reported to have shot his brother—and more things of this
sort. But one thing everyone knew: that he busied himself
now, very intently, with matters scientific.

I had already heard much about him and recognized him
immediately when, one day, I encountered him on Vesuvius, and watched him knocking stones down and then going over to the new crater and smilingly looking down at
the blue curling smoke as it rose from the opening and out
between the cracks. I crossed over the yellow gleaming
clods to him and called him by name. He answered amiably
and a conversation quickly ensued. Really, at that time
there was a terrible and dark wasteland around us—made
all the harsher since the indescribably pleasant, deep blue
southern sky stood directly over it and the little puffs of
smoke drew off sideways toward it. We spoke together a
long while that time, but we left the mountain separately
afterward.

Later I again found an opportunity to get together with
him. Thereafter we visited one another often and finally
we were almost inseparable until I left for home. I found
that he was rather blameless for the effects created by his
outward appearance. Out of his inmost being there often
broke forth something childlike, unconscious, lonely, and
even simple. He was unaware of his gifts and often, with
the utmost naturalness, spoke the most beautiful words I
ever heard from human lips, and never in my life—not even
later when I had opportunities to consort with poets and
artists—did I meet with such a responsive sense of beauty:

one which could be goaded to the point of irascibility by crudeness and ugliness. It may have been these unconscious gifts of his, too, which caused the hearts of the other sex to fly toward him—for the very reason that this splendor and glamour is so very rare in men of his years. This may have been the reason, too, for his liking to consort with me, still quite a young man, who in those days had not yet really learned to evaluate all these things properly—in fact, many of them did not really dawn upon me until I was older and had set about putting together this account of his life. I was never able to learn how far his legendary and fabulous good fortune with women actually went, since he never spoke about these things, and I never had an opportunity to observe on my own part. Neither could I perceive anything of the melancholy which was supposed to shadow his brow, nor could I learn anything at that time of his earlier history, apart from the one fact that he had once made extensive journeys but was now resident in Naples for many years, gathering specimens of lava and various antiquities. He himself told me, later, of his estates in Hungary and, as I have said, invited me repeatedly to visit him there.

We lived side by side for some time and when I left him our parting was not without emotion. But so many types of human beings and countries afterward passed across my consciousness that, in the end, I should not even have dreamt that one day I would be crossing a Hungarian steppe on my way to see this man as, in fact, I was now actually doing. In my thoughts I kept adding strokes to my memorized portrait of him. I became absorbed with this occupation and consequently often had trouble realizing that I was not in Italy; it was so hot, so silent, on that plain where I was walking, and the blue layers of mist in the distance conjured up a mirage of the Pontine marshes.

However, I did not strike out in a direct line for the estate which the Major had described to me in his letter. I undertook several crisscross excursions in order to have a better look at the country. Although on account of my friend, the Major, the image of this country had always

been mingled with impressions of Italy, now more and more
it emerged in its own peculiar way as something independ-
ent and complete. I had crossed a hundred brooks, creeks,
and rivers; I had slept among shepherds and their shaggy
dogs; I had drunk from those lonely springs on the heath
which are marked against the sky by their high, crossed
poles; and I had sat under many a low-hanging roof
thatched with reeds—yonder leaned the bagpiper, the swift
coach driver flew across the heath, the white cloak of the
horseman gleamed—often I thought to myself, wonderingly,
how my friend would look against the background of this
country. I had seen him only in society, among people who
were as like each other as the pebbles in a brook. There
he had appeared outwardly as the smooth and elegant gentleman; here, however, everything was different and often,
when I had seen nothing all day long but the distant red-
dishly blue twilight of the steppes and the thousands of
tiny white dots in it which were the cattle of that country,
when at my feet lay the dark black earth and so much
wildness, so much lushness—in spite of the ancient history
of the place, so much beginning and originality—I wondered how he would act here. I circled through that country, adapting myself more and more to its manners and
customs and peculiarities until it seemed to me that I heard
the ring of the hammer with which the future of its people
would be smithed. Everything in this country pointed to
coming times, everything dying was weary, everything on
the way toward becoming was on fire. That is why I was
glad to see these endless villages, these vineyards rising,
these marshes and reed banks and, far in the distance, its
gentle blue slopes.

After a month of wandering I one day finally felt that
I must now be very near the estate of my friend. Tired,
after all, of so much looking, so many things seen, I decided to end my pilgrimage and turn directly to my future
host. I had walked all afternoon through a sun-bathed,
stone-strewn landscape; at my left rose the far-off blue
heads of mountains against the sky—I took them to be the
Carpathians—and to my right lay rough torn land with that

peculiarly reddish coloration so often produced by the wind breathing across the steppes. But the two did not join together, and between them continued the endless picture of the plains. Finally, just as I was climbing up out of the hollow in which lay the bed of a dried-out stream, there jumped into my view to the right a forest of chestnut trees and a white house, both hidden from me till now by a sand dune. Three miles, three miles: almost all afternoon that is what I had heard when I asked about Uwar—this was the name of the Major's castle. Three miles: but since I knew from experience the nature of Hungarian miles, I had walked at least five of them, and so I wished with all my heart that the house before me might be Uwar. Not far off the fields rose up toward a ridge of earth on which I could see people. I proposed to ask them, and started across a strip of chestnut woods for this purpose. It was here I realized something that the frequent optical illusions of this country had already taught me; as I had suspected, the house was not situated by the woods at all, but behind a plain which ran off from the woods, and that it must be a very large building. Across the plain I now saw a figure coming at a gallop, directly toward those fields where the people were working. All the workmen gathered about the figure after its arrival as they might about a master—but this person looked nothing at all like my Major. I walked slowly up toward the ridge of earth, which was also at a greater distance than I had thought, and just as I reached it, the whole splendor of the sunset began to glow behind the dark waving corn fields and the group of bearded workmen grouped around the rider. The latter, however, I now made out to be a woman, about forty years old, who, strangely enough, was wearing the wide trousers customary to that country and was sitting astride her horse like a man. Since the hired hands were already dispersing, and she had remained almost alone in that place, I directed my question to her. Pushing my heavy knapsack up with my staff, I looked up at her and, as it were, brushed the light of the sunset out of my eyes as I wished her good evening in German.

She answered with the same greeting in the same language.

"Please do me the favor of telling me: is that building called Uwar?"

"That building is not called Uwar. Are you supposed to go to Uwar?"

"As a matter of fact, I am. I want to visit my friend, the Major, there, whom I met on my travels and who invited me to come."

"Then walk along awhile next to my horse."

With these words she started walking her horse, proceeding slowly so that I could follow her up the slope between the high green clumps of corn. I walked along behind her and had an opportunity to look around at the immediate landscape—which actually gave me more and more cause for surprise.

The higher we climbed, the more visibly the valley opened up; a great enormous garden-like forest extended from the castle into the mountains that began behind it. Avenues stretched out toward the fields; one piece of property after another came into view and seemed to be in excellent condition. Never had I seen such long juicy fresh leaves of maize with not a single blade of grass growing between the stalks. The vineyard, at whose edge we were just arriving, reminded me of those along the Rhine, except that I had never seen such luxuriant leafage and grape bunched on the Rhine as I saw it here. The plain between the chestnut trees and castle was a meadow, as soft and pure as though velvet were spread out. It was crossed by hedged paths, along which wandered the white cattle of that country, as smooth and slim as deer. All of this contrasted strangely with the stony fields that I had crossed during the day and which now lay out there in the evening air and in the reddish beams of the sun, hot and dry, looking in at all this cool green freshness.

By this time we had arrived at one of the white buildings I had noticed among the green of the vineyards, and the woman addressed a young man who, in spite of the hot June evening, was wearing a shaggy fur coat and busying

himself near the door of the cottage: "Milosch, the gentleman wants to go to Uwar this very evening; suppose you
take the two brown horses from the pasture, give him one
and accompany him as far as the gallows."

"All right," answered the fellow, straightening up.

"Just go with him now; he will get you there all right,"
the woman said, turning her horse to ride back the same
way she had come with me.

I took her to be some kind of inspector and wanted to
give her a large silver coin for the service she had done
me. But she only laughed and, in doing so, showed her
beautiful teeth. She rode slowly down through the vineyard, after which we heard the quick hoof beats of her
horse as she flew across the plain.

I put my money away again and turned to Milosch. He
had meanwhile put on a broad hat; he now led me some
distance into the vineyards; we began to climb the twisting
valley path until we came to a farm building from which
he pulled two of those small horses one customarily finds
in that heath country. Mine he saddled, mounting his as it
stood, and at once we rode into the evening twilight toward
the darkening east. It must have been a strange sight: the
German wanderer with knapsack, knobby stick, and cap
sitting astride his horse and, next to him, the slender Hungarian with his round hat, mustaches, shaggy fur coat, and
fluttering white trousers—both riding into the darkness and
wilderness. Actually it was a wilderness into which we entered beyond the vineyards, and this settlement was like
something legendary in the midst of it. As a matter of fact,
the wilderness was my old stony field which had remained
so much like itself that I had the illusion of riding back the
very same way I had come, except that the dirty red that
still glowed in the sky over my shoulders made me realize
that we were really traveling eastward.

"How far is it still to Uwar?" I asked.

"Another mile and a half," answered Milosch.

I was satisfied and rode along behind him as well as I
could. We rode past the same countless gray rocks that I
had counted all day long by the thousands. They slipped

past me on the dark ground in the false light, and because
we were actually arriving on dry firm moor land, I heard
not a hoof beat of our horses except when they might
chance to strike a shoe against stone, although these animals, used to paths of this kind, knew how to avoid that
very well. The ground remained level except where we had
to go down into two or three hollows and climb up again
out of the dry and pebbly beds of vanished streams.

"Tell me," I asked my companion, "who owns the property we have just left?"

"Marosheli," he answered.

I did not know, since he had spoken quickly while riding
ahead of me, whether this was the name of the owner, or
whether I had even understood him correctly since speaking and hearing were hindered by our riding.

Finally, a blood-red piece of a moon rose up, and in its
weak light there stood the slender scaffold which I took to
be our place for parting company.

"Here are the gallows," said Milosch. "Down there,
where you see it glittering, there is a brook. Next to it is
a black clump. Go toward that—it is an oak tree on which
criminals used to be hanged. Now it is no longer allowed
since we have a gallows. From the oak a road leads off,
with young trees planted on either side. Follow this road
somewhat less than an hour; you will reach a gate with a
bell pole. Even if the gate is not locked, do not go in—on
account of the dogs. Just tug at that bell pole. Now you
had better dismount, and button your coat tighter, so that
you don't catch a fever."

I dismounted, and even though I had not been successful
in attempting to give a reward to the inspector for her services, I nevertheless offered one to Milosch. He accepted and
put the money in his shaggy coat. Then he grabbed the
reins of my horse, turned and hurried away before I could
even ask him to give the owner of the horses my thanks.
Apparently he had wanted to get away from this place. I
took a look at it. Two columns stood upright and on them
was a crossbeam; thus it jutted up into the yellow moonlight. On the top lay something that looked like a head.

Actually it may have been almost any sort of an object. I went on; the heath grass behind me seemed to whisper and something stirred at the foot of the gallows. Of Milosch not the slightest sign remained, as if he had never been there. I arrived at once at the dead men's oak. The brook glittered and gleamed with an iridescence and circled around the reeds like a dead serpent. Next to the brook stood the black trunk of the tree. I went around it and, on the other side, came upon a straight white road, lit up by the moon. This road was packed down with much travel and had ditches and an avenue of young poplars. It did me good to be able to hear my steps echoing again as they usually do on the hard roads at home in our own country.

I walked along slowly; the moon rose more and more and finally stood clear in the warm summer sky. The heath stretched out beneath that light like a pale flat disk. Finally, after the passage of a good hour, black clumps, like a forest or a garden, rose before my eyes and soon the road came to a grill which was fixed in a wall, running out of the woods, and behind the wall were gigantically tall tree tops standing deathly still in the silver of the night air. Near the grill was a bell pole; I pulled it and could hear a ringing. Immediately I heard what was hardly to be called a barking, but rather the deep, resolute, and curious sniffing of noble dogs—a muffled jump—and then the largest, most beautiful dog I had ever seen in my life stood before me inside the grill. He stood up on his hind legs, seized the iron rods between his four paws, and looked out at me without uttering the slightest sound, quite in the usually serious manner of these beasts. Soon two smaller and younger animals of the same breed came running and growling, smooth-haired bulldogs, and all looked at me without turning their heads away. After a while I heard approaching steps and a man in a shaggy coat came and asked me what I wanted. I asked whether I was in Uwar, and I mentioned my name. He must have had instructions, because he immediately said some soothing words in Hungarian to the dogs and then opened the grill.

"The master has letters from you and has been expecting you for some time," said the man as we walked on together.

"I wrote him that I wanted to have a look at your country," I answered.

"And you have had a long look at it!" said he.

"Indeed," I answered. "Is the Major still awake?"

"He is not even at home, but attending a meeting. Tomorrow morning he will ride back home. He has had three rooms made ready for you and told us to take you to them in case you came in his absence."

"Very well, then lead me inside."

"Good."

These were the only words we exchanged on the long walk we were taking through what I should rather have termed a virgin forest than a garden. Gigantic firs stretched toward the sky and the oak boughs were as thick as a man's body. The largest of the dogs trotted quietly next to us; the others sniffed at my clothes and chased each other from time to time. When we had walked through the grove in this manner, we came to a treeless rise on which the castle stood; as nearly as I could make out, it was a large square building. A flight of broad stone steps led up; the most beautiful moonlight was reflected from them. Back of these steps was a somewhat flat open place and then a large grill, which served as gate to the house. When we arrived at this gate my companion spoke a few words to the dogs, whereupon they scooted off into the garden. Now he unlocked the grill and took me into the building.

On the stairway a light was still burning and shone upon strange high statues with broad boots and long hanging garments. I took them to be Hungarian kings. Then we entered a long corridor covered with reed mats. This was in the second story. We went along this corridor and then climbed another stairway into another such corridor. Opening one of a pair of doors, my companion said that these were my rooms, and we went in. After he had lighted several candles in each room, he wished me a good night and left me. After a while a servant brought wine, bread, and a cold joint, after which he, like his predecessor, offered

me a good night. I took this, along with the completeness
with which the rooms were furnished, to mean that I would
now remain alone and I therefore went to the doors and
locked myself in.

While I ate, I surveyed my apartment. The first room,
where my food had been placed on a large table, was spacious indeed. The candles, beaming brightly, lighted everything up. Furnishings and implements were different from
those we at home are accustomed to seeing. In the middle
stood a long table, at one end of which I was sitting.
Around this table oak-wood benches were placed, not
really very comfortable-looking, but rather as if intended
for meetings. Otherwise only here and there was a chair
visible. On the walls hung weapons from different periods
of history, presumably Hungarian. Among them were many
bows and arrows. Beside the weapons, clothes—also Hungarian—hung there, preserved from earlier times, including
those loose-hanging silk garments which must have been
either Turkish or Tartar in origin.

When I was finished with my night's supper, I went into
the two rooms adjoining this large hall-like one. They were
smaller and, as I recognized at once when my guide had
first shown them to me, were furnished more domestically
and more comfortably than the hall which I have just described. Everything was there that a lonely wanderer could
wish for in his dwelling: chairs, tables, wardrobes, wash-
stands, writing materials. Books lay on the night table, all
in the German language. In each of the two rooms stood a
bed, but instead of a bedspread, each one was covered with
the wide folk costume called a *bunda* spread upon it. This
is usually a coat or cloak of hides or pelts, with the raw side
worn inside, the smooth white one turned outward. The
latter frequently has all sorts of colorful trimming and is
decorated with colored leather designs that are sewed on.

Before I went to sleep, I stepped once more, as is always
my habit in strange places, to the window, in order to have
a look outdoors. There was not very much to be seen. But
this much I could make out in the moonlight: that the
landscape did not look German. Like another gigantically

magnified *bunda,* the dark area of the forest or garden was
spread out upon the steppe beneath—further off shimmered
the gray of the heath—then came all sorts of strips. I did
not know whether they were objects of this earth or layers
of cloud.

After I had allowed my eyes to wander for a while over
these things, I turned away again, closed the window, undressed, went to the nearest bed, and stretched out.

As I drew the soft fur of the *bunda* over my tired limbs,
and as I closed my eyes, I thought to myself: "Now I am
eager to know what things—pleasant or unpleasant—I shall
experience under this roof." Then I fell asleep and everything was dead, both what had been in my life and that
which I longed for.

II. *The House on the Steppes*

How long I slept, I do not know, but I do know that
it was not soundly. My all too great weariness must have
been to blame for this. All night long I was walking about
on Vesuvius, seeing the Major one moment in Pompeii
dressed as a pilgrim, the next in a frock coat among the
rubble, looking for stones. In a dream at dawn there were
the neighing of horses and the barking of hounds, then I
slept soundly for a time and when I woke up bright day
was streaming into the room and I looked out into the hall-
like outer room in which the weapons and clothes on the
walls were reflecting the bright sunshine. Down below, the
shady park was alive with the noise of birds, and when I
had got up and gone to one of the windows I saw the
heath sparkling in a net of sunbeams. Before I was completely dressed there was a knocking at my door; I opened
it and my old friend stepped in. I had been curious, especially during the last few days, as to how he might look;
now I found him looking no different than he naturally had
to look, namely, fitting so well into the whole environment
that I might have thought I had always seen him that way.

On his upper lip he wore the customary mustache, which made his eyes all the more sparkling. His head was covered by a broad round hat and he wore the loose white trousers of that country. This costume seemed so natural that suddenly I could no longer remember how he looked in a frock coat; in fact his dress seemed so charming to me that my German pilot coat which lay, dusty and worn, across a bench (but fortunately hidden by the silk garment of a Tartar) was now remembered almost with pity. His coat was shorter than the customary German coat but fitted in very well with his outfit. My friend appeared to have aged, certainly—for his hair was mixed with gray and his face was covered by those delicate and short lines which, in the case of well-built and well-preserved men, finally do indicate the growing count of the years—but he struck me as being as charming as ever.

He greeted me in a very friendly, very hearty, almost intimate manner—and after we had chatted for half an hour we were already as well acquainted as before. It seemed as though we had never separated since our Italian journey. While I was dressing, I made the remark that a trunk with my other things would arrive; he proposed that until such time, or if I so desired during my entire sojourn, I should wear Hungarian costume. I accepted the idea and the necessary articles were soon procured—with the added remark on his part that he would shortly provide for changes of linen. As we now came down into the courtyard among the servants, who were dressed exactly as we, they looked up at us, their faces with the dark mustaches and the bushy eyebrows expressing great approval as they brought us our horses for a morning ride. There was something so noble and calming in the whole scene that I felt myself inwardly truly refreshed by it.

Accompanied by the great gentle dog, we rode about among the Major's holdings. He showed me everything and handed out orders and words of praise occasionally to the workers. The park, through which we first rode, was a friendly sort of wilderness, very well cared for, kept clean, and traversed by paths. As we rode out onto the fields, they were billowing in the darkest shade of green. Only in England have I seen anything like it; but there, so it seemed to me, it was softer and more delicate, whereas this before me appeared stronger and more penetrated by the sun. Behind the park we rode gently uphill, and along the crest of this gentle rise, which stretched toward the heath, the vineyards were spread out. A dark broad leafage covered everything, the plantings took up a considerable stretch of ground; in all sorts of places peach trees had been inserted and, from the proper places, just as in Marosheli, the white of the small gleaming watchmen's houses, peeked through. Once out on the heath, we saw the Major's cattle, a huge, scattered, almost endless-looking herd. An hour of riding brought us then to the stud farms and the sheepfolds. As we crossed the heath, he pointed to a narrow black strip, which, far in the west, cut into the stretching gray of the steppe, and he said: "Those are the vineyards of Marosheli, where you got your horses yesterday."

We took a different way back, and now he showed me his gardens, his orchards, and his greenhouses. Before we reached them we rode past a rather mean-looking tract of land on which a considerable number of persons were working. To my question he explained that those were beggars, vagabonds, even tramps, whom he had won over through punctual payment to the point of working for him. They were just draining a swampy section and laying a road.

At noon, arriving home, we ate with all the men—and maidservants—in a kind of loggia, or rather, under a monstrous shelter next to a perfect giant of a walnut tree. By a wooden railing beside a wall, a gypsy was playing his music. At the table sat a stranger, a youth who caught my attention by his extraordinary beauty. He had brought letters from the neighborhood and he rode away again after the meal. He had been treated very respectfully by the Major; almost tenderly, in fact.

We passed the hot afternoon in the cool rooms. In the evening my host showed me the sunset on the heath. We rode out expressly for the purpose after he had advised me to put a fur around me, as he was doing, against the fever-

ish air of the plains, even though the yet warm air might
seem to make this unnecessary. We waited, after we had
ridden out, at a point indicated by him, until the sun had
gone down. And actually it was a view of splendor which
now followed. Over the entire black disk of the heath, the
giant shell of the burning, flaming, yellow sky came down,
flooding and overcoming the eyes so completely that every
object of earth became black and strange. A blade of heath
grass stands like a beam or girder against the glow, any
cattle straying past are sketched out like so many black
monsters against the golden background, and miserable
juniper or wild plum bushes are painted as distant cathe-
drals and palaces. Then, after a few moments, the damp
cold blue of night begins to climb up from the east and
cuts with dull opaque haze the actual gleam of heaven's
dome.

This spectacle lasts longest in the June days, when the
sun stands high for a long time. When we were already
back home and had eaten our evening meal, and passed
some time chatting together, and after I had gone to my
own room and was standing at the window and midnight
was already approaching, a dull yellow bit of light still
stood in the west, while in the blue east the red curve of
the half moon already was glowing.

On this evening I decided that the following day, or the
day after that, or whenever, in the succeeding days, the
opportunity presented itself, I would ask the Major about
the goal which, according to his letter, he claimed finally
to have found, saying that it bound him to his homeland
permanently.

The next morning he awakened me before dawn and
asked whether I wished to spend the day alone, or whether
I wished to share it with him. Either choice lay open to
me in the future as well. If I wished to take part in the
affairs and endeavors of the establishment, then I need only
—on that particular day when I had such an intention—
arise at the sound of the bell in the courtyard (which they
rang every morning) and join them all at the common
breakfast table. If, however, I should happen to have spe-

cial plans on any particular day, then his people were already instructed accordingly, in case he himself should not be on hand, to stand by with horses, escort, or anything else I might need. He would, he said, appreciate it if I could always tell him in advance about such things, especially whenever they involved extensive absences from the house, so that he might save me detours, difficulties, and perhaps even little dangers that might be involved. I was grateful to him for his readiness and explained that for today and tomorrow and, in fact, until such time as I might change my mind, I wished to share the time with him.

I therefore got up, dressed, and went down to breakfast under the projecting shelter. The work people were already almost finished and were separating to go to their various assignments. The Major had been waiting for me and delayed until I was finished eating my breakfast. Then the horses were brought up, all saddled. I did not ask what he was going to do, but merely followed him as he rode.

This day we did not ride around so much at random, to look at his possessions and undertakings in general, but rather he said he wanted to do what the day's duties demanded of him and I might watch, unless it bored me.

We came to an extensive meadow land on which they were haying. This beautiful Hungarian bay which the Major was riding bore him along on the lovely, soft, close-mown green turf, dancingly. He dismounted, while a groom held the horse, and examined the hay of several different stacks. The remark was made by the groom that it was ready to be carted in that afternoon. The Major gave orders that as long as the meadow was so close-mown, several ditches should be dug so that superfluous water might drain off and, in other places, so that it might be collected. From the meadow he took the path to the greenhouses, which were not, as is usually the case, near the mansion itself, but in a suitable place, where a gentle slope turned a sheltering side toward the east and the south. There was a neat little stable built next to these greenhouses, where the Major and his party, whenever anyone was with him, could leave their horses; for not infrequently he was forced to stay here a long time and when visitors were there who wanted to inspect the plantings, it often happened that several hours were thus occupied. We put our horses into this stable, leaving them saddled, and the Major first set about examining several plants and slips which had been requested and were being prepared for sending away; then he went into the gardener's room, where writing materials lay, and spent considerable time there at the desk. Meanwhile I looked at the things about me, understanding as much and as little of them as a constant traveler can who looks at one greenhouse after another. Later, however, when I went through the works in his library a little and looked at the illustrations of this subject matter, I recognized how little I actually knew about the care of this specialty.

"If one wants to have these charming things really bear fruit," said the Major one time, "one must pursue the matter thoroughly and try to excel the others who work in the same branch of endeavor."

Coming out of the gardener's room, he watched several women for a while as they were busied dusting and cleaning the green leaves of the camellias. This plant was still rare and expensive at that time. He examined those that had been cleaned and made some remarks. From there we went past the many clean white sand beds of the greenhouses in which stood the very young seedlings; then we passed all the flowers and varieties whose cultivation he had made his special interest. At the opposite exit our horses were waiting—a gardener's boy had meanwhile brought them around the back way. Here were places for mixing and preparing soils, brought from different regions in baskets by donkeys —sometimes from distant conifer forests all through the year. There were special places for heating earth, and near by the oak logs were stacked for the winter's fuel.

Since, as I had noticed the day before, it was not far from the greenhouses to the heath, we now rode out onto it. The good pace of our slim horses soon carried us so far out upon the monotonous plain, still in the haze of morning,

that we now saw castle and park only as a dim spot in
the distance. Here we came upon his shepherds. A few
poles, so thin that they were useless as protection, formed
a hut, or perhaps merely a sign which could be easily seen
and found on the steppe. Under these poles burned, or
rather glimmered, a fire, which was kept going by tough
branches or roots of the juniper, wild plum, and other
dwarfish plants. Here the shepherds, already at eleven
o'clock, were preparing to eat their noon meal. Brown figures, whose sheepskin coats lay about on the ground, were
standing in their shirt sleeves and dirty white trousers
around the Major and answering his questions. Others, who
had noticed his arrival on the wide flat plain, came hurrying
up on little, insignificant-looking horses, which had neither
saddle nor blanket, and instead of reins and halter often
only a rope. These shepherds dismounted and, holding their
animals, they surrounded the Major, who had likewise dismounted but given his horse for someone to hold. They
talked to him, not only about their work, but also about
other things, and he knew them almost all by name. He
was as amiable with them as if he were one of them, and
this, I believe, awakened a kind of enthusiasm among these
people.

As with us in the hills, so here, too, the animals were
out in the open all summer long. They were those white,
long-horned cattle who live on the grasses of the steppes
and which have a spiciness and a flowery smell which we
Alpine people can hardly believe. The men who tend these
animals likewise remain in the open and often have nothing
above them but the skies and the stars of the heath, often
—as we have seen—only a few sticks, or a hut dug out of
the sod. They stood before the Major and listened to his
orders. When he mounted his horse again one of them,
whose eyes blazed from a dark face and dark brows, held
his horse, while another, with long hair and thick mustaches, bent over and held his stirrup. "Farewell, children,"
he said as he rode away, "I will visit you soon again and
when our neighbors come over we shall spend an afternoon
on the heath and eat with you."

He had spoken these words in Hungarian and then translated them for me at my request.

As we rode away, he said to me: "If you should care sometimes to look at this heath and the life on it in detail, and should like perhaps to come out here alone sometime to live awhile, as it were, with these people, you would have to watch out for the dogs they keep. They're not always as tame and as patient as you have seen them today and they might give you a bad time. You must tell me beforehand so that I can accompany you, or, if I am not able to, I can assign a shepherd to guide you—one whom the dogs like!"

As a matter of fact, while we were standing by the shepherds' open fire, I had admired the unusually large, slender, shaggy dogs, of a kind I had never yet seen on all my wanderings, and which sat about next to us and among us, so well behaved by the fire, as if they understood what was going on and were taking part in the conversation.

As we rode away, we turned again toward the castle, since dinner time was already approaching. When we came past, as we had done the day before, that stretch where the people were at work draining the swamp and laying the outlines of a road, the Major, pointing to a wheat field close at hand where the grain stood extraordinarily ripe and beautiful, said: "This good ground, if it does its duty, must earn us the money to do other work elsewhere. These people work there on the heath all year. They have their daily wage and do their cooking outdoors, right next to their work. For sleeping, they go into those wooden huts which you see. In the winter, when ice forms, we go to the deeper spots which we cannot reach now on account of the softness of the ground, and we fill in rubble stones from the heath and stones that we have taken from the vineyards."

And, to be sure, as I looked over the peculiar prospect, I caught sight of the wooden huts he had been telling about and at several places on the broad back of the heath I saw a faint trace of smoke rising, which apparently indicated the simple hearths where the people were cooking their noon meal.

As we rode into the park, with the great and small hounds jumping about us, the bell was just ringing in the manor house, calling us and the others to the table.

On the evening of this day I did not ask my friend and former traveling companion about his finding of an ultimate goal, as I had so firmly resolved the night before as I went to sleep.

The afternoon passed as usual in a manor house, except that toward five o'clock the Major disappeared down the paved avenue of poplars on which I had arrived in the night; I do not know where he went. I was examining the books which he now ordered sent in increasing numbers from his library to my room.

The next day the Major had much writing to do and I passed the entire day inspecting those of his horses which he had at home, and making the acquaintance of his workmen.

On the day that followed this one, I was with him in the sheepfolds, an area two hours' ride away, where we spent the entire day. He had several people there who seemed to have considerable training and to be willing to enter wholeheartedly with him into the essentials of this enterprise which they loved so much. It was here, too, that I saw that each branch of the Major's many activities had its own financial administration; he advanced a sum to the sheep-raising division which had obviously been taken out of the earnings of another department. The matter was taken up and entered very exactly and correctly in writing. The folds were very extensive and the different flocks and breeds arranged according to their peculiar needs.

Another time I visited the stud farms and we were on the meadow where his colts and fillies and younger horses of ordinary breed stood about among the herdsmen, much as the cattle do elsewhere.

In this manner I came bit by bit to know the whole circle of his activities which truly was anything but small. I was surprised that he was able to pursue these affairs with such attentiveness and circumspection, the more so since I had known him earlier as a dreamer who dabbled and made researches in various branches of knowledge.

"I believe," he once said to me, "that one must start working with the very ground of a country. Our government, our history; these are very old, but there is still much to be done; we are, in our history, just like a flower that has been stuck for safekeeping in some old album. This broad land is a greater jewel than one might think, but it still is in need of the proper setting. The whole world is moving into a struggle to make itself useful, and we must move along with it. What beauty, what a blossoming is the body of this country capable of producing, in and of itself—and these things need to be drawn out of her. You must have seen it as you traveled here to visit me. These plains are the finest black arable earth, and in these hills full of glittering stones as far as to those blue mountains which you see in the north, sleeps the fiery fountainhead of the wine and, surrounded by the rich earth, slumbers the gleam of metal. Two noble rivers cross through our land; above them the air is, so to speak, still dead, and is waiting for countless many-colored banners to flutter in it. Many tribes live in this land—some of them still children who need to be shown what to do. Since I have been living in the midst of my people, over whom I actually have more power and more rights than you imagine, since I have been walking in their midst in their costume, have been sharing their customs, and have gained their esteem—it really seems to me as though I have achieved that happiness which I used always to be seeking in one or another distant region."

Now I no longer needed to ask the man about his goal, that goal he had mentioned to me in his letter.

It was especially the different sorts of grain to which he had turned his attention. And they stood there, too, in such abundance and beauty that I was already becoming curious to know when these ears would become ripe and when we should be able to harvest them home.

The solitude and power of these occupations reminded me rather frequently of the sturdy old Romans who had also loved the cultivation of the soil so much and who, at

least in their earlier period, had enjoyed their solitude and
power.

"How beautiful and how primitive," I thought, "is the
destiny of the countryman, if he but understands it and
ennobles this destiny. In its simplicity and multiplicity, in
living closely together with a nature that is dispassionate,
his destiny borders most nearly on the legend of Paradise."

After I had been for a protracted time on the Major's
estate, when I had learned to have a kind of overall view
of its parts and to understand them, as I saw things growing before my very eyes and partook of their flourishing:
then the uniformly gentle, flowing passage of these days
and occupations had so enmeshed me that I felt both
calmed and mildly stimulated, and I forgot all about our
great cities, just as though what went on in them were but
a trifle.

When we had been out again on the heath among the
horses, and when the herdsmen had been joined by the
cattlemen so that quite a crowd of these people were gathered together around us on the heath, the Major said to
me on our way home—for this time he had a beautiful team
harnessed and hitched before a wagon which, with its wide
wheel base, went rolling securely on the grass of the heath:
"These people I could lead even to the point of shedding
their blood for me, if I were to place myself at their head.
They are completely devoted to me. These others too, the
hired hands and workmen I have at home, would sooner
lose their limbs than let a hair of my head be touched. If
I count also the ones who are subject to me through rights
of property, along with those who are devoted to me (as
I have been able to learn on many occasions) from the bot-
toms of their hearts—then I think I would be able to gather
together a rather large number of people who really love
me. Think of it! And I did not come to them until my head
was already gray, and until I had forgotten them many
years. How must it be to lead hundreds of thousands like
them, and to lead them toward the Good; for mostly, when
they trust, they are like children, and follow toward the
Good as they might toward the Evil."

After a while he went on: "Once I believed I would be an artist or a scholar. But I came to see that such people must have a deep and serious message for mankind that will inspire them and make them nobler and greater. Or, that at least the scholar must bring things to light and invent things that will further men in their earthly and material good. In both cases it has to be that such a man himself first have a simple and a great heart. But since I do not possess such a heart, I let everything go again, and now it is all past."

It seemed to me that a gentle shadow passed over his eyes as he spoke these words, and as though he were looking at this moment out into space with the same ardor as once upon a time when we used to sit idly on the Epomeo together while an ocean of blue sky gleamed about us and sea below gleamed back, and he had talked of all sorts of wishes and dreams of young hearts. That is why the thought suddenly came to me that perhaps that happiness he had been telling me about having found was, after all, not yet quite there.

This had been the only time since our acquaintance that he referred to his past, something he had never before done in all our association. Nor had I ever asked; nor did I later. A person who travels much learns to spare others, and to let them have their own way within the inner household of their lives, whose doors never open except voluntarily. I had now been rather a long while at Uwar and liked being there, because I participated in the things that were going on—at least with passive interest, and often with real activity—and because I passed the rest of the time writing the memoirs of my experiences and the diaries of my travels. But this much I thought I could make out: that in the straightforward and busy life of the Major there lay some residue or other, some sediment, which would not let the pure essence of it clear, and I felt that some sort of sorrow was there, though of course the man expressed it only through his calm and seriousness.

Otherwise his life and his contacts with me were very plain and simple and without the slightest trace of reticence or disguise. There stood on the writing table in his study—a room I often entered and where we would frequently sit and chat about various things during the hot afternoons, or by candlelight in the evening—a certain picture. This, in its beautiful gold frame, was the miniature of a girl of perhaps twenty or twenty-two years, but it seemed strange that, no matter how the painter of it may have tried to conceal the fact, it was not the picture of a beautiful, but of an ugly, girl! The dark tone of the face and the structure of the forehead were strange, but they had something strong and forceful about them, and the look in the eyes had the wildness of a creature of resolution. That this girl must have played a role in his earlier life became clear to me, and the thought occurred to me that it was odd that this man had never married: the same thought I had had during our acquaintance in Italy. But just as my principles had forbidden my asking then, I did not ask now either. He could well allow the picture to stand there on his writing table, since none of his people came into the study, but were required to stop in the antechamber where a little bell rang as they entered, whenever any one of them had any business with him. Not even his acquaintances or callers ever came into that room, since he always received them in his other apartment. Therefore it betokened a degree of familiarity that I was allowed there and could look at everything that stood or lay in view. This familiarity was probably owing to the fact that I never inquired or dwelled upon these things.

Meanwhile the harvest time had come, a time I shall never forget for its joyfulness. The Major had found it necessary to make several little trips into surrounding country and invited me to accompany him. In no country are the distances between inhabited points frequently as great as here. But with their fast horses they can be covered in a relatively short time—either riding or driving them hitched to light carriages across the heath. On one occasion the Major was wearing the close-fitting Hungarian folk costume; he was in gala attire, with his saber at his side. His costume was very becoming to him. He made a speech in

Hungarian in the midst of a gathering of his district, discussing affairs of general interest. Since it has always been my habit, in every country which I visited, to learn quickly as much of the language as I could, I had already picked up some Hungarian from the Major's people and from all with whom I came in contact, with the result that I understood quite a bit of the speech. It seemed to call forth great admiration among one part of the audience, but among the other, equally violent disagreement. On our drive home, he translated his remarks completely into German for my benefit. That afternoon, at table, I saw him in his dress coat, as I had formerly seen him in Italy, and I noticed that most of those present had changed their folk costume and were wearing the generally accepted European formal attire.

I also accompanied him on other visits he made in the vicinity. Here I now learned that four country seats similar to the Major's existed. Some years before, a compact had been made for the improvement of agriculture and the production of goods, the basic idea being that each owner at first carried out his best efforts on his own estate and in this way set an example for the others by letting them see how prosperity developed. The compact had its own laws, and the members of it held agricultural meetings. Beside these four large model establishments, which actually up until now constituted the only members of the compact, several smaller owners had begun to imitate the procedures of their larger neighbors, without thereby becoming actual members of the compact itself. A meeting could be attended by all the farm operators and other people, if they but announced their intention beforehand, but they could come only as listeners-in, or, at times, as persons in need of advice. And they participated far from sparingly, as I learned from one gathering which was held four hours' ride away from Uwar on the estate of one member, Gömör, where the only members were the Major and Gömör, but where there was a considerable crowd of listeners. After this I was with Gömör twice by myself, the last time even passing several days with him.

Since the harvest was nearing its end and the work was decreasing somewhat, the Major said to me one day: "Now that we shall have a little leisure, we are going to ride over next week to my neighbor, Brigitta Marosheli, and pay a call on her. In the person of my neighbor Marosheli you will make the acquaintance of the most splendid woman on this earth."

Two days after this conversation, he introduced me to Brigitta's son, who by chance had come over. This turned out to be the same young man who, on the first day of my stay in Uwar, had taken noon dinner with us, and who had struck me at that time by his extraordinary beauty. He stayed the entire day and went with us to several different parts of the estates. He was, as I had already noticed the first time, in the earliest years of his youth, scarcely in the transition from boyhood to young manhood, and I liked him very much. His eyes were dark, gentle, and eloquent, and when he rode he was somehow both powerful and submissive. I was very much taken with the young fellow. I had had a friend very much like him and in the earliest years of his youth he had gone into his cold grave. Gustav, as Brigitta's son was called, reminded me vividly of him. Since the Major had spoken as he did about Brigitta, and since I now knew her son, I was very curious and eager to see her too, in person.

I had learned a little about the past of my host, the Major, from Gömör, when I had been with him. Gömör, like many of the Major's friends, was of an open, friendly, and conversational nature, and he told me what he knew without being asked. The Major had not been born in that region. He stemmed from a very rich family. Since his youth he had been almost constantly on his travels; one could not actually say where—just as one did not rightly know in whose services he had earned his rank of Major. In his entire earlier life he had never been on his estate of Uwar. A few years before, he had arrived, settled down in Uwar, and joined the confederation or compact of the friends of agriculture. At this time there had been only two members: he, Gömör himself, and Brigitta Marosheli. Actually it was not then a confederation or compact; the meetings and the laws did not come into being until later, but the two neighbors Gömör and Brigitta had jointly agreed to begin a better conduct of their estates in this waste region. Actually it had been Brigitta who had made the start. Since she was more readily called unbeautiful than even pleasant-looking, her husband, a young and frivolous man to whom she had been married at an early age, had left her and never returned. At that time she had appeared, with her child, at her estate, Marosheli, had set about, like a man, managing and making alterations, and down to this very time still dressed and rode like a man. She took care of her servants, was active and at work from morning until well into the night. One could see by this what uninterrupted work could accomplish, for she had almost brought about miracles out of the stony ground. Gömör had become her imitator as soon as he came to know her; he had introduced her methods on his estate, and had not, up to this time, ever been sorry for it. When the Major first settled in Uwar, he had not come over to see her for several years. Then one time when she was deathly sick, he had ridden across the heath to her and made her well again. From this time on he went constantly to see her. The people said at the time that he had used the healing powers of magnetism of which he had some knowledge, but nobody knew really anything at all about the whole affair. An unusually deep and friendly bond had developed—the woman was worthy, too, of the highest friendship—but whether the passion which the Major had conceived for the ugly and already aging Brigitta was a natural one or not, that, said Gömör, was another question. But passion it surely was, as everyone recognized who chanced that way. The Major would surely marry Brigitta if he could—he obviously was deeply grieved that he could not. But since nobody knew anything about her lawful husband, no death certificate and no certificate of divorce could be produced. This fact spoke strongly in Brigitta's favor and condemned the husband who once had left her so frivolously, whereas now such a serious man was longing to possess her.

These things Gömör had told me about the Major and Brigitta and I met Gustav, her son, several times more on the occasion of a visit which we made to neighbors, even before the day dawned that was appointed for us to ride over to his mother's estate.

On the evening before this day, when already the thousand-voiced chirping of the heath crickets fell upon my sleepy ears, I was thinking of her. I then dreamed all sorts of things about her, but especially I could not get free of a dream that I stood upon the heath before that woman rider who had loaned me the horse at the beginning of my visit, that she held me spellbound with her beautiful eyes, that I had to keep standing there, unable to stir a foot, and that all the days of my life I would never be able to budge from that spot on the heath. Then I fell tight asleep, awakened the next morning refreshed and strengthened, our horses were brought, and I rejoiced that I would now see face to face the one with whom I had been united in dreams so much the night before.

III.   *A Story of the Steppes*

Before I tell how we rode to Marosheli, how I made the acquaintance of Brigitta, and how I afterward was often a guest on her estate, it will be necessary for me to recount a part of her earlier life without which what followed would not be understandable. How I was able to acquire a really penetrating knowledge of the conditions narrated here will become clear from my relationship to the Major and to Brigitta, without its being necessary for me to disclose ahead of time what I did not learn ahead of time but only through the natural development of circumstances.

The human race possesses that wonderful thing called beauty. We are all drawn to the sweetness of this phenomenon and we cannot always say where the attractiveness lies. It is in the universe, it is in an eye, then again it is not in features formed in accord with every reasonable rule.

Often the beauty is not seen because it is in the desert, or because the proper eye for it is lacking—often it is worshiped and deified without being there. But never dare it be lacking wherever a heart beats in ardor and ecstasy, or where two souls take fire from one another; otherwise the heart stands still and the love of these souls is dead. From what ground this flower will blossom is a thousand times different in a thousand different cases; but when beauty is once there, one can take every opportunity of budding away from her and she will yet break forth in some new budding place, unsuspected before. This quality is peculiar only to man and it ennobles man as he kneels before it; everything that is rewarding and worth prizing in life, beauty alone pours into that man's trembling heart. It is sad for the one who does not have this thing called "beauty," or does not know it, or has no eye for it. Even a mother's heart turns away from her child if she is unable to find a single shimmer of this radiance in him.

Thus it was with the child Brigitta. When she was born, she did not appear as the beautiful angel which every child usually seems to be in the eyes of its mother. Later she lay in a beautiful golden cradle, among the snow-white linen, with an unpleasantly gloomy little face, as if she had been breathed upon by a demon. The mother turned her glance away, without knowing, and looked upon the two little angels who were playing on the rich carpeting. When strangers came, they did not criticize the new child, nor did they praise her; they merely asked for her sisters instead. In this way she continued to grow. Her father often crossed through the room as he went about his business, and when the mother often embraced the other children warmly (perhaps out of a despairing sense of affection), she failed to see the fixed black eyes of Brigitta focused upon her as if the tiny child already understood the insult. When she wept, they came to her assistance; if she did not weep, they let her lie. They all had enough to do for themselves, and she turned her big eyes to the gilt decorations of her crib or the arabesques of the wall tapestries. When her little limbs had become strong, and she could remain no longer in her narrow little bed, she would sit in a corner, playing with stones and uttering sounds that she had heard from no one. As she progressed in her games and became quicker, she would often roll her great wild eyes as boys do who already inwardly are acting out dark deeds. She hit at her sisters if ever they tried to mix into her games—and when her mother now, in a rush of belated love and pity, took the little creature into her arms and let her tears fall upon her, the child showed no joy at all, but rather wept, and twisted out of the embrace. Her mother, however, became both more loving and more embittered; she did not know that the roots of the little soul, which once had sought the warm soil of a mother's love and had not found it, had had to force their way into the rock of her own heart, there to remain defiant.

Thus the desert became even wider.

As the children grew up and pretty clothes were brought into the house, Brigitta's were always said to be "all right," while those of her sisters were becomingly altered. The others received rules of conduct and praise; she not even blame when she soiled or wrinkled her dress. When the time came for learning things and the hours of the morning were filled, she sat and stared with the only thing of beauty she possessed, with her really beautiful darkling eyes, at the corner of a distant book or map. And whenever the teacher put a quick question to her, which happened rarely, she became frightened and could give no answer. But on long evenings or at other times when everyone was in the parlor and no one noticed her absence, she was lying on the floor among heaps of books or looking at pictures and torn maps which the others no longer used. In her heart she must have hatched a fanatical and crippled world. From the bookcases of her father, where he had left the keys, she had read nearly half the books without anyone's suspecting it, and the greater part of them she could not even understand. In the house one often found papers on which strange wild things were written or drawn, which must have been her work.

When the girls entered young womanhood, she stood

among them like a strange plant. The two sisters had become soft and lovely—she merely slim and strong. Her body held an almost masculine power which revealed itself when one or the other sister wanted to say some teasing trifling thing to her, or wanted to caress her, and Brigitta merely turned her away calmly with her strong arm, or when she took up (as she liked to do) some work worthy of a hired man and kept at it till the drops of sweat stood out on her brow. She did not learn to play any musical instrument, but she rode well and boldly and like a man; often she lay in her best dress on the turf of the garden and made fragmentary speeches or shouted into the foliage of the bushes. And now it happened that her father began to admonish her about her stubborn and silent ways. And then, if she were in the middle of speaking at last, she would suddenly break off; she became even more silent and even more stubborn. Nor did it help at all that her mother gave certain signs and signals to her, or showed her displeasure by wringing her hands in bitter frustration. The girl would not speak. When her father once so far forgot himself as to chastise her—a grown girl—physically, on an occasion when she absolutely refused to go into the sitting room, she merely gazed at him with hot dry eyes and still did not go, no matter what he might do with her.

If only there had been but one person who might have had an eye for her veiled soul and might have seen its beauty, so that she should not despise herself! But there was no one; the others could not do it, and she could not either.

Her father lived in the capital, as was his wont, and indulged himself in a life of splendid luxury. When his daughters were grown, the reputation of their beauty spread throughout the country. Many came to see them, and the assemblies and social evenings in the house became more frequent and more lively than they had been before. Many a heart beat violently and coveted the possession of the jewels which this house sheltered—but the jewels themselves paid no heed to it all, they were too young to understand such homage. All the more did they give themselves to the pleasures which such gatherings bring, and a gala ball dress or the arrangements for a festive occasion could keep them busy for days in the most complete and utter absorption. Brigitta, being the youngest, was never asked about anything, as though she did not understand the business at hand. She was often present at the gatherings and assemblies and, when she was, she always wore a broad black silk gown which she herself had sewn. Or she avoided the occasion and sat alone the while in her room and nobody knew what she was doing there.

In this way several years passed.

Toward the end of this period of time, a man appeared in the capital, a man who excited attention in the various circles of that city. His name was Stephan Murai. His father had brought him up in the country in order to prepare him for life. When his education was completed, he had first begun to set out upon various journeys. Then he was supposed to become acquainted with the elite society of his fatherland. This was the reason that he came to the capital. Here he soon became almost the sole topic of conversation. Some praised his mental powers, others his behavior and his modesty, still others vowed that they had never seen anyone so handsome as this man. Several insisted that he was a genius and, since there was no lack of slander and gossip, many said that there was something wild and shy about him, and that you could tell by looking at him that he was brought up in the woods. A few were also of the opinion that he was proud and, so far as that was concerned, certainly false as well. Many a girlish heart was, to say the least, curious to catch just one glimpse of him. The father of Brigitta knew the family of the new arrival very well; in earlier years, when he still traveled a good deal, he had often visited on their estates and it was only later, when he constantly lived in the capital, to which they never came, that he had lost contact with them. When he inquired about the condition of their estates, which had once been excellent, and learned that they were now in an even better condition than previously and, in view of the family's simple way of living, were continuing to improve —he thought to himself that if the fellow were otherwise as well a man, so to speak, to his own liking, then he might well provide a worthy bridegroom for one of his daughters. However, since quite a number of fathers and mothers were thinking the same thing, the father of Brigitta made haste to win the advantage of time over the others. He invited the young man to his house. Murai accepted and had come to several soirées there. Brigitta had not seen him, because just at that time she had not entered the sitting room for quite a while.

One time she went to her uncle's house when he arranged a sort of festivity and invited her to it. Previously she had often enjoyed going to see her uncle's family. On that particular evening she was sitting there in her usual black silk dress. She was wearing a headdress which she herself had made and which her sisters said was ugly. At least it was not the custom anywhere in the whole city to wear one of this kind, but it did go very well with her dark complexion.

There were many people present and when, at one time, she looked through a group of them, she perceived a pair of dark and gentle youthful eyes fixed upon her. She looked away immediately. When, later on, she looked again in that direction, she noticed that the same eyes were again directed toward her. It was Stephan Murai who had looked at her.

About a week later there was a dance at her father's house. Murai was among those invited and arrived when most of the people were already there and the dance had begun. He stood and watched and when everyone was taking their places for the second dance, he walked toward Brigitta and asked her in a modest tone for a dance. She said that she had never learned to dance. He bowed and mingled again among the spectators. Later he was seen to dance. Brigitta sat down behind a table on a sofa and watched the goings on. Murai talked to different girls, danced and joked with them. On this evening he was especially affable and obliging. Finally the amusements were over, people dispersed in all directions, each to his house. When Brigitta arrived in her bedroom, which, after much begging and defiance, she was finally permitted to occupy as her very own, and when she had begun to undress herself, she happened to glance in the mirror and saw her brown forehead glide across its surface and the raven black curl about her brow. Then, since she could not bear to have a serving maid near her when she dressed or undressed, she went toward her bed, threw the snow-white linen back, lay down upon the hard mattress and put her slim arm under her head. There she lay with sleepless eyes staring at the ceiling.

When, in the days and weeks that followed, there were parties and Brigitta attended them, she was again noticed by Murai, greeted by him with the greatest respect; when she left the room, he brought her her scarf and when she was gone one immediately heard his carriage wheels roll and he went home.

This went on for quite some time.

She was at her uncle's again one evening and, finding the salon very warm, she had stepped out onto the balcony whose doors always stood open. Dense blackness lay all about her and she heard Murai's step coming toward her and saw even in the dark how he took his place next to her. He spoke of nothing but the most ordinary things and yet, if one listened to his voice, it seemed as though there were something frightened in its quality. He praised the night and said that people did not do the night justice when they complained about her, since she was so beautiful and mild; the night alone could cloak, soothe, and calm the heart. Then he was silent and so was Brigitta. When she entered the room again, he came in with her and stood for a long time by a window.

After Brigitta had arrived home that evening, gone to her room and taken her finery piece by piece from her body, she stepped before the mirror in her nightgown and gazed for a long, long time. Tears came to her eyes, tears that did not stop, but gave way to more tears that came trickling down. These were the first tears of the soul in her whole life. She wept more and more violently; it seemed as if she had to catch up on her entire neglected life and as if this would all be much easier if she could only weep her heart out. She had sunk down upon her knees, as she was often accustomed to do, and she was sitting on her own feet. On the floor next to her there chanced to lie a little picture; it was a children's picture showing one brother sacrificing himself for the other. She picked it up and pressed it to her lips until it was crushed and wet.

When finally the springs had dried and the candles had burnt down, she was still sitting on the floor in front of her mirror table, like a child who had cried its eyes out, and she sat there thinking. Her hands lay in her lap, the bows and frills of her nightgown were damp and hung without beauty about her chaste breast. She became quieter and more motionless. Finally she drew several deep breaths, passed the flat of her hands over her eyelids, and went to bed. As she lay there with the night lamp, which she had placed behind a little screen after the candles were out, burning dimly, she said these words: "It is not possible, it is not possible!"

Then she fell asleep.

When, in the future, she met Murai again, things were as they had been; only, he took even more notice of her, but otherwise his behavior was shy, almost hesitant. He hardly said anything to her. She herself did not take a single, not even the slightest, step toward him.

When, after a time, another opportunity offered itself for him to be alone with her and to speak with her, after having let many such slip by unused, he took courage, addressed her and said that it seemed to him that she was disinclined toward him—and if this were true, then he had but one request, namely, that she become acquainted with him—she might find him after all not entirely unworthy of her attention, perhaps he had qualities—or could acquire such—as might gain him her esteem, if indeed not something that he desired even more devoutly.

"Not disinclined, Murai," she answered, "oh, no, not disinclined; but I, too, have one request to make of you: do not do it, do not do it, do not court me, you would regret it."

"But why, Brigitta, why?"

"Because," she answered softly, "I can desire no other love but the highest. I know that I am ugly, therefore I would demand a higher love than would the most beautiful girl in this world. I do not know how high, but it seems to me as though that love ought to be without measure or end. Now you see—and since this is impossible, you must not court me. You are the only one who has asked whether I, too, have a heart and toward you I cannot be false."

She would probably have said still more if some people had not come up to them, but her lips were trembling with pain.

That Murai's heart was not calmed by these words, but only set afire the more, is readily understood. He honored her like an angel of light; he remained withdrawn, his eye passing over the greatest beauties that surrounded him, merely seeking her eyes with a gentle plea. This went on without any change. In her, too, the dark power and majesty of emotion began to make the poor soul tremble. It appeared evident in both. Those in their environment began to suspect the unbelievable, and people were openly astonished. Murai definitely exposed his soul before the eyes of the world. One day, in a lonely room, when the music for which people were gathered together sounded from a distance, as he stood before her saying not a word, he took her hand and drew her gently toward him. She did not resist, and when he bent his head and his face closer to hers and she suddenly felt his lips upon hers, she pressed her lips sweetly upon his. She had never before felt a kiss, since she herself had never been kissed, even by her mother or her sisters—and Murai, many years later, once said that he never again experienced such a pure joy as at that time when he first felt those lonely, untouched lips upon his mouth.

The curtain between the two of them was now rent and fate went its way. Within a few days, Brigitta was the declared fiancée of the celebrated man; the parents on both sides had agreed. An easy, friendly atmosphere prevailed. Out of the deep emotional nature of this previously unknown girl, a warmth emerged, timidly at first, then de-

veloping richly and serenely. The instinctive feeling that
had drawn this man to this particular woman had not
deceived him. She was strong and chaste beyond other
women. Because she had not weakened her heart prema-
turely by thoughts of love and imagined images of love,
the breath of an unadulterated strength of life was carried
to his soul. Her society was charming. Because she had always been alone, she had built her world alone too, and
he was now introduced into a remarkable new realm that
belonged to her alone. As she allowed her nature to unfold
before his eyes, he came to recognize her peculiarly sincere
and warm lovingness, which welled up like a golden stream,
high and full between its banks, full but lonely; as the
hearts of other human beings were split and scattered to
half the world, hers had remained together and since only
a single person had recognized it, it was now the sole
property of this one person. And in this way he lived in a
great joy and an exaltation through the days of their engagement.

Time passed on rose-colored wings and, within time, fate
on her darker pinions.

Finally the wedding day had arrived. When the religious
service was over, Murai took his silent bride into his arms
on the threshold of the church, lifted her into his carriage,
and drove with her to his house, which, since the young
people had decided to remain in town, he had furnished
most beautifully and most elegantly, making use of some of
the money which his father had placed at his disposal.
Murai's father had come in for the wedding from the country estate which was his chosen place of permanent residence. His mother unfortunately was not alive to share in
the joy of the occasion; she had long since passed away.
Of the bride's family, the father, the mother, the sisters,
uncle, and several close relatives were present. Both Murai
and Brigitta's father had wanted the day to be celebrated
publicly and resplendently and that is exactly the way it
had gone.

When finally the last guests had departed, Murai conducted his wife through a suite of brilliantly lighted rooms

(she herself had, up to now, always had to be contented
with a single one) into a rear living room. There they were
sitting and he was speaking these words: "How well, how
splendidly everything went! And how beautifully everything has been fulfilled! Brigitta! I knew you for what you
are. The very first time I saw you, I knew that this woman
would not remain an object of indifference to me; but I
could not yet make out whether I would love you eternally
or eternally hate you. How happily it all turned out that
it was love!"

Brigitta said nothing; she held his hand, letting her glistening eyes wander calmly about the room.

Then they ordered the servants to clear away the re-
mains of the celebration, to extinguish the great number of
superfluous lights, so that the festive rooms could become
a more usual kind of living place. And it was done; the
servants retired to their quarters; and upon the new household and upon the new family, consisting of but two and
still only a few hours old, the first night settled down.

From now on they lived within their own household. Just
as, when they had first come to know one another, they
had met only in company, at parties, and just as during
their engagement they had appeared together only in public, now they remained at home all the time. They did not
feel that anything extraneous was necessary to their happiness. Although the house was well provided with everything they needed for their convenience, still there remained
many little things that could be improved upon and beau-
tified. They figured these things out, thought over what
they could add here and there, helped each other with
word and deed, until finally their rooms acquired a better
arrangement and lay ready to receive visitors in beautiful
simplicity and hospitality.

When a year had passed, she bore him a son; and this
new wonder kept them at home more than ever. Brigitta
took care of the child; Murai attended to his business since
his father had turned over to him a good part of the estates and these he managed from town. This necessitated
his taking many trips but he was also able to combine, in

this way, many problems which would otherwise have demanded separate solutions.

When the boy was far enough along in his development not to need much immediate care, and after Murai had his affairs set in order, he began to take his wife out more often into public places, to soirées, on walks, to the theater—even more than he had done before. She noticed that he treated her with more elaborate tenderness and attentiveness in front of others than at home. She thought: "Now he knows what is the matter with me," and kept her choking heart to herself.

The following spring he took her and their child along on a journey and when, toward autumn, they returned, he proposed that they live permanently on one of his estates, it being much more beautiful in the country and much more pleasant than in the city.

Brigitta followed him to the country estate.

Here he began to manage, to make changes and introduce innovations on the estate, and the rest of the time that was left to him he spent in hunting. And here fate brought before him a very different woman from the kind he was accustomed to seeing. On one of the lonely hunting trips he now often made, walking or riding alone with his gun through this landscape, he had caught sight of her. Once when he was slowly leading his horse a little off the road, through a strip of marshy pasture land, suddenly, through the thick foliage, he came face to face with two eyes, frightened and beautiful, exotic as the eyes of a gazelle, and next to the green leaves shone the rosy dawnlike glow of her cheeks. It was only for a moment; before he could really see her clearly, this creature, who was likewise on horseback, turned her mount out of the bushes and flew across the plain.

This had been Gabriele, the daughter of an old count who lived in that neighborhood; she was a wild creature; her father had brought her up out in the country where he allowed her to enjoy every freedom, because it was his idea that this way and this way only could she unfold herself as Nature willed her to be, and not turn into one of those doll-like personalities he found unbearable. The beauty of this Gabriele was already famous far and wide, but her fame had not reached Murai's ears because up to this time he had never been on this one of his estates and had recently, in fact, been on his travels.

After several days the two of them met again on the very same spot, and then more and more often. They did not ask one another who they were or where they came from; the girl, with boundless unconcern, joked, laughed, and teased him and egged him on to bold and reckless races, during which she flew along beside him like a divinely mad and feverishly glowing will-o'-the-wisp. He joined in with her teasing play and mostly let her win. But one day, when she was so breathless with exhaustion that she could only indicate by repeatedly trying to reach his reins that she wanted him to stop, and when, dismounting, she had whispered languishingly that she was beaten—on that day, after he had adjusted something on her stirrup strap that had gone awry, and looked up and saw her leaning against a tree trunk, panting—he suddenly seized her, pulled her close, pressed her to his heart, and before he could tell whether she was angry or happy about it, he sprang to his horse and galloped away. It had been presumptuous, perhaps, but the dizziness of an ecstasy beyond description was his at that moment, and before his soul's eye, as he rode home, hung suspended the image of her gentle cheek and the memory of her sweet breathing and the brightness reflected in her eyes.

From then on they did not attempt to see one another. But one time when, quite by chance, they met in the house of a neighbor for a brief moment, their blushes turned their cheeks almost scarlet.

Murai now went to one of his more distant estates; once there he made extensive alterations and occupied himself there for a long time.

But Brigitta's heart was near expiring. There had grown and welled up in her bosom a whole round world of shame as she kept her silence and walked about in the rooms of their house like the shadow of a cloud. And then, finally, she took this swollen screaming heart into her hand, as it were, and pressed it to death.

When he came back from the distant estate, she went into his room and with gentle words she proposed their divorce. When he showed how greatly shocked he was, when he begged her and offered other solutions, she only kept saying the same words, "I told you that you would live to regret it, I told you that you would live to regret it!"—until he jumped up, took her by the hand, and said with deep conviction in his voice, "Woman, I hate you unutterably, I hate you unutterably!"

She did not say a word, but merely looked at him with dry inflamed eyes. When, three days later, he had packed and dispatched his trunks—when he himself, in his traveling clothes, had ridden away toward evening—then she lay again, as once when she had whispered the poetry of her heart to the bushes in the garden, stretched out now with grief upon the carpet of her room. The tears that ran from her eyes felt so hot that they must surely have been capable of burning through her gown, the carpet, and the boards of the flooring; but they were the last tears she ever sent after the man she still loved so hotly. Meanwhile he rode across the darkened plain and a hundred times the thought came to him to take up his saddle pistol and blow his own brains out. And as he rode, and while it was still day, he came past the home of Gabriele; she stood on the balcony of her castle, but he did not look up; he rode on.

After half a year he sent Brigitta his consent to a divorce and gave up his rights to the boy, too, either because he knew him to be in better hands with her, or because it was the old love that did not want to rob her of everything and leave her completely alone while the whole world lay open before his feet. In regard to their fortune, he had taken care of her and the boy as generously as could possibly have been done. With his consent to the divorce, he sent papers along regulating these financial matters. This was the first and the last sign that Murai had ever given of his existence; after this, nothing more was heard, nor did he appear again. The moneys which he needed were turned over to a firm in Antwerp, as his attorney later explained, but more than this even the attorney did not know.

At about this same time, in very quick succession, Brigitta's father, her mother, and both her sisters died. Murai's father, who already was very advanced in age, also died a short while afterward. Thus Brigitta was left, in the literal sense of the phrase, completely alone with her child.

Far from the capital she had a house on a desolate heath, where she knew no one. The place was called Marosheli and it was from here that the name of the family stemmed. After the divorce she resumed her original name, Marosheli, betook herself to the house on the heath, to remain there in concealment.

Just as once when, out of pity, they had given her a beautiful doll, she threw it away again after a brief period of joy over it, and replaced it in her bed with a few miserable things such as stones, bits of wood, and the like, so now she took her chief possession along with her to Marosheli, namely, her son, took care of him and protected him and the glance of her eyes hung continually and solely above his small bed.

As he grew bigger and as his eyes and his heart opened wider, hers did likewise; she began to see the heath country, the moors round about her, and her mind began to work at the wilderness. She began wearing men's clothes, she took again, as once in her youth, to riding horseback and appeared often among her working people on the estate. As soon as the boy could even sit on horseback, he went along with her everywhere, and the active, creative, commanding soul of his mother gradually flowed into him. This soul reached out in an ever-widening circle; the Creator's heaven sank down and seemed to become a part of her: green hills rose up, springs ran, the leafy vineyards whispered, and the powerful crescendo of a heroic epic was written into what had been a wilderness of stony fields. And the heroic strains of this living poem, as is the wont of poetry, bore blessings. Many followed her example; the society, or compact, came into existence; more distant persons became enthusiastic, and here and there on the desolate blind heath land a kind

of free human activity opened up like a beautiful eye opening in the desert.

After fifteen years, during which Brigitta lived at Marosheli, the Major came, arriving to take residence at his
country estate of Uwar, where he had never been before.
From this woman he learned, as he himself told me, activity
and effective work—and for this woman he conceived a
deep and belated attachment.

IV. *Time: The Present; Place: The Steppes*

We rode to Marosheli. Brigitta had really been that
woman on horseback who gave me the horse for my first
ride to Uwar. She remembered our previous acquaintance
with a friendly smile. There were no other visitors but the
Major and I. He introduced me as a traveling acquaintance,
with whom he had once spent a good deal of time, and
added that he flattered himself that I was on the point of
graduating from an acquaintance into a friend. I had the
joyful experience—and to me it was no small joy—of finding
that she knew almost everything about my former contacts
with the Major, that he obviously must have told her a
great deal about me, that his memories still liked to linger
upon those days, and that she herself took the trouble to
notice and remember all these details.

She said that she wished to conduct me through her castle and show me around her estate and that I should have
a chance to see everything, either while we walked about
now, or if I should care to come over often from Uwar,
which she cordially invited me to do.

She reproached the Major for not having come over in
such a long while. He excused himself on the grounds of
having been occupied with many things, but chiefly because, as he said, he did not want to ride over without me
and yet wished to ascertain first whether or not I might
be a congenial person for her to meet and know.

We went into a great hall, where we sat down and re-

laxed a bit after our ride. The Major produced a tablet
and began to ask her about various things. She answered
clearly and simply and he noted down a number of her answers. After this, he asked her some questions in reference
to her neighbors, to the business of the present and the
meeting that was to convene in a short time. This gave me
an opportunity to see with what deep seriousness she conducted her affairs and what attention the Major paid to her
opinions. Whenever she felt on unsure ground on some
question, she admitted her ignorance and asked the Major
for the correct answer.

When we had rested a bit and the Major put his writing
pad away, we went for a walk through the estate. There
was much discussion of recent changes in her establishment. Whenever she happened to refer to matters of the
Major's household, it seemed to me that there was a kind
of tenderness in the concern she showed for these things.
She took us to the new wooden arcade, level with the con-
servatory of the house, and asked whether she should plant
and train grapevines up the sides of it. She said she thought
it would make a pleasant place by the court-side windows,
where one could sit in the late autumn sunlight. She took
us into the park, which had been a wild forest of oak trees
ten years before; now paths crossed through it, channeled
springs flowed, and the deer were wandering. By indescribable perseverance, she had built a high wall all around the
immense perimeter to keep the wolves out. The funds to
pay for it she drew gradually from her cattle raising and
from her fields of maize, whose cultivation she had advanced very greatly. When the wall was finished, a closed
rank of hunters went through the whole park, step by step,
to see whether, by chance, perhaps one wolf might have
been left walled in inside the park, which could have meant
an entire brood of wolves in the future. But there was not
a one to be found. After that they put deer into the enclosure and it seemed almost as if the deer knew all about
these provisions and thanked Brigitta for them. Whenever
we met one on our walk, it did not shy away but stood and
looked over at us with dark and shining eyes. Brigitta

loved the park and enjoyed taking guests and friends there. From there we came into the adjoining subdivision where the pheasants were kept. As we walked along the paths under tall oaks, with white clouds peering down between the tree tops, I observed Brigitta. Her eyes seemed more black and gleaming than those of the deer and they must have been especially bright this day because the man walking beside her was the one man who best appreciated her efforts and her creativity. Her sound snow-white teeth, her figure—still slender for her years—showed health and vigor and inexhaustible energy. Since she had been expecting the Major, she was wearing women's clothes and had put all business aside for that day, in order to devote her time entirely to us.

In the midst of talk on the greatest variety of subjects— the outlook for the country, the betterment of the common man, the cultivation of the soil, the regulation and control of the Danube, outstanding patriotic personalities—we had crossed through the largest part of the park; she had not really wanted to conduct us through her holdings, but more to bear us company as we walked. We arrived back at the house just as it was time to eat. Gustav, Brigitta's son, joined us at the table: a fine-looking slim youth, with sunburnt cheeks; he was the very picture of flourishing health. That day he had taken his mother's place in making the rounds through the fields, dividing up and assigning tasks, and now he reported to her, briefly and to the point. Then he sat modestly at the lower end of the table, listening. In his fine eyes one could read enthusiasm for the future and infinite kindness toward the present. Just as at the Major's, the retainers all sat with the masters at the table; among them I noticed my friend Milosch, who waved a greeting in sign of old acquaintance.

The greater part of the afternoon was spent inspecting various new alterations which the Major had not seen before; after that we took a turn through the gardens and then toured the vineyards.

We took our leave toward evening. As we were gathering our wraps together, Brigitta scolded the Major for having

ridden home recently from Gömör in the night air wearing
lightweight clothes—didn't he know, she asked, how tricky
the dewy winds of these plains were, exposing himself to
them like that? He did not defend himself and promised in
future to be more cautious. But I knew very well that
on that particular occasion he had forced Gustav (who had
come without one) to borrow his *bunda*, pretending to him
that he had an extra one in the stable. This time, however,
we parted well provided with everything. Brigitta took care
of every detail in person and did not go back into the house
until we were on our mounts, well covered by our thick
overcoats. The moon was rising. She had given the Major
a few last-minute errands or requests and she said good-bye
to us with a friendliness that was both plain and noble.

The conversations of these two had been calm and serene
all day long, and yet it seemed to me as though some secret
and inward thing trembled through, something which they
were both ashamed to express because they considered
themselves too old. But on the way back, the Major said to
me, when I couldn't help making a few frank and com-
plimentary remarks—well deserved, too—about this woman:
"My friend, often in my life I have been hotly desired,
whether as hotly loved or not, I cannot say; but the company and the esteem of this woman have become to me a
greater happiness in this world than any other in my whole
life that I may at one time have taken to be such."

He said these words without trace of passion, but with
such a calm certainty that, in my heart, I was utterly convinced of their truth. What came close to happening to me
at that moment is not usually characteristic of me: I prac-
tically envied the Major this friendship and his way of life
and life activity; for at that time I had no firm existence
of my own in this wide world, nothing to lay hold of but
my wanderer's staff, so to speak, which I had set into motion in order to visit this land and that land, but which was,
in the long run, beginning to be a burdensome thing.

Back at his home, the Major proposed that I stay on with
him through the summer and the coming winter. He had
begun to treat me in a very confidential manner and to

allow me to look more deeply into his life and heart; as a consequence, I conceived a strong inclination, a great love for this man. And so I consented to stay. And once I had done so, he said that he wanted immediately to assign the management of one branch of his establishment regularly to my supervision—that I should not be sorry, and that it would most certainly be of advantage to me in the future. I agreed to this too, and as things worked out, it was actually of advantage to me. That I now have a household of my own, a beloved wife for whom I live and work, and that one good thing after another has come our way and been drawn into the charmed circle of our lives, all of this I really owe to the Major. At that time, when I formed a part of his harmonious plan, I wanted to do my little part as well as I possibly could. With practice, I improved constantly; I became really of use to him and I gained some self-confidence and self-esteem. Once I had tasted the joy of creative work, I came to recognize how much more valuable the achievement of an immediate end can be, rather than the endlessly dragging procrastination I had previously been guilty of—something I had called "gathering experience"—and now I accustomed myself to activity.

In this way time passed day by day and I was boundlessly glad to be in Uwar and the country around it.

In the course of my work I often got over to Marosheli. They were fond of me and I was almost a member of the family and came to know the situation better there. Of those things of which I had heard—a secret passion, a feverish desire, or even a definite magnetism—there was not a trace. On the contrary, the relationship between Brigitta and the Major was of a most remarkable sort; I have never seen anything quite like it. It was—there is no denying—what, between persons of opposite sex, we should call love, but it did not appear as such. The Major treated this woman, as she grew older, with a tenderness, a respect, that reminded one of devotion to a higher being. She was visibly filled with an inner joy at this: a joy which made her countenance blossom like a late autumn flower, spreading a breath of beauty over it that was incredibly lovely, yet as firm as the hardy rose of serenity and health. She returned the same respect and esteem to her friend, the Major, yet mingled at times with a trace of worry about his health, about his little daily needs and such matters— a worry that really belonged in the particular sphere of a woman and of love. But the behavior of both of them did not go a hairsbreadth beyond this—and in this way they went on living almost side by side.

One time the Major told me that, in such an hour as is rare between human beings, he and Brigitta had had a deep discussion about themselves and had determined that friendship of the most beautiful sort, frankness, an equal striving and mutual sharing, should obtain between them, but nothing further. At this morally firm altar they wished to stand, perhaps happily until the end of life. They would ask no more riddles of fate nor beg that she lose her sting and never play her wily tricks again. This, said the Major, was the way it had been for several years and the way it would remain.

So much he had told me—and yet, a little while after that, fate gave an answer unbidden and of her own free will, an answer that solved everything quickly and in an unexpected manner.

It was already well along in autumn, one could call it the beginning of winter; a thick mist lay one day over the already hard-frozen heath, as I rode with the Major on one of those newly built roads lined with poplars. Our intention was to do a little shooting, when we suddenly heard the report of two shots, dully through the mist.

"Those are my pistols and none other!" shouted the Major.

Before I could either grasp his meaning or ask a question, he spurred his horse along the avenue of poplars as madly as ever horse was galloped. I followed after him, fearing some misfortune, and when I reached him, I was met by a spectacle so terrible and so splendid that even today my soul still shudders and rejoices. At the spot where the gallows stands and the willow brook quivers like quicksilver, the Major had found the boy Gustav, weakening, but still

defending himself against a pack of wolves. He had shot
two of them; one, which was springing at his horse's throat,
he fought off with his weapon; the others he held momen-
tarily at bay by the blazing anger of his wild frightened
eyes that bored down upon the pack. They stood about him
waiting and drooling, so that one turn, one false glance, a
mere nothing, might have been enough to set them all upon
him—when, in the very moment of desperate crisis, the
Major appeared. By the time I arrived, he was already like
a miracle of destruction, like a meteor, in their midst. The
man was terrible to look at; without a thought of himself,
he threw himself on them like another beast of prey. I did
not see how he had got off his horse; I had heard the crack
of his double pistols, and when I appeared on the scene I
saw the gleam of his hunting knife flashing against the
wolves, as he stood on foot. Three or four seconds it must
have taken; I only had time to discharge my hunting rifle
at them, and the uncanny beasts had scattered into the
mist as if they had been sucked in and swallowed by it.

"Load up again!" shouted the Major. "They will be back
in a hurry."

He had gathered up the pistols that had been thrown
down and was pushing the cartridges in. We also loaded,
and in the very first moment that we were a bit quiet we
heard uncanny trotting around the gallows oak. It was clear
that the hungry fearful beasts were circling about us until
such time as their courage had grown to the attacking
point. Actually these animals are cowardly when they are
not spurred on by hunger. We were not equipped for a
wolf hunt. The miserable mist lay close to our eyes, therefore we struck out on the path for the manor house. The
horses—scared half to death—fairly shot along, and while
we rode I more than once saw a scurrying shadow next to
me, gray within the gray mist. With indescribable patience,
the pack of wolves was hastening along beside us. We had
to be constantly alert and ready. I heard the Major, over on
my left, shoot one time. But I could make nothing out and
there was no time to ask questions and so we arrived at the
park gate. As we rushed through, the beautiful noble dogs,

waiting behind the gate, broke forth and their angry howls already were echoing out of the mists as they swept out into the heath in pursuit of the wolves.

"Mount at once!" shouted the Major to the servants who were scurrying to meet us. "And unleash all the wolfhounds, so that my poor dogs come to no harm. Rouse the neighbors and go on and hunt to your hearts' content—as many days as you want. For every dead wolf, I'll give double bounty, with the exception of those that lie already at the gallows oak. We killed those ourselves. Near the oak you may also find one of the pistols which I gave to Gustav last year; I see only one in his hand and the saddle holster for the other pistol is empty; look about and see whether you can find it where I think it is."

Turning to me, he went on, as we continued riding through the park: "In the last five years no wolf has ventured so close to us; up to now it was quite safe here. There must be a hard winter coming and it must already have begun up in the north country, since they have already penetrated so far down south."

The servants had heard their master's orders and, in less time than I should have thought possible, a company of huntsmen was ready; near at hand were those beautiful shaggy hounds of a race peculiar to the Hungarian heath lands and so indispensable to them. The men conferred about fetching the neighbors; then they left, to commence a protracted hunt from which they might not return for a week, two weeks, or even longer.

All three of us had watched the greater part of these preparations without dismounting from our horses. But now, as we turned from the outbuildings toward the manor house itself, we noticed that Gustav was, after all, wounded. Just as we arrived under the archway of the gate, from which we had intended going to our rooms, he became ill and threatened to drop from his horse. One of the men caught him as he slumped and lifted him gently down, and it was then we saw that the flanks of his mount were red with blood. We had him carried into an apartment on the ground floor which opened on the garden; the Major or-

dered that a fire at once be laid in the fireplace and the
bed prepared. Meanwhile the wound had been found and
laid bare and the Major himself examined it. It was a bite
in the thigh, not deep, not dangerous, but the loss of blood
and the excitement that had gone before left the young
fellow struggling to keep from fainting. He was brought
to bed, and immediately a messenger was sent for the doctor and another messenger dispatched to Brigitta. The
Major remained at the bedside and saw to it that the fainting spells didn't get the better of the patient. When the
doctor arrived, he administered a stimulant, diagnosed the
business as absolutely without cause for concern, and explained that the loss of blood had itself acted as a remedial
agent, since it lessened the inflammation that very frequently followed wounds of this sort caused by bites. The
only bad thing about such illnesses, he declared, was the
force of the emotional impact, but a few days of rest should
completely end the fever and the tension. Everyone was
relieved and happy and the doctor left with the thanks of
everyone present; there wasn't a person that didn't love the
boy. Toward evening Brigitta appeared and, in her characteristic decisive way, she would not rest content until she
had examined her son's body limb by limb and convinced
herself that, except for the bite wound, there was nothing
that might threaten trouble. After her examination was
completed, she still sat at the bedside and administered the
medicines the doctor had prescribed. For the night, a make-
shift bed had to be set up for her in the sickroom. The next
morning she was sitting once more next to the young fellow
and listening to his breathing while he slept—and slept such
a sweet refreshing sleep that he didn't seem to want to wake
up, ever again. At this point a heart-shaking scene occurred.
I can still see it before my eyes. I had gone down to inquire
about Gustav's condition and walked into the room which
was next to the sickroom. I have already explained that the
windows gave upon the garden. The mists had lifted and
a red winter sun peered through the leafless branches into
the room. The Major was already there, standing by the
window, his face turned toward the glass as though he were

looking out. Inside the sickroom, through whose door I
could look and whose windows were somewhat darkened
by rather thin curtains, Brigitta was sitting, looking at her
son. Suddenly there came from her lips a happy sigh; I
looked more closely and saw that her glance was fixed
sweetly upon the boy's face and that he had opened his
eyes. He had awakened after his long sleep and was looking about serenely. But also from the place where the Major
had stood I had heard a slight stirring, and when I looked
over, I saw that he had turned half around and that two
hard tear drops clung to his lashes. I went toward him and
asked him if he were all right. He answered softly: "I have
no child."

Brigitta, with her sharp hearing, must have heard the
words, for at that moment she appeared in the door of the
room, looked very shyly at my friend, and, with a glance
that I cannot describe, and which seemed in its hesitant
anxiety not to venture a plea in words, she said nothing but
the single name: "Stephan!"

The Major turned around completely—they stared at one
another for a second—only a second—then, stepping forward, he suddenly lay in her arms, which encircled him
with positive violence. I heard nothing but the deep gentle
sobbing of the man, during which the woman embraced
him more and more firmly and pressed him closer to herself.

"No more separation now, Brigitta, for here and eternity."

"No more, my dear friend!"

I was in the greatest embarrassment and wanted to leave
quietly; but she lifted her head and told me: "Stay, stay
here."

The woman, whom I had always seen serious and strict,
had wept on his shoulder. Now she lifted her eyes, still
shimmering with tears—and so wonderful is that most beautiful of all things that poor erring humanity can do here
below: forgiving—that to me her features beamed with a
beauty beyond equal, and I was truly stirred.

"Poor, poor wife," he was saying, "for fifteen years I had

to do without you and for fifteen years you were the victim."

But she folded her hands and said pleadingly, looking into his face: "It was I who failed, Stephan, forgive me the sin of pride! I did not know how good you were—it was merely natural; it is a gentle law, the law of beauty which draws us."

He put his hand on her mouth and said: "How can you speak this way, Brigitta? Yes, it draws us, the law of beauty, but I had to go through the whole world until I learned that beauty lies in the heart and that I had left beauty at home within a heart, a heart that meant only well with me, that is firm and true, that I thought was lost, and that yet through all the years and through all the lands of earth had traveled with me. O Brigitta, mother of my son! Day and night your image stood before my eyes."

"I was not lost to you," she answered, "I passed through sad years of regret! How good you have become, now I know you, how good you have become, Stephan!"

And again they rushed into each other's arms, as though they could not get enough, as though they could not believe in the happiness won. They were like two human beings from whom a great burden is taken. The world stood open again. There was a joyfulness about them such as one only finds in children and in that moment they, too, were innocent as children are; for the most purifying, the most beautiful flowering of love, but only of the highest love, is forgiveness; that is why it is always found in God and in mothers. Beautiful hearts accomplish it often—bad ones never.

The man and wife had forgotten me once more and turned toward the sickroom, where Gustav, who had a vague intuition of all this, lay like a glowing, blossoming rose and waited breathlessly for them.

"Gustav, Gustav, he is your father and you did not know it," Brigitta called to him as she and Stephan walked over the threshold into the darkened room.

I went out into the garden and thought to myself: "How sacred, how very sacred the love of man and wife must be, and how poor am I, not to have known anything of it in my life thus far, having at most felt my heart held in the dull glow of passion."

I did not return to the manor until late and then I found everything solved and aired. A busy joy, like the serenest sunlight, seemed wafted through every room. I was received with open arms as the witness of that most beautiful of scenes. They had been looking for me everywhere after I had slipped away at a moment when they were naturally busy only with themselves. They told me everything—part of it immediately, in broken sentences, part of it the next few days in a calmer context—everything that had happened and all the things that I have already related above.

So the friend of my travels had been Stephan Murai. He had traveled under the name of Bathori, assumed from one of his maternal ancestors. Under this name I had known him, but he always preferred to be addressed as Major, a rank he had won in Spain, and everyone knew him simply as that. Since he had been all over the world, he returned —drawn by some inner magnetism—under that same name to his heath-land country seat of Uwar, where he had never yet been, where nobody knew him, and where he, as he very well knew, would become the neighbor of the wife from whom he was separated. In the same spirit, he did not go over to see her, already so well settled on her estate at Marosheli, until the news was brought to him that she was lying at death's door. Then he betook himself to her; he rode over, went to her; she, in her fever, failed even to recognize him. He stayed with her night and day at her bedside, watching over her, taking care of her until she was well again. It was at that time, touched by the sight of each other, driven by an impulse of love and yet fearful of the future, because they no longer knew one another, and because again something terrible might happen—it was at that time they made the strange pact of mere friendship which they had kept for years and which, up to this time, neither one of them had dared be the first to infringe, until fate, by a sharp stab into the hearts of both, broke the pact and joined them together again in a more beautiful, more natural bond.

Now all was well.

After two weeks had passed, this all was made known in the neighborhood and the burdensome well-wishers came from near and far.

I, however, remained the entire winter with my friends and, moreover, at Marosheli, where, for the time being, they all lived and from which the Major had no intention of ever taking Brigitta away, because she lived there in the midst of her creation. Happiest of all was Gustav, who had always clung so to the Major, had always insisted, stubbornly and passionately, that he was the most marvelous man on this earth, and who now could call him and honor him as his father: the very man he looked up to as to a divinity.

That winter I learned to know two hearts that now opened up to form one single, full—even if delayed—flower of happiness.

These hearts I shall never, never forget!

In the spring I put my German clothes on again, took my German staff, and wandered back toward my German fatherland. On the way back I passed Gabriele's gravestone and learned that she had died twelve years before, at the peak of her youthful beauty. On the marble stood two large white lilies.

With thoughts both gentle and sad, I went on until I had crossed the Leitha and the lovely blue peaks of my country dawned upon my sight.

Meret

GOTTFRIED KELLER

TRANSLATED BY MARY HOTTINGER

Fragments from a Pastor's Journal, 1713

TODAY, having received from the godly and noble
Madame de M. the first Quarter's Payment for
Board, I did immediately make acknowledgment of
it, along with my Report. Further, administered to the
Child Meret (Emerentia) her weekly *Correction*, though
more rigorous than before, laying her upon the Bench and
applying a new Rod, not without Lamentation and Sigh-
ings to the Lord God, that He might bring this grievous
Task to a good End. Whereby the Child did indeed cry
most pitifully and pray in Abasement and Pain for Pardon,
yet afterward resumed her former Obstinacy, deriding the
Hymn Book which I presented to her to learn from. Therefore I allowed her a short Respite and then locked her in
the dark Bacon Larder, where she began to whimper and
complain, but then fell silent, till she suddenly set to singing and jubilating not otherwise than the three Blessed
Men in the Fiery Furnace, and I, listening to her, heard
that she sang those same Psalms in Verse which she did
at other times refuse to learn, though in the idle and
wanton Fashion as were fitting for foolish and meaningless
Rhymes for Children, so that I could not but recognize the
Devil at his old Wiles again."

Further:

"A most lamentable Letter from Madame, who is indeed
a most excellent and godly Lady. She had wetted the Letter

with her Tears, and told me of the great Sorrow her godly
Spouse was in because the Child Meret showed no Betterment. It is in truth a sore Calamity that has befallen this
most famous and honorable Family, and I would be so bold
as to opine, saving their Respect, that the Sins of the
Child's Grandfather on her Father's side, who was an Evil-
Liver and a great Lecher, will be visited on the head of
this wretched little Creature. Have changed my *Method*
with the Child and will now essay the Hunger Cure. Have
also caused my own Wife to make a Shift of coarse Sack-
cloth, and have forbidden Meret to wear any other Attire,
this penitential Shift being most suited to her. Stubbornness
at the same *Puncto*.

"Today was forced to prevent the little Demoiselle from
all Association and Play with the Village Children, she having run with them into the Wood and there bathed in the
Pool, hanging the penitential Shift I caused to be made for
her on the Branch of a Tree and dancing before it naked,
provoking even her Playmates to Impudence and Wantonness. Considerable *Correction*."

"Today, a day of stir and hubbub. There came to me a
big strong Lad, our Miller's Son, and sought a Quarrel with
me because of Meret, whom he declares he hears moaning
and crying every Day, and as I was disputing with him,
who should come up but the young Schoolmaster, the Dolt,
who threatened to take me before the Justice, and fell on
the evil Creature's neck, kissing and caressing her, etc., etc.
Had the Schoolmaster arrested forthwith and taken before
the Magistrate. Will have to deal with the Miller's Son, but
he is rich and quarrelsome. Were almost fain to believe
myself that the Child is a Witch, if such Opinion were not
contrary to Reason. In any case the Devil is in her, and I
have taken sore Trouble upon myself."

"This whole week I have had in my house a Painter, sent
to me by Madame, who is to paint the Portrait of the little
Lady. The afflicted Family is not minded to take the Creature back, but will keep her Picture for the purpose of
melancholy Contemplation and because of the Child's great
Beauty. Monsieur in particular clings fast to the Notion.

My wife serves the Painter two measures of Wine daily,
which seems not to satisfy him, for he goes every Evening
to the Red Lion, where he plays with the Surgeon. Is a
vainglorious Fellow, wherefore I often serve him up a
Woodcock or a Pike, the same noted in the quarterly Account for Madame. At first he made much of the Child and
at once engaged her Affections, till I warned him that he
must not interfere with my *Method.* When we took out
from the Chest the Dress and Sunday Finery of the Child,
and put it on her with her Crown and Belt, she made show
of great Pleasure and began to dance. But this her Joy soon
turned to Bitterness when I, upon the order of her Lady
Mamma, sent for 1 Skull and placed it in her Hand, she
resisting with all her Might, and then holding it in her
Hand weeping and trembling, as if it were glowing Iron.
The Painter declared that he could paint the Skull by
Heart, the same being one of the Elements of his Art, but
I would not allow it, Madame having written: 'What the
Child suffers, we suffer also, and in her Suffering lies our
Opportunity of doing Penance, provided we do it for her
Sake; for that reason we would have Your Reverence make
no Change in your Care and Education. If, as I hope to
the Almighty and Merciful God, the Child shall one Day
receive Enlightenment at one Point or other and be saved,
she will doubtless rejoice greatly that she has done with a
great Deal of her Penance by her present Habit of Stubbornness, which Our inscrutable Lord has been pleased to
afflict her with.' With these brave words before me, I considered the time had come to use the Skull as a means of
serious Penance for the Child. For that Matter, it was a
small, light, Child's Skull, the Painter having complained
that, by the Rules of his Art, the big, Man's Skull was too
uncouth for the little Hands, and indeed she did hold it
more readily after. The Painter also laid a white Rose in
her Hand, which I suffered because it can be taken as a
favorable *Symbol.*

"Received today sudden Counterorders respecting Portrait and am not to send the same to Town, but to keep
it here. 'Tis a pity for the fine Work the Painter has done,

for he was delighted beyond Measure by the Child's
Gracefulness. Had I but known this before, the Fellow
could have painted my own Portrait on the Canvas, seeing
that the good Victuals and Payment will be wasted any-
how."

Further:

"I have received Orders to cease all worldly Instruction,
especially in the French Language, the same being regarded as no longer necessary, and my Wife is to stop the
Spinet Lessons, which seems to sadden the Child. I shall
from now on treat her like any other charge, taking care
only that she give no more Cause for Public Annoyance.

"The Day before Yesterday, little Meret ran away, and
we were in great Fear till she was found today at Noon on
the Top of the Beech Hill, where she sat naked on her
penitential Shift, warming herself to a Turn in the Sun. She
had unplaited her Hair and set a Wreath of Beech Leaves
on it, and had draped a Scarf of the same round her Body;
she had also a quantity of fine Strawberries lying before
her and was quite tight and round from eating of them.
When she saw us, she started up again to flee, was
ashamed of her Nakedness and would have put on her
Shift, this giving us time to capture her. Now she lies sick
in Bed and seems confused in Mind, giving no reasonable
Answers.

"Great Betterment in the Child Meret, yet she changes
more and more and seems bereft of all Sense. The Report
of the *Medicus* is that she is losing her Mind or going mad,
and that she should be placed in Medical Treatment, he
offering himself to undertake such Treatment, and promising to restore the Child to Health if she should be placed
in his House. But I have noted that *Monsieur Chirurgeon*
hath an eye only for the good Payment and the Presents
from Madame, so I replied what I thought best, namely
that the Lord seemed about to make an End to His Plan
concerning His Creature, and that Human Hands could
and should change nothing, as is in Truth so."

Five or six months later:

"The Child seems to enjoy excellent Health in her sense-

less Condition, having fresh rosy Cheeks. Stays the whole
Day now in the Bean Field where we cannot see her, and
we trouble no more about her, the more so as she occasions
no further Nuisance.

"In the Midst of the Bean Field the Child Meret has arranged a little *Salon,* where the village Children pay their
Duties to her, carrying to her Fruit and other Victuals
which she has most daintily buried and keeps in Store. And
we did also find there that little Child's Skull which was
lost long since so that it could not be restored to the Sexton.
She has also enticed to her and tamed the Sparrows and
other Birds, which have made much Havoc among the
Beans, but I dare not shoot into the Bean Field now because of its little Inmate. *Item,* she has played with a
poisonous Snake which broke through the Hedge and made
its Nest beside her. *In Summa,* we have had perforce to
take her into the House again and keep her there.

"The rosy Cheeks have faded from her and the Surgeon
declares that she will not be with us long. Have written to
the Parents.

"Today, before Daybreak, the poor Child Meret must
have escaped from her Bed, crept out to the Beans and
died there, for we found her lying there as dead in a little
Grave she had dug in the Earth, as if preparing to crawl
into it. She was stiff as a Rod and her Hair and Nightgown
damp and heavy with Dew, which lay in clear Drops on
her faintly rosy Cheeks, as it might be on apple blossom.
We were overcome by great Fear, and I myself suffered this
Day great Distraction and Confusion because Monsieur and
Madame arrived from Town just when my Wife was gone
to K. to buy Cakes and other Victuals wherewith to offer
them becoming Refreshment. Did not know where to turn,
all being at Sixes and Sevens, the Maids having to wash and
shroud the little Corpse and at the same time prepare suitable Refreshment. In the End I had the green Ham roasted
which my Wife laid in Vinegar a Week since, and Jacob
caught three of those tame Trout that still come to our Garden now and then though we had forbidden our blessed
(?!) Meret to go to the brook. To my great Happiness,

these Dishes brought me some Credit, and Madame ate
of them with great Pleasure. Great Mourning; we spent two
Hours in Prayer and the Contemplation of Death, and the
same in melancholy Discourse of the Sickness which afflicted dead Child, since we must now believe, to our great
Consolation, that the same arose from a fatal Disposition
of the Blood and Brain. And we also spoke of the Child's
great Gifts and of her oftwhile ingenious and delightful
Conceits and *Caprices*, but we, in our earthly Blindness,
could make no Sense of it all. Tomorrow Morning the Child
is to have Christian Burial, the Presence of the Parents
being most desirable in this Point, since the Villagers would
otherwise have refused to suffer it."

"This is the strangest and most dreadful Day, not only
since the wretched Creature came to us, but in the whole
of my peaceful Life. For when the time was come and ten
had struck, we set out behind the little Corpse for the
Graveyard while the Sexton tolled the Bell, though not
with much Fervor, for it rang most dismally and half of
the Sound was swallowed up by a great Wind which raged
furiously. And the Sky also was dark and lowering, and
the Graveyard empty of People save of our little Company,
while outside its Walls all the Villagers had gathered,
stretching their Heads curiously over it. But just as we were
about to lower the little Coffin into the Grave, a most dole-
ful Cry broke from the Coffin, so that Terror overcame us
and the Gravedigger took to his Heels. But the Surgeon,
who hastened up to the Grave, removed the lid in all
Speed, and the dead Child rose up as if alive and climbed
quite nimbly out of the Grave and looked at us. And as at
that very moment the Beams of Phoebus broke through the
clouds with unaccustomed Power, she looked, in her yellow Brocade and glittering little Crown, like an Elfin or a
Goblin Child. Her Lady Mother fell forthwith into a deep
Swoon and Monsieur dashed himself to the Earth, weeping.
I myself stood rooted to the Spot in Wonder and Fear, and
did at that moment firmly believe in Witchcraft. But the
Child soon regained her Self-Command and scampered
away over the Graveyard and out of the Village like a Cat,

till all the People fled to their Homes in Horror and bolted
their Doors. At that very moment, School came out, and
the Children entered the Lane, and when the Little Ones
saw this Thing we could not hold them back, but a great
Company of Children ran after the Corpse and pursued it,
with the Schoolmaster and his Birch Rod after them. But
she had twenty paces' start and did not stop until she
reached the Beech Hill, and there fell dead, while the Children scrabbled about her and caressed her in vain. This all
we learned later as we, in our Terror, had taken refuge in
the Parsonage, remaining there in profound Desolation till
the Corpse was brought back to us. It was laid upon a
Mattress, and Monsieur and Madame departed, leaving a
small stone Tablet on which nothing is engraved but the
Family Crest and a Date. And now the Child lies there as
dead again, and we dare not go to Bed for Fear. But the
Medicus sits by her Bed, and now believes she has at last
found **Peace**."

"Today the *Medicus* declared, having made many ex-
periments, that the Child is truly dead, and she has now
been buried quietly, and nothing further has happened,
etc., etc."

Mozart on His
Way to Prague

EDUARD MÖRIKE

TRANSLATED BY MARY HOTTINGER

I N the autumn of 1787, Mozart, accompanied by his wife, set out for Prague, where he was to conduct the first performance of *Don Giovanni* in person.

On the third day of their journey, the happy and hopeful couple were still not much more than thirty hours away from Vienna. Traveling northwest, they had left the Mannhardsberg and the Dyja behind them and were approaching Schrems, where the road at last surmounts the ridge of the lovely Moravian Mountains.

"Their carriage, drawn by three post horses," the Baroness von T. wrote to her friend, "was a fine yellow and red equipage belonging to a certain Madame de Volkstett, an old general's lady, who seems to have always derived great satisfaction from her association with the Mozart family and the services she was able to render it." Anyone familiar with the taste of the time will be able to supplement this somewhat scanty description of the vehicle in question. The carriage was red and yellow and had nosegays painted in natural colors on both doors, left and right, which were edged with narrow gilt moldings. There was, however, as yet no luster on the paint such as is given by the varnish used in the Viennese workshops in our time, nor had the box swelled to its present proportions, though it tapered below in a very daring but elegant curve. The whole was covered by a high canopy with stiff leather curtains, which were, at the moment, drawn back.

And now we may take a glance at the costume of its
two passengers. Madame Constanze, in order to save her
husband's fine new suit, had packed it in the trunk, and
had selected a very quiet one for the journey. With his
embroidered waistcoat of rather faded blue, he wore his
everyday brown coat with large buttons of brass foil which
shimmered reddish through the star-shaped openwork of
their stuff covering, black silk knee breeches and stockings
and gilt shoe buckles. For the last half hour he had laid
aside his coat on account of the heat, which was quite extraordinary for the time of year, and, shirt-sleeved and bare-
headed, was chatting contentedly. Madame Mozart wore a
comfortable green and white striped traveling dress, and
her hair, only half bound up, fell in rich waves on her neck
and shoulders. Never in her life had it been touched by
powder, which lay deep, and rather more wildly dabbed
than usual on her husband's thick plait.

They had made a leisurely ascent of a gentle slope between fertile fields interrupted here and there by spurs of
the spreading woodland, and had reached the edge of the
forest.

"How many forests," said Mozart, "have we passed
through today, yesterday, and the day before! I hardly gave
them a thought, and it never occurred to me to set foot in
them. Let us get out here, my dear, and pick some of those
pretty blue flowers which look like bells there in the shade.
Your beasts will be glad of a breather, coachman."

As they rose, a small mishap occurred which brought
down a scolding on the head of the master. By a careless
movement on his part, the stopper had fallen out of a phial
of precious perfume which had seeped out unnoticed onto
their clothes and the cushions.

"I might have known," she lamented. "There has been
such a strong scent this long time past. Oh dear! oh dear!
A whole bottle of genuine *rosée d'amore* simply wasted! I
was treasuring it up as if it had been gold."

"My dear little simpleton," he replied, by way of consolation, "this may be the only way for that celestial smelling-
schnapps of yours to be any use to us. We were sitting in

an oven and that busy little fan of yours was no good at all. Then it was as if a cooling breath had invaded the carriage, and you thought it came from the drop or two I had dabbed on my ruffles. It was as if fresh life had come into us, and we drove along talking to our hearts' content. Otherwise we should have drooped our heads like the sheep on the butcher's cart. And now this coolness will bless us for the rest of our journey. But come and let us poke our two Viennese noses here, at this very spot, into the green wilderness."

Arm in arm they climbed over the roadside ditch and plunged into the shade which, as it deepened into gloom, was broken only here and there by flecks of sunshine on the mossy velvet of the earth. The refreshing coolness, following so suddenly on the torrid heat outside, might have been dangerous to the thoughtless husband if it had not been for his wife's precautions. With some difficulty she induced him to put on the coat she held in readiness.

"Heavens! How glorious!" he cried, looking up the tall tree trunks. "We might be in church. I feel as if I had never been in a forest before, and can only realize now what it is to see a whole nation of trees together. No human hand planted them. They grew of themselves, and stand there just because it is joyous to live and work together. When I was young, you know, I traveled through half of Europe, saw the Alps and the sea, the greatest and most beautiful things in creation; and now here I stand like a simpleton in an ordinary pine forest on the Bohemian border, lost in wonder and delight just because life like this exists in the world, and is no mere poetic fancy like your nymphs, fauns, and all the rest of it, and no scenery in a theater either. It sprang from the earth and grew tall only by moisture and the warming light of the sun. The stag lives here with his wonderful jagged antlers, and the lusty little squirrel, and the woodcock and jay."—He bent and picked a mushroom, praising the vivid scarlet of its cap and the delicate whitish gills underneath. He also put several pine cones in his pocket.

"Anyone would think," said Madame Constanze, "that

you had never looked twenty feet into the Prater, which
has beauties of the kind to show too, after all."

"The Prater! My child, how can you even pronounce the
name here! What with equipages, dress swords, gowns and
fans, music and all the noise in the world, how can anyone
see anything there? And as for the trees, whatever airs
they put on—I don't know how it is, but the beechnuts and
acorns on the ground look as if they were of the same race
as all the old corks they lie among. The place smells of
waiters and sauces two hours off."

"Well, I declare!" she exclaimed. "And that's the man
whose greatest pleasure is a dinner of fried chicken in the
Prater."

When the two had taken their seats in the carriage
again, and the road, after a short level stretch, sloped down
to a beautiful and smiling plain which stretched away to
the farther mountains, our master, after a few minutes'
silence, began again:

"The earth is very beautiful, and we can hardly take it
ill of anybody who wants to stay on it as long as he can.
I am, thank God, as fresh and well as I have ever been,
and I feel in the mood to start a thousand things, and so
I will, one after the other, once my new work is finished
and has been produced. There is so much that is wonderful
and beautiful that I know nothing about as yet, marvels
of nature, science, art, and useful handicrafts. The black
charcoal burner's boy there knows many things as well as
I do, in all their particulars, while I really have the heart
and the mind to have a look at many a thing that has nothing to do with my daily round."

"A day or two ago," she replied, "I found an old pocket
calendar of the year 1785. You had jotted four or five notes
in it. First there comes: 'In the middle of October the great
lions are to be cast in the imperial bronze foundry.' Then,
underlined twice: 'See Professor Gattner.' Who is he?"

"Ah yes! I know—the old gentleman in the observatory
who asks me there now and then. I have wanted to take
you to see the moon and the little man in it this long time
past. They have got a great telescope up there now, and

they say you can see the huge disk, as bright and clear as your hand before your face, with mountains, valleys, ravines, and on the side the sun cannot reach, the shadows cast by the mountains. I have had it in mind to pay that visit for the last two years, but, to my shame be it said, I never went."

"Well," she said, "the moon won't run away. We have several things to catch up with."

After a pause, he went on: "But isn't that the way with everything? A pest on it! I dare not even think of all we miss, postpone, push aside. I am not speaking of our duties to God and men. I mean pure pleasure, the small innocent pleasures which lie there at hand every day."

Madame Mozart neither could nor would distract his impressionable mind from the train of thought it was pursuing, and unfortunately she could only feel he was right when he went on:

"Have I ever enjoyed one whole happy hour with my children? Only with half my mind and hurrying on to something else. Ride-a-cock-horse with the boys for one minute, galloping round the room with them for two, and then it is over and I have to shake them off again. I do not believe that we have ever had a whole happy day together, at Easter or Whitsun, in the country, in a garden or a wood or in the fields, by ourselves, playing with the children among the flowers as if we were children again ourselves. And all the time life hurries, rushes by. Good Lord! Even to think of it makes you shiver."

With these rueful reflections, the conversation took an unforeseen and very serious turn, though in all confidence and kindness. We will not give it in detail, but rather review the circumstances which were in part the actual topic, and in part only the conscious undertone of their talk.

The first painful observation that must be made is that this ardent spirit, attuned to all the beauty of the world and unbelievably responsive to the loftiest aspirations of mankind, never knew, in his short span of life, what it was to be at peace with himself for one single hour.

Unless we wish to seek deeper reasons for this state of

affairs than probably exist, we shall in all likelihood find
them in those apparently ingrained habits of weakness
which we are apt, and not without reason, to associate in
Mozart with everything we find most admirable.

He was a man of simple tastes, but his relish for the
pleasures of society was inordinately strong. His incompara-
ble gifts made him a welcome and honored guest at the
best houses in the town, and he seldom or never neglected
invitations to fêtes, salons, and evening parties. At the same
time he was extremely hospitable within the circles of his
closer friends. An old-established musical evening at home
on Sundays, an informal dinner at his own well-appointed
table two or three times a week, were things he did not
like to miss. Sometimes, to his wife's discomfiture, he would
bring home, unannounced, friends he had met in the street,
all sorts and conditions of men, dilettantes, fellow musicians,
singers and poets. The idle parasite whose sole merit was
his vivacity, wit, and humor, even of the cruder sort, was
as welcome as the true connoisseur and the real musician.
Most of his recreation, however, Mozart sought outside of
his home. Day after day he could be found after dinner
playing billiards in the coffeehouse, and many an evening
too at the inn. He was extremely fond of long drives and
rides with friends in the country. Since he was an excellent
dancer, he went to balls and routs, and several times a year
had a genuine frolic on St. Bridget's day, where he appeared in the costume of Pierrot.

Such diversions, sometimes gay and boisterous, sometimes congenial to quieter moods, were necessary if his
mind, overwrought by the long strain of an enormous expenditure of energy, was to find some relaxation. Besides,
in the mysterious ways in which genius pursues its unconscious ends, they did not fail to communicate the delicate,
fleeting impressions by which it is sometimes fertilized. But
unfortunately, at such times, when all that mattered was
to drain the merry moment to its dregs, no other consideration, whether of prudence or duty, of self-preservation or
the home, could make itself heard. Whether at work or
play, Mozart never knew when it was time to stop. Part

of his night was always devoted to composition. In the
morning, often in bed, some hours were spent finishing the
work of the night. Then, from ten o'clock on, he made his
round of lessons on foot, or in carriages sent for him, and
they took up several hours of the afternoon. "We strive like
Christians," he once wrote to a patron, "and sometimes it
is hard for me to keep my temper. As a well-known cem-
balist and teacher of music I take on say a dozen pupils,
then another and yet another without asking who they are,
if only they pay their thaler per lesson. Any Hungarian
mustachio from the corps of engineers is welcome if only
the devil drives him to acquire thorough bass and counter-
point for no conceivable reason; the most spirited little
Contessa, who meets me crimson with fury, as if I were
Maître Coquerel the hairdresser, if for once she does not
hear my knock on the stroke of the hour," and so on. And
when, worn out by this and other professional work, by
academies, rehearsals, and the rest, he longed for relaxation, it seemed as if his jaded nerves could only derive
a factitious strength from fresh excitement. Invisibly his
health suffered; his recurring fits of melancholy may not
have sprung from this source, but they were certainly fed
by it, and so the foreboding of an early death, which never
left him toward the end, was fated to be fulfilled. Cares
of every kind, remorse among them, were the bitter spice
to every joy he knew. Yet we know that even these cares
flowed together, transfigured and purified, in that deep
fountain which, gushing inexhaustibly from a hundred
golden jets, poured forth all the torment and all the bliss of
the heart of man in the profuse riches of his music.

The evil effects of Mozart's manner of life came out most
clearly at home. Of the charge of reckless expenditure he
cannot be acquitted; it was in fact the result of one of the
most endearing traits in his character. If anyone came to
him to borrow money in some dire need, or to beg him
to stand warrant for them, they had generally assumed that
he would not trouble about pledges or securities; such
things would have been less natural to him than to a child.
His immediate impulse was to give, and always with smil-

ing largesse, especially when he imagined he was in funds.

The means which such expenditure required over and above the daily needs of home were out of all proportion to his income. What he earned by operas and concerts, publications and lessons, and his imperial pension, was still inadequate because the taste of the public was not yet wholeheartedly won over to Mozart's music. This purest beauty, fullness, and depth alienated a public accustomed to the very digestible musical fare popular at the time. True, Vienna had been beside itself with delight over *Belmonte and Constanze* owing to the popular elements in the piece; on the other hand it was not only due to the intrigues of the manager if, a few years later, *Figaro* fell miserably flat in competition with the charming but much more trivial *Cosa Rara*. It was that very *Figaro* which the more cultivated or less conservative theater goers at Prague were to receive soon after with such enthusiasm that the master, touched and grateful, resolved to write his next great opera specially for them. But in spite of the temper of the time and the influence of enemies, Mozart, given more prudence and wisdom, could have made a very considerable income by his art, but as it was, he even failed to make a profit on those productions which were received with jubilation even by the crowd. In short, everything, fate, his nature, and his own failings, were in league to prevent this one man from prospering.

It may well be imagined that such circumstances would be hard to bear for any wife who knew her business. Although she was herself young and gay, thoroughly artistic by temperament as the daughter of a musician, and accustomed to privations from childhood up, Constanze did everything that lay in her power to check the evil at its source, to forestall many a wrong step, and to make up for general losses by small economies. But it was perhaps just at this point that she lacked both skill and experience. It was she who managed the money and kept the household accounts; every bill, every reminder of a debt, or anything else unpleasant went to her and her alone. From time to time it threatened to overwhelm her, especially at times when all this distress, this poverty, painful embarrassment, and the dread of public dishonor, was rendered unbearable by her husband's fits of despondency. Then he would sit idle for days at a time, sighing and complaining by his wife's side or mute in a corner, revolving like an endless screw the one idea of death. But she seldom lost heart; her bright eyes found some way out, if only for the time being. In the general situation there was little or no real improvement. Gravely or gaily, with entreaties or caresses, she might prevail on him to take tea with her, or enjoy his supper at home with the family without going out afterward, but what was gained by it? When he caught a glimpse of his wife's reddened eyes, he would, in a wave of compunction, sincerely abjure a bad habit and promise the best—more than she even wanted—but in vain; unwittingly he fell back into the old rut. One is tempted to think that it was not in his power to change, and that if he had been forced in some way to adopt an absolutely different manner of life, such as would have been right and proper for the rest of mankind, his wonderful being would have destroyed itself.

Constanze, however, always hoped for a turn for the better in outward circumstance; the growing fame of her husband could not but bring an improvement in their financial status. If only, she thought, the troubles that weighed on him more or less directly from that source were at an end, if only he could live wholeheartedly for his vocation instead of wasting half his time and strength in mere earning, if only he no longer had to seek for pleasure, but could enjoy it freely with a good conscience, it would refresh him, body and soul, and his whole state would be easier, calmer, and quieter. She actually considered moving to another town, since his unconquerable love of Vienna, where she was sure he would never prosper, might be ultimately overcome.

There was one thing, however, on which Madame Mozart was counting as the next decisive step in the realization of her plans and hopes, namely the success of the new opera which was the occasion of their present journey.

More than half of the composition was finished. Familiar

friends of sound judgment, who had witnessed the birth of the great work and had been able to form an adequate idea of it, spoke of it everywhere in such terms that a great many people, opponents among them, were assured that this *Don Giovanni*, before six months had passed, would shake the whole of musical Germany to its foundations, and take it by storm. Other, equally good friends were more cautious and temperate; in view of the state of musical taste at the time, they hardly hoped for a sweeping success. In his heart of hearts the master shared their doubts, which were only too well founded.

As for Constanze, like all women of lively temperament who are under the spell of a justified wish, and who are less likely than men to be troubled by misgivings, she clung firmly to her faith, and took the opportunity, at this very moment in the carriage, of proclaiming it anew. She did so in her fresh and lively manner all the more eagerly because Mozart's spirits had visibly sunk during their previous conversation, which could in any case lead to no useful end and had broken off in the most unsatisfying fashion. She at once explained to her husband, with unabated vivacity and in detail, how she proposed to use the hundred ducats, the price agreed on with the Prague impresario for the score, to meet the most urgent demands and in other ways, and how, according to her calculations, she should manage very well for the whole of the coming winter.

"Your Monsieur Bondini will turn a pretty penny with the opera, believe me; and if he is half the man of honor you always make him out to be, he will hand a nice little percentage over to you later on what the theaters will pay him, one after the other, for the copies. If not, thank God, we have other good prospects, which are a thousand times more reliable. I foresee all kinds of changes."

"For instance?"

"A little bird told me not long ago that the King of Prussia was looking for a Kapellmeister."

"Oho!"

"I mean a general director of music. Let my fancy run wild a little. It's a weakness I got from my mother."

"Then go on. The wilder the better."

"No, just as it comes. . . . Introduction: a year today."

"Children and fools speak the truth, they say."

"Now be quiet, clown. What I was trying to say was that in a year's time, on St. Egidius's day, there will not even be the shadow of an imperial chamber composer by the name of Wolf Mozart in all the length and breadth of Vienna."

"Wishes will never fill a sack, my dear."

"I can hear our old friends talking about us and passing the news round."

"For instance."

"For instance, early one morning, not long after nine, our old admirer Madame Volkstett comes pounding along at her fieriest visiting gallop. She has been away for three months; the great visit to her brother-in-law in Saxony that she was always talking about has at last taken place. She arrived back last night, and, with overflowing heart—it is bubbling with holiday pleasures and the impatience of friendship and all the most delightful titbits of gossip—off she charges to the Colonel's lady—up the stairs, never even waits for 'Come in!' Imagine the mutual rejoicings and embracings!—'Now, my dearest, my best Mrs. Colonel,' she begins, regaining her breath after a few preliminary remarks. 'I have a pile of messages for you—can you guess from whom? I didn't come straight from Stendhal, I took a little way round—to the left—toward Brandenburg—'—'What? Is it possible? You have been to Berlin and seen the Mozarts?'—'Ten days of Heaven'—'Oh, my dear, my sweet, my own Mrs. General—tell—describe. How are our dear young people? Do they like it there as much as they did at first? Even now it seems incredible, unimaginable, and all the more so now you come from them . . . Mozart a Berliner! How does he bear himself? How does he look?'—'Oh he! You should see him. This summer the King sent him to Karlsbad. Can you imagine such an idea even coming into the head of his beloved Emperor Joseph? They had only just come back when I arrived. He is radiant with health and good spirits, he is round and a little portly and as lively as quicksilver. You can see happiness and contentment beaming in his very eyes.' "

And now the speaker, in her pretended role, began to describe the new situation in the brightest colors. Everything, from his home in Unter den Linden, from his garden and country cottage to the most brilliant scenes of his appearances in public and in the more intimate circles of the court, where he had to accompany the Queen on the pianoforte, became present reality. She poured forth whole conversations, the most charming anecdotes. She actually seemed to be more at home in that royal residence of Potsdam and at Sans Souci than at Schönbrunn and the Emperor's castle. And in between she had wit enough to adorn the person of our hero with quite a number of unprecedented domestic virtues which had developed in the security of his life on Prussian soil, and among which the said Madame Volkstett had noted, as the supreme phenomenon and the proof that extremes do meet at times, the makings of a regular little miser, which became him extremely well.

" 'Well, now, let us assume that he has his regular salary of three thousand thalers—what for? For conducting a chamber concert once a week and the grand opera twice.' —'Ah! my dear Mrs. Colonel, I saw him, our own dear, precious, good young man, surrounded by his wonderful orchestra which he has trained in his own ways and which adores him to a man. I sat with Madame Mozart in their box—*almost* facing royalty itself! And what was on the program?—Look—I brought it with me wrapped round a little holiday souvenir from me and the Mozarts—there, look, read—there in letters a yard high.'—'Good Heavens be merciful! What? *Tarar!*'—'Yes, there you are, my good friend, you never can tell what will happen. Two years ago, when Mozart was writing *Don Giovanni* and that venomous serpent Salieri was plotting in private to repeat the Parisian triumph of his own piece as soon as he could on his own ground, and his accomplices were muttering darkly among themselves how they would produce *Don Giovanni* in the same way as they did *Figaro* in its time—plucked like a fowl

and neither dead nor alive—will you believe me, I made a
vow that if that unspeakable piece were given, I would not
go, no, not for the world. And kept my word. When everybody was fighting for seats, even you, my dear Mrs. Colonel, I sat by my fire with my cat on my lap, over a dish
of stewed tripe; and I did the same every time it was given.
But now, just fancy, *Tarar* at the Berlin opera, the work
of his mortal enemy conducted by Mozart! You simply must
go, he cried in the first quarter of an hour, if only to be
able to reassure our beloved Viennese that I have not hurt
a hair of the boy Absalom's head. Oh! if he were only there
himself, the arch-green-eyed monster, he would see that I
don't need to botch somebody else's work in order to be
myself for the rest of time!'"

"Bravo! Bravissimo!" cried Mozart, took his little wife by
the ears, kissed, fondled, and caressed her, till the bright
soap bubbles of a future dreamed of, but never, alas! to be
fulfilled in the smallest degree, dissolved in gaiety, noise,
and laughter.

Meanwhile they had long since reached the valley, and
were approaching a village they had noticed from the top
of the hill, immediately behind which there could be seen,
in the smiling plain, a small château of rather modern as-
pect, which was the seat of a Count Schurzburg. They had
decided to make a halt at the village, to have the horses
fed and to rest and dine themselves. The inn at which they
stopped stood alone at the end of the village, on the road
from which a poplar avenue turned off and led in not more
than six hundred steps to the Count's garden.

When they had alighted, Mozart, as usual, left the ordering of dinner to his wife. In the meantime he ordered a
glass of wine for himself in the inn parlor, while all she
wanted, beyond a glass of fresh water, was a quiet nook
for an hour's sleep. She was conducted up a staircase, her
husband gaily humming and whistling behind her. In a
freshly aired, whitewashed room, there stood, among other
furniture of nobler lineage—which had no doubt found its
way to the inn from the château at some time—a clean light
bed with a painted canopy on slender green varnished

posts, whose silk curtains had long since been replaced by
others of commoner stuff. Constanze settled in comfortably;
he promised to wake her in time; she bolted the door after
him, and he went down on the search for entertainment
in the inn parlor downstairs. But there was not a soul there
except the innkeeper, and since the guest relished his conversation as little as his wine, he mentioned that he was
going for a walk in the château grounds to pass the time
till dinner. They were open to well-behaved visitors, he was
told; besides, the family had driven out that day.

He left, and had soon covered the short distance to the
open wrought-iron gates. Then he paced slowly through an
ancient lime walk, at the end of which he was suddenly
faced with the façade of the château. It was Italian in
style, lime-washed in a light color, and approached by a
great double flight of steps; the slate roof was adorned with
a few statues of the ordinary kind, gods and goddesses, and
a balustrade.

From between two flower beds in full bloom, our master
turned toward the shrubbery, passed close by a few fine
clumps of dark pines, then strolled along winding paths to
the open parts of the garden again, drawn on by the lively
plashing of a fountain which he reached in very little time.

Round its fairly large oval basin there was an orangery
consisting of orange trees in tubs alternating with laurels
and oleanders; round it there ran a soft sanded path on
which a small latticed arbor opened. The arbor was the
most inviting of resting places; a small table stood in front
of the seat and Mozart sat down at its entrance.

His ear caressed by the sound of the water, his eyes fixed
on a splendid orange tree of medium size, loaded with
fruit, which stood by itself on the ground outside of the
row, and close to his hand, our friend had before him a
vision of southern lands which plunged him into a lovely
reminiscence of his childhood. Smiling thoughtfully, he
stretched out his hand to the nearest orange, as if to feel
its glorious roundness and juicy fullness in his hollowed
hand. Closely associated with that remembrance of childhood, however, there was a faint, half-forgotten air which

he dreamily sought to recapture for a time. But his eyes
began to glitter, to wander hither and thither, an idea had
flashed into his mind, at once he was on its track. Absent-
mindedly he grasped the orange again, it broke from the
branch and remained in his hand. He saw, and saw not.
Indeed, he was so lost in his musical musings that, constantly turning the sweet-smelling fruit under his nose, humming now the opening, now the middle of a tune between
his lips, he drew without thinking an enameled case out of
his side pocket, took a little silver knife out of it, and slowly
cut the soft yellow mass through from top to bottom. He
may have been moved by some feeling of thirst of which
he was only half aware, but his awakened senses were
satisfied by merely breathing in the delicious perfume. For
minutes he gazed at the two inner surfaces, he laid them
together again very gently, took them apart, then reunited
them.

Then he heard steps approaching, he started, and was
overwhelmed by the realization of where he was and what
he had done. In the very act of hiding the orange, he
stopped, whether out of pride or because it was too late.
A big, broad-shouldered man in livery, the gardener of the
château, stood before him. He had certainly seen the last
suspicious movement, and stood still for a few seconds in
outraged silence. Mozart, speechless too and as if nailed to
his seat, looked him in the face, half laughing, visibly blushing, yet with a certain jauntiness in his large blue eyes;
then—for a third person the scene would have been un-
speakably comic—he placed the apparently undamaged
orange in the middle of the table with a kind of defiant
flourish.

"Pardon," said the gardener, with suppressed annoyance, having mustered the not very promising clothes of the
stranger, "I do not know whom I . . ."

"Kapellmeister Mozart, from Vienna."

"A friend of the family, no doubt?"

"I am a stranger here, passing through. Is the Count at
home?"

"No."

"His lady?"

"Is occupied and is unlikely to receive anyone."

Mozart stood up as if to go.

"I beg your pardon, sir. How did you come to help yourself in this place and in this manner?"

"What?" cried Mozart. "Help myself? The devil, man! Do you believe I wanted to steal and devour that object there?"

"I believe what I see, sir. These oranges have been counted. I am responsible for them. The Count selected this tree for a fête. It was just about to be carried away. I will not let you go until I have reported the matter and you have stood witness yourself to what has happened here."

"Good. I will wait here till then. You may be sure of it."

The gardener looked round him hastily, and Mozart, thinking that a tip might settle the matter at once, put his hand in his pocket, but had not a single coin on him.

Two gardeners' boys now actually came up, loaded the tree onto a barrow, and rolled it away. Meanwhile our master had drawn out his writing case, taken out a sheet of white paper, and, while the gardener stood motionless at his post, wrote in pencil:

"Most honored Lady,

Here I sit, unhappy that I am, in your Paradise, like Adam after he had eaten the apple. The Fall has happened, and I cannot even put the blame on a kind Eve who at this moment is sleeping the sleep of the innocent at the inn enframed by the graces and cherubs of a four-post bed. You have but to command and I will myself answer to your Ladyship for a misdemeanor I cannot even understand myself.

In sincere contrition,

Your Ladyship's most humble and obedient servant,

W. A. MOZART

on his way to Prague."

He folded the note rather clumsily and handed it to the sternly waiting servant with the necessary instructions.

Hardly had the monster gone when a carriage could be

heard rolling into the courtyard behind the château. It was
the Count, bringing his niece and her betrothed, a young
Baron from the neighboring estate. As the Baron's mother
had not been able to go out of doors for years, the be-
trothal had been celebrated that day in her presence; it
was to be followed by a fête with other members of the
family at the château, where Eugenie had been at home
like a daughter since her childhood. The Countess had returned home a little earlier with her son, Lieutenant Max,
to give sundry directions, and now everybody in the château
was on the move, along the corridors and up and down the
stairs, and the gardener had some difficulty before he could
at last hand over the note to the Countess in the anteroom.
She did not, however, open it, but hurried past without
paying much attention to what the messenger said. He
waited and waited, but she did not return. One servant after
the other, footman, lady's maid, valet, ran past him; he
asked for the master—he was dressing; he sought and found
Count Max in his room, but he was deep in conversation
with the Baron, and, as if he feared that something might
be said or asked which was still to be kept secret, silenced
him with a hasty: "Go now—I'm coming." It was some time
before the father and son came along together and heard
the dreadful news.

"That would be the very devil," cried the fat, jovial, but
somewhat hasty Count. "It's beyond belief. A musical vaga-
bond from Vienna, you say. Most likely some rogue who
runs about to find a living and pockets whatever comes his
way."

"By your leave, sir. He does not look quite like that. To
my mind he is not quite right in the head; besides, he is
very high and mighty. He says his name is Moser. He is
waiting below for an answer. I told Franz to hang about
and keep an eye on him."

"What good is that now, damn it! Even if I had the fool
locked up, the damage could not be made good. I've told
you a thousand times that the front gate should always be
kept locked. But the thing would never have happened if
you had made your preparations in proper time."

At this moment the Countess, looking pleased and excited, hurried out of the adjoining cabinet with the open note in her hand.

"Do you know," she cried, "who is down there? For goodness' sake read this letter—Mozart from Vienna, the composer. Somebody must go down at once and ask him up —I'm only afraid he's gone already. Whatever will he think of me? Velten, you were polite to him, I hope. What actually happened?"

"Happened!" returned her husband, whose vexation was not to be conjured away on the spot by the prospect of a visit from a famous man. "The madman picked one of the nine oranges off the tree I had set aside for Eugenie. H'm, the monster! That simply means that our fête has lost its whole point and Max can tear up his poem straightaway."

"No, no," said the lady, pleading. "The gap can easily be filled; just leave it to me. Go now, both of you, release the good man, bid him as kind and flattering a welcome as you can. If we can keep him here at all, he must not travel farther today. If you cannot find him in the garden, look for him at the inn and bring him here with his wife. Chance could have given us no greater gift and no more wonderful surprise for Eugenie today."

"Of course," replied Max, "that was my very first thought. Come, Papa, make haste. And," he added as they turned toward the stairs, "don't trouble about the poem. The ninth muse need not be slighted. On the contrary, I shall make good use of the mishap."—"You cannot."—"Of course I can."—"Well, if that's so—but mind, I take you by your word—then we shall show this madman all the honor we can."

While this was going on in the château, our captive, not greatly troubled about the outcome of the matter, had spent some time writing. But as nobody appeared, he began to pace restlessly to and fro. Then an urgent message came from the inn, dinner had been ready this long time past; he was to come at once; the postilion was growing impatient. He therefore collected his things and was just

on the point of leaving when the two gentlemen appeared
at the entrance to the arbor.

The Count bade him a hearty welcome in his loud ringing voice, almost as if he had been an old acquaintance,
refused to listen to apologies, but at once expressed his wish
to have the couple to dine and spend the evening in the
bosom of his family. "You are no stranger to us, my dearest
Maestro. I can vouch that there are few places where the
name of Mozart is mentioned more often and with greater
enthusiasm than here. My niece sings and plays, spends
nearly the whole day at her pianoforte, knows your works
by heart. Her dearest wish is to see you closer than was
possible at any of your concerts last spring. Since we are
leaving very soon to spend a few weeks in Vienna, relatives
promised her an invitation to Prince Gallizin's, where you
are often to be found. But now you are on your way to
Prague, you will not leave it in a hurry, and God knows if
your return journey will bring you our way. Take a rest
for today and tomorrow. We shall send your vehicle back
and take the liberty of providing for your journey from
here."

The composer, who would sacrifice more than ten times
what was asked of him here for the sake of friendship or
pleasure, had soon made up his mind; he accepted gladly
for the present day; on the other hand, he said, he would
have to continue his journey very early in the morning.
Count Max asked for the pleasure of calling for Madame
Mozart and making all the necessary arrangements at the
inn. He went, and a carriage was ordered to follow him
immediately.

It might be remarked of this young man by the way that,
with a naturally cheerful disposition inherited from his father and mother, he united a talent and love for the fine
arts, and though he had no real inclination for a military
career, distinguished himself among his fellow officers
merely by his knowledge and good breeding. He was familiar with French literature, and at a time when German
poetry was disregarded among the upper classes, he was
liked and admired for his uncommon facility for writing

verse in his mother tongue after good models such as Hage-
dorn, Götz, and others. As has already been mentioned, the
present day had offered him a particularly delightful opportunity of putting his talent to use.

He found Madame Mozart chatting with the innkeeper's
daughter at the dinner table, where she had made a start
with a plate of soup. She was too accustomed to extraordinary incidents, to headlong improvisations on her husband's part, to be more than commonly overcome by the
appearance of the young officer and the message he
brought. With unfeigned good will she took the situation
in hand at once, discussed and arranged everything that
was needful herself. She unpacked, packed, dismissed and
paid the postilion, dressed without too much anxiety as to
her own toilette, and drove happily to the château with her
escort, not dreaming in what a strange manner her husband had introduced himself there.

He, for his part, was perfectly at home there and enjoying himself highly. Soon he saw Eugenie, a grave and
very lovely girl in the bloom of youth, with her betrothed.
She was fair and slender and wore for the fête a brilliant
crimson silk dress trimmed with costly lace; her forehead
was bound with a white ribbon and pearls. The Baron, who
was not much older than she, seemed, with his gentle candid ways, to be worthy of her in every respect.

The jovial whimsical master of the house took the lead
in the early part of the conversation, a shade too exuber-
antly, maybe, owing to his somewhat noisy way of larding
it with jokes and anecdotes. Refreshments were brought,
and our traveler, for one, did them full justice.

Someone had opened the pianoforte, *The Marriage of
Figaro* lay ready, and the young lady, accompanied by the
Baron, prepared to sing Susanna's garden aria, that aria in
which the spirit of sweet passion pours forth as richly as
the scented air of a summer evening. For the space of two
breaths, the delicate color in Eugenie's cheeks faded to extreme pallor, but with the first rich tone that passed her lips
all nervous constraint fell from her. Smiling and secure she
held the crest of the wave, savoring to the full a moment

which was perhaps destined to remain unique all the days
of her life.

Mozart was obviously surprised. When she had finished,
he approached her and said, with the warmhearted unaf-
fectedness which was natural to him: "What shall I say,
my dear young lady? It is as if I should speak of the beloved sun, which we should leave to praise itself, since everybody is equally happy in it. Listening to singing like
that, one feels like a child in its bath; it laughs and wonders
and cannot imagine anything more delightful in the world.
Besides, believe me, it is not every day that one of us Viennese hears his own music rendered with such purity, simplicity, and heart, indeed, so utterly—" With that he took
her hand and kissed her warmly. The sovereign goodness
and kindness of the man, no less than the tribute he paid
her art, moved Eugenie with one of those moments of emotion which are like a sudden vertigo, and she felt as if her
eyes were filling with tears.

At that moment Madame Mozart entered, and soon
afterward other expected guests appeared, a noble family
living close by, related to the family, with a daughter,
Franciska, who had been attached to the young bride since
childhood by the most tender affection, and was almost at
home in the château.

There were general greetings, embraces, and congratu-
lations, the two Viennese guests were presented, then Mozart took his place at the pianoforte. He played part of one
of his own concertos, which Eugenie was just learning.

The effect of a performance of the kind in a small and
intimate circle differs from any similar one in a public place
by the infinite pleasure given by the presence of the composer and his genius within the familiar walls of home.

It was one of those brilliant pieces in which pure beauty,
as if by a whim, lends itself for once to the service of ele-
gance, yet in such a way that, although apparently veiled
behind the fanciful movements of outward form, or out-
shone by its dazzling flashes, it still betrays its own innate
nobility in every movement and pours forth a profusion of
glorious feeling.

The Countess noticed that the attention of most of the audience, including Eugenie herself perhaps, though rapt and silent as the enchanting music went on, was very much divided between eye and ear. Watching the composer in spite of themselves, his unaffected, rather stiff posture, his kindly face, the rounded movements of his little hands, they could hardly resist the thousand confused wonderings which beset their minds about the man of wonders.

Turning to Madame Mozart, when the master had risen, the Count said: "It is not given to everyone to turn a fine phrase of praise for a famous musician. For kings and emperors it is easy. Everything they say sounds rare and exceptional. They can afford to say what they like, and how easy it is, for instance, standing just behind your famous husband's chair at the last chord of a brilliant fantasia, to clap the modest little servant of the classics on the shoulder, saying: 'You're a damned clever fellow, my good Mozart.' Hardly has he spoken when the whisper spreads through the hall like wildfire: 'What did he say to him?'—'He said he was a damned clever fellow.' And every man in the place who can fiddle and flute and compose is beside himself just because of those few words; in short, it is the grand style, the familiar, inimitable, imperial style, that I have always envied the Josephs and the Fredericks, and never more than at this minute, when I am desperate because I find not the least coin of intellectual brilliance in all my pockets."

But his way of saying such things was so captivatingly droll that there was a general burst of laughter.

At the invitation of the mistress of the house, the company now moved to the round dining room, from which a festive scent of flowers and a cooler, more appetizing air wafted to meet the guests.

They took the seats allotted to them in due order, the distinguished guest facing the young couple. On one side he had a small elderly lady, a maiden aunt of Franciska's, on the other, the charming young niece herself, who soon won his heart entirely by her gaiety and intelligence. Madame Constanze sat between her host and her obliging escort, the Lieutenant; the rest took what seats were left, and so eleven of them managed to find room round the table, the lower end of which remained empty. In its middle there stood two huge porcelain vases painted with figure scenes, holding large dishes overflowing with fruit and flowers. Rich garlands festooned the walls of the room. Whatever else was there, or followed in its turn, seemed to promise a prolonged banquet. Among the dishes on the table, or on the sideboard in the background, noble wines twinkled, from the richest red up to that golden white whose sparkling foam crowns by tradition the latter end of every feast.

Until that time was reached, the conversation was general and lively. But the Count, from the very beginning, had made distant allusions to Mozart's adventure in the garden, which became more open and pointed as time went on, so that some of the guests smiled to themselves, while others racked their brains for what he might mean. There was nothing for our friend, therefore, but to tell his story.

"Well, if it must be, I will confess," he began, "how I actually had the honor of becoming acquainted with this noble house. My part in the matter is anything but dignified, and but for the grace of God, instead of sitting at this pleasant table, I should be languishing in one of the château dungeons, contemplating spiders on an empty stomach."

"What is all this?" cried Madame Mozart. "What fine story is coming now?"

First he described in detail his parting from his wife at the White Horse, his stroll into the park, the ill-starred moment in the arbor, the quarrel with the garden watchman, in short more or less what we know already, telling it all with perfect honesty and to the huge delight of his hearers. There was no end to the laughter; even Eugenie, in spite of her reticence, was convulsed.

"Well," he went on, "you know the saying—let him laugh that wins. I have gained by the incident, as you will hear. But first of all you will hear how it came about that an old dotard like me could so forget himself. It all goes back to my childhood.

In the spring of 1770, when I was a boy of thirteen, my

father took me to Italy. We went from Rome to Naples.
I had played twice at the Conservatorium, and several
times elsewhere. The nobility and clergy were very gracious, and one abbot in particular attached himself to us
who set himself up as a connoisseur and had some standing
at court in other ways. The day before our departure, he
took us and some other gentlemen to a royal garden, the
Villa Reale, which stood on a magnificent road by the sea-
shore, where a troop of Sicilian commedianti were performing—Sons of Neptune, they called themselves, among other
highfalutin names. Together with many people of rank, including even the young and charming Queen Caroline with
two princesses, we sat on a long row of seats in a low gallery
shaded by a kind of awning, with the waves lapping at
the foot of its walls. The sea, with its bands of many colors,
was a glorious mirror of the blue sky of summer. Just in
front of us was Vesuvius; to the left, the shimmering curve
of the lovely coast.

The first part of the performance was over; it was given
on the dry boards of a kind of raft on the water and was
in no way remarkable. But the second and better part consisted of feats of rowing, swimming, and diving and has
remained fresh in my memory, in all its details, ever since.

From opposite sides, two pretty, very light boats approached each other, both, it seemed, out for pleasure only.
The rather larger one was half decked and carried, in addition to the rowing benches, a slender mast and a sail, beautifully painted like the rest, while the figurehead was gilt.
Five ideally handsome youths, lightly clad, their arms,
chests, and legs apparently bare, were occupied either in
rowing or in sporting with an equal number of pretty
maidens, their sweethearts. One of these girls, who was sitting in the middle of the half-deck winding garlands, stood
out from the others by her taller figure and greater finery.
The others served her willingly, held up a cloth to shade
her from the sun, and handed her flowers from the basket.
A girl playing the flute sat at her feet, accompanying the
others' song with the clear tones of her instrument. This
remarkable beauty had a protector too, but the couple

seemed rather indifferent to each other, and, to my eyes, the youth looked rather coarse.

Meanwhile the other, plainer boat had approached. It was manned only by youths. While those in the first boat wore scarlet costumes, those in the second wore sea-green. They stopped short at the sight of the lovely maidens, waved greetings to them, and showed their desire to be better acquainted. Thereupon the liveliest of the girls took a rose from her bosom and held it aloft, as if to ask whether such gifts were welcome, and was answered by all in the other boats with eager gestures. The scarlet youths looked on this interplay with somber contempt, but they could do nothing when several of the girls agreed to throw something to the poor creatures, if only to relieve their hunger and thirst. There was a basket of oranges on the deck; probably they were only yellow balls made to imitate the fruit. And now a delightful masquerade began, accompanied by the orchestra which had taken its place on the embankment.

One of the girls began by lightly tossing a few oranges over; caught in the other boat with equal ease, they were soon returned, and as more and more girls joined in the sport, little by little dozens of oranges were flying to and fro at ever greater speed. The beautiful maiden in their midst took no part in the contest but watched the contest with great curiosity from her seat. The skill of both sides moved us beyond admiration. At a distance of about thirty feet, the boats circled round each other, presenting now their sides to full view, now only their slanting sterns. Some two dozen balls were in the air, but as they flew hither and thither, there seemed to be many more. Sometimes a regular cross fire developed, or again they rose and fell in high curves. Very few missed their mark. It was as if they fell into the opened fingers by the mere power of attraction.

While our eyes were so delightfully occupied, lovely melodies charmed our ears: Sicilian airs, dances, saltarelli, ballads, a whole fantasia woven as lightly as a garland. The younger princess, a beautiful artless creature of about my own age, kept time by a pretty nodding of her head;

I can see her smile and her long eyelashes before me today.

However, I must tell you the rest of this merry masquerade, although it has little to do with my adventure. You cannot imagine anything more charming. The skirmish drew to an end, only a few balls were flying to and fro, and the girls were gathering their golden apples together and putting them back in the basket when a youth in the other boat picked up, as if in play, a large green net and held it under water for several minutes. He drew it up, and to the astonishment of all it held a great fish shimmering in blue, green, and gold. The other youths hurried to pull it on board, but it slipped out of their hands as if it had been alive and slid back into the sea. It was a stratagem planned to distract the scarlet side and lure them out of their boat. The Scarlets, as if spellbound by the wonder, once they realized that the fish would not sink but would continue to play on the surface, cast prudence to the winds and all dived into the sea, followed by the Greens, and then we saw twelve supple and handsome swimmers pursuing the fleeting fish as it flitted over the water, vanished under it for minutes at a time, and reappeared now here, now there, between the legs of one, between the chest and chin of another. Just when the Scarlets were most eager in the chase, the others seized their opportunity and, quick as lightning, boarded the boat which had been abandoned to the girls, who uttered loud cries as they did so. The noblest of the youths, a very Mercury, his face radiant with joy, sped to the beauty, embraced and kissed her, while she, for her part, far from joining in the cries of the others, enfolded the youth, who was no stranger to her, in an ardent embrace. The defeated side swam up as quickly as they could, but were driven from the deck with oars and weapons. Their vain fury, the cries of the girls, the struggles of some of them, their prayers and entreaties, almost stifled by the rest of the hubbub, the water, the music, which had suddenly changed its tone—it was all beautiful beyond description, and the spectators broke out into a storm of applause.

At that moment the sail, till then lightly reefed, opened,

a rosy boy appeared, with silver wings, with bow, arrow, and quiver, hovering freely and gracefully on the mast. The oars rose and fell, the sail swelled, but still greater power was in the presence of the god and the eager gestures with which he waved the boat on, till the swimmers, following almost breathless, with one holding the fish high over his head in his left hand, soon relinquished their pursuit and, almost spent, took refuge in the abandoned boat. Meanwhile the Greens had reached a small bushy islet where, quite unexpectedly, a splendid boat manned by armed comrades issued from ambush. Realizing their peril, the little troop hoisted a white flag as a sign that they were ready to negotiate on friendly terms. Encouraged by a similar signal from the other side, they rowed to the stopping place, and soon the maidens—excepting the one who stayed behind of her own free will—could be seen boarding their own boat happily with their lovers. That was the end of the masquerade."

"It seems to me," whispered Eugenie with flashing eyes to the Baron during a pause devoted to general applause of what they had heard, "that we have had a kind of symphony in picture form from beginning to end, and a perfect allegory of the spirit of Mozart in all its joyousness! Am I not right? Is not all the grace of Figaro there?"

Her betrothed was just about to tell the master what she had said when the latter continued his story.

"It is seventeen years now since I saw Italy. Nobody, I think, who has once seen that country, and especially Naples, can ever forget it, though he saw it only in childhood. Yet that last wonderful evening on the Bay of Naples has never yet come so vividly back to me as it did today in your garden. When I closed my eyes, the last veil dissolved and the lovely scene lay before me—sea and shore, mountain and town, the motley colors of the crowds on the shore and the exquisite dance of the golden balls. I seemed to hear that very music, a whole rosary of joyous melodies passed through my mind, other men's and my own, helter-skelter, one fading as the next rose. Then somehow a dance tune flashed out, six-eight time, quite unknown to me.—

Stop, I thought, what is this? It seems a devilishly pretty tune.—Good Heavens! It's Masetto, it's Zerlina!" He smiled at Madame Mozart, who guessed at once.

"It's all very simple," he went on. "In my first act I had left out one short light number, the duet and chorus of a rustic wedding. Two months ago, when I set to work to put the whole in order, I could not at first hit on the theme I wanted. It had to be simple, childish, all sparkling with merriment like a fresh nosegay with a fluttering ribbon on the bride's breast. But not a note will come by force, and trifles of the kind often create themselves. So I put it aside and as the more important work went on, it slipped out of my mind. Just before we entered the village today, the words flitted through my head, but led to nothing, so far as I was aware at the time. Well, an hour later, in the arbor by the fountain, I caught a theme on the wing, more joyous and more true than I could have discovered at any other place or time. Artists sometimes have odd experiences, but I have never had a trick of the kind played on me. For a tune which seemed to flow into the words—but we mustn't anticipate, we haven't got so far yet, the chick had only put its head out of the egg, so there and then I set about hatching it for good. As I did so, Zerlina's dance seemed to take shape before my eyes and the smiling beauty of the Bay of Naples joined in. I heard the antiphony of the bridal couple and the chorus of men and maidens."

At this point Mozart warbled very quaintly the beginning of the song:

> "Maidens born to love, born to love,
> Let not the summer pass, the summer pass.
> If your hearts are bowed in sadness,
> Here is healing—tra-la-la.
> Oh the pleasure! Oh the pleasure!
> That's to be—tra-la-la.

"Meanwhile my hand had committed the crime. Nemesis was lurking in the hedge and now appeared in the guise of the monster in the blue-braided coat. If, on that divine

evening by the sea, Vesuvius had buried forever, in one
sudden downpour of black ashes, the spectators and the
actors and the whole splendor of Parthenope, the catas-
trophe would not have been more sudden and appalling.
The ogre! I cannot remember, in all my life, anyone ter-
rifying me out of my wits by simply being there. A face
of bronze—not unlike the cruel Roman Emperor Tiberius.
If the man looks like that, I thought, after he had gone,
what will the master look like? However, to tell the truth,
I was actually counting on the help of the ladies, and had
reason to. For Constanze, my little wife there, who is by
way of being rather inquisitive, induced the fat landlady
at the inn to tell her everything about every single member of the family at the château while I was still with her.
I stood, I listened, I heard—"

Here Madame Mozart broke in, declaring most vehe-
mently that he, not she, was the questioner: there were
lively exchanges between husband and wife, which gave
rise to great laughter.

"Well, however that may be," he said, "to cut a long
story short, I heard vague reports of a foster daughter who
was betrothed, very beautiful, the soul of goodness, and
who could sing like an angel. Per Dio, it flashed through
my mind. That's the way out of my plight! I shall sit down,
write the song as best I can, give a truthful account of the
idiotic mishap, and it will all be a splendid frolic. I had
plenty of time and managed to discover a clean sheet of
green-lined paper! And here is the result. Let me lay it in
those lovely hands, an impromptu bridal song, if you will
accept it as such."

With that he handed his beautifully neat sheet of music
to Eugenie over the table, but her uncle's hand forestalled
him; he snatched it away, crying: "A moment's patience,
my dear."

At a sign from him the double doors of the drawing room
opened wide and a few servants appeared, carrying the
fateful orange tree carefully on noiseless feet into the dining room. They placed it at the foot of the table on a chair;
two slender myrtle saplings were placed to left and right

of it. A billet fixed to the trunk of the orange tree declared it to be the property of the bride, but in front of it, on its mossy soil, there lay a china plate covered with a serviette on which, when the serviette was removed, the halves of an orange were revealed. With a sly smile, the uncle slipped the Maestro's autograph beside it. There was a burst of general applause.

"If you ask me," said the Countess, "I don't believe that Eugenie even knows what that is standing before her. She actually cannot recognize her old beloved tree in its new trappings of flower and fruit." Half dismayed, half incredulous, the young lady looked at the tree and her uncle by turns. "It is impossible," she said. "I knew it was beyond rescue."

"And therefore," he replied, "you think we are trying to palm off a changeling on you. Perish the thought! No— come and look. I shall have to take a leaf out of the recognition scenes in the comedies, in which the sons and brothers, believed dead, prove their identity by moles and scars. Look at that bole there, and this slanting scar. You must have seen them a hundred times. Come now, is it your tree or not?"

She could doubt no longer; her amazement, emotion, and joy were beyond description.

For the family, this tree was associated with a memory, more than a century old, of a remarkable woman who deserves a brief tribute here.

The uncle's grandfather, celebrated for his services to the Viennese cabinet, honored by the equal confidence of two succeeding rulers, was not less happy at home in the possession of an excellent wife, Renate Leonore. Her many visits to France gave her the entrée to the brilliant court of Louis XIV and brought her into touch with the most eminent men and women of that remarkable epoch. Though she took part without reserve in the ever-changing and cultivated diversions of the court, she never belied, in word or deed, the strict sense of honor and the moral seriousness of her German ancestors which can be so clearly seen in the still existing portrait of the Countess. By dint of this

way of thinking, she set up, in that society, an oddly naïve
kind of opposition, and the correspondence she left at her
death bears many a trace of the gallantry and ready wit
with which she advocated her sound principles and beliefs
in matters of religion, literature, politics, or anything else,
and attacked the foibles of society without giving the least
offense. Her lively interest in all the people she met at a
house such as Ninon's, the living focus of the most refined
intellect was thus, by its own nature and her keen sense of
values, in no way at odds with her friendship with one of
the greatest ladies of the time, Madame de Sévigné. In the
grandmother's ebony casket, there were found, after her
death, many a witty verse by Chapelle, scribbled by the
author's own hand on paper edged with silver flowers, and
the most warmhearted letters from the Marquise and her
daughter to their outspoken friend from Austria.

It was from Madame de Sévigné's hand too that, one
day at a fête at the Trianon, she received a blooming
orange twig which she at once planted haphazard in a pot,
where it struck root and was flourishing when she took it
to Germany.

For twenty-five years the little tree grew steadily under
her care and was later tended by her children and grandchildren with the greatest devotion. Beyond its value as a
personal keepsake, it was the living symbol of the cultivated pleasures of a kind of Golden Age, though we find
nothing very much to praise in it, and it bore within it the
seeds of an ominous future which was to burst upon the
world not long after the time of our harmless tale.

It was Eugenie who lavished the greatest care on the
bequest of her worthy ancestress, and for that reason her
uncle had often hinted that it would one day be her own.
It was all the more painful for the young lady when, during the preceding spring which she had spent away from
home, the tree began to droop; its leaves faded and many
twigs fell off. No possible cause could be discovered for its
decay, and no remedies availed. The gardener therefore
soon gave it up for lost, although by the nature of its kind
it could have lived to two or three times its age. The Count,

however, on the advice of a neighbor, had it treated in a
separate room by a curious and mysterious method such
as countryfolk often use, and his hope of surprising his beloved niece one day with her old friend in renewed strength
and perfect fertility was fulfilled beyond all expectations.
Mastering his impatience, and not without anxiety lest the
fruit, some of which was fully ripe, should not hang on the
branches so long, he deferred his pleasure for several weeks
until the fête now being celebrated, and we need waste no
words on the feelings of the good man when he saw his
happiness mutilated by a stranger at the last moment.

The Lieutenant had seized the time and opportunity before dinner to put the finishing touches to his poetic contribution in preparation for its ceremonial presentation, and
to adapt, as far as he could, his perhaps rather overserious
verses to circumstances by changing the end. He now
produced his paper, and, rising from his seat, turned to
his cousin and read his poem. Its contents were briefly as
follows.

A descendant of the famous tree of the Hesperides, which
had sprung up in olden times on a western isle in the garden of Juno as a bridal gift to her from Mother Earth, and
was guarded by the three nymphs of music, had always
longed to become a bridal gift in his turn, for the custom
of presenting a lovely bride with one of his kind had descended from the gods to mortals long ago.

After long, vain waiting, it seemed at last that he had
found a maiden on whom his eyes could rest with favor.
She was kindly disposed to him and was often by his side.
But the Laurel of the Muses, his proud neighbor by the
fountain, awakened his jealousy by threatening to deprive
the beautiful votary of the arts of her mind and heart for
the love of men. The myrtle tried in vain to console him
and teach him patience by her own example; in the end it
was the lasting absence of his beloved that deepened his
grief and, after long sickness, cost him his life.

With summer the absent fair one returned, her heart
happily changed. The village, the château, the garden, all
welcomed her with untold joy. Roses and lilies, in richer

effulgence, looked up to her in humble worship; bushes
and trees waved joy to her; for one, alas, she came too late;
his garland was withered, her fingers touched a lifeless
trunk and the rattling tips of twigs. He no longer saw or
heard his muse. How she wept! How her tender complaint
poured forth!

From far off, Apollo heard his daughter's voice. He came,
approached and saw her mourning with compassion. Then,
with his all-healing hand he touched the tree; it trembled,
the dried sap in its bark swelled mightily, young leaves
sprouted, white flowers unfolded here and there in ambro-
sian fullness. Yes—for what can the Heavenly Ones not do—
beautiful round fruit appeared, nine in number for the nine
sisters, swelling till their childish green passed into the color
of gold. Phoebus, the poem concluded:

> Phoebus counts the golden harvest,
> Sacred to the sisters nine,
> Then his mouth begins to water,
> And his eye begins to shine.
>
> With a smile, the god of music
> Plucks the juiciest from the tree.
> Come and share it, gracious beauty—
> Cupid, here's a leaf for thee!

Delighted applause greeted the poem, and nobody
blamed the poet for the rather fanciful turn at the end
which seemed to efface the truly serious feeling of the
whole.

Franciska, whose merry wit had been provoked more
than once by the master of the house or Mozart, suddenly
ran off as if something had flashed into her mind, and returned with a very large English sepia engraving which
hung, almost unnoticed, framed and glazed in a remote
cabinet.

"What I have always heard must be true after all," she
explained, setting up the picture at the end of the table.
"There is nothing new under the sun. Here is a scene from
the Golden Age. Have we not been living in a Golden Age

this very day? I only hope that Apollo will recognize himself in this situation."

"Excellent," cried Max in triumph. "There he is, the beautiful god, in the very act of bending pensively over the divine spray. And that is not all. Can you see there the old satyr back in the bushes, listening to him? You would swear that there has just come into Apollo's mind some long-forgotten Arcadian dance which old Chiron taught him to the lyre in his boyhood."

"That's it, exactly as we see it here," applauded Franciska, who was standing behind Mozart. "And," she went on, turning to him, "can you see the fruit-laden branch bending down to the god?"

"Of course; it is the olive, his sacred tree."

"Not a bit of it. Those are the loveliest of oranges. The very next minute, in his reverie, he will pluck one of them."

"No!" cried Mozart. "He will close that roguish mouth with a thousand kisses."

So saying, he caught her by the arm and swore not to release her till she had yielded him her lips, which she did without overmuch persuasion.

"But Max," said the Countess, "tell us what is written there under the picture."

"Those are lines from a famous ode by Horace. Ramler, the Berlin poet, gave us a matchless rendering of them in our own language not long ago. It is supremely vivid. How beautiful those lines are:

> ". . . here, on his shoulder
>   bearing no idle bow,
> He who lives in the verdure of Delos' grove
>   And on the shady shores of Pataras,
>   Who plunges his gold-curled head
>   Into Castalian springs."

"Beautiful, indeed beautiful," said the Count. "But an explanation is necessary here and there. For instance, 'no idle bow' would, of course, simply mean: who fiddles away more industriously than anyone else. But what I wanted to

say was, my dear Mozart, that you are sowing seeds of dis-
cord between two tenderly devoted hearts."

"I hope not. How?"

"Eugenie envies her friend, and has every reason to."

"Aha! You have marked my weakness. But what does
the bridegroom say?"

"He can close an eye now and then."

"Very well. We shall not let the opportunity slip. Meanwhile, do not be alarmed, Baron. There is no danger until
the god there lends me his face and his long yellow hair.
I wish he would! He could have in exchange, on the spot,
Mozart's plait and his finest ribbon."

"But then I hope Apollo will look on," laughed Franciska, "to see how he manages to plunge his new French
coiffure with decorum into the Castalian spring."

With these and other pleasantries the general mood grew
merrier and more exuberant. The men gradually warmed
up to their wine, a host of healths was drunk, and Mozart
relapsed into his old habit of speaking in rhyme, the Lieutenant seconding him and Papa unwilling to be left out.
Once or twice he made admirably happy hits. But such
things can hardly be reported in a story. All that makes
them irresistible in their time and place, the general gaiety, the brilliance, the joviality of the personal expression
in word and look, is lacking.

Among other things a toast was proposed in honor of the
Maestro by the elder lady, who foretold a long series of
immortal works by him.

"*A la bonne heure!* It shall be so!" cried Mozart, clink-
ing glasses with spirit. Thereupon the Count began to sing,
with great vigor and self-assurance, and inspired only by
himself:

> May the gods his soul inspire
> To fresh works of heavenly fire.

> MAX (*continuing*)
> To Da Ponte and our own
> Schikaneder still unknown.

MOZART

And the poor composer too,
By God! has not a note in view.

COUNT

May that scoundrel from the south
Hear them all with watering mouth,
Hear them till he rends his hair,
Our Signor Bonbonnière!*

MAX

He shall live a hundred years,

MOZART

Unless, with all his quips and sneers

ALL THREE (con forza)

The Devil fetches him away.
Bonbonnière has had his day!

As the Count's delight in his own voice grew, the trio,
which had come about haphazard, by the repetition of the
last four lines, developed into a canon finale, which the
aunt had sufficient humor or self-assurance to embellish
with all kinds of ornaments in her cracked soprano. Afterward Mozart promised that when he had time he would
write down the whole impromptu according to all the rules
of his art, and later did so, sending it to them from Vienna.

Eugenie had by now become familiar with her jewel
from the arbor of Tiberius. There was a call for the duet to
be sung by her and the composer, and the uncle was glad
of the opportunity to display his voice again in the chorus.
There was therefore a general move to the pianoforte in
the neighboring salon.

Though the delicious piece gave exquisite delight, its
words, by a swift transition, brought the festivity to that
climax at which the music in itself hardly counts, and our

* This was the name given by Mozart among friends to his
fellow musician Salieri, partly because of his habit of nibbling
sweets at all times and places, and partly as an allusion to his
dainty person.

friend was the first to give the signal by jumping up from the pianoforte, approaching Franciska, and asking her to dance a waltz with him, which she did with great willingness, while Max needed no pressing to take up his violin. The master of the house promptly invited Madame Mozart. In a moment, bustling servants had carried away everything movable so as to make more room. One by one, all had to take their turn, and Mademoiselle the aunt was by no means outraged when the obliging Lieutenant led her out for a minuet, which restored her entirely to her youth. Finally, when Mozart closed the dance with the bride, he took his toll in due form of her beautiful lips.

Evening had come, the sun was setting, the cool of the evening had replaced the heat of the day, and the ladies proposed a little rest in the garden. The Count, for his part, invited the gentlemen to the billiard room, since Mozart was known to be passionately fond of billiards. Thus the party separated, and we will follow the ladies.

After strolling up and down the drive for some time, they climbed a round knoll which was half surrounded by a vineyard; from it there was a prospect of the open country, the village and the high road. The last red rays of the autumn sun were gleaming through the vine leaves.

"This would be a place for confidences," said the Countess, "if Madame Mozart were to tell us something about herself and her husband?"

Madame Mozart at once complied, and they all settled down on the chairs which had been drawn into a circle.

"I will entertain you with a story you will certainly come to hear of, because it is connected with a little joke I have up my sleeve. I have in mind to present the young Countess, in happy remembrance of this day, with a love token, and one of a peculiar kind. Love tokens are neither costly nor fashionable today, so that it can only be of interest for the story behind it."

"What can it be, Eugenie?" asked Franciska. "It can be nothing more nor less than the inkwell of a famous man."

"Very near the mark! You shall see it within an hour. I

shall begin my story, and with your permission, start some time back.

"The winter before last I had grown really anxious about Mozart's health because of his increased irritability and frequent fits of depression. While he was often in high spirits in society—sometimes more than was natural—at home he was self-absorbed and gloomy and sighed and complained. The doctor prescribed a diet, Pyrmont water and exercise in the country. The patient had very little confidence in this good advice; the cure was uncomfortable, wasted his time, and was entirely at variance with his daily routine. Then the doctor tried to put the fear of the Lord into him, held a long discourse on the constitution of the human blood and the little spheres in it, on breathing and phlogiston, in short, incredible things, and what nature's purposes were in eating, drinking, and digestion, which Mozart had up to then taken as naturally as his own five-year-old son. Actually the lecture made an impression. The doctor had hardly been gone an hour when I discovered my husband in his room, thoughtful, but with a brighter expression, and contemplating a walking stick which he had looked for in a cupboard among old rubbish and had actually found. I would not have believed that he remembered it. It had belonged to my father, and was a beautiful cane with a high lapis lazuli knob. Mozart had never been seen with a walking stick in his hand, and I could not help laughing.

" 'Look!' he cried. 'I am on the point of plunging boldly into my cure. I shall drink the water, take exercise every day in the open air, and this shall be my staff. I have been thinking. There must be some reason why men who have reached years of discretion cannot do without their sticks. The Councilor, our neighbor, will not so much as step across the street to visit his crony without his stick. Professors, men of letters, officials, civil servants, grocers, and peddlers on their Sunday walk into the country with their families all take their good and trusty sticks with them. In particular, I have often noticed honest burghers standing about in groups in St. Stephen's Square before sermon and mass, and you can see how every one of them has his stick as a kind of prop and support for his unnoticed virtues, his industry, orderliness, his quiet courage and contentedness. In a word, some blessing, some special comfort must reside in this outmoded and not very tasteful custom. You can believe it or not, but I can hardly wait until I can use this good friend on my first cure promenade over the bridge and on to the Rennweg. We are not quite strangers to each other, and I hope that our love will last forever.'

"The love was not long-lived; the third time they went out together, the friend did not return. Another was bought, which was faithful rather longer. In any case, I attributed to this flirtation with walking sticks a good deal of the perseverance with which Mozart quite tolerably obeyed the doctor's orders. The good results appeared too; we had hardly ever seen him so fresh, so bright, and so equable. But unfortunately he went too far again. So I had trouble with him every day. It so happened one day that, tired by strenuous work, he went out late in the evening to a musical soirée just to satisfy some inquisitive travelers—only for an hour, he promised me faithfully, but those are always the times when the people, once he is stuck at the piano and is in the mood, are most likely to take advantage of his good nature, for there he sits like the little man in a balloon, six miles above the earth, hovering where nobody can hear the clock strike. I sent our servant twice in the middle of the night; it was useless, he could not gain admittance to his master. The latter came home at three in the morning. I made up my mind that he should be in real disgrace the whole day."

Here Madame Mozart omitted to mention certain circumstances. We must know that it was not unlikely that a young singer, Signora Malerbi, would be present at the musical evening, and Madame Constanze was perfectly right in feeling seriously annoyed with her. She was a Roman and had been engaged at the opera on Mozart's recommendation, and her blandishments had certainly played no small part in winning the Maestro's favor. Some people, in fact, declared that she had kept him attached to her for several months, roasting him hot on her grill. Whether that be true, or a great exaggeration, one thing is certain: her later behavior was insolent and ungrateful. She even went so far as to make fun of her benefactor. It was quite like her to call him straight out *un piccolo grifo raso* (a little, smooth-shaven pig's snout) in comparison with a more fortunate admirer. The idea, which was worthy of a Circe, was the more wounding because it must be confessed that there was a grain of truth in it.*

As he went home from that evening, at which, by the way, the singer did not appear, a friend, in the exuberance of the moment, was indiscreet enough to repeat the malicious remark to the Maestro. He was anything but edified by it, for it was, for him, the first unequivocal proof of his protégée's utter heartlessness. For sheer indignation he did not at first notice the frosty reception that awaited him at his wife's bedside. Breathlessly he related the insult and this candor certainly betrays some small degree of compunction. He almost made her feel sorry for him. But she did not weaken; he was not to get off scot-free. When he awoke from a heavy sleep soon after midday, his wife and the two boys were not at home, but the table was laid neatly for him alone.

There were few things that ever made Mozart so unhappy as any breach in the serenity of the relations between him and his better half. And if he had only known what a burden she had had to bear for the last few days—one of the heaviest, which, by old habit, she had refrained from disclosing as long as she could. Her ready money was long since at an end, and there was no prospect of more coming in soon. Though he had no inkling of this domestic extremity there was a heaviness in his heart which was not unlike her own forlorn and helpless state. He could not eat, he could not sit still. He dressed hurriedly, only to escape from

* This can be seen in an early profile portrait which, well executed and engraved, figures on the title page of one of Mozart's piano works, and is unquestionably the best likeness of all his portraits, even of those which have lately appeared among art dealers.

the stifling air at home. On a slip of paper he left her a few
lines in Italian: "You have paid me out thoroughly, and it
served me right. But please, love me again and laugh again
when I come home. I tell you, I feel as if I could turn
monk, Carthusian or Trappist, or bellow like an ox." Then
he picked up his hat, though not the stick; its time was
past.

Since we have followed the thread of Madame Constanze's story thus far, we may continue a little farther.

Turning to the right toward the Arsenal from his house
near the Schranne, the lovable creature—it was a warm,
rather cloudy summer afternoon—sauntered thoughtfully
across the so-called Hof and past the church house of Our
Lady toward the Schottentor, where he turned left and
climbed the Mölker ramparts, thus escaping the necessity
of speaking to a number of acquaintances and patrons who
were just on their way into town. He did not spend long
enjoying the beautiful prospect from the green slope of the
glacis and the outskirts of town toward the Kahlenberg
and southward to the Styrian Alps, though the sentry who
was pacing silently to and fro by the guns left him in
peace. The beautiful serenity of nature found no echo in
his own feelings. With a sigh he continued his aimless walk
over the esplanade and then through the Alser Vorstadt.

At the end of the Währinger Gasse there stood an inn
with a skittle alley, the owner of which, a rope maker, was
very well known to his neighbors and the countryfolk who
passed his inn for the good quality of his wares and his
wine. The sound of skittles could be heard; since there were
not more than a dozen people in the place it was fairly
quiet. A hardly conscious impulse to forget himself in the
company of natural and simple-minded people moved the
musician to enter. In the scanty shade of the trees he sat
down at a table already occupied by a Viennese inspector
of fountains and two other honest citizens, ordered a glass
of wine, and entered wholeheartedly into their very hum-
drum conversation, rising from time to time to stroll about
or watch the game in the skittle alley.

At the side of the house, not far from the skittle alley,

was the rope maker's shop, a narrow room bursting with wares, since, in addition to the immediate products of his trade, there were all kinds of wooden tools for the kitchen, cellar, and garden; there was oil and cart grease, while some seeds, dill and caraway, stood or hung about for sale. A girl who was both waitress at the inn and shopgirl was busy with a farmer who, leading his little boy by the hand, had come in to buy a few things, a peck measure, a brush, a whip. He would select one from among many others, try it, lay it aside, take up a second, then turn irresolutely back to the first. The girl left him several times to serve in the inn, came back, and was tireless in helping him to choose what he needed without making too many words about it.

Seated on a bench by the skittle alley, Mozart watched and heard the little scene with pleasure. The good sensible manner of the girl, the serious cast of her pleasant features, pleased him, but he was still more interested in the farmer, who remained in his mind long after he had trundled off satisfied. He had entered completely into the man's mind, felt what importance the trivial incident had for him, felt how gravely and conscientiously he had weighed up the prices, though there was but a copper of difference between them. And, he thought, that man will go home to his wife, display his bargain, and the children will watch for his canvas bag to open, for there may be something there for them too, while she, for her part, will hurry to fetch him his meal and the cooling glass of home-made cider he has saved up his appetite for so long.

Who else could be so happy, so free of men, so dependent on nature only, and on her bounty, however hard it must be won!

Yet with my art another kind of daily toil has been entrusted to me, and, all things considered, I would not change it for any other in the world; then why must I live in circumstances which are the exact opposite of his innocent and simple life? A little estate, if I had it, a little house near a village in some beautiful place, would mean fresh life to me. All morning working hard at my scores, the rest of the time with my family, planting trees, inspecting my fields, picking apples and pears in autumn with my boys, now and then a trip to town for a performance, from time to time a friend, or friends, to visit me. What bliss! Well, after all, who can foretell the future?

He walked up to the shop, spoke kindly to the girl, and began to inspect her wares more attentively. Since most of them were closely akin to his idyllic flight of fancy, the cleanliness, the bright smooth surface, the very smell of the wood delighted him. It suddenly occurred to him to choose some things which he imagined his wife might like and find useful. First of all he looked for gardening tools, since Constanze, on his suggestion, had rented a plot of land in front of the Kärntner Gate and planted some vegetables in it, so that a large new rake, a smaller ditto, and a spade seemed most appropriate. Then, stretching his hand out farther, it must be recorded to the credit of his thrift that, after a few minutes' consideration he abandoned, though with reluctance, a butter barrel which smiled at him very temptingly; on the other hand a tall vessel with a lid and finely carved handle took his fancy, though what it was for he could hardly have said; it was made of alternating bars of dark and light wood, was wider below than above and beautifully finished inside. The needs of the kitchen were provided by a beautiful selection of spoons, rolling pins, carving boards, and a very practical hanging saltcellar.

Finally he contemplated a stout stick, the handle of which was equally stoutly mounted with leather and brass nails. Since the odd customer seemed on the point of succumbing to temptation, the girl remarked with a smile that it was hardly the thing for a gentleman. "You're right, my child," he replied. "I rather think that butchers take such things on their travels; take it away, I don't want it. But please bring everything else we have chosen to me at my home today or tomorrow." He gave her his name and the street he lived in, then he went back to his table to finish his glass; only one of the three, a tinsmith, was still there.

"The servant is doing well today for once," the man remarked. "Her cousin allows her a penny in the crown on all the profit the shop makes."

Mozart was doubly pleased with his purchases, but his interest in the girl was soon to become greater. For when she was again within speaking distance, the man called to her: "Well, Crescentia, how do things stand now? What is the locksmith doing? Will he soon be filing his own iron?"

"As if he could!" she answered as she hurried past. "That iron's still in the mountain, and back in the farthest cave too, I believe."

"She's a good girl," said the tinsmith; "she kept house for her stepfather for years, and nursed him when he was ill, and when he was dead it turned out that he had spent everything she had. Since then she's been here in her cousin's service. She's the heart and soul of the business, waits in the inn and looks after the children. She walks out with a decent kind of fellow and would marry him tomorrow, but there's a difficulty in the way."

"What kind of difficulty? Is he quite penniless?"

"They've both saved, but not quite enough. And now half a houseful of furniture with a workshop is being put up to auction in town in a few days' time. The rope maker could easily advance what they haven't got to buy it up, but of course he doesn't want to lose the girl. He has good friends on the town council and in the gild, and the locksmith finds all kinds of obstacles in his way."

"The devil take it!" cried Mozart, making the other start and look round to see if anyone was listening. "Isn't there anybody to see that they get their rights, to shake his fists at those gentlemen? The scoundrels! Just you wait! You'll be caught in your own trap some day."

The tinsmith was on tenterhooks. He made blundering efforts to tone down what he had said; he nearly took it all back. But Mozart was not listening.

"Take shame to yourself for what you say. You rascals are all the same when it comes to standing up for somebody else." And with that he turned his back on the poltroon without a word of good-bye. To the serving girl, who had her hands full with new guests, he merely whispered in passing: "Come early tomorrow, salute your sweetheart from me. I hope your fortunes will mend." She was merely taken aback and had neither the time nor the presence of mind to thank him.

Walking more quickly than was his habit, for the scene had roused his blood, he first went back the way he had come till he reached the glacis, then, slackening his pace, he made a wide semicircle round the ramparts. Entirely engrossed in the affair of the poor lovers, he ran over in his mind a number of his friends and patrons who might be able to do something for them in one way or another. But since he had to have more particulars from the girl before he could take any step, he decided to put the whole matter aside till he knew more about it; then, his heart and mind outstripping his feet, he was at home with his wife.

In his heart of hearts he was looking forward to a warm, even a joyous welcome, a kiss and embrace on the very threshold, and his expectancy doubled the pace of his feet as he entered the Kärntner Gate. Not far from it the postman called to him and handed over a small but heavy packet on which he immediately recognized a clear and neat handwriting. In order to pay the postman, he went into the next shop with him, then, back in the street, he could not wait till he reached home; he broke the seals and devoured the letter, now standing, now walking.

"I was sitting," Madame Mozart continued her story to the ladies at this point, "at my sewing table, heard my husband come upstairs and ask the servant where I was. His step and voice sounded more vigorous and cheerful than I expected, and, to tell the truth, than I quite liked. First he went to his room, but soon came down. 'Good evening,' he said. I replied demurely without looking up. After pacing up and down in silence for a time, he took the fly whisk from behind the door—a thing he never did—pretended to yawn, and murmured: 'Wherever do the flies come from?' Then he started to hit about with it, right and left, as hard as he could. That was a noise he could not bear, and I never dared make it in his presence. Well, I thought, what we do ourselves is always right, especially if we are men. For that matter, I had not noticed that there were so many flies about. I was really annoyed by his strange doings. 'Six at a blow!' he cried. 'Come and look.' No answer. Then he laid something on my sewing cushion in such a way that I could not help seeing it without raising an eye from my work. It was nothing more dreadful than a little pile of gold coins, as many ducats as you could hold between two fingers. He went on with his nonsense behind my back, giving a thwack here and there, muttering to himself: 'Beastly, useless, shameless creatures! What are they in the world for—thwack—just to get killed—thwack—and I'm a pretty good hand at that, I can tell you. Natural science teaches us how amazingly the creatures multiply—thwack, thwack —in my house there's summary judgment on them. Ah, *maledette! Disperate!* There's another ducat. Do you like them?' He came and did as before. Up to then I had managed to stifle my laughter, but now I could do so no longer; I burst out, he fell on my neck, and we giggled and laughed ourselves helpless.

'Where does the money come from?' I asked, as he shook the rest out of the roll.

'From Prince Esterházy, forwarded by Haydn. Read the letter.' I read it.

'Eisenstadt, etc. My very dear friend, His Excellency, my gracious patron, has charged me, to my great delight, with forwarding to you these sixty ducats. We played your quartets again lately, and His Excellency was still more enchanted with them than the first time, three months ago. The Prince remarked to me (I must give his own words): When Mozart dedicated this work to you, he thought he was honoring you alone, but he can hardly take it ill if I see a compliment to myself in it. Tell him that I shall soon have as great an idea of his genius as you yourself, and more he cannot desire for immortality.—Amen! I added. Are you pleased?

P.S. A word in your dear wife's ear. Be so kind as to see that a letter of thanks goes off at once. It might be better from him to present his thanks in person. We must keep the good wind blowing.'

'Angelic, heavenly soul!' cried Mozart again and again, and I cannot say what pleased him most, the letter, the Prince's tribute, or the money. For my part, to tell the honest truth, the last came in the nick of time. We spent a very merry evening.

On that day I heard nothing of the affair at the inn, nor the next day. The whole week passed, and no Crescentia appeared, while my husband, in a whirlwind of work, soon forgot the incident. One evening we had company; Captain Wesselt, Count Hardegg, and a few others came in for music. During a pause I was called out—and there it all lay! I went in and asked: 'Did you order all kinds of wooden things in the Alser Vorstadt?'—'Good Lord, so I did! Did a girl bring them? Tell her to come in.' So in she came, most amiably, a full basket on her arm, holding the rakes and spade. She apologized for the long delay, she had forgotten the name of the street and had not been able to discover it before. Mozart relieved her of her wares one by one and handed them to me with great complacency. I was pleased and grateful, but wondered why he had bought the gardening tools. 'For your kitchen garden on the river, of course,' he said. 'But my goodness, we gave that up long ago. The water spoilt everything and we got no good out of it. I told you—you didn't object.'—'What about the asparagus we had this spring?'—'All from the market.'—'My goodness, if I had only known! I praised it out of pure kindheartedness because I really pitied you and your gardening. Little sticks they were, the size of quills.'

The gentlemen enjoyed the joke immensely. I even had to present some of them with what I could not use as a remembrance of the evening. But when Mozart came to ask the girl about her marriage, encouraging her to speak quite frankly, since anything that was to be done for her and her sweetheart would be done quietly, discreetly, and without blame to anybody, she began to speak with so much good sense, modesty, and forbearance that she completely won the hearts of all present, and was finally sent off with high promises.

" 'Those young people must be helped,' said the Captain.

'Those dodgers in the gild won't cause much trouble: I know somebody here who will soon put that right. Our business is to make a contribution to the house and furniture and so on. Suppose we advertised a public concert in the Trattner Hall with seats for as much as people liked to pay for them?' The idea was received with great acclamation. One of the gentlemen picked up the saltcellar, saying: 'Somebody will have to introduce the concert with an amusing story of the whole affair, describing Maestro Mozart's purchase and his kind intentions, and this splendid saltcellar will be set up on a table as an alms box, guarded left and right by the two rakes *croisés.*'

"Well, that part of the plan did not come to anything, but the concert did. A good sum was realized by it, various contributions followed, so that the happy couple had more than they needed, and even the other obstacles were soon removed. The Duscheks, our closest friends in Prague, where we are going to stay, heard of the story. And she, the kindest-hearted, most generous of women, demanded some specimen of the collection just as a curio. So I put aside something suitable for her, and have seized this opportunity of bringing it along with me. But as we have meanwhile discovered, to our own surprise, an unknown and generous lover of music, who is soon to install her own home and who will certainly not despise a piece of household goods chosen by Mozart's own hand, I will halve what I have brought, and you can choose between a beautifully pierced chocolate whisk and the famous saltcellar, which the artist has taken the pains to decorate tastefully with a tulip. I would certainly advise the latter. Salt is a noble thing and, as far as I know, is a symbol of domesticity and hospitality, and there go with it all our best wishes for you."

So far Madame Mozart. You can imagine the gratitude and delight with which the story was heard and the gift accepted by the ladies. The rejoicings doubled immediately afterward when the articles were displayed to the gentlemen upstairs and the symbol of patriarchal simplicity was ceremoniously presented, the uncle prophesying that its place in the silver closet of its present owner and her descendants would be no less honorable than that of the famous work by the Florentine master in the Ambras collection.

It was nearly eight o'clock; the company was at tea. Soon our musician was urgently reminded of his promise, given at midday, to introduce the company to "Don Juan's Descent into Hell," which was carefully locked away in his traveling trunk, though fortunately not too far down. He needed no pressing. The plot of the piece was soon explained, the book was opened, and the candles stood burning on the pianoforte.

If only our readers, at this moment, could feel a touch of that strange thrill which holds us spellbound when, passing an open window, we hear a single but unmistakable chord of music, or of that sweet and tremulous anticipation in the theater when the orchestra is tuning up and we sit facing the curtain! If the threshold of every sublime tragedy, be it Macbeth or Oedipus or anything else, be haunted by a premonition of immortal beauty, where could it be as moving, or even more moving, than here? Man desires, yet fears, to be shaken out of his daily self. He feels the finger of infinity touch him like a load on his heart as it strives to draw his spirit into itself. The reverence for art in its perfection, the thought of experiencing a heavenly wonder which is yet akin to him, brings with it a kind of exaltation, even of pride, which is perhaps the happiest and purest he can ever know.

Our friends, however, were hearing for the first time a work that we have possessed since childhood. Apart from their good fortune in hearing it performed by its creator, therefore, their situation was far less privileged than ours, since none of them could gain a clear and untroubled conception of it, nor could they have done so even if it had been possible for them to hear the whole.

Of eighteen finished numbers* the composer gave not more than half. (In the account on which our story is based

---

* This enumeration takes account of the fact that Elvira's recitative and aria and Leporello's catalogue aria were not contained in the original version of the opera.

we find only the last piece of the series, the sextette, mentioned by name.) He executed them, it appears, in a free adaptation for the pianoforte, singing from time to time as occasion arose. His wife is mentioned as having sung only two arias. Since her voice was as powerful as it was sweet, we may imagine that they were Donna Anna's first (*Ah! mi tradi*) and one of the two given to Zerlina.

In spirit, understanding, and taste, Eugenie and her betrothed were certainly the only listeners the master could have truly wished, and she far more than he. They both sat far back in the room, the young lady motionless as a statue, rapt in the music to such a degree that, even in the brief pauses when the others paid their modest tribute, or gave vent to their feelings in involuntary exclamations of admiration, she could hardly give a coherent reply when her betrothed spoke to her.

When Mozart's performance had come to an end in the ravishing beauty of the sextette, and conversation had been gradually resumed, he seemed to listen with special interest and pleasure to some detached remarks of the Baron's. They spoke of the finale of the opera, and of the performance which had been provisionally fixed for the beginning of November, and as someone remarked that certain parts of the finale would involve immense labor, the Maestro smiled, but Constanze said to the Countess, though it was for her husband's ear: "He has something in petto which he is keeping secret, even from me."

"My dear, you forget yourself," he retorted, "in bringing that up now. Suppose the fancy took me to start again? I feel my fingers itching already."

"Leporello!" cried the Count, starting up in high good humor, and beckoning to a servant. "Wine, Sillery, three bottles!"

"None of that, I beg you. It's too late. My young nobleman is at his last glass."

"Much good may it do him—and to every man his due!"

"Oh dear! what have I done?" lamented Constanze, looking at the clock. "It is nearly eleven and we start early tomorrow. How shall we do it?"

"You cannot, my dear young lady. You simply cannot."

"Sometimes," Mozart began, "things happen very strangely. What will Constanze say when she hears that the very work she is about to hear made its first appearance in the world at this very hour of night and just before a journey too?"

"Can that be? When? I know! It was three weeks ago when you were setting off for Eisenstadt."

"Right! It came about in this way. I came home after ten from the judge's dinner. You were already fast asleep, and I wanted to go to bed early, as I had promised, so as to be up and on my way early in the morning. Meanwhile Veit, our servant, had lit the lights on my desk. Without thinking, I put on my bedgown, and suddenly it occurred to me to run over again the last passage I had finished. But what a misfortune! A pest on all your accursed, untimely housewifery! You had tidied up and everything was packed. I had to take it with me, the Prince had demanded a specimen of the work—I sought, I growled, I grumbled—in vain! Suddenly a sealed envelope caught my eye—to judge by the hideous flourishes in the handwriting of the address, from the abbot. It was! He had returned the revised ending of his libretto which I had not hoped to see for a month. Then and there I sat down greedily, and was delighted by the way the odd fellow had felt what I wanted. It was all far simpler, denser, and richer. The churchyard scene and the finale up to the hero's damnation had improved in every respect. (Excellent poet! I thought, you shall not conjure up Heaven and Hell a second time without reward.) Now as a rule, it is not a habit of mine to compose out of order, no matter how enticing it may be; that is a bad habit that can lead to very unhappy results. But there are exceptions. To cut a long story short, the scene at the Commander's statue, the threat, which is suddenly interrupted from the grave of the dead man by the grisly and raucous laughter of the drunkard—suddenly it all flashed into my mind. I struck a chord and felt that I had knocked at the right door, for behind it there lurked the legions of horrors which were to break loose in the finale. The first thing to come to the surface was an adagio, D minor, only four bars, then a second phrase of five—that, I imagined, should have startling effects on the stage, where the voices are accompanied by the strongest wind instruments. Meanwhile, listen to it, as far as it can be given here at all."

Without further explanation he extinguished the candles on the two candelabras standing beside him, and that dreadful chorale, "Thy laughter ends before the dawn of day," burst into the deathlike silence in the room. As if from distant orbits of stars, the notes fall down through the blue night from silver trumpets, icy cold, piercing heart and soul.

"Who is there? Answer!" Don Juan's voice is heard.

Then it begins again, monotonous as before, commanding the ruthless youth to leave the dead in peace.

After the last vibration of the thundering notes had died away, Mozart went on: "You will understand that I could not even dream of stopping then. When the ice once cracks at some spot by the shore, the lake bursts asunder and the echoes ring into its farthest reaches. Involuntarily I picked up the same thread again farther on at Don Juan's banquet, just when Donna Elvira has retired and the ghost answers the summons.—Listen."

Then there followed the whole ghastly dialogue, which carries the soberest mind to the very frontiers of the human imagination, and beyond them, where we see and hear the supernatural, and feel in our own breasts how helplessly we are tossed from one extreme to the other.

Already a stranger to the speech of men, the immortal voice of the dead deigns once more to speak. Soon after the first terrible greeting, when, halfway to immortality, he spurns the earthly food offered him, with what strange terror his voice wavers up and down the steps of an ethereal scale! He demands an instant resolution to make atonement. The ghost's time is short, and long, long, long the way. And then, when Don Juan, defying eternal laws in his monstrous self-will, writhes helplessly as the hosts of hell press closer, writhes and struggles and at last succumbs, yet with sublimity in every gesture—who could refrain from shudder-

ing to the very marrow of his bones in mingled delight and
terror? It is a feeling of astonishment such as we have
when watching the glorious spectacle of an ungovernable
force of nature, or the burning of a splendid ship. Against
our will we range ourselves on the side of this blind greatness, and, with clenched teeth, share its agony in the headlong course of its self-destruction.

The composer had finished. For a time no one ventured
to break the general silence.

"Give us," the Countess at last began with a tremor in
her voice, "please give us some idea of your feelings when
you laid down your pen that night."

As if awakened from a deep reverie, he raised his clear
eyes to her, thought for a moment, then said, half to the
lady and half to his wife: "Well, at the end, my head was
reeling. I had written that desperate dibattimento up to the
chorus of spirits in one heat beside an open window, and
after a short rest stood up to go to your room, and talk to
you to calm my blood. Then suddenly I was brought up
short in the middle of the room." (At this moment he lowered his eyes for a second or two, and when he went on
his voice betrayed an almost imperceptible emotion.) "I
said to myself: if you were to die tonight, with your score
as it stands, would it leave you peace in the grave? My
eyes were fixed on the wick of the candle in my hand and
on the heaps of melted wax. For a moment, I felt a pang
at the idea, then I thought—let us imagine that sooner or
later another man, perhaps even an Italian, is given the
opera to finish, that, except for one piece, he finds everything in perfect order from the Introduction to Number 17,
and all of it ripe fruit, shaken down into the grass for him
to pick up; but, just before the middle of the finale, his
heart almost fails him—then he discovers with a sigh of relief that the huge boulder has been cleared out of his way,
in part, at any rate. He chuckles with satisfaction. He might
even be tempted to cheat me of the honor. But that would
be a dangerous game; there would still be a host of good
friends who know my hand and would secure to me what
is mine.—Then I went away, thanked God from a full heart,

and thanked your good genius, my beloved wife, because he had laid his two hands gently on your forehead for so long that you slept on like a rat and could not call me one single time. But when at last I came and you asked me the time, I cheerfully lied you a few years younger than you were, for it was nearly four o'clock. And now you will understand why you could not drag me out of bed at six, and had to send the postilion home and tell him to come the next day."

"Of course," retorted Constanze, "but you needn't be so self-complacent as to imagine I had not noticed anything. There was really no reason to hide from me the beautiful march you had stolen on your own work."

"That wasn't the reason either."

"I know. You did not want your treasure to be cried abroad for the present."

"What pleases me," cried their kindly host, "is that we shall have no reason tomorrow to wound the noble heart of a Viennese coachman if Monsieur Mozart is absolutely incapable of getting up. The order, 'Hans, take the horses out again,' always hurts."

This indirect plea for a longer stay, which was acclaimed by the rest of the party, gave the travelers the opportunity of putting forward very grave reasons against it; however, there was a general agreement not to break the party up too early and to breakfast at their leisure together.

For a time the company stood talking in groups. Mozart was looking for somebody, apparently the bride, but as she was not present at the moment, he innocently asked Franciska, who was standing at his side, the question he had meant to put to her: "Well, what do you think of our *Don Giovanni* as a whole? What good fortune can you prophesy for him?"

She laughed as she answered: "I will answer as well as I can in my cousin's name. My opinion, for what it is worth, is that if *Don Giovanni* does not transport the whole world, it means that God has simply shut up His musical box—for an indefinite time, I mean—and is telling humanity—."—"Or rather," her uncle broke in, "is handing out the bagpipes to all mankind and hardening men's hearts to worship Baal."

"God preserve us!" laughed Mozart. "Well, in the next sixty or seventy years, many a false prophet will arise."

Eugenie now joined them with the Baron, the conversation once more took on a graver tone and more serious themes, and the composer's heart was gladdened, before the party broke up, by many a beautiful and telling remark which flattered his hopes.

It was long past midnight when they separated; till that moment nobody had noticed how much they needed rest.

The next morning (the weather was still lovelier than the day before), a pretty traveling chariot, packed with the luggage of the two Viennese guests, was to be seen standing in the courtyard of the château at ten o'clock. The Count was standing in front of it with Mozart before the horses were led out, and asked him whether he liked it.

"Very much; it looks most comfortable."

"Excellent. Then do me the pleasure of keeping it in memory of me."

"What! Are you serious?"

"Why not?"

"By Saints Sixtus and Calixtus! Constanze, here!" he called up to the window where she was looking out with the other ladies. "This carriage is to be mine! You shall ride in your own carriage now."

He embraced the smiling giver, contemplated his new possession, inspected it all round, opened the door, threw himself in and cried:

"I am as noble and rich as Prince Fortune himself! How they'll stare in Vienna!"

"I hope," said the Countess, "to see your carriage again on your way back from Prague buried in laurel wreaths."

Not long after this last pleasant scene, the much-praised equipage really drove off with the departing couple, and trotted briskly toward the main road. The Count's horses took them to Wittingau; from there they were to proceed with post horses.

When men of eminent heart and mind have brightened our home for a time by their presence, have poured fresh

vigor into our own being by the breath of their spirit, and
have made us feel the blessing of hospitality in full measure, their departure always leaves a strange stagnation behind it, at any rate for the rest of the day and if we are
quite thrown back on our own resources.

This was not the case with our friends at the château.
True, Franciska's parents left immediately, but her friend,
the bridegroom and Max still remained. One would imagine that Eugenie, of whom we must speak now, would feel
no void and no dismay because the precious experience had
moved her more deeply than all the rest. Her pure happiness in the man she truly loved, which had just received
its official sanction, would, we must think, swallow up every other feeling, or, to put it differently, the noblest and
most beautiful feelings must blend into one with that overflowing bliss. And that would certainly have been so if she
had been able to live entirely in the present for those two
days, and afterward in the joy of their memory. But even
in the evening, when Madame Constanze was drawing an
enchanting portrait of her husband in her story, a secret
dread for him crept into her heart, and later this foreboding
lurked in the background of her consciousness all the time
that Mozart was playing, through the ineffable beauty, the
mysterious horror of the music, and she had been surprised and moved when he had spoken of his own premoni-
tions. She was so sure, so utterly sure, that this man would
burn himself up in his own flame, rapidly and irresistibly,
that he could be but a transient visitor on earth because it
could not, in reality, support the riches he poured forth on
it.

These and many other thoughts rose and fell in her heart
after she had gone to bed the evening before, while confused echoes of *Don Giovanni* long held her inward ear captive. It was nearly daylight when she fell asleep, exhausted.

The three ladies had sat down in the garden with their
needlework, the men kept them company, and since the
only topic of conversation for the time being could be Mozart, Eugenie made no secret of her fears. Not one of the
others shared them in the least, though the Baron under-

stood her perfectly. In happy hours, when our hearts are overflowing with pure gratitude to some human being, we are prone to ward off with all our might any idea of misfortune which does not affect us directly. The most striking, the most smiling proofs to the contrary were brought forward, especially by her uncle, and how gladly Eugenie listened to them! It wanted but little to make her believe that she had foreseen the future too darkly.

A few minutes later she passed through the large salon upstairs which was being cleaned and restored to order; its green damask curtains diffused a gentle twilight. She remained standing sadly by the pianoforte. The thought of who had sat there a few hours before seemed to her a passing dream. Her eyes rested on the keys his had been the last hands to touch, then she closed the lid softly and removed the key, so that no other hand should open it for some time to come. As she left the room she stopped to put away a few song books; an old sheet of music fell out, the copy of a Bohemian folk song which Franciska and even she herself had often sung. She picked it up with dismay. In a mood such as hers, mere chance will speak with the voice of an oracle, and the burden of the simple lines was such that, as she read them through, the hot tears fell from her eyes.

> In woodland green
>   A pine tree grows;
> In a garden plot
>   A rose bush blows.
> One day the tree and bush will grow
>   Above your head,
> When you are dead and gone, my soul,
>   And in graveyard laid.
>
> Two brave black horses leap
>   In the field beyond;
> And lustily toss glittering hoofs,
>   Galloping home.
> They will pace slow, my soul,
>   When you are dead;

And you will go behind them
To your graveyard bed,
Maybe before those shoes
That glitter now
Are shed.

Notes on the Authors

JEAN PAUL RICHTER 1763–1825

Son of a poor teacher and organist, Jean Paul Richter abandoned his theological studies after many a lean year of poverty to devote himself to literature, attaining success with the novels *Die unsichtbare Loge* (The Invisible Lodge, 1793) and *Hesperus* (1795), after which the doors of the cultured aristocracy opened to him when a patroness, Charlotte von Kalb, invited him to Weimar (1796), where he lived for some years pampered by the philosopher-critic Herder and in touch with Goethe and Schiller, who treated him rather coldly, however, perhaps seeing in him a strong potential competitor. Here Richter's most ambitious works were written: *Quintus Fixlein* (1796), *Blumen, Frucht und Dornenstücke* (Flower, Fruit and Thorn Pieces, 1796), *Der Kampaner Tal* (The Campaner Thal, 1798). Pensioned by Prince Dalberg and later by the Bavarian government, he settled in Bayreuth, where he wrote *Flegeljahre* (Walt and Vult or The Twins, 1804), the educational novel *Levana* (1807) and *Des Feldpredigers Schmelzle Reise nach Flätz* (Army-Chaplain Schmelzle's Journey to Flätz, 1809).

Richter's collected works run to 65 volumes, and the name of Jean Paul, as he is known to literature, ranked at one time with that of Goethe. In England his books were eagerly received and translated by men like Carlyle and De Quincey, and he was regarded as a German Sterne, though lacking that Englishman's light touch and sparkling conviviality. Today his long meandering works seem to have a baroque remoteness and an antique ring, though his shorter pieces such as *Leben des vernugten Schulmeister-*

leins Maria Wuz (Life of the Cheerful Schoolmaster Maria Wutz, 1793) hold the reader's attention with their fusion of ironic humor and whimsical pathos.

About Richter: M. R. Altenheim, *Jean-Paul's Reception in the Nineteenth and Twentieth Century,* N.Y., 1938; E. V. Brewer, "The Influence of J. P. Richter's on Meredith's Conception of the Comic," *Journal of English and Germanic Philology,* XXIX (1930); E. V. Brewer, "Jean Paul's *Unsichtbare Loge* and Early German Romanticism," *Germanic Review,* VIII (1933), pp. 165–77; E. V. Brewer, *The New England Interest in Jean Paul Friedrich Richter,* University of California Press, 1943; Thomas Carlyle, *Critical and Miscellaneous Essays,* N.Y., Munro & Co., 1838; Thomas De Quincey, *Essays on Philosophical Writers & Other Men of Letters,* Boston, Ticknor, Reed & Fields, 1854; R. H. Fife, "Jean Paul Richter and E. T. A. Hoffmann," *PMLA,* XXII (1907), pp. 1–32; J. C. Hayes, *Lawrence Sterne and Jean Paul,* N.Y., 1942; E. B. Lee, *Life of Jean F. Richter,* N.Y., C. C. Little, 1842; E. B. Lee: *Life of Jean Paul Frederic Richter,* N.Y., D. Appleton & Co., 1850; H. Walden, *Jean Paul and Swift,* N.Y., 1940.

HEINRICH VON KLEIST 1777–1811

Descendant of a Prussian military family which included two field marshals and eighteen generals, Kleist served in the Prussian army (1792–99), "a monument of tyranny" from which he resigned as a second lieutenant. After a brief sojourn at the University of Frankfort, during which Kant's philosophy brought him to a crisis, he retired to a Rousseauistic farm life in Switzerland where he wrote a play *Die Familie Schroffenstein* (1802) which began his brief and tragic literary career (seven plays, eight tales, a sheaf of poems and articles). Kleist's life was beset with serious illness, incessant anxiety, and constant travel. He was arrested by Napoleon's soldiers (1807) as an alleged spy and sent to a French jail; his political intransigence brought to a quick end both his literary journal *Phoebus* (1808) and his daily *Berliner Abendblatt* (1810–11); embittered by lack of literary recognition (especially Goethe's hostility) and the victories of his archenemy Napoleon, he twice broke his engagement, remaining a bachelor until his suicide at the age of thirty-four. Kleist's genius found fullest expression in the existentialist play *The Prince of Homburg* (1810) and *Michael Kohlhaas* (1808). This dramatic novelette, based on a sixteenth-century historical figure, may be considered a peak of German literature because of its fusion of awesomeness with matter-of-fact realism and objectivity, as well as its deft psychological analysis. Kleist's works mirror the conflicts of a fiercely nationalistic Prussian, driven to despair by the titanic shadows cast upon him by his contemporaries, Napoleon and Goethe, who acts anarchistically while flirting with both Paganism and Catholicism; and who, like Pascal, Kierkegaard, Dostoyevsky, and Kleist's spiritual son, Franz Kafka, seems to have peered into "the Abyss."

About Kleist: Richard March, *Kleist,* Cambridge, Bowes & Bowes, 1954. **Others:** E. N. Anderson, *Nationalism and the Cultural Crisis in Prussia,* N.Y., Farrar & Rinehart, 1939; Fairley Barker, "Heinrich von Kleist," *Modern Philology,* XIV (1916), pp. 65–84; H. K. Becker, *Kleist and Hebbel: A Comparative Study,* N.Y., Scott, Foresman, 1904; John C. Blankenagel, *The Attitude of H. von Kleist toward the Problems of Life,* Johns Hopkins University Press, 1917; J. C. Blankenagel, *The Dramas of H. von Kleist,* University of North Carolina Press, 1931; S. Flygt, "Kleist's Struggle with the Problem of Feeling," *PMLA,* LVIII (1943), pp. 514–36; N. Furst, "The Structure of Kleist's Plays," *Germanic Review,* XVII (1942), pp. 48–55; E. G. Fürstenheim, "The Sources of Kleist's *Prinz Friedrich von Hombourg,*" *German Life & Letters,* January 1955, pp. 103–9; Michael Hamburger, *Reason and Energy,* N.Y., Grove Press, 1957, pp. 107–44; William H. McClam, "Kleist and Molière as Comic Writers," *Germanic*

Review, XXIV (1949), pp. 21–33; Charles E. Passage, *Michael Kohlhaas*, "Form Analysis," *Germanic Review*, October 1955, pp. 181–97; W. Silz, *Early German Romanticism: Its Founders and H. von Kleist*, Harvard University Press, 1929; E. L. Stahl, *Heinrich von Kleist's Dramas*, Oxford, Blackwell, 1948; S. Zweig, *Master Builders*, N.Y., Viking, 1939.

E. T. A. HOFFMANN 1776–1822

Hoffmann had a painful and insecure childhood in an unhappy and somewhat turbulent home. Dissatisfied with his government post, he aspired to a glamorous musical career like that of Beethoven, of whom he was one of the earliest supporters. Recognizing his shortcomings in music, however, he turned to literature and upon the success of his novel *Die Elixiere des Teufels* (The Devil's Elixir, 1815) wrote copiously until his death, twelve years later, scores of tales dealing with the supernatural, the hypnotic, and the world of dreams. Hoffmann's fabulous inventive genius and myth-making successfully fused the Gothic element which had flowered, so stiltedly, in eighteenth-century England, with a dramatic realism full of psychological overtones. His influence has been ubiquitous, extending from the Russia of Gogol and Dostoyevsky to the America of Poe and the Spain of Becquer. At his most felicitous moments, as in "Der goldne Topf" (The Golden Pot, 1814) or that little gem "Die Bergwerke zu Falun" (The Minds at Falun, 1818) or the less known *Lebensansichten des Katers Murr* (Life of Murr the Cat, 1820) and *Meister Floh* (Master Floh, 1822), one recognizes the hand of a storyteller virtuoso, perceptive observer of the human heart and master of suspense.

About Hoffmann: Harvey W. Hewett-Thayer, *Hoffmann, Author of the Tales*, Princeton University Press, 1948. **Others:** P. Cobb, *The Influence of E. T. A. Hoff-*

mann on the Tales of Edgar Allan Poe, University of North
Carolina Press, 1908; Robert H. Fife, "Jean Paul Richter
and E. T. A. Hoffmann," *PMLA,* XXII (1907), pp. 1–32;
W. F. Mainland, "The Legacy of Hoffmann," *German Life
& Letters,* I, 4, 1937; A. R. Neumann, "Musician or Author?
E. T. A. Hoffmann's Decision," *Journal of English & Ger-
manic Philology,* LII (1953), pp. 174–81; Ralph Tymms,
German Romantic Literature, London, Methuen, 1955, pp.
347–66.

JEREMIAS GOTTHELF 1797–1854

Jeremias Gotthelf (Albert Bitzius was his real name) spent
most of his life as a Protestant minister, like his father, in a
Swiss village north of Bern, zealously looking after his pa-
rishioners' welfare and adding to his intensive work of
practical Christianity with his literary labors which were
equally bound with his preaching and moral uplifting. Already thirty-nine and father of three children when his first
book, *Der Bauernspiegel* (The Peasants' Mirror), was published, he wrote during the next seventeen years twelve long
novels, forty tales, and sundry essays dealing soberly and
often unsentimentally with the trials and tribulations of his
farming community. Of these works none is as powerful as
Die schwarze Spinne (The Black Spider, 1842) which
Thomas Mann considered one of the outstanding examples
of narrative fiction in the German language. With the
moralist and practical theologian in full command of his
imaginative faculties, his lesson—*exemplum* or cautionary
tale—assumes the proportions of a hair-raising myth com-
parable to one of Kafka's allegories or Freud's dream cases.

About Gotthelf: H. M. Waidson, *Jeremias Gotthelf,* Oxford, Blackwell, 1953. Others: J. S. Andrews, "The Reception of Gotthelf in British and American Nineteenth-
Century Periodicals," *Modern Language Review,* LI
(1956), pp. 543–54; J. R. Foster, "J. Gotthelf's Reputation

Outside Switzerland," *German Life & Letters*, April 1955,
pp. 208–11; G. T. Hughes: *"Die schwarze Spinne* as Fiction," *German Life & Letters*, July 1956, pp. 250–60;
R. E. Keller, "Language and Style in J. Gotthelf's *Die
schwarze Spinne,*" *German Life & Letters*, n.s. X (1956),
pp. 2–13; Roy Pascal, *The German Novel*, University of
Toronto Press, 1956, pp. 101–42; H. M. Waidson, "Gotthelf's Reception in Britain and America," *Modern Language
Review*, XLIII, 2, (April 1948).

ADALBERT STIFTER 1805–1868

Of humble origin, Stifter upon the death of his parents
left his native village of Oberplan in the Bohemian forest
of Upper Austria (now Czechoslovakia) to study in the
Benedictine school attached to the Kremsmünster Abbey,
and later at the University of Vienna (1826), where he
never obtained the law degree he needed for earning a
living, being more interested in painting, mathematics, and
natural science. As a result he became a tutor of children
of the nobility, including one Richard Metternich, son of
the Prince. For a while he enjoyed the charm of aristocratic
salons and the café conviviality of writers and painters
(Grillparzer, Lenau, Grün), but he was often homesick and
had to return to his native countryside. Rejected as a drifter
by the father of his fiancée, Fanni Greipl, he finally married
Amalia Mohaupt in 1837. The marriage was a fiasco,
chiefly because it was childless, and it deteriorated when
their adopted daughter, the strangely inaccessible Juliana,
committed suicide. Stifter's first stories appeared shortly
after this tragedy. Couched in a poetically harmonious language and suffused with genuine feeling for Nature, his
quiet human dramas gained him an ever-widening circle
of readers. But he was unhappy and sighed for Vienna. In
1850 he was appointed inspector of the elementary schools
in Linz, but the bureaucratic life of the provincial capital
nearly annihilated him, and he took refuge in his literary

endeavors, writing one masterpiece after another: *Bunte Steine* (Bright Stones, 1853), *Der Nachsommer* (Indian Summer, 1857) and *Witiko* (1865–67). But a cancer of the liver drove him one winter morning in 1868 to cut his throat with a razor. Neglected for half a century for flashier and more spectacular writers, in recent years Stifter has been universally acclaimed as Austria's greatest writer.

About Stifter: Eric A. Blackall, *Adalbert Stifter*, Cambridge University Press, 1948. Others: J. S. Andrews, "The Reception of Stifter in Nineteenth-Century Britain," *Modern Language Review*, LIII (October 1958), pp. 537–44; C. O. Arndt, *The Changing Appreciation of the Writings of A. Stifter*, University of Illinois dissertation, 1937; H. G. Barnes, "The Function of Conversation and Speeches in *Witiko*," *German Studies Presented to Prof. H. G. Fiedler*, Oxford, 1938; U. E. Fehlan, "Symbolism in A. Stifter's Works," *Journal of English & Germanic Philology*, XXXIX (1940), pp. 239–55; Roy Pascal, *The German Novel*, University of Toronto Press, 1956, pp. 52–75; H. H. Schneider, *The Use of "Dinge" in the Creative Art of A. Stifter*, Princeton University dissertation, 1955; W. Silz, *Realism and Reality. Studies in the German Novelle of Poetic Realism*, University of North Carolina Press, 1954, pp. 52–66; A. Spalding, "A. Stifter," *Modern Languages*, XXXII, 2, (1951); F. J. Stopp, "The Symbolism of Stifter's *Kalkstein*," *German Life & Letters*, n.s. VII, January 1954, pp. 116–25; W. E. Umbach, *Natural Science in the Work of A. Stifter*, University of Kentucky Libraries Occasional Contributions, No. 15 (1950); "J. Urzidil, A. Stifter and Judaism," *Menorah Journal*, XXXVI (1948), pp. 327–38.

GOTTFRIED KELLER 1819–1890

Born in Zurich in 1819 in rather humble circumstances, Keller lost his father at five and was expelled from school at fifteen. Deciding to devote himself to painting, he spent two years in Munich 1840–42; only after six painful years of vacillation and frustration was his real vocation revealed when his verse collection *Gedichte* (1846) won him a scholarship from his cantonal government enabling him to study at Heidelberg. From there he moved to Berlin where during the fruitful years 1850–55 he completed his autobiographical novel *Der grüne Heinrich,* the humorous earthy tales *Die Leute von Seldwyla* (The People of Seldwyla) which included the well-known "Romeo und Julia auf den Dorfe" (A Village Romeo and Juliet) and the comic masterpiece "Die drei gerechten Kammacher" (The Three Righteous Comb Makers). From 1861 to his retirement in 1876 he occupied the lucrative position of cantonal chief clerk, writing then leisurely his *Sieben Legenden* (Seven Legends), seven pious legends retold with truculent verve, and a group of tales collected as Volume II of *Die Leute von Seldwyla.* During the last few years of his life Keller revised *Der grüne Heinrich* (1879) and wrote some of his raciest tales: *Züricher Novellen* (1878), stories in a framework *Die Sinngedicht* (The Epigram, 1881), and the political novel *Martin Salander* (1886). Without any doubt Keller towers over all other Swiss writers and will continue to hold a lofty position in world literature for his extraordinary narrative power and astringent realism, sprightly fantasy, and rugged humor. "Meret," the brief excerpt from *Der grüne Heinrich* included here, brilliantly illustrates Keller's piquancy, comic spirit, and almost surrealist imagination.

About Keller: H. Adolf, "A Mid-Century Duel: G. Keller and Heine," *Germanic Review,* XXVIII (1953), pp. 180–89; L. Forster, "G. Keller," *German Life & Letters,* X, pp. 177–82; E. F. Hauch, *G. Keller as a Democratic Idealist,* Columbia University Press, 1916; M. Hay, *The Story of a Swiss Poet,* N.Y., F. Wyss, 1920; R. Heller, "G. Keller and Literary Criticism," *German Life & Letters,* October 1958, pp. 39–45; V. J. Lemke, "The Deification of G. Keller," *Monatshefte,* XLVIII (1956), pp. 119–26; Roy Pascal, *The German Novel,* University of Toronto Press, 1956, pp.

30–51; R. H. Phelps, "Keller's Technique of Composition in *Romeo and Juliet*," *Germanic Review*, February 1949, pp. 34–51; H. W. Reichert, *Basic Concepts in the Philosophy of G. Keller*, University of North Carolina Press, 1949; J. M. Ritchie, "The Place of *Martin Salander* in G. Keller's Evolution as a Prose Writer," *Modern Language Review*, LII (1957), pp. 214–22; J. G. Robertson, *Essays and Addresses on Literature*, London, Routledge & Sons, 1935; Walter Silz, *Realism and Reality*, University of North Carolina Press, 1954, pp. 79–93.

EDUARD MÖRIKE 1804–1875

Son of a distinguished doctor, Mörike was educated in his native Ludwigsburg, in Württemberg, and, after the death of his father (1818), at the seminaries at Urach and Tübingen, where he preferred the company of poets and musicians to that of his fellow theological students. Here he also developed an ineradicable passion for Mozart's genius, and fell in love with a Swiss girl, Maria Mayer, who had been disowned by her family for joining an itinerant religious sect. Dostoyevskian saint-sinner, mixture of mysticism and sensuality, Maria became inextricably bound to the poet's creative and symbolic world under the name of "Peregrina." After graduation (1826) Mörike wrote the autobiographical novel *Maler Nolten* (1832) and held numerous curacies, in 1834 becoming parson of the parish of Cleversulzbach, where he remained for almost a decade, with frequent self-imposed illnesses and absences which permitted him to write some of the most perfect lyrics in the German language. In 1843 he retired to Stuttgart on a small pension which he supplemented by teaching German literature in a girls' school. At the age of forty-six he married the Catholic Margarethe von Speeth, by whom he had two daughters and from whom he separated twenty years later only to be reunited before his death. In addition to his novel and flawless lyrics (many set to music by Schubert, Brahms, Hugo Wolf), Mörike wrote the delightful fairy tales "Historie von der schönen Blau" (1837) and "Das Stuttgarter Hutzelmännlein" (1853), and the little masterpiece *Mozart auf der Reise nach Prag* (Mozart on His Way to Prague), written in 1850–51 but not published until 1855, in which he weaves his old love for Mozart into a fragrant tale fraught with verve, humor, and imaginative splendor.

About Mörike: Margaret Mare, *Eduard Mörike, His Life and Work*, London, Methuen, 1957. Others: T. M. Campbell, "E. Mörike, A Neglected German Classic," *Sewanee Review*, XXV (April 1917), pp. 171–86; A. Closs, *The Genius of the German Lyric*, London, Allen & Unwin, 1938, pp. 350–54; F. Gundolf, "E. Mörike," *The Criterion* (London), X (1931), pp. 682–708; H. W. Hewett-Thayer, "Mörike's Occultism and the Revision of *Maler Nolten*," *PMLA*, July 1956, pp. 386–413; R. Immerwahr, "Apocalyptic Trumpets: The Inception of *Mozart auf der Reise nach Prag*," *PMLA*, June 1955, pp. 390–407; J. H. Kneisel, *Mörike and Music*, Columbia University dissertation, 1949.

UE

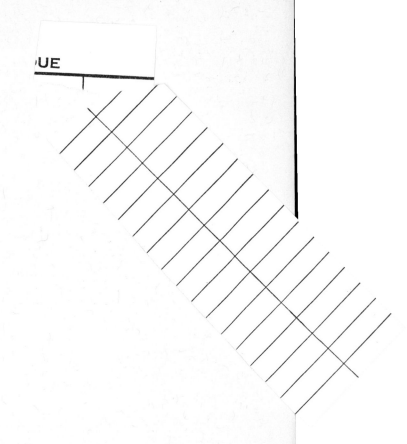